PENGUIN

The Bomb Girls' Secrets

Daisy Styles grew up in Lancashire, surrounded by family and a community of strong women. She loved to listen to their stories of life in the cotton mill, in the home, at the pub, on the dance floor, in the local church, or just what happened to them on the bus going into town. It was from these women, particularly her vibrant mother and Irish grandmother, that Daisy learnt the art of storytelling.

By the same author

The Bomb Girls
The Code Girls

The Bomb Girls' Secrets

DAISY STYLES

PENGUIN BOOKS

PENGUIN BOOKS

UK | USA | Canada | Ireland | Australia
India | New Zealand | South Africa

Penguin Books is part of the Penguin Random House group of companies
whose addresses can be found at global.penguinrandomhouse.com

First published 2017
001

Copyright © Daisy Styles, 2017

The moral right of the author has been asserted

Set in 12.5/14.75 pt Garamond MT Std
Typeset by Jouve (UK), Milton Keynes
Printed in Great Britain by Clays Ltd, St Ives plc

A CIP catalogue record for this book is available from the British Library

ISBN: 978-1-405-93792-4

www.greenpenguin.co.uk

Penguin Random House is committed to a
sustainable future for our business, our readers
and our planet. This book is made from Forest
Stewardship Council® certified paper.

*For the real Kitty, my beloved Grandma,
who, against all the odds, refused to have her son,
Bill, adopted and loved him passionately till
the day she died. Bill, my father, loved swing
band music, so Daddy, if you're 'In the Mood',
this is for you too!*

1. Kit

On a freezing January night, twenty-four-year-old Kitty Murphy lay in her berth and prayed for death. The biting howling gale whipped around the passenger ship bound for Heysham, sending it tossing and spinning over the churning grey sea. As it plunged and rose like a monstrous sea serpent in the rolling waves, Kit stopped thinking about the possibility of being torpedoed by a German warship or bombed by a German Luftwaffe flying low over the Irish Sea. Instead, she groaned as her stomach went into yet another spasm of dizzying nausea. She'd been sick since the moment of departure from Dublin, and all through the wretched dark night too. In the bunk beds on either side of the cabin that smelt of vomit and cigarettes two other women lay sprawled and groaning on their berths, whilst a third cheerfully sat upright on her bed chain-smoking.

'She must have guts of steel,' thought Kit as sleep mercifully engulfed her.

She suffered tormented dreams of Billy, new born, pink and warm in her arms. The baby she had had to leave behind, only a matter of weeks after a hard birth. Tears rolled unchecked down Kit's thin cheeks; it was less than twenty-four hours since she'd left Billy at home in Chapelizod and it already seemed like a lifetime. Rosie had escorted her sister to the bus stop, where they'd stood in the rain, waiting for the bus that would take Kit to Dublin. Clutching Billy tightly in her arms, she'd inhaled the sweet baby smell of him for the last time, and as the bus loomed up she'd kissed him over and over again, before Rosie had literally wrenched the screaming child from her arms and Kit stumbled on the bus, blinded by tears.

Kit could scarcely remember how she got from the bus station to the Dublin docks. All her instincts had told her this was wrong: she should be walking in the opposite direction. Even her body had protested. Her breasts were sore and engorged with milk, food that Billy, she was quite sure, would be wailing for right now. The thought of him lying in his makeshift crib, a drawer taken from the dresser, crying for food, nearly killed her. Would her younger sister have time to change Billy's nappy and give him the bottle she'd left with instructions on how to sterilize it with boiling water after Billy's feeds? Her womb throbbed from the long walk to the docks; the sensation reminded her so much of when she'd first fed her son. As he caught on the nipple and sucked greedily, she'd felt her womb contract. Just the thought of his birth, the sweet memory of him entering the world, brought a brief barely visible smile to her lips.

Kit's father had refused point-blank to pay out money for a midwife.

'To hell with a feckin' midwife!' he'd announced. 'You'll not find me paying out for your bastard child.'

It was a long hard labour for Kit, who was small and narrow hipped, and Billy, a big bouncing boy, almost tore her apart, but all the pain and fear had been worthwhile.

She cherished the moment of holding Billy for the first time, of putting him to her breast, and worn out by the long labour he slept peacefully in her arms.

As the rain had started to fall and the Dublin docks loomed up in the wet mist that suddenly shrouded the city, Kitty vividly recalled how she'd marvelled at Billy's dask eyelashes fanned out on his soft, pale cheeks. Could this miracle of a child really be the product of Lionel Fitzwilliam?

'He's like an angel, Ma,' she'd whispered to her mother when the labour was over. 'A gift from God.'

After a prolonged spell of coughing, Mrs Murphy had remarked in a frightened whisper, 'Don't be after letting your da hear you talking like that – you've brought shame upon this house.'

When she'd missed her first monthly, Kit wilfully told herself that the shock of Fitzwilliam's brutal attack had upset her body, but when she missed the second and was sick every morning she knew she was pregnant.

'Mi da will kill me,' she whispered to Rosie as they lay together in the single bed they shared, covered with old coats to keep them warm.

'Jesus, Kit! He'll crucify you,' Rosie whispered in a voice full of fear.

Lying in her narrow berth in one of the cheapest cabins, which were close to the engine room, she remembered the long queue of passengers she'd joined the previous day, all poor families hoping for a better life in England. Kit's eyes had instantly picked out the babes in their mothers' arms. She would willingly have sailed around the world and back again if she could only have her baby safe in her arms. She should have known it would end badly after her father's reaction to her pregnancy, which he'd discovered when she started to show in her fifth month. He hadn't crucified her, as Rosie had predicted, but he'd bounced Kit off every wall in the cottage, then hit her repeatedly until stars blazed in her head. The sound of her mother's high-pitched screams finally brought him to a halt. As he stood panting and swearing over his daughter's battered body, Kit tried to tell him what had happened to her.

'It wasn't my fault!' she sobbed.

'WASN'T YOUR FAULT?' he roared like a raging bull. 'It was YOU that opened yer legs, yer filthy little tramp!' he sneered.

'Da, as God's my witness –'

Kit got no further: after giving her a final kick, her father turned away and left the house.

Despite all the terrible things going on in the war-torn world, for Kit the 7th of December 1941 had been the start of a whole new wonderful world; for the first time in her life she felt complete. With her son's arrival the sky was bluer, the grass greener, and the birds sang more sweetly. In a state of blissful infatuation, Kit had no idea that her son's birth date was the fateful day the Japanese bombed Pearl Harbor, an event that, she would later learn, changed the entire course of the war.

When Billy slept in his dresser-drawer cradle, Kit ached to hold him; when he woke, she waited for his blue eyes to open and search out hers. As he grew, his little hands reached for her, and Kit was the first to see his heart-stopping, lop-sided smile. Mrs Murphy, who was weak and breathless after having suffered for two years from tuberculosis, advised her daughter to let Billy cry.

'He can't be having you all of the time,' she chided.

Kit was shocked by her mother's harsh words. 'I don't want to let him cry!' she exclaimed. 'If he's hungry I want to feed him; if he's sad I want to cuddle him.'

'Picking him up and mollycoddling him every five minutes will turn the little lad into a big softie,' her mother warned.

'Ma, he's a few weeks old – what harm can a kiss and a cuddle do?' Kit protested as she scooped Billy out of the drawer and put him to her breast, where he suckled eagerly.

'Mark my words, you'll ruin the boy,' Mrs Murphy said as she shook her head in deep disapproval.

Staring up at the ceiling, trying to stop the waves of nausea overwhelming her, Kit was glad that she had spent those precious first weeks with Billy, responding to his every cry, examining every inch of his soft warm body, kissing his little toes and stroking his rosy cheeks until he drifted off to sleep. As if sensing they would be parted, she had imprinted her baby into her memory: his irresistible smell, his sky-blue eyes, his dimpled chin, the way he sighed when falling asleep, the arch of his small strong back. There was nothing about her son that went unnoticed by his adoring mother.

Only the night before she'd stood at the quayside, standing on Irish soil for as long as she could, clinging to the thought that she and her son were still breathing the same air, still living in the same country.

'All aboard! All aboard!' a sailor had cried, startling Kit, who realized she'd been staring into space, unaware of fellow passengers bustling by.

'Come along, young lady,' the cheerful sailor said as he helped Kit on to the gangplank. 'England awaits!'

'England!' Kit had groaned as she leant over the rails and watched the crew raise the anchor. 'It's Ireland where I should be,' she whispered as the ship's engine powered the massive propeller and they headed her out to sea. As the dark and misty coastline of the land she'd grown up in faded into darkness, Kit wondered if drowning herself in the crashing waves far below would be easier than living without Billy.

And the misery hadn't dissipated. Drifting in and out of a restless sleep, Kit recalled with a shudder how she had come to be on this boat in the first place.

When Billy was almost three weeks old, Mr Murphy had returned rolling drunk from the pub, threatening to send the child away for adoption. Kit, wild and fearless as a tigress guarding her cub, had fought her father with every fibre of her body.

'He's my son!' she protested. 'He belongs to me – I'll never let him go.'

A few days later, and this time stone cold sober and therefore more dangerous, her mercenary father had come up with an alternative plan.

'We'll take care of your bastard in return for five pounds a week.'

Kit's jaw dropped in disbelief.

'That's impossible. You know how much I earn working on the farm: not even half of that!'

'I'm not talking about working on the feckin' farm, yer eejit!' her father snapped. 'It's the Lancashire mills you'll be heading for.'

Kit's incredulity changed to blind panic.

'Lancashire!' she exclaimed. 'My baby's not a month old – I can't leave him.'

Ignoring her words, her father continued. 'There's good money to be had in England.'

'But I want to be with Billy,' Kit said as she started to cry. 'Please don't make me go, Da. *Please, please* let me stay.'

'You've brought disgrace to the family with your dirty little bastard. The only way you can keep him is by going to work in England and sending money home to us to look after him.'

Kit knew full well that any money she sent to her father would disappear down the pub; none of it would go to Billy, who'd be left with her sickly mother whilst her self-seeking father drank himself into oblivion. She bit back the words which, if spoken, would only make her position worse. Through distant relations who'd recently crossed the waters to settle in Manchester, her father had heard of the comparatively high wages paid to workers in the Lancashire cotton mills, and his mind was set on sending Kit there. No matter how much she sobbed and implored, ranted and wept, Mr Murphy's remained resolute, until she slowly realized that leaving home and providing her family with money was really the only way she could keep Billy and avoid his adoption.

After the longest and loneliest night of her life, the ship finally heaved to a halt and Kit, briefly unaware of where she was, thought for a split second that she was back home in bed with Billy.

'Don't cry, my darling,' she said as she reached out to comfort him.

She pictured him gurgling and cooing in her arms, smiling trustingly at his mother, the person who loved him most in the world. Grasping thin air, Kit wept. She had shattered that innocent new-born trust, abandoning him to her mother, who'd be lucky if she lived to see the year out, and her cruel father, who didn't care if the child lived or died. Her only hope was that Rosie would have the time and patience to look out for her precious son.

'Thank Jesus! We've landed,' the chain-smoking girl announced.

Weak and shaky, Kit found a bathroom, where she washed her ashen face and combed her hair. Staring at her reflection, she hardly recognized the girl she'd been a year ago. Her dark hair was still long but it had lost its rich lustre, as had her dark brown eyes. The worry of leaving her son had dramatically reduced her appetite, though she'd still managed to breastfeed Billy until the day she left. Her breasts tingled with the milk seeping from her nipples, sustenance for the baby she'd abandoned, she thought bitterly as she stuffed handkerchiefs into her ragged vest to absorb the liquid. Bone weary, Kit returned to her cabin, where she picked up her cheap, battered suitcase, then she walked down the ship's gangplank and on to English soil with her heart as heavy as lead.

2. Gladys

Gladys Johnson opened her beautiful dark blue eyes wide so she could sweep black mascara on to her long lashes.

'Be sharp now, or you'll miss the bus,' her mum nagged from the back kitchen, where a sheep's head bubbling in a pan on the back burner made the air unpleasantly sickly. Though Gladys knew her mum would later drain the stock off the boiled head and use it to enrich her meat pies, the sight and smell of the sheep's brains always turned her stomach.

'Come on, our Glad,' said Leslie, her handsome young brother, as he flicked her long hair on his way to pick up his coat. 'I'll walk to't bus stop with you.'

'You won't if you keep messing up my hair!' she laughed. 'Gimme a minute to finish mi make-up.'

Les shook his head and smiled fondly as he watched his beautiful big sister apply red lipstick to her full pouting lips, then pull a comb through the rich, glossy brunette ringlets that framed her smiling face.

'Thou art vainest lass in't th'ole of Leeds!' he mocked.

Gladys gave him a cheeky wink. 'You've got to make the most of what you've got, our kid!'

Calling a cheery goodbye to their mother, brother and sister swung down the cobbled terrace street where they'd grown up. With only a couple of years separating them in age, they'd always had a strong bond: they shared the same sense of cheeky humour, they both regularly played in the local Sally Army band along with their dad, and they both had a passion for swing music. They also shared the same good looks: tall and strong, they both had thick curling brunette hair, stunning deep blue eyes, a dimple in the right cheek and a wide smiling mouth.

'Don't mention owt to our mam, but I'm thinking of joining the Yorkshires,' Les said in a whisper. 'I might even get a chance to play my trumpet in the regimental band,' he added excitedly.

Gladys stopped dead in her tracks. 'I knew this was coming!' she exclaimed.

'Come on, Glad,' he reasoned. 'A lot of lads I know joined up as soon as war was declared.'

'Aye!' she said angrily. 'And a lot of them lost their young lives at Dunkirk in 1940.'

'It's my duty, Glad,' he said flatly.

She knew he was right; there were hardly any young men in evidence in Leeds these days, not unless they were briefly home on leave. Of course Les should fight for his country, even though he was her kid brother whom she used to protect from the bullyboys at primary school. As if reading her thoughts, Les added, 'I'm not a kid any more.'

Gladys nodded. 'I know . . .'

Tears filled her eyes at the thought of him going away. The house often rang with his laughter and the sound of his trumpet blasting out of his bedroom. 'God, how I'll miss him,' she thought to herself, but she knew that he was of the age for conscription. Nobody could miss the stern government posters all over the city: BRITAIN NEEDS YOU.

Standing up to kiss Les she gave a brave smiled as she said, 'In that case, I wish you good luck!' She hugged him hard, praying that God would keep him safe. Bravely she swallowed her tears for his sake.

They went their separate ways: Les to the factory where he worked as a welder and Gladys to the Lyons Café on Hudson Road. Lyons employed over a hundred staff to serve food throughout the day and into the evening in a restaurant arranged on four levels. Whilst an orchestra played in the background, Gladys offered hungry customers a dizzying choice of starters, main courses and puddings, followed by coffee, and all for one shilling and sixpence. Wearing a black dress and an immaculately starched and pressed white apron and cap, Gladys glided through the noisy dining room packed with tables, all draped with snowy-white cloths and laid with gleaming cutlery. Skilfully balancing a heavy tray loaded with fish cakes, vegetable hotpot, baked currant pudding and apple turnovers plus a pot of tea, Gladys gracefully circumnavigated boisterous children, impatient old ladies and flustered Nippies to bring food to her expectant customers.

Happy as she was at Lyons, nothing equalled the thrill of her evening job, when she played the alto saxophone in Jimmy Angelo's Swing Band. Gladys had always loved music. From the time they were just tots, she and Les had joined their dad, who played the booming drum for the Salvation Army, in marching through the streets of Leeds, singing hymns and collecting money for the homeless. When his children were still small, Mr Johnson had bought each of them a tiny trumpet, which they proudly tooted as they strode along beside him through the streets of Leeds city centre. In their teens, much influenced by the American swing bands which they both adored, Gladys had moved from the trumpet to the alto sax, whilst Les stuck with his beloved trumpet. Brother and sister loved to play duets: up in their bedrooms they'd take it in turns to pick a dance number and experiment with harmonies until their mother banged on the ceiling with a brush.

'Will you stop that din up there – the neighbours will have us thrown out!' she bellowed.

The Andrews Sisters were their all-time favourites, especially 'Boogie Woogie Bugle Boy of Company B', which they played with wild abandon whenever they could get away with it. Les loved his music and was good at it but his talented sister had bigger ideas; Gladys wanted to take her musical skills to a professional level.

'Perform in public! You must be joking,' Les had laughed when she confessed her burning ambition. 'Our dad'll go crackers!'

'Nothing ventured, nothing gained,' she'd said with a shrug of her pretty shoulders.

When she'd seen an advert in the General Post Office for a dance band saxophonist, Gladys had immediately applied. The dance bandleader, Jimmy Angelo, though born and bred in Leeds, had a Sicilian father and spoke in a thick Northern dialect interspersed with snips of Italian.

'*Eh! Non credo che sia una ragazza!*' he laughed when Gladys turned up to audition.

Not having a clue what he was talking about, Gladys,

in a tight-fitting black crêpe dress with her long dark hair swinging around her shoulders, took her saxophone out of its leather case and played a powerful rendition of 'You are My Sunshine' that took the indulgent smile off Angelo's cocky face. Dropping the Italian, he blurted out, 'Blood 'ell, kid! Who taught you 'ow for't play yon sax?'

'My dad,' she replied proudly. 'There's more,' she added as she launched into 'Oh, Lady Be Good' without any sign of sheet music.

At the end of her performance, Angelo applauded loudly, then blew kisses in the air.

'*Favoloso! Eccellente!* When can you start?'

She was required to play each evening from Friday to Sunday at the Mecca Locarno in the County Arcade in Leeds.

Les had been right when he'd warned Gladys about the family's reaction to her playing in public. Her mother, a born worrier, was appalled by the thought of her twenty-year-old daughter having two jobs.

'You'll kill yourself!' she exclaimed.

But it was her father who was the biggest obstacle. He adored his little girl and wasn't happy about her performing with an all-male band.

'That's not a job for lasses,' he announced as he lit up his pipe and buried his head in the *Yorkshire Evening Post*.

'Lots o' lasses play in the Sally Army band!' Les said in his sister's defence.

Gladys shot him a loving smile. 'Thanks,' she mouthed.

'That's different,' Mr Johnson retorted. 'That's for the Lord.'

Gladys cuddled up to her dad. 'Come on,' she coaxed.

'It's you that taught me music; it's not my fault if I'm good at it – it's a gift from God!'

Mr Johnson finally relented – on condition that he accompanied Gladys to the Locarno and stayed throughout the night to keep an eye on her. He became a regular feature in the ballroom, sitting in a corner drinking warm lemonade and puffing on his pipe. If the truth were known, he loved his nights out watching his dazzling daughter playing the alto sax, which had almost become an extension of her bright, vibrant personality. The complicated melodies that poured out of the instrument when Gladys was playing solo sometimes brought the dancers to a stop; they'd gaze in amazement at the good-looking young girl in her full-length satin ballroom dress embellished with sequins and bows playing the alto saxophone like they'd never heard it played before. Though surrounded by men, Gladys was rarely approached for a date or a dance. Her father's glowering presence frightened off potential suitors, which suited Gladys down to the ground. Her passion was music – men would just get in the way of her secret ambition, which was to lead her own all-female swing band.

Ironically, it wasn't men that got in the way of her dreams: it was female conscription. There was no denying that Gladys, a staunch patriotic Yorkshire lass, wanted to do her bit for the war effort; her only condition was that she wanted to stay in Leeds, where she could continue to play for Jimmy Angelo at the Locarno in between her shifts. So it was with horror that she read her call-up letter, which instructed her to report to a munitions factory in Pendleton, on the other side of the Pennines.

With tears spilling from her lovely blue eyes, she blurted out, 'I don't want to go, Dad!'

Mr Johnson choked back a tear too: not only had his son recently announced he had joined up but he was now losing his daughter. Frightened of betraying his emotions, he replied more brusquely than was necessary. 'Thou's got no choice, our lass.'

'Why can't I do my war work here in Leeds?' she sobbed.

Mr Johnson sighed as he gave her hand a squeeze. 'The government are sending you where you needed, Glad, that's all that's to it.'

On her final night at the Locarno, Gladys played her heart out. After a show-stopping rendition of 'Rhapsody in Blue', she took to the floor with Jimmy, who was a superb ballroom dancer, and, to the strains of 'I Only Have Eyes for You', she leant her head against his shoulder and wept.

'I'll die without my music,' she said as he dabbed away her tears with his red silk handkerchief.

'Come on, amore, it won't be forever,' he assured her. 'The war has to end one day, eh, certo? We'll be waiting for you when you get back.'

Gladys gave a brave smile . . . Little did she know that night in January 1942 that she'd never be coming back.

3. Manchester

Kit arrived in Manchester soaked to the bone. Confused and cold, she'd sat on the train from Heysham to Victoria surrounded by troops laughing and joking as they chain-smoked cigarettes. Scared by their loud male voices, Kit huddled deeper into the ragged tweed coat that she'd taken from the bed she and her sister slept in. Her shoes leaked so much she couldn't even feel her feet, and her long black hair lay in wet streaks around her ashen white face. Seeing the wretched-looking girl squeezed into the corner of the compartment, the jovial troops tried to cheer her up with offers of soggy sandwiches, a Woodbine, even a swig of beer from a bottle. Too frightened to speak, wide-eyed Kit shook her head, then turned to the window, where she kept her eyes firmly fixed until the train puffed its way into Victoria Station. The troops shouldered their kit bags and disembarked as Kit dragged her case from the overhead netted luggage rack. Then she walked in the drizzling rain to her cousins' house in Moss Side. Loud and noisy, they welcomed her into their filthy two-roomed flat in a crumbling tenement block, where Colleen, the eldest of the cousins, showed Kit to a bed that was crawling with bed bugs and cockroaches.

Early the next morning Kit was given a slice of stale grey bread and a cup of black tea, after which she hurried through the sooty streets along with her chattering cousins to the Majestic Mill, where bossy Colleen shoved her through the door.

'Go and ask for a bloody job,' she said.

Cringing with embarrassment, Kit shook her head.

'You ask him,' she begged.

Colleen threw back her head and roared with laughter. 'I've already got a bloody job! Go and get one yerself.'

As Colleen and her younger sister made their way into the weaving shed, Kit hung back, too frightened to approach the foreman. She waited, hoping he might notice her.

'What can I do for you?' he asked when he caught sight of her lurking in a dark corner.

'I . . . I . . . I . .'

'Spit it out, lass, I 'aven't got all day,' he said good-naturedly.

'I need a job!' she blurted out.

Looking her up and down, he shook his head.

'You're not the size of two pennies' worth of copper,' he joked.

Thinking he was going to turn her down, Kit took a bold step forwards. 'I'm stronger than I look: I've been picking potatoes twelve hours a day in all weathers in Ireland,' she told him.

The foreman's eyes raked up her thin body draped in rags, but it was her eyes that arrested him. Large and dark in her pale anxious face, they showed the desperation of her situation.

'Aye, go on, then,' he said with a shrug. 'We're short in't card room – clock on there.'

Kit's first day was a nightmare. Fibres from the fluffy white cotton that they combed and separated floated in the air, covering the workers' clothes and hair in a layer of greasy white specks. Kit returned to the tenement block coughing and gagging from the fibres she'd inhaled and sometimes swallowed.

'Keep your trap shut,' Colleen advised. 'Swallow too much cotton and you'll clog your lungs and die coughing your guts up.'

Terrified of leaving her son an orphan, Kit kept her mouth firmly shut, but it didn't stop the evil fibres from going up her nose and covering her from head to foot. The combination of the dirty work in the carding room and life in the squalid tenement block was intolerable. After Kit picked up her first wage packet, she carefully counted out the money she'd agreed to send to her father, then realized all she'd got left to live on till payday was ten shillings and sixpence. She knew she had no choice but to continue working and living the way she was, but she seriously wondered if she'd survived the hazards of her daily life. Dysentery and tuberculosis were rife in the slums, and byssinosis was a virulent mill-related disease. Somehow she HAD to survive if only for Billy.

After shyly consulting an older woman in the carding room, Kit discovered there was a place in town called the Labour Exchange, where she was told she might be able to find alternative work. In her short dinner break Kit ran all the way up the steep hill to the Exchange. A woman behind the desk asked her age.

'I'm twenty-four.'

'You look about fourteen,' the woman said as she shoved a form across the desk to Kit. 'Do you know about female conscription?'

Feeling stupid and ignorant Kit dumbly shook her head. 'No,' she answered. 'I've just arrived from Ireland.'

'Lasses are being called up by the government to do men's work,' the helpful woman explained. 'Working on the land, or in factories, building planes and tanks and bombs. Though we can't force you into subscription seeing as you're from Ireland,' she quickly added.

Worried about the amount of money she might get paid, Kit asked, 'Do the government pay lasses to do this men's work?'

The woman laughed. 'Oh, aye!' she cried. 'Munitions work is good money. Mind you, you could be sent anywhere, Scotland, Wales, down South – and you have to live on site, working shifts around the clock.'

A slow smile lit up Kit's tired face as she realized she'd get more money doing war work; plus, if she was posted elsewhere, she could leave the slum where she was presently living. Smiling with hope, she asked one final question.

'When can I start?'

Kit had to endure the misery of her cousins' tenement block for two more weeks before a letter from the Labour Exchange arrived, instructing her to report to the Phoenix Munitions Factory in Pendleton. Fortunately Kit had had the foresight to warn her cousins in advance that she might be 'flitting', moving on to another mill job in Salford, where she told Colleen she planned to stay with friends she'd met on the boat coming over to England.

'God forgive me for lying,' she thought guiltily.

Kit had no choice but to deceive Colleen, as she knew

full well that she would be obliged to pass the information back to her father, whom she had every intention of keeping in the dark. She'd send home the money her dad expected every week, but what was left over from her munitions work she would save for herself and Billy. Luckily she was on the other side of the Irish Sea from her dad, who'd be unable to learn of her plan to squirrel away money for her future.

'What the eye doesn't see the heart can't grieve over,' she said gleefully to herself as she formed the bold plan to deceive her tyrannical father.

As the Pendleton bus rumbled out of the damp smoky city, the air began to clear and the slum blocks receded; and, though the black-faced mills with their tall sooty chimneys were still in evidence, they grew fewer and fewer as the bus drove further away from Manchester. When she saw skudding white clouds over the high misty ridges of the Pennines, Kit's heart lifted.

'Sweet Jesus,' she fervently prayed. 'Let this be a better place to live.'

4. Violet

Violet Walsh left Coventry Hospital, where she worked in the filing department, with a heavy heart. The last thing she wanted to do was return to her matrimonial home in Wood End. Beautiful, slender Violet, with widely set pale blue eyes and long silver-blonde hair, had married young, too young.

Seeing the Wood End bus approaching, Violet forced herself to join the queue at the bus stop, and when it pulled up at the shops a block away from her house she got off and bought some stringy sausages with her ration coupons. It was a relief to find the house empty, and, feeling the tension drain out of her, Violet switched on the radio, lit the fire and started to cook tea. When she heard the key turning in the front door, her heart skipped a beat and her pulse started to race. Panicking, she began to think about what he could find wrong. She was home, cooking his tea; the house was warm and welcoming. She jumped as Ronnie snapped off the radio, killing the music that she'd been enjoying. He peered at the stringy sausages in the frying pan, which he grabbed from her hand and threw at the wall.

'NO!' she cried in shock.

'Don't argue with me, bitch!' he cried as his hand came down and smacked her hard across the face.

After a few more blows to the head, Ronnie turned his

back on his wife and without another word walked out of the house. Reeling in pain, Violet slumped on the sofa, where she took out her handkerchief to wipe the blood dripping from her mouth and nose.

'God help me,' she prayed out loud, wondering for the millionth time how she could have made such a terrible mistake and ended up in this mess.

At eighteen she had been swooped off her feet by Ronnie, ten years her elder, a handsome bus driver who charmed her every day to and from work. How could Violet, a clever, educated girl brought up by a gentle mother, a music teacher and a widow, ever have guessed the enormity of the mistake she was making? The minute the wedding ring was on her finger, sweet-talking, romantic Ronnie kept her a virtual prisoner in the house, allowing her out only to go to work or to shop for food. She'd learnt early on in the marriage that to question or disobey him brought on a flash of temper, which resulted in a beating. Violet, previously so happy and carefree, was soon reduced to a nervous wreck.

There wasn't a day went by when Violet didn't ask herself WHY she'd ever allowed herself to be seduced by Ronnie. She remembered being flattered by the advances of a handsome older man, who showered her with gifts: nylons, chocolates, a gold watch and finally a diamond engagement ring, which a month after they'd married he pawned along with the watch. What a fool she'd been, flying in the face of her family's advice and ditching the devoted boy whom she'd been shyly dating since her grammar-school days.

Since the war started three years ago, their marriage had become even worse. Ronnie had successfully dodged conscription, claiming bad eyesight, which was a cowardly lie. As if that wasn't shaming enough, Ronnie had started meeting up with dodgy local spivs. Many a time Violet had come home from work to find her home stinking of cigarettes and black market whisky.

Nursing her new bruises and wiping blood from her broken lip, Violet felt something rustling underneath her; shifting position, she saw she was sitting on the *Coventry Evening Telegraph*. Her eyes blearily scanned the headlines, then stopped as something caught her eye.

CONSCRIPTED WOMEN MAKING A
DIFFERENCE

Churchill's secret army of female conscripts are stepping into men's shoes. Women across the nation are building bombs, tanks, planes and artillery for our brave boys on the front line. Massive residential sites are going up across the Midlands, Wales, Scotland, Lancashire and Yorkshire to house hundreds of women forced to move away from home in order to work in munitions factories.

Violet read no further: the paper fell from her hands, and she sat staring at the embers flickering in the hearth. Could conscription be her way out of the hell of a life she shared with Ronnie?

When Violet signed up at the Labour Exchange the next day, she specified that she wanted to be posted as far away from Coventry as possible.

'You could end up in Dumfries or Swansea,' the woman in the Exchange told her.

Violet smiled as she replied, 'The further away from Wood End the better!'

When she received instructions to sign on immediately at the Phoenix Munitions Factory in Pendleton, Lancashire, Violet hugged the letter to herself. After the first rush of euphoria, she wondered how she'd make it out of the house without Ronnie breaking both her arms. Predictably he went berserk when she told him, but after he'd hit her the first time Violet pointed out that neither she nor he had any choice: it was obligatory work, and she had to go.

'Over my dead body!' he'd roared, then slapped and kicked her until he got bored and went to the pub.

Violet managed to withstand the beating, safe in the knowledge that when she'd signed on at the Labour Exchange she'd begged the woman behind the desk to help her hide details of her posting from her husband. The middle-aged woman had looked at her through her dark bottle-top glasses before she quietly replied, 'You're not the only one, sweetheart.'

Violet's pale blue eyes had opened wide in surprise. Could it be that other women were on the run from their abusive husbands?

'I can bury your papers at the back of the filing cabinet; what you say to your husband is down to you,' the woman added kindly.

So Violet had lied to Ronnie. If she was ever going to escape him, the time was now. She'd made up a fictitious name and address for an armaments factory in Lincolnshire and planned to tell him she'd been posted there. Knowing how suspicious her husband was, she was sure he'd look it up and investigate its whereabouts in order to track her down, but the wonderful and fortuitous thing that gave Violet the confidence to lie was that the location of armaments factories was kept under wraps by the government. It was thought that spies infiltrating local neighbourhoods could pass on vital information to the Germans, who would happily bomb every munitions factory in Britain. LOOSE LIPS SINKS SHIPS the War Office slogans read, and in the case of bomb factories loose lips really did cost lives, so the less the Germans knew about the numerous munitions factories springing up all over the country the safer the workers were.

After bathing her wounds, Violet checked her suitcase, which she'd hidden for fear Ronnie would burn the contents. Underneath her clothes and shoes was her mother's silver clarinet – picking it up, Violet played a few discordant notes which brought tears to her bruised eyes. Maybe one day she'd play it again, when she was free of Ronnie and a hundred miles from Coventry. With her head ringing from her husband's repeated blows, Violet undressed and crawled into bed, where huddled under the blankets, she counted down the days to her departure. One thing was sure – she was never coming back, unless it was in a coffin.

5. The Phoenix

When the bus pulled up in Pendleton town centre, Kit alighted and looked eagerly around. It was a smaller, cleaner place than Manchester, she noted with relief; there was a tidiness to the town, with its rows of identical grey stone terrace houses stacked back to back, row upon row, reaching up to the foothills that dominated the landscape. Though there was a sharp wind blowing down from the Pennines, under which Pendleton nestled, the air felt clean and healthy, and the sky above her was bright and blue.

The smell of frying chips made Kit's tummy rumble. In her rush to get out of the city she hadn't stopped to eat and she was starving hungry. Following the tantalizing aroma, she made her way to a chip shop just off the town square and joined a long queue that snaked all the way from a cotton mill. Customers chatted to each other as they progressed down the line holding tin bowls. As Kit got nearer to the shop entrance, she could see a tall smiling woman behind the counter cheerfully filling the bowls with chips and peas, gravy, potato pie and butter beans. When it was her turn to stand in front of the cooking range from which steam rose in a great cloud, Kit fumbled with her purse. The good-natured, middle-aged woman gave her a knowing look.

'You're a stranger to these parts,' she said cheerily. 'What can I get you?'

Kit looked at the few pence in her purse before she answered hesitantly, 'A bag o' chips please, missis.'

Seeing a blush spreading across the girl's thin cheeks, the woman shovelled a generous portion of chips into a greaseproof bag which she lavishly sprinkled with golden scraps, then dolloped the lot with salt and vinegar.

'There you go, lovie,' she said as she handed the bag to Kit, who was salivating at the sight of so much good food.

'How much?' she asked nervously.

'Nothing!' the generous woman laughed. 'You look like you could do with a hot meal.'

Kit smiled gratefully before she was jostled away by the next customer. As she walked out of the shop, she gazed up at the board nailed above the steamy shop window: EDNA'S CHIPPIE – BEST IN LANCASHIRE!

'Thanks, Edna,' Kit murmured as she appreciatively polished off the delicious crispy chips.

Back in the town square, Kit asked an old man in a flat cap for directions to the Phoenix factory.

'They'll 'ave for't walk t'ot top of th'ill up yonder,' he said in the thickest Lancashire accent Kit had ever heard. 'It'll take thee a good 'alf 'our to get theer.'

Seeing Kit's confused expression, the old man simply pointed towards a steep cobbled street.

'Go up yon, lass.'

By the time she was halfway up the street, Kit was panting, but the view as she climbed got better and better. When she reached the top, where the street ended and the moors began, she followed a well-worn track through bracken and heather that led her towards a red-brick factory. Pushing open the heavy double doors, Kit stood in the entrance hall, wondering which way to go. From deep within the building there was a steady clattering noise, which Kit would later discover was the conveyor belt carrying bomb parts around the factory. Kit nervously crept towards a door which stood slightly ajar. Tapping on it gently, she jumped in alarm when a smart, formidable women appeared from behind it. Looking down her long hooked nose at Kit she snapped, 'Yes?'

'I'm Kit Murphy. I've come to sign on.'

'Papers?'

Kit produced the letter, now creased and dirty, which she'd received from the Labour Exchange. The woman scanned it, then nodded towards the entrance area.

'You'll find your digs on the noticeboard in the hallway.' With that she slammed the door hard in Kit's face.

After some searching Kit found her name amongst the hundreds of women's names typed on several long lists.

'Kit Murphy . . . Moor House Digs'.

A female worker coming off her shift kindly pointed out the direction of Kit's new accommodation, which was situated some distance from the Phoenix, on the edge of a moorland track. When she finally found it, Kit tentatively pushed open the front door and gazed in delight at a large spacious sitting room with an old sofa, a couple of chairs and a dining table. There were three very small bedrooms, each with a single bed made up with sheets, blankets and an eiderdown. When Kit walked into the bathroom, which had running hot and cold water, she cried out in delight. And then she caught sight of the indoor privy. This was a place that was fit for the KING!

There was an old wood-burning stove, which Kit (used to working the black lead range at home) immediately set about cleaning. When that was done, she lit a fire using some wood that had been stacked up by the side of the gable end of the house. When she looked at it from the outside, it became clear to her that the building was a renovated cowshed. Filling the rusty kettle perched on top of the wood-burner, she boiled water for tea, which she had carried from Manchester in a twisted piece of newspaper in her old canvas bag. Holding a tin mug of hot black tea, Kit sat back on the sofa and, as she did so, she felt her whole body relax.

'Holy Mother of God, thank you,' she said softly and, laying aside her tea, she put her head on the arm of the sofa and fell into the sweetest sleep she'd had in weeks.

Violet arrived in Pendleton just four hours after Kit. Her journey North had been fraught with fears; her major terror was that Ronnie would turn up at one of the stations the train stopped at and force her to return home with him. Once they'd cleared Stafford, Violet began to feel safer, and, as they approached Manchester and the Pennine Hills loomed up in the far distance, Violet let out a long sigh of relief.

'I've made it!' she murmured incredulously.

Hours later, when the bus from Manchester finally dropped her off in Pendleton, Violet felt giddy and light-headed. Like a convict released from a long dark imprisonment, she smiled in delight at the bright, rolling countryside. Following the bus driver's directions, Violet almost skipped up the cobbled street that led on to the moors, where, with only skylarks for company, she laughed with joy as she ran all the way to the Phoenix, a place she prayed would give her shelter from the storm.

After finding her name on the digs' rota in the factory, Violet, like Kit before her, made her way along the moorland track to her accommodation, where she found the door standing ajar. Nervous of disturbing anybody who might be sleeping off a long shift, Violet knocked gently, then, after getting no reply, she cautiously pushed the door open. She smiled with pleasure when she saw the sparse but clean sitting room and the crackling wood-burning stove with a little kettle steaming on top. Hurrying towards the heat to warm her chilled hands, Violet stopped in her tracks when she thought she saw a sleeping child curled up on the sofa. When she peered more closely, she realized with a shock that it was in fact a young woman with a mass of long dark hair which fell around her lovely pale face.

'Poor soul,' she murmured as she gazed at her dirty, ragged clothes and broken shoes.

Afraid of waking her Violet took a step backwards, but in doing so she caught the side of the table, which scraped on the floor, and Kit jumped up like a startled animal.

'HAHHH!' she gasped.

'Oh! I'm so, so sorry,' Violet cried. 'I never meant to frighten you.'

Kit gazed in amazement at the tall, slender woman with hair the colour of angels' wings and eyes as blue as the sky.

'Are you real or am I dreaming?' she asked as she rubbed her eyes.

Violet couldn't help but burst out laughing.

'I'm real all right, and I think I'll be sharing this place with you,' she said warmly. 'I'm Violet Walsh, by the way.'

Happy to have such delightful company, Kit smiled back.

'I'm Kit Murphy and I swear to God this is an owd cowshed,' she said in her lilting Irish voice. 'Don't get me wrong,' she added hastily. 'It's far and away the best place I've ever lived in. Come and see for yourself,' she said and, like an eager impulsive child, she took Violet by the hand and led her into the bathroom. 'Will you be looking at the indoor privy and running hot water and . . .' she cried as she pulled Violet into one of the bedrooms. 'A bedroom all to ourselves,' she exclaimed in delight.

Violet's thoughts flew back to the semi-detached house she'd shared with Ronnie for four nightmare years. It had a tiled pink bathroom, three double bedrooms, fitted carpets and a gas oven; she had fine crockery, good cutlery, clean linen and a full pantry thanks to Ronnie's under-the-counter dealings. But, for all its apparent luxuries, her former Wood End home in Coventry had been a place of torture and humiliation for her. This clean, airy cowshed open to the sky and the moors was heaven by comparison.

'Will you be after havin' a cuppa tea?' Kit asked when they returned to the cosy sitting room.

The warmth and sincerity of her new housemate brought tears to Violet's eyes.

'Thank you,' she replied.

She couldn't have asked for more.

6. Raw Recruits

Though their looks, clothes and backgrounds were vastly different, Violet and Kit instinctively bonded, each unaware that they had one essential thing in common: fear. After several cups of strong black tea, they decided it was time to take a tour of the factory.

'We need to get our bearings,' Kit said as she pulled a ragged misshapen shawl around her bony shoulders.

'It's raining,' Violet said as she pointed to the window, through which they could see a light drizzle falling. 'You'll get wet through.'

Kit shrugged. 'I'm used to that,' she said with a laugh. 'It never stops raining in Ireland!'

Violet noticed that though Kit had a wide, open smile that revealed her small white teeth, her dark eyes – more black than brown – remained broodingly sad.

'Poor kid,' Violet thought to herself as she noticed Kit's pale face and hollow cheekbones. 'With a bit of food inside her she could be quite a beauty.'

Grabbing a raincoat from her suitcase, she handed it to Kit, saying, 'Put that on. I've got a coat, and I don't need both.'

The black raincoat drowned Kit, but it kept her dry, though the sole on one of her shoes flapped as she walked along, something Violet ignored for fear of further embarrassing Kit.

Both girls were astonished at the size of the factory complex, which was like a town within a town. In order for the female munitions workers to remain on site, it was essential they had everything they needed to hand. Precious time would be wasted if they had to run up and down the hill into Pendleton to pick up food, go to the dentist or see the doctor. If the three rotating shifts spanning twenty-four hours were to run like clockwork, the world had to come to the Phoenix. The doctor, dentist, nursery, post office, small infirmary, chapel, pub, laundry and cinema were housed in the low camouflaged buildings close to the factory.

'They've thought of everything,' gasped Kit in amazement.

'They're obviously keen to accommodate us Bomb Girls,' Violet joked.

Kit's eyes flew wide open. 'Is that what we are, Vi?' She'd shortened the name within half an hour of meeting Violet, who was surprised how much she liked it. 'Bomb Girls?'

'For sure,' Violet replied. 'We're here to make bombs for the boys on the front line.'

More about the work of the Bomb Girls was explained to the recently arrived new recruits by the factory manager later that day. In the massive echoing canteen Mr Featherstone, a little man with a twirly moustache and a little twitch, stood on a metal chair to address the newcomers.

'Welcome, ladies!' he started.

Violet and Kit sneaked a look at the other girls assembled in the canteen – one of them, a tall glamorous brunette with a scowl on her face, caught their attention.

'She looks like she's just walked into a brick wall!' cheeky Kit remarked.

'Shhh!' Violet giggled as Mr Featherstone continued with his usual welcoming speech, which always laid great emphasis on factory safety.

'You'll be working round-the-clock shifts, six in the morning till two in the afternoon, two till ten, then ten till six in the morning. For this you'll be paid between two pounds and four pounds a week. With overtime and bonuses, your pay packet could amount to nearly eight pounds.'

Kit's heart skipped a beat with excitement. If she did get bonuses and overtime, she'd be able to save as much as four pounds a week for herself and Billy, sixteen pounds a month, over two hundred pounds a year! She dragged her attention back to Mr Featherstone.

'You'll be issued with white overalls and turbans; all jewellery, slides, grips and clips are banned.'

'What about us that're wed? Can't we wear our rings?'

Mr Featherstone nodded. 'Yes, but they must be securely covered with a sticking plaster. You'll be working with dangerous materials – cordite, TNT, gunpowder, amatol and fuses. I cannot emphasize enough, ladies, how the tiniest spark could cause an explosion that could take out the entire factory.' He paused dramatically so that his heavy warning could sink in, then drew the meeting to a close. 'You'll find a list of your shifts and your section on the canteen noticeboard.' Before he clambered off the chair he was standing on, Mr Featherstone concluded with a curt, 'Thank you for your co-operation.

Kit and Violet joined other women checking the

noticeboard. Tall Violet, who was able to peer over their heads, spotted their names.

'We're in the filling shed,' she told Kit. 'We start on the two o'clock shift.'

A girl beside them with flaming red hair that tumbled all around her very pretty face introduced herself.

'Hiya, I'm Maggie Yates. Mi sister, Emily, ses the filling shed's a right mucky job.'

'What's your section?' Violet asked curiously.

'I work with mi sister on the cordite line, filling bombs – that's mucky too – and it turns your skin yellow!' Maggie said with a cheerful laugh.

Kit's eyes had drifted from the noticeboard to the canteen counter, where a line of women was queuing up for their tea. On the menu were chips, bread and marg, pies and puddings, spam and corned-beef fritters and peas. For most of the workers what was on offer was common enough rationed fare but for Kit, who'd lived on a poor diet most of her life, it was an abundance of food. Sidling away from Violet, she joined the queue at the serving hatch. Ravenous, she picked up two chip butties and two pint-pot mugs of scalding hot tea, then hurried towards Violet, who was talking to the glamorous brunette they'd seen earlier.

'This is Gladys Johnson, Kit,' Violet explained when Kit joined them. 'She's been allocated accommodation with us in the cowshed.'

With her mouthful of chips, Kit could only mumble, but after she'd swallowed her food she said, 'Will I get you a chip butty too?'

Gladys shook her head, smiling. 'No, thanks, I'm not hungry.'

'This is the second lot of chips I've had today,' Kit confessed. 'God only knows how many I'll get through once I start working shifts!'

Violet got Gladys some tea and they all sat down together. After their meal Violet and Kit lit up Woodbines, which Gladys, a non-smoker, refused.

'I'd have preferred to have done my war work at home in Leeds,' Gladys confessed without giving a reason why.

'I couldn't get away from home quick enough,' Violet confessed.

Kit's eyes grew wide with unshed tears; she would have given a limb to have stayed at home with Billy, but that was her secret.

Violet and Kit helped Gladys carry her luggage to the digs, which she surveyed with undisguised horror.

'Oh, God! It really is a cowshed,' she groaned.

Kit, who simply adored her new home, pointed out its finer points.

'It's got a good roof, a dry floor – and it doesn't smell of cow muck!' she chuckled.

Gladys was grateful to her new friends, who made her welcome and lifted her spirits, which had sunk to an all-time low on her journey over from Yorkshire.

'I suppose I'll get used to it,' she said with a wistful sigh as she laid her suitcase on the narrow single bed in her room.

'It's a case of having to, sweetheart,' Violet said as she hung Gladys's smart coat on the back of the bedroom door. 'We're Bomb Girls now – our country needs us!'

7. The Filling Shed

Violet, Gladys and Kit had a fairly leisurely morning, unpacking and doing a bit of handwashing before their two o'clock shift began. After a plate of potato hash and pickled red cabbage in the canteen, where *Workers' Playtime* virtually drowned out the steady buzz of female conversation, they made their way to the stores and picked up their white overalls, turbans and heavy rubber shoes. In the changing room they stripped off their jewellery and hair slides, then slipped into their new factory outfits.

'These bloody boots are so heavy I can barely walk,' Kit giggled as she stomped around the changing room like Frankenstein.

'You'll be glad of 'em,' one of the girls changing shifts said. 'The factory floor's always kept wet, and the big doors to the dispatch department are wide open for the bombs on the overhead conveyor to shunt through. When a freezing cold wind blows in off the moors, it can take the frill off your drawers!' she joked.

Stuffing their hair into their turbans, the girls entered the filling shed, where they saw groups of women sitting around large tables. As the new girls stood uncertainly in the doorway, a tall handsome young man with cropped dark blond hair approached.

'I'm Arthur Leadbetter, the factory's safety manager,' he said. 'Welcome to the filling shed.'

'He's a bit of all right,' Gladys muttered behind her hand.

Violet hissed, 'Shhh!' as Arthur, who had fingers missing on both his left and right hands, pointed to trays of dark powder on the tables.

'That mucky grey stuff is gunpowder. Your job is to blend it with your fingers, then pack it into metal fuses – these' he said as he waved a fuse in the air. 'Further down the production line the loaded fuses will be attached to a variety of bombs and explosives, which will be dispatched to air bases around the country before they're flown out to the front line.' All the time he talked Arthur's gaze drifted to Violet, who even in her overalls looked lovely. 'Each of you will be working with a tray of twenty-five fuses which, when filled, will be collected by Malc, the overseer. Any questions ask Ivy – she's your supervisor,' he said as he pointed out a stout middle-aged woman who beckoned to them.

'Come and get yersels sat down,' she said as she dug her hand into a tray of gunpowder. 'It's a bloody dirty job, but some poor bugger's got to do it.'

The new girls watched her smooth the gunpowder under her fingertips and tap it into one of the empty fuses; then, all fingers and thumbs, they tried to copy her. It was close, demanding work that was expected to be done at speed. Concentrating hard, Violet, Kit and Gladys filled the fuses, then stacked them in trays ready for collecting. When the whistle went for their shift break, they hurried to the bathroom to wash out the gunpowder from underneath their finger nails; then they enjoyed ten minutes in the canteen, where Kit and Violet immediately lit up a Woodbine each.

'I feel like my eyes are crossing with concentrating so hard,' Kit sighed as she covered her mouth to hide a huge yawn.

Violet nodded as she exhaled a cloud of smoke. 'I can hardly see straight after peering down so many narrow fuses.'

Gladys appeared with a tray loaded with mugs of scalding hot tea and beef-paste sandwiches.

'Grub's up,' she said as she set the tray down on the table.

'Thanks, Glad,' said Kit, who had an endearing habit of shortening everybody's name. 'Is it only me that's hungry?' she said as she wolfed down a sandwich and hungrily reached for another.

'I'm hungry, but the smell of gunpowder makes me feel sick,' Gladys replied as she played with her food.

Violet smiled: it was good to see Kit eating well. The girl already had colour in her cheeks, and she looked less gaunt than when Violet had first met her in the cowshed.

Arthur Leadbetter approached their table.

'How did it go?' he said, addressing the question directly to Violet, who nervously stubbed out her cigarette.

'Fine, fine,' she mumbled.

Ignoring her friends, Arthur looked her straight in the eye. 'That accent of yours suggests you're not from these parts?'

Violet blushed and shook her head; there was no way

she was going to start up a conversation about where she came from with a total stranger. Scraping back her chair, she muttered, 'Excuse me!' and hurried into the ladies' toilets.

Standing at one of the sinks that ran in a line the length of the room, Violet looked at the give-away dent on her wedding finger. She'd thrown the ring out of the carriage window as the steam train pulled out of Coventry Station, but the mark of the ring was still there. Muttering under her breath, she rubbed her finger hard under the cold-water tap.

'The past is dead and gone – nobody must ever know my secret.'

Handsome as he was, Violet wished Arthur Leadbetter would not single her out – as far as she was concerned the less she had to do with men the better.

Back in the canteen, Gladys was asking Ivy why Arthur had not joined up. 'He looks strong and healthy enough,' she remarked. 'The forces are crying out for fit young men!'

'He was with the Cheshires, working with explosives,' Ivy said in a low voice. 'He had a terrible accident during the Battle of Dunkirk, lost three of his fingers.' She shook her head as she made sympathetic clucking noises. 'After being declared unfit for war work he were sent up here. He's the safety officer; he makes sure we don't all go up with the bloody rockets we're making!' she cackled. 'There's no more decent a fella than Arthur Leadbetter. He could have any woman in't factory if he set his mind to it, but he never puts a foot wrong. He's a proper gent,' she concluded.

When Kit and Gladys returned to the filling shed, Violet was already sat at the table, filling fuses.

'You shot off,' Kit said with a smile.

'I felt a bit sick,' Violet explained.

'Sick of Arthur Leadbetter?' Gladys teased.

'Sick of bloody men in general,' Violet muttered under her breath.

8. Gladys's Secret

Gladys desperately missed playing her alto sax, which she'd played every night in her bedroom at home. For her it wasn't just a question of practising new numbers in readiness for the weekend shows with Jimmy Angelo; the saxophone was like a limb to Gladys, an extension of herself. It reflected her changing moods: it could be soft and seductive, loud and vampy, sad and lilting, wild and reckless, haunting and romantic. Without her music, Gladys felt incomplete and out of sync with herself, and soon she realized she was depressed, a feeling she'd never experienced in her life before. She knew the only person who would understand her mood was her brother, Les, so she wrote to him and he immediately wrote back, sending her a black-and-white photograph of himself in a smart Yorkshire Regiment uniform.

'Play the damn thing, our Glad! You say you can't play the sax in your digs for fear of upsetting your mates, who work long shifts, fair enough, but you've got the moors right outside your front door. Get yourself up yonder – you'll be bothering nobody if you play on't tops but the birds and the bees!'

Gladys burst out laughing when she read Les's funny, warm insightful letter. Why hadn't she thought of that? She gazed proudly at his picture: he did look handsome, and so young and hopeful.

'God keep him,' she prayed as she tucked the photograph in her pocket.

The next day, after finishing an early-morning shift, she grabbed a spam sandwich in the canteen, then hurried back to the digs, where she pulled her music case out from under the bed. Opening the lid, she smiled at her precious sax lying in its navy-blue velvet bed.

'Hi, stranger!' she giggled. 'We're going for a walk!'

Swinging the brass instrument in her hand, and wrapped up against the bitter cold, she skipped along the worn rabbit trails, passing shoots of bracken breaking through the cold earth. She walked for a good ten minutes before she stopped and looked around. Les was right: the only signs of life on the cold wind-swept moors were hopping rabbits and wheeling skylarks. Wetting her lips, she gave the instrument an experimental toot.

'You're out of practice, lady,' she chuckled.

Taking a deep breath, Gladys put her lips to the mouthpiece, and tapping her foot on the heather she launched into the Andrews Sisters' 'Beat Me, Daddy, Eight to the Bar'. As the music got louder and more complicated, Gladys moved her body to the rise and fall of the notes; and towards the end of the song she was dancing along to the sound of her beloved saxophone. Laughing joyfully, she flung herself down on the soft springy heather, where she lay until she got her breath back. Even though it was a chilly February day, she felt hot after her exertions, but slowly began to cool down as she gazed up at the cold, ice-blue sky dotted with scudding grey clouds.

'That's *much, much* better,' she sighed contentedly.

Dusting twigs and leaves off her skirt, she rose to her

feet and swaying to the beat she played 'Don't Fence Me In'. Halfway through she stopped playing and, clicking her fingers, she sang solo as she had done with Jimmy Angelo's band. Her young strong voice floated out across the moors. Then she returned to the sax to conclude the song with an ear-splitting finale. Feeling a thousand times happier, Gladys skipped back home to the cowshed with a radiant smile on her face.

After carefully returning her instrument to its case under the bed, Gladys put the kettle on the wood-burner, which she stoked with logs so the house would be warm and welcoming when Kit and Violet returned.

'Where did you rush off to?' Violet asked as she flopped on to the old sofa.

Gladys shrugged as she answered with a smile. 'Oh, you know, out and about, shooting the breeze, as the Yanks say!' she joked.

Gladys's secret might never have been discovered had Violet not run on to the moors in order to avoid Arthur Leadbetter's advances. It wasn't that she didn't like the fella – who couldn't like the handsome, young man whose priority was keeping the Bomb Girls safe in a very unsafe environment? But Ronnie had been irresistibly attractive at first, and look where that had got her! In order to avoid engaging with Arthur, Violet made a habit of leaving the factory as soon as her shift was over.

One afternoon, restless and nervy after a bad dream about Ronnie, Violet could barely concentrate on her work. She couldn't stop thinking about what Ronnie would do if he managed to track her down. If he ever found out that she'd tricked him, outfoxed him and lied to him, he would kill her. Regardless of the consequences – being arrested, possibly hanged – Ronnie's temper would get the better of him and he'd strangle the life out of her. Arthur and her friends couldn't help but notice Violet's trembling hands and tear-filled eyes.

'Are you all right, lovie?' Gladys asked over their tea break.

Violet shrugged as she tried to answer with a cheery smile, 'That time of the month, you know.'

Back in the filling shed, Arthur was getting anxious. 'Don't overfill the fuses,' he warned when he saw her hands shaking as she worked. 'Take a break if you're not feeling well,' he added in a low concerned voice.

Violet ignored both his concern and his advice; instead she stayed on. But as soon as the hooter went for the end of her shift, she shot out of the building and ran up the hill to the safety of the cowshed. Once inside, too restless to sit down and worried that Arthur might take it into his head to follow her, she grabbed a coat, which she threw over her shoulders, then set off at a brisk pace over the moors. In the February sunshine, which had a sharp cold edge to it, she wandered along, criss-crossing paths, not really paying attention to where she was going. Swinging her arms and throwing back her shoulders, she quickened her pace, and, as she did so, felt the fear flow out of her. Oh, it felt good to be free!

As the sun, a ball of brilliant, bright orange, started to slide over the western hills, Violet stopped dead in her tracks as she heard the sound of music sweeping across the moors. Clear as a bell, strong and melodic, it made her catch her breath in amazement.

'Where's it coming from?' she said out loud as she hurried up the hill towards the source of the music.

Violet's jaw dropped when she saw Gladys on a grassy mound, surrounded by heather and sprouting fronds of green bracken, blowing on a saxophone!

'Oh, my God!' she gasped as Gladys, totally unaware that she had an audience, played her heart out.

When Gladys stopped for breath, Violet loudly applauded before walking towards her flabbergasted friend to say, 'That was unbelievable, Glad!'

Blushing and embarrassed, Gladys hugged the sax to her chest as she shyly asked, 'What're you doing here, Vi?'

'I haven't followed you, if that's what you mean,' Violet answered quickly. 'I just fancied a walk, I was wandering around when I heard music, wonderful music,' she added with a smile. 'And I followed it to you.'

Throwing an arm around her friend, she gave her a hug. 'Why are you keeping all this wonderful talent a secret?' she whispered.

Gladys slumped to the ground; tugging at Violet's hand, she pulled her down to sit beside her.

'It's only a secret here in Pendleton,' she said. 'At home in Leeds I played in a swing band. I loved it more than anything in the world,' she finished sadly.

'So WHY keep it a secret here? You've got a real gift – you should play for me and Kit!' Violet suggested excitedly.

'Oh, yeah, and keep you both awake all night blasting out "In the Mood"!' Gladys joked.

'I wouldn't mind,' Violet assured her. 'Come on,' she said as she pulled Gladys to her feet. 'Let's go and surprise Kit!'

Back in the cowshed, Violet couldn't help but notice that once Gladys started playing her sax the rippling melodies even seemed to chase away the habitual sadness from Kit's dark eyes.

'MORE! MORE!' she cried as she clapped her hands like an excited child.

Happy and relaxed, Gladys began regularly practising in the cowshed till late into the night, and Kit especially loved her wild boogie numbers. When she abandoned herself to dancing around the room with Violet, she suddenly felt young and elated; and, though it was a fleeting sensation, it always left her racked with guilt afterwards. How could she experience even the smallest joy when she wasn't with her baby? But Gladys's gentler numbers, serenades and love songs sent Kit drifting into a dream world where she was united with Billy and lived happily ever after, so all round the music was a real tonic for her.

News of Gladys's skills spread around the canteen, and it wasn't long before she was standing on a metal table entertaining the Bomb Girls during breaks. It made a pleasant change from the heated conversations that had been stirred up amongst the workers about the rights and wrongs of area bombing that had been issued by RAF Bomber Command. Its directive, to allow legitimate bombing in civilian areas, divided the munitions girls.

'I don't like it,' Violet protested. 'It makes us no better than the Germans during the Blitz; randomly killing innocent civilians has to be a sin in the eyes of God.'

Kit, fresh off the boat from Éire, which had declared its neutrality at the beginning of the war, was a little baffled.

47

'Will somebody be after telling me what the feck's the problem here?'

'In the past there's been an understanding about steering clear of bombing civilian areas, but, since the Germans don't share that feeling, Churchill's allowed Bomber Command, that's the RAF,' Gladys explained, 'to legitimately bomb civilian areas in Germany.'

'And who decides what's legitimate and what's not?' Kit asked in all innocence.

'That's the burning question!' Violet exclaimed. 'Some think that what's good enough for Jerry is good enough for us, whilst others say it's not war but mass murder.'

It was a relief to drown out the heated discussions with loud music. When the Bomb Girls heard their top wartime favourites, 'Tuxedo Junction' and 'PEnnsylvania 6-5000', they simply couldn't sit still. Jumping to their feet, they spun and twirled around the canteen until the hooter sounded, calling them back to work.

By popular demand, if she wasn't on the night shift, Gladys played and entertained her co-workers every Friday lunchtime. It was sweet to watch her pals relax to her music; it made Gladys happy to see the fear and tension fall away from them. For a few precious minutes they could forget about the misery of war and rationing and briefly abandon themselves to the magic of her music.

'Thanks, lovie,' cried the women as they returned, a lot happier, to the cordite line or the dispatch sheds. 'Your music brings a bit of joy and romance into our lives.'

One evening in the digs, as they drank cocoa around the cosy wood-burner, the three friends talked about the future.

'I just can't imagine life without war,' Gladys sighed.

'You know,' Kit confessed, 'with Ireland being neutral, I have to say I was hardly aware of it till I arrived here. I couldn't believe the terrible bomb damage in Manchester, and I hear things on the radio every day that frighten the bejesus out of me.'

'There's only one thing we can do, Kit, and that's "Keep calm and carry on!"' Violet advised as she quoted the familiar wartime phrase.

'Peace has to come one day,' Gladys said wistfully. 'Then what will we do when we're not building bombs?'

'I've always wanted to run my own dress shop,' Violet confessed with a blush.

'With a figure like yours you could be a model!' Kit insisted.

Violet shook her head. 'Nice of you to say so, Kit, but I hate people staring at me,' she admitted. 'I'd rather be behind the camera than in front of it,' she said with a modest laugh.

'Have you ever worked in a shop?' Gladys asked.

'No, I've only ever worked in the records office in the local hospital,' she answered; then feeling uncomfortable talking about her past, she quickly changed the focus of the conversation. 'What about you, Kit? Have you got any secret plans, dreams you hope that one day will come true?'

Kit's eyes opened wide as she held Violet's trusting gaze. How she longed to tell her the truth, to reveal her secret and speak openly and with pride about her son in Ireland. Instead she prevaricated with a joke and a smile.

'I'd like to have enough money to buy a new pair of shoes!' she answered.

'Your turn, Gladys,' Violet said, letting Kit off the hook yet knowing instinctively that she was keeping something back. 'What's your secret ambition?'

Gladys's dark blue eyes grew big and dreamy. Answering the question with a slow smile, she said, 'I've been dreaming for years of creating my own all-female swing band.'

Predictably, Kit, who loved just about every song on *Workers' Playtime* or *Music While You Work*, cried excitedly, 'You mean like Ivy Benson's women's dance band?'

'Exactly!' Gladys replied, then slumped as she added, 'But how's that going to happen now that I'm up here on the moors, working in a munitions factory?'

There was a pause as Kit thoughtfully stoked the burning embers in the wood-burner before she added a few more logs. 'You're in an all-female bomb factory,' she pointed out. 'If there's one thing you're not short of at the Phoenix, it's women!'

Gladys stared at her friend as she took in what she was suggesting. 'You mean audition for musicians in the factory?'

Kit nodded her head. 'Why not? You can't be the only musician in the Phoenix.'

Gladys sprang to her feet. 'You're right, Kit! You're absolutely right! Why didn't I think of that before?'

Kit smiled with pride. 'It just seemed obvious to me,' she answered modestly.

'I could put up a poster in the canteen asking for volunteers,' Gladys continued excitedly.

When Violet suddenly stood up and walked out of the room, Kit and Gladys turned to each other in surprise.

'Did I say something wrong?' Gladys whispered.

Before Kit could reply, Violet returned holding her mother's silver clarinet.

'I can play this,' she said awkwardly.

Gladys and Kit gazed at her in astonishment.

'You never said,' gasped Gladys.

'You never asked!' Violet laughed. 'I'm a bit rusty, but I'm sure I'll soon pick it up.' She gave a cautious toot-toot on the instrument, then smiled as she recalled the past before her marriage to Ronnie. 'It belonged to my mother; she was a music teacher,' she said with a proud ring in her voice. 'She taught me how to play the instrument when I was a little girl.'

Gladys flung her arms around Violet and hugged her. 'We can practise together,' she said, then she turned to Kit. 'Have you got any dark secrets you're keeping from us?' she asked with a cheeky smile.

Shocked by the question, Kit caught her breath, then realized with relief that Gladys was talking about music. 'Well . . .' she said cautiously.

'Spit it out!' Gladys urged.

'I had to learn to play the drums at school,' Kit admitted. 'The parish priest needed a drummer for the Catholic processions and I got landed with the job.' She laughed as she remembered. 'To tell you the truth I really loved it. I felt so grand and important marching along banging the drum at the head of the processions.'

Gladys shook her head in disbelief. 'WHO would have thought there was so much talent right under one roof!' she cried in delight.

Kit raised her hands in alarm. 'Don't go running ahead

of yerself, Glad,' she warned. 'I've not played in years – and I haven't even got a drum!'

Gladys paced the room, talking to herself. 'We'll need more players. Trombone, trumpet – and piano too.' With her cheeks blazing, Gladys turned to her smiling friends. 'You know something,' she said breathlessly, 'this could be REALLY good.'

9. Edna

Down in Pendleton, Edna Chadderton – a clever independent woman in her late forties, with arresting green
eyes and a mass of curling auburn hair flecked with grey –
was having a quiet smoke and a strong brew before she
opened the shop doors for the Dove Mill customers to
pour in for their dinners. She'd been giving a lot of thought
to the Bomb Girls up on the moors, and as an astute business woman she realized she was missing a seriously good
opportunity.

Glancing at the row of numbers she'd jotted down on
the back of a chip bag, Edna calculated that if she sold all
200 Bomb Girls a two-penny bag of chips every night,
she'd make a pound and thirteen shillings. Sadly, the busy
girls hadn't time to pop down into Pendleton, which
sorely grieved Edna.

'One pound and thirteen shillings a night,' she said as
she bit the stub of her pencil. 'Multiply that by five
nights . . . that would bring my takings up to more than
eight pounds a week.' Pausing to stand up and light the
gas underneath the cooking range, Edna muttered out
loud, 'I could make as much as ten pounds a week if any
of them lasses splashed out on a potato pie or a pastie.'

Watching the slabs of lard in the big pans break up like
polar ice caps, then dissolve in the heat and start to bubble, Edna wondered how she could entice the Bomb Girls

into town; then realized how slow and short-sighted she was and burst out laughing. 'You silly bugger, they can't come to you – you've got to go to them!'

After a busy lunchtime opening, Edna washed down the range, mopped the floor and then closed the shop before heading to the only motorcar-repair shop in Pendleton. After a good half-hour of bartering with the manager, a lanky middle-aged man she'd known from her school days, Edna finally got what she wanted: an old blue van big enough to be adapted into a mobile chip shop!

'Who's going to drive it?' the garage owner asked as Edna counted out her hard-earned five-pound notes.

'ME!' she replied.

His eyes widened.

'YOU?'

'Whilst you lads were away fighting on the French battlefields, us lasses were working to feed the nation. I drove a tractor all through the last war when I was working as a Land Girl,' she reminded him.

'Yon van will be a damn sight easier than driving a tractor,' the manager chuckled.

'As long as it's got gears and a steering wheel I'll manage,' Edna retorted with a confident smile.

Two weeks later Edna set off in her new mobile chip shop for the Phoenix. Under her instructions a local carpenter, again another lad she went to school with, fixed up a worktop that could accommodate a neat little chip range. The carpenter had widened the side window so Edna could serve her bags of chips to customers, and he'd added an external ledge for bottles of salt and vinegar. Inside the van, there was a small sink that could be filled up with a bucket of water and a tea urn – wherever Edna went tea went too! With a pink-and-blue checked pinafore wrapped around her voluptuous body and her unruly hair stuffed under a turban, Edna boldly parked in the dispatch yard and, after announcing her arrival by ringing a hand bell, she lit up her range and started to cook. As the mouth-watering smell of frying chips drifted across the yard, girls hurrying home after finishing their shifts were drawn to the van like iron to a magnet. They smiled when they saw Edna, arms akimbo, standing behind her cooking range.

'Best chips in Lancashire!' she called out as she beckoned to the workers. 'Tuppence a bag, scraps and salt and vinegar on the house!'

Kit, who'd hurried to the van with Gladys and Violet, grinned when she recognized Edna.

'You make marvellous chips, missis!' she enthused.

'Call me Edna.'

'Thanks, Edna!' said Kit as she handed over her twopence, then doused her chips in salt and vinegar.

After the girls had polished off their supper, they lingered by the van, which was warm from the bubbling cooking range. Lighting up a cigarette, one of the customers remarked, 'You're new round here, aren't you?'

'New up here, mebbe,' Edna replied. 'But I've been running my own chip shop in Pendleton for nearly five years now.'

'Did you drive up here especially for us?' Kit asked incredulously.

Edna grinned as she replied, 'You know what they

say? "If Mohammed won't go to the mountain then the mountain must go to Mohammed."' Seeing Kit's blank expression, she quickly added, 'I reckoned you hard-working girls wouldn't have the time to come to my shop in town, so I got myself a van and came up here to fry chips just for you Bomb Girls!'

'I hope you'll come often,' Kit said with genuine enthusiasm.

Looking at her takings in a tin box on the worktop, Edna smiled as she replied, 'I think you'll be seeing a lot of me and my mobile chippie, lovie!'

Edna's original calculations had been based on visiting the Phoenix five times a week but because she enjoyed the company of the appreciative Bomb Girls, who looked forward to the sound of Edna's bell ringing out her arrival, she got into the habit of driving to the factory nearly every night. As the weeks passed Edna's mobile chippie standing in the dispatch yard in all weathers became a communal hub. It didn't take the Bomb Girls long to realize that Edna dished out sound advice along with her chips.

There was no doubt that working at the Phoenix increased Edna's takings, but it didn't take long for her to realize just how much she enjoyed the company of these big-hearted women. They made her laugh; they told her about their husbands, brothers, fiancés and boyfriends fighting on the front line in north-west Europe. With every passing week Edna's affection and admiration for them grew.

'I might not be building bombs but I'm feeding the brave lasses that do!' she often joked.

Little Kit loved Edna's motherly warmth and humour.

When she wasn't working, she'd watch out for the blue van, and when she saw it approaching she'd smile and wave as she hurried out into the yard, eager for a chat with Edna, whom she instinctively trusted. It made Edna smile to see Kit with her silky black hair flying loose around her sweet heart-shaped face.

'Can I help you tonight?' Kit asked one evening as Edna poured the potatoes she'd previously peeled and chopped into the sizzling cooking range.

'Haven't you done enough already, filling fuses all day?' Edna asked.

Kit shrugged as she replied with an easy smile, 'This is different – this is fun!'

'Well,' Edna said, grinning, 'if you put it like that, how can I refuse?'

So an easy pattern was established: Kit regularly popped into the van to help Edna serve tea or wrap up bags of chips in newspaper when her shifts allowed.

'I don't know what I'd do without you, little lass!' Edna said fondly as they shared a cigarette during a lull one evening.

'Honest to God,' Kit enthused, 'I enjoy your company – and your chips!'

After she'd taken a drag on her Player's, Edna said, 'So where do you hail from, sweetheart? I can tell from that soft lilting voice of yours that you're not from these parts.'

Seeing Kit blush, Edna realized she might have overstepped the mark.

'Sorry, lovie, you don't have to answer – ignore me and my cheeky questions.'

Suddenly seized with an overwhelming desire to speak

of her son without shame or condemnation, Kit burst into floods of tears.

'I trust you, Edna, more than I've ever trusted anybody, and I want to tell you my secret,' she said unsteadily.

Frightened of saying anything, Edna held her breath as Kit told her what she'd never told any living creature before.

'I come from Chapelizod, just outside Dublin. Me and mi family live and work on a farm out there. I have a pig of a dad, a poor mammy who's dying of the consumption and' – she took a deep shuddering breath – 'a baby.'

Edna gently squeezed Kit's trembling hand. 'How old's your baby?'

As a slow smile spread across Kit's face and her eyes glowed with pride. 'He'll be three months old in March.'

Edna was visibly socked. 'Three months!' she exclaimed.

The glow faded from Kit's eyes as quickly as a light being turned off.

'Mi da forced me to leave my son; he forced me to travel to England to work in the mills so that I could send money back to him.'

Edna shook her head in confusion. 'Surely you and the child's father can refuse his demands?' she asked softly.

The colour rose in Kit's pale face; crimson with shame she murmured, 'The father is the landlord of the estate we live on; he raped me but mi da thinks I egged him on. As God's my judge I never did!'

Kit paused as Edna gently wiped her streaming face with a clean handkerchief. 'There, there, my sweetheart,' she said tenderly to the trembling girl.

Determined to get to the end of her story, which she

had bottled up for too long, Kit stared up at Edna with wild innocent eyes. 'I always thought the thing that goes on between a man and a woman would be beautiful and romantic, like the songs and poems say, but that' – she shuddered in horror – 'that was a nightmare.'

Edna softly stroked Kit's long silky black hair. 'And your father never once thought you were telling the truth?' she said incredulously.

'He always thinks the worst of me. But, for all the shame and humiliation, my Billy's the loveliest child you've ever seen,' she added passionately. 'I could have spent the rest of my life kissing and holding him but' – she concluded with a long sad sigh – 'it wasn't meant to be.'

Edna took Kit into her arms and slowly rocked her back and forth. 'You poor, poor girl,' she whispered, almost in tears herself. After a few minutes she asked a question that had been troubling her. 'How come you ended up here at the Phoenix, when your father sent you to work in the mill?'

'I hated the mill, so I looked for other work,' Kit said with a bleak smile. 'Mi da knows nothing about my whereabouts, and as long as he gets mi wages every week he doesn't care where I am or what I do,' she added angrily.

'And what about your bonny little lad?' Edna inquired.

'Da says he'll keep him as long as he gets his money,' Kit replied. 'He doesn't know that munitions girls get better paid than mill girls,' she added with a wicked wink. 'I save every penny I don't send home.' She dropped her voice to a whisper. 'My secret plan is to bring my son to live with me in England.'

Edna smiled widely as she nodded in approval. 'Hold on to that plan. If you believe in something enough, it'll happen.'

Kit gazed hopefully at her friend. 'Do you REALLY think that?' she gasped.

'I most certainly do!' Edna retorted robustly.

Smiling, Kit shook her head. 'Nobody's EVER believed in me before,' she whispered.

'Then it's about time they did,' Edna said as she rose to her feet and pulled Kit to hers. 'Look at me,' she commanded.

Kit's brown eyes locked with Edna's green ones. 'YOU CAN – AND YOU WILL! Repeat those words,' she urged.

'I can and I will,' Kit responded shyly.

'LOUDER!'

'I CAN – AND I WILL!' Kit almost shouted.

As Edna hugged Kit, she could feel the girl's sharp skinny bones through her overalls. Her heart ached for the tragic young woman whom nobody seemed to love or want. With a passionate expression, Edna caught Kit's tear-stained face in her hands.

'I understand about secrets, sweetheart,' she said with an intensity that surprised Kit. 'Don't worry, yours is safe with me.'

10. Gladys's Launch

On a blustery cold March morning in the steamy canteen Gladys gave Violet a sharp nudge.

'Time to make the announcement,' she whispered as she waited impatiently for the news to finish, then she boldly switched off the Bakelite radio before *Workers' Playtime* claimed the air space. Standing on one of the canteen's metal tables, Gladys tapped a spoon against her pint-pot mug.

'Sorry to interrupt, ladies,' she called over the din. 'May I have your attention for just five minutes?'

Gradually the noise subsided long enough for Gladys to speak.

'I'm looking for musicians,' she blurted out in a nervous rush.

'You've come to't wrong place,' a woman at a nearby table chuckled.

'Try the Hallé Orchestra in Manchester,' another cried.

'Here me out,' Gladys begged. 'I want to set up an all-girls' dance band, you know, like Ivy Benson's,' she explained.

The name caught her audience's attention; everybody loved Ivy Benson's dance numbers, especially 'Stardust' and 'I'm Getting Sentimental Over You'.

Seizing the moment, Gladys quickly said, 'I need women who can play the trumpet, trombone, piano, guitar.'

'Bloody hell!' a woman guffawed. 'You'll be lucky!'

Before ribald laughter drowned her out, Gladys cried even louder, 'If you're interested, meet me by the notice-board during the next break.'

The hooter recalling the girls back to work sounded, and Gladys stepped down from the tabletop.

'Do you think anybody will turn up?' she anxiously asked her friends.

Violet giggled as she replied, 'Let's face it, a bomb factory's not the likeliest of places for recruiting musicians!'

'But it's worth a go,' said Kit hopefully.

When Gladys returned to the canteen during the next tea break, she was met by two young women.

'I'm Maggie Yates,' the pretty redhead said. 'I can play the trumpet.'

'And I'm Nora Barnes,' said the other girl. 'I play the trombone – a bit,' she added nervously.

'We're both on the cordite line – Canary Girls,' Maggie, the bolder of the two, said. 'I work with mi sister, Emily.'

Gladys smiled as she replied, 'I know Emily, she's a great cook.'

Maggie smiled proudly. 'She likes making pies and pudding when she's not building bombs!' she joked. 'Best cook in Lancashire, our Em.'

Gladys quickly jotted down their names on a scrap of paper.

'Thanks for turning up, I'll be in touch soon,' she promised.

When she joined her friends, who were halfway through their break, Gladys gratefully accepted the mug of tea that Kit had saved for her.

'I suppose I should be grateful for small mercies – looks as if I've found myself a trumpet player and a trombonist. Let's just hope they can actually play!'

'That's a start,' said Kit enthusiastically.

'No pianist, though,' Gladys added. 'We won't get far without a pianist,' she added gloomily.

'One thing at a time,' Violet insisted. 'Audition the new girls, then worry about the pianist.'

The next day Gladys auditioned Maggie and Nora in the cowshed. Luckily both girls had their own instruments.

'Okay, ladies, let's hear what you can do,' Gladys said as she settled herself on the sofa in between Kit and Violet.

Maggie on trumpet was loud and brash, but she had genuine rhythm and could sing like a bird.

Gladys smiled as Kit gave her a gentle dig in the ribs.

'She'll do,' she said with a wink.

Nora, on the other hand, was not so good. She was a wildly over-enthusiastic amateur who would need a lot of training, but her heart was in the right place.

'I know I'm not up to scratch,' she said bluntly. 'But if you give me something to practise, I'll improve – I'll work at it,' she declared with a winning smile that showed the gap between her big front teeth. 'I won't let you down.'

Gladys reached for her alto sax.

'Let's try playing together. I've only got one music sheet but not to worry,' she added as she saw Nora's anxious expression. 'We'll peer over each other's heads and do our best.'

Kit didn't have any drums to play, but, as Violet and Gladys swung into 'Moonlight Serenade', she kept up a steady beat on the wooden dining table. Swaying to the rhythm, wriggling their bottoms and tapping their toes, Violet and Gladys set the tempo, which Maggie immediately picked up from the music sheet. Winking at Nora, Maggie encouraged her to join in whenever she could. It was impromptu but Gladys could see that with plenty of regular practice sessions they could pull together as a group – if only they had a pianist!

It was Kit who discovered the pianist. Shift work didn't allow her time to go to St Columba's Catholic Church in Pendleton, so occasionally she'd sneak into the little chapel on the Phoenix factory site and say a prayer to herself. Whilst she was on her knees saying the 'Our Father', her eyes strayed to a drum kit half hidden behind a curtain.

'BEJESUS!' she thought to herself. 'That could be a godsend.'

Another time, when Kit was hurrying down one of the many labyrinthine corridors that threaded through the factory site, she'd stopped dead in her tracks at the sound of accomplished piano playing ringing out. Curious, she'd followed the music to the chapel and tentatively opened the door to see who the pianist was. Seated behind the upright piano was a tall, middle-aged and big-boned woman wearing glasses that swooped up at the sides like silver diamanté wings. Creeping closer so as not to disturb her, Kit watched, fascinated, as the pianist's long, flexible fingers persuasively caressed the keys, drawing life and sound from the old upright that had been neglected for years.

After the final chords had faded away, Kit approached the woman.

'You play beautifully,' she enthused.

The lady bowed graciously. 'I was a piano teacher before the war, and a Sunday school teacher too,' she said as she stretched out a hand to Kit. 'Pleased to meet you. I'm Myrtle Tindal. I'm in packing.'

'Kit Murphy, filling shed.' Determined not to let this precious opportunity pass her by, Kit blurted out, 'Have you ever thought of playing in a swing band?'

Myrtle burst out laughing. 'I heard the announcement in the canteen, an all-girls' dance band,' she said and then added, 'I think I missed that boat.'

Kit stared at her in confusion. 'Why, what's wrong with you?'

'I'm a middle-aged woman, serving my country in the only way I can. I am *not* a young gadfly in a short skirt!'

'It's your music that counts,' Kit insisted. 'You play like a film star!'

Myrtle actually blushed with pleasure; she rather liked being called a film star.

'Come and meet Glad,' Kit begged, then she stopped short. 'No, other way round, Glad should come here and meet you and hear you play the piano.'

Myrtle quickly checked her glittering marcasite watch. 'I was just having a brief practice – I'm due in the dispatch yard soon,' she said sharply.

'Wait there!' cried Kit. 'I'll be ten minutes.'

Tearing across the site, Kit didn't pause for breath until she got to the cowshed, where she flung open the door and yelled, 'Glad! Come to church now!'

Gladys appeared with her gorgeous brunette hair in rollers. 'Are you joking?' she laughed.

Kit grabbed her arm. 'No, I've got a surprise for you,' she said breathlessly. 'Violet!' she called. 'You come too.'

Not wasting a second to explain, she dragged her friends across the site to the chapel, where they found Myrtle still at the piano. Panting for breath Kit said, 'Can you play a swing number, Myrtle?'

Myrtle paused for a second, then without sheet music she launched into Woody Herman's 'Woodchopper's Ball'. The girls stood open mouthed as Myrtle beat out the rhythm, and, finding it impossible to stand still, they started to dance around the piano. Gladys's fine strong voice soared out as she harmonized alongside Myrtle, who finished the piece with a series of rippling chords.

'Wonderful!'

'Marvellous!' the girls cried as they applauded Myrtle, who was now on her feet, clearly in a hurry to get back to work.

'So do you think you could be our swing-band pianist?' Kit sweetly asked.

'I'm far too old,' Myrtle said again, though the glint in her eye belied her demure reply.

'You're not!' Gladys cried as they hurried down a corridor after her. 'It's about the music, not age.'

Before they parted ways at the workshop door, Gladys said, 'Please just think about it?'

'You'd make all the difference,' Violet assured her.

'Pleeeease,' begged little Kit.

Myrtle nodded. 'I'll think about it,' she said with a smile.

By the end of her shift, Myrtle had decided she would join the swing band on condition that she would never have to wear a short skirt or dye her hair blonde.

'You're perfect as you are,' said Kit as she hugged the new band member.

Kit later showed Gladys and Violet the dusty drum kit she'd noticed behind the curtain in the chapel.

'It needs a good clean up,' she said as she sat down before it. 'But it plays well.' Pressing the pedal, she hit the base and the snare drum and clashed the cymbals.

'We're in business!' Gladys laughed.

'Though we'd better check with the chaplain,' Violet added.

'You're not telling me that he comes here on a regular basis to knock out a few jazz numbers?' Kit joked.

'No, but he might get a shock if you suddenly start up drumming during one of his sermons,' Violet teased.

Later that night, as they boiled milk for their bedtime cocoa, Gladys was still worried.

'If we can get Nora up to scratch on the trombone, we'll be in business; if not we might be looking for a new trombonist and that would break poor Nora's heart.'

It was Myrtle who took Nora under her wing. Having taught music for years, she was experienced in bringing on young musicians. With Myrtle in packing and Nora on the cordite line, their shifts didn't always overlap, but that didn't stop the determined couple from meeting at least once a day, whether it was an early-morning practice or last thing at night. Myrtle taught Nora the techniques she needed, such as how to blow down the trombone instead of puffing at it.

'You have to purse your lips like this,' she explained as she puckered up her own lips to demonstrate. 'You need to get a steady stream of air into your instrument if you're to produce a clear note,' she added. 'At the moment we're getting a lot of flat notes.'

Nora chuckled, 'More like rude noises!' she joked.

'Practise positioning your fingers on the valves,' Myrtle advised as she took up Nora's trombone. 'Keep your fingers soft and supple so you can stretch to the furthest valve,' she said as she demonstrated the move. 'And try not to get flustered; if you do you'll hit the wrong one.'

'And that'll be another rude noise,' Nora commented.

Myrtle discovered that if she played a soft piano accompaniment to Nora's trombone pieces, the girl visibly relaxed and her confidence grew.

'Excellent,' Myrtle said in praise of her student after she'd completed her best piece of music to date.

Nora's big round face grew pink with pleasure.

'Now,' Myrtle added. 'Let's try that Gracie Fields song you love so much.'

Nora nodded enthusiastically. '"Sing as We Go" – it's my big sister Nellie's favourite song,' she said as she pursed her lips exactly as Myrtle had taught her and blew a series of clear melodious notes.

As Myrtle made progress with her student, Gladys and Maggie practised backing harmonies, whilst Violet accompanied Kit to the chapel, whenever it was available to them, so Kit could play the drums and Violet her clarinet.

It took over two weeks of hard concentration and repeated practice sessions (in between their long gruelling shifts) before they really began to swing as a band. After a lively rendition of 'South of the Border', with Gladys and

Maggie singing in beautiful harmony to Violet's lilting clarinet, Kit's seductive drumming and Nora's gritty trombone playing, Gladys smiled in approval.

'I think it's time we launched ourselves on the public,' she announced.

'You mean perform?' Maggie gasped.

Gladys nodded. 'Put on a show at the canteen, open it up to the public as well as the workers.'

Nora paled. 'Are we ready for that so soon, like?'

'We could be waiting forever for the right moment,' Gladys replied.

Myrtle nodded in agreement. 'There's nothing like a performance to focus the mind,' she said knowingly.

'Well, then, we'd better come up with a name for ourselves,' Kit giggled.

Gladys, who'd spent months day-dreaming about her band, grinned as she answered without a moment's hesitation. 'I've got one already: The Bomb Girls' Swing Band.'

Myrtle, Nora, Maggie, Violet and Kit smiled at each other.

'It's got a nice ring to it,' Myrtle said approvingly.

'Let's take a vote,' cried excited Gladys. 'Show of hands, ladies!'

As five hands shot up in the air, Gladys clapped her hands excitedly.

'YESSSS! The Bomb Girls' Swing Band is launched!'

11. Swing Band Debut

A Saturday night at the start of May was suggested to Mr Featherstone, who promptly agreed that the Phoenix canteen could be thrown open to the public to attend a dance there, on condition that he and his wife could attend too.

'This will boost war-time morale,' he enthused to Malc, who'd been delegated by Gladys to approach the factory boss.

'I should think half of Pendleton will be there when they hear it's an all-lasses band,' Malc commented.

'Just make sure you get me tickets. I wouldn't miss this show for the world,' Featherstone replied.

With their debut night less than a fortnight off, Gladys was getting cold feet.

'It was you that suggested going public in the first place,' Edna reminded her after Gladys had poured out her woes one wet breezy evening in the dispatch yard.

'I thought it would boost our morale,' Gladys replied limply.

'And it clearly has,' Edna remarked. You might well have up to 200 people to entertain if all the Phoenix girls show up.'

'They won't all come!' Gladys answered dismissively.

'Don't count your chickens,' Edna teased.

Gladys groaned. 'Stop tempting fate, Edna,' she begged.

Lighting up a Player's, Edna got down to brass tacks. 'What's worrying you most, our kid?' she asked bluntly.

'The amount of numbers we've got to learn,' Gladys blurted out. 'The song list is SIXTEEN!' she cried.

'They're not *all* songs, though, are they?' Edna asked.

'A mixture of dance numbers and songs,' Gladys told her.

'Do the girls already know the songs?'

Gladys nodded. 'I purposefully chose the songs we use for our practice pieces.'

'Well, then, that's not so bad if they're already familiar with them,' Edna said as she pushed a clean chip bag and pencil towards Gladys. 'Write down all the songs you know off by heart.'

After Gladys had scribbled down eight song titles, Edna stubbed out her cigarette and studied the list.

'So that only leaves eight more to learn; make them dance numbers,' she suggested. 'That way you won't have to worry about any lyrics.'

Gladys's lovely face lit up with a happy smile. 'Why didn't I think of that?'

'Because, Miss Panic Drawers, you're working too hard and you're not thinking straight.'

Gladys blew her grinning friend a big kiss. 'Thanks, Edna. I don't know what we'd do without you!'

Feeling better for her discussion with her older friend, Gladys walked slowly home, all the time chastising herself for her unprofessional behaviour. Edna was right: she had panicked; as bandleader she was solely responsible for not spreading alarm amongst her fellow musicians, who were gaining in confidence day by day.

Nora was thriving under Myrtle's careful supervision; Maggie's trumpet playing had improved too, and she picked up quickly on their backing harmonies; Kit and Violet were fine, as were she and Myrtle – well, Myrtle was flawless!

Once they'd established what they were going to play, the band decided to do four dance numbers and four songs in the first half of the show; then, after a thirty-minute supper break, an equal number of song and dance pieces in the second half of the evening.

'We'll end the show with Nora's favourite. "Sing as We Go!"' Gladys announced. 'That'll have 'em all on their feet.'

Confident about their repertoire, the Bomb Girls' thoughts turned to clothes.

'What are we going to wear?' asked Maggie.

'Ivy Benson's girls wear identical ball gowns,' Kit replied knowingly.

'Oh, yeah, and we've got plenty of them tucked away in the back of our utility wardrobes!' Maggie teased.

'Well, actually . . .' Gladys rose to her feet. 'I'll be back,' she said. 'Don't go away.'

When she returned she was holding one of the glamorous ball gowns she'd worn when she was singing in Jimmy Angelo's band.

'GOD!' Maggie gasped as she leapt to her feet to examine every detail of the full-length pink satin dress trimmed with little pink bows and sequins. 'It's gorrrrrgeous,' she murmured.

'I designed it and had it made,' Gladys explained. 'This is what I *used* to wear,' she said, emphasizing the past tense.

'Could we wear something like that?' starry-eyed Nora begged.

Gladys shook her head. 'We haven't got the money to spend on six posh frocks,' she said firmly. 'Nor the time to get them, for that matter,' she added as an afterthought.

Kit, who was the least vain person in the world, waved her hand dismissively. 'We should be concentrating on our music, not clothes.'

'We should at least try to wear similar clothing,' Myrtle insisted.

'The only clothes we've got in common are the Phoenix uniforms – white overalls and turbans,' Violet pointed out.

Gladys snapped her fingers, 'You know, that's not such a bad idea.'

'I hope you're joking!' Maggie exclaimed.

'Seriously,' Gladys continued. 'We're the Bomb Girls' Swing Band, so why not dress as the genuine thing?'

'And there was I dreaming of gorgeous ball gowns,' sighed Maggie.

'When we're famous, we'll be dressed like princesses,' Gladys promised. 'But for now we'll dress like the Bomb Girls we are – but without the big rubber boots!'

'Thank God for small mercies,' chuckled Myrtle.

The days whizzed by in a flurry of frantic activity. When they weren't filling fuses, they were practising their numbers, and when they weren't doing either they were sleeping deeply from exhaustion.

'Oh, dear,' sighed Violet one morning as they staggered into work with dark circles around their eyes. 'I hope we're not going to disappoint our workmates.'

'Don't say that, Vi!' Kit protested fiercely. 'We must all do our best; they need us.'

All eyes turned to Kit in surprise. Blushing, she tried to explain herself. 'It's our job not to disappoint our audience,' she said firmly. 'If we can give them a break, a chance to dance and relax, that would be enough for me.'

What her friends didn't know was that Kit spoke from real experience. The more she played with the band, the more she loved the music, which alleviated, however briefly, the constant gnawing anxiety of how much she missed Billy and how much she worried about his well-being. She'd put all her faith in her sister, Rosie, but being so far away she had no real idea of what was going on back at home, something she found agonizing. If music gave her some respite, maybe it would have the same effect on her fellow workers, even if it was only for five minutes.

'Kit's right,' Gladys agreed. 'We hear bad news every day on the radio; only yesterday we heard the bloody Huns are doing everything they can to take Sevastopol. We can do nothing to stop them killing and slaughtering thousands of innocent civilians but what we can do,' she declared with passion ringing in her voice, 'is rally the workers: take them out of their miserable, humdrum worlds and allow them to be carefree and happy, even if it is just for a few hours.'

Violet smiled. 'Point taken,' she said, then added as she took a deep breath to steady her nerves, 'KEEP CALM . . . AND DANCE!'

On the morning of their debut, Gladys was thrilled to find a letter from her brother, Les, in her pigeon-hole. It had been opened by the censors, and there was no date or location, but it was full of news and hope.

Hiya, our kid,

Well, I don't know where to start. I'm in a country where I don't speak the language, but me and our battalion get by and, as you well know, I'm an expert when it comes to smiling at pretty girls!

'Typical!' giggled Gladys.

I miss playing in the regimental band with Captain Horrocks directing us. He's a good bloke – sent us off with a smile and a wave of his baton! I miss home and Ma's grub and you and Pa but I'm happy fighting for my country and I enjoy the joshing that goes on between me and the lads in between the fighting. When they saw my trumpet in my kit bag they asked could I play. I told 'em I just lugged it round for the fun of it! After I'd entertained them with a few numbers they called me the Yorkshires' 'Bugle Boy'! They have me playing regularly, which is good for my practice, they say my music cheers them up when they're missing their girlfriends! In fact me and a couple of lads who play trombone and guitar do a lot of serenading in between the action. It makes me think of you, our Glad, and the duets we played which drove poor Ma crackers! Hope you're keeping up with your music and not letting your saxophone grow rusty. Also hope you're not meeting too many fellas, they'd better not put a foot wrong or I'll sort 'em out next time I'm home.

Lots of love,
Your loving brother,
Les
xxxxx

Gladys hugged the letter to her and she said out loud, 'Wish me luck, Les. Today's the big day! Wish you could be here to cheer us on,' she added wistfully.

Malc and a group of volunteers had made an attempt to transform the utilitarian canteen into a dance-hall. They'd hung paper decorations around the room, and Malc had somehow got hold of some mirrored silver balls, which twirled and glittered when the lights were dimmed. A makeshift stage had been built at one end of the room and a space cleared for dancing. Hot and cold drinks would be served from the kitchen along with Edna's tasty meat pies and mushy peas.

When the big day dawned, the girls hurried home at the end of their shift and shared tepid baths before slipping into clean white overalls.

'I don't know why we don't wear our usual overalls,' Maggie said as she stuffed her thick hair underneath her turban.

Myrtle rolled her eyes in despair. 'Think girl — THINK!' she scolded.

Seeing Maggie's blank expression, Myrtle elaborated. 'You and Nora work with cordite; Gladys and the others work with gunpowder. Particles of explosives remain on your overalls, which would most certainly go up in flames if somebody were to light a cigarette near you.'

'OH!' Maggie gulped as the penny dropped.

After helping each other with their hair and make-up the girls made their way to the empty canteen, where they found Arthur and Malc setting up Kit's drum kit and Myrtle's piano, which they had just moved from the chapel.

'Thank you for helping us out,' Gladys said gratefully.

'I hope the move hasn't made it even more out of tune,' Myrtle fretted as she ran her fingers along the keys of the ancient piano.

Arthur's eyes were on Violet, who, with her silky fine hair flying loose from her turban, was practising her clarinet. His heart ached as he caught sight of the sadness in her eyes as she played. For the hundredth time he wondered what he could do to make her happy. He longed for her to open up to him, trust him, be his friend, but it was like trying to catch a wild bird: the nearer he got to her, the further away she flew.

'That's beautiful,' he said as she finished the piece.

Blushing with pleasure, Violet didn't hurry away; instead she briefly held his gaze.

'I'm looking forward to hearing you play more later,' he added softly.

Malc interrupted their exchange. 'Come on, Arthur, let's be having you,' he called out. 'Doors open at half past seven, sharp,' he told the girls as he and Arthur left the room.

As a warm-up exercise the band played their opening and closing songs; then the canteen doors were thrown open and an eager crowd poured in. Leading them was Mr Featherstone with his plump smiling wife on his arm.

'Good evening – may I introduce you to my wife, Sybil, and these, my dearest, are the Phoenix's very own swing band.'

Mrs Featherstone shyly bobbed a curtsey, then followed her husband to a table positioned as close to the stage as possible.

As the audience drifted around the space, lighting cigarettes, greeting friends and checking out the talent, Myrtle played a light waltz on the piano; then, as people gathered expectantly near the stage, Gladys gave a nod to her fellow musicians. Tapping her right foot, she chanted, 'A-1, a-2, a-1, 2, 3, 4.'

And, raising her alto sax to her lips, Gladys played her solo introduction to the Andrews Sisters' 'Tuxedo Junction'. The audience, which consisted of female munitions workers and a large local crowd, immediately grabbed partners, male or female, and started to dance. The girls smiled and nodded at their friends in their best dresses with their hair washed and dried, swirling and twirling on the dance floor, happy and lost in the moment, just as Gladys had hoped. As one number followed another, the dancing varied from foxtrot to waltz, then a quick-step followed by a tango, but the all-time favourites were the jive numbers – 'PEnnsylvania 6-5000', 'In the Mood', 'Beat Me, Daddy, Eight to the Bar' all sent the audience wild.

When the Bomb Girls stopped for a well-deserved break, they were hot and sweaty but very, very happy.

'It's going well!' Nora gasped. 'They like us.'

'They bloody love us!' laughed Maggie, who'd lost her turban halfway through their first song and had strands of her thick hair flying loose around her glowing face.

Myrtle rose from the piano and said with almost regal dignity, 'I must pay a visit to the lavatory.'

'And I must get something to eat,' said hungry Kit, who could smell Edna's meat pies from halfway across the canteen.

After trips to the ladies' and, in Kit's case, polishing off one of Edna's meat pies, the girls reassembled on stage as Malc dimmed the lights for their foxtrot number, 'A Nightingale Sang in Berkeley Square'. After this the night flew by, and before they knew it they were on their final song, Nora's all-time favourite, 'Sing as We Go'. After a rousing introduction from the brass section, the girls broke into song, as did the audience. The canteen echoed with the happy, hopeful sound of young voices, which gave way to applause as Gracie Fields's spine-tingling song drew to a close.

'MORE! MORE! MORE!' yelled the audience.

Gladys winked at the girls. '"Tuxedo Junction" one more time?' she asked.

The audience clapped and cheered as they took to the floor, and if it hadn't been for Mr Featherstone finally calling a close to the proceedings, the Bomb Girls might have been forced to play till dawn.

'That's enough now,' said the manager kindly but firmly. 'These lasses have to be on the bomb line first thing in the morning. Thank you, ladies,' he said as the lights came up, causing the audience to blink like baby owls startled from their sleep. 'You've done the Phoenix proud. Good night and God bless.'

As the tired but triumphant musicians packed up their instruments and collected their music sheets, Arthur appeared again by Violet's side.

'May I have the honour of walking you home?' he said as he relieved her of her clarinet case.

As Violet hesitated, Arthur quickly added, 'Just a walk up the hill, then I'll be on my way,' he promised.

Seeing the pleading in his dark blue eyes, Violet relented.

'That would be nice,' she said as she followed him out of the canteen and into the starry night.

12. The Sisters of Mercy

Exhausted but happy, Violet, Gladys and Kit fell into their beds, grateful that they had an afternoon shift the next day. As they made their usual breakfast of tea and toast around the wood-burner, Gladys and Kit teased Violet about walking home with Arthur.

'He was the perfect gent,' Violet cried. 'Never laid a hand on me.'

'He's been after you since the first time he set eyes on you,' Kit giggled. 'I think he's lovely, and good-looking too.'

'With his looks he could have any girl in the factory,' Gladys added.

'It's not his looks that impress me,' Violet replied sharply. 'It's what's inside the man that matters.'

'You can say that again,' said Kit bitterly.

After they'd clocked on at the Phoenix, Gladys went to check her pigeon-hole in the hope she'd find another letter from her brother. Finding none, she checked her friends' pigeon-holes and returned with a letter for Kit, who went as white as a ghost when she saw the Irish stamp and postmark on the envelope. The only person in the world who knew her address in Pendleton was her sister, Rose, who was sworn to secrecy.

'Never, never tell mi da,' Kit had begged when she'd given it to Rose. 'And only use it in an emergency.'

Knowing instinctively that it could only be bad news,

Kit's hands began to shake. Was her mother dead or Billy sick? Hurrying into the ladies' toilets, she dashed into a cubicle; then, after bolting the door, she ripped open the envelope.

Dear Kit,

Come home right away. Da's got plans for Billy that you must stop. He'll flay me alive for telling you but I have no choice.

Your loving sister
Rosie.

Sitting on the toilet seat, Kit groaned as she rocked back and forth in a turmoil of fear. What on earth had happened? She felt a visceral need to get home to her darling boy as soon as she possibly could. 'Blast this war,' she thought. How would she manage to get time off work and secure an urgent passage to Ireland as quickly as she needed to? She didn't even know where to start, and the increasing sense of panic she felt wasn't helping her to think logically.

'EDNA!' she suddenly thought. 'Edna will help me.'

After her shift, Kit stood outside in the wind and the rain waiting for Edna to show up. When she caught sight of the blue van, frantic Kit ran in front of it to flag it down.

'God Almighty!' cried Edna as she slammed on the brakes.

Sobbing uncontrollably, Kit showed Edna her sister's letter. Staying calm and focused Edna said, 'I'll sort out your travel arrangements; your priority is to get compassionate leave off Mr Featherstone.'

'I can't tell him I've got a baby!' Kit gasped.

'Tell him the truth – your mam's dying.'

'He might sack me and not let me come back,' Kit fretted.

'Don't be daft,' Edna chided gently. 'Everyone's entitled to compassionate leave, especially in these circumstances.'

So Kit, a shaking nervous wreck, went to see Mr Featherstone in his office the next morning before her shift started. First, she had to circumnavigate his officious, bossy secretary, Marjorie, who kept her waiting in the cold corridor a good half-hour before she could tremblingly present her case to Mr Featherstone in his cosy office, where a fire crackled in the hearth and tea and biscuits were served to him by the devoted Marjorie.

'I'm sorry, sir, I've got to go home – Ma's dying, as we speak.'

Seeing the poor girl weeping and distraught, Mr Featherstone granted her leave.

'But only for three days, mind,' he said as he helped himself to a second biscuit. 'We need you back on the bomb line ASAP.'

Grateful for anything, despite knowing the travelling time would take up much of those three days, Kit ran back to her digs, where she frantically packed a few belongings and some of the money she'd saved into her old suitcase. She left a brief note on the dining table for Violet and Gladys, who had already left for work.

Bad news from home. Got three days of compassionate leave.

Love,
Kit.

Breathless, she ran down the hill into Pendleton, where she banged on Edna's shop door. When it was thrown open, Kit fell into Edna's arms.

'Everything's going to be all right,' the older woman soothed as she led Kit into the back of the shop, where she made her a cup of tea. 'I've booked your passage and here's your train ticket to Heysham,' she said as she handed Kit a ticket.

'Thank you, oh, thank you,' gasped Kit. 'I'll pay you back; I've got plenty of money saved up.'

Kit waved goodbye to Edna at Clitheroe Station. As the plumes of sooty black smoke enveloped the platform, Kit slumped wearily into an empty seat. What could her father be planning to do with her son, she wondered as the train gathered speed. What was it that had frightened her sister so much she'd disobeyed her father just to inform her? Kit shuddered in dreadful foreboding; a terrifying urgency suddenly gripped her and she willed the train to go faster and faster, for she knew with overwhelming certainty that if she didn't get to Billy soon it would be too late.

'Holy Mother of God!' she prayed out loud. 'Please take care of my son.'

In the Phoenix canteen there was much discussion about the Germans' strategic bombing of Britain's cathedral cities, which had systematically been targeted by the Luftwaffe since April.

'The brutes have studied their guide books and ticked off the oldest and most historical English cathedrals, then bombed them into the ground,' Myrtle sighed with tears in her eyes. 'Ancient buildings which have stood as a symbol of our Christian faith for over a thousand years are going up in flames.'

'As if it's not enough for the Third Reich to slaughter our brave lads – now they're hell-bent on destroying our national landmarks,' Gladys seethed as she pulled Myrtle's newspaper closer so that she and Violet could see the black-and-white photograph of Exeter Cathedral.

'Coventry's been bombed over and over again,' said Violet as she recalled the tragic sight of her city's cathedral destroyed by repeated German bombing attacks.

'It looks like it took another beating last night,' Gladys said as she pointed to a boldly headlined article lower down the page: COVENTRY'S WOOD END STREET AND RESIDENTS BLASTED!

Violet's eyes widened as she read the article.

Wood End, with its engineering works and factories, has yet again been targeted by enemy bombers who dropped high-explosive bombs on Tuesday night whilst innocent civilians slept in their beds. Utilities were knocked out, the water supply, electricity network, telephones and gas mains; many roads in the area were cratered. One entire street, Sawley Avenue, was wiped off the map. Fire workers are sifting through the wreckage, but ambulance crews have stated there are no survivors in the tragic ruins of Sawley Avenue; all seventy-two residents, including innocent women, children and babies, all perished.

Violet caught her breath. 'Sweet Jesus!' she gasped.
Her friends turned to her in alarm.
'What's the matter, Vi?' Gladys asked.

Hating herself for lying to her friend, Violet prevaricated.

'I just can't believe these terrible pictures,' she said as she pointed to the photographs of the bombed cathedral cities.

She was relieved when the hooter went and she could return to the filling shed; she automatically filled dozens of fuses with gunpowder, all the time thinking, 'My neighbours, my friends. And Ronnie.' Dare she really hope that Ronnie was dead? Blown up along with everybody else in Sawley Avenue? They had said there were no survivors. They must have checked; they wouldn't publish something like that without being sure of their facts. Her heart ached for all her former neighbours – mothers, sisters and fiancées of lads who had joined up. She'd known them all, and they'd been kind to her, even though they knew her husband was a liar and a coward. They'd seen her cuts and bruises after his savage attacks and understood all too well what went on behind closed doors. Even though Violet grieved for the innocent civilians, she couldn't help but feel the beginning of a flame of hope licking through her. Could it be that, at last, God had released her? Could she really be FREE of Ronnie?

Her eyes turned to Arthur, who was checking the fuses in the trays waiting to be collected.

'Everything all right?' he said cheerily.

Not wanting anybody to know the teeming conflicting thoughts in her head, Violet gave a little shrug. She was anything but all right; in fact, she didn't know whether to laugh with guilty relief at the thought of her possible freedom or weep with grief at the loss of so many innocent lives. Keeping her eyes firmly fixed on the fuse cases she was packing, Violet answered guardedly, 'Everything's fine!'

After yet another nightmare journey across the Irish Sea, with an agonizing sense of impatience at every small hold-up that delayed her journey home, Kit finally landed in Dublin. In a frenzy now to get where she needed to be, Kit ran straight for the bus to Chapelizod, drumming her fingers on her small travel bag as she willed the driver to go faster. When it finally pulled up, she grabbed her belongings and raced down the lane to the gates of the vast Fitzwilliam estate, shuddering as she recalled her rapist's bloated face and stinking breath.

'Surely no day could ever be worse than that day?' she muttered to herself as she crossed the park to her former home, hoping against all hope that this would prove to be the case.

Minutes later, she ran into the family cottage, out of breath and bedraggled, barely noticing what a stinking hovel her old home was in comparison with her clean, bright new home on the Lancashire moors. Kit feverishly cast about the room, but could see no sign of Billy. Frantic and trembling, she barged into the bedroom she'd shared with her sister, where she saw with horror that the drawer that Billy had slept in was now back in its original place.

'Billy!' she cried, hoping still that there could be an innocent explanation. Billy must be too big for the drawer now, she told herself; they must have got a crib for him. But where was he? There was no sign of his things either, not a bottle or a toy or even a dirty nappy. And where was Rosie, who had urged her to come? She wouldn't have told her to return if there was nothing wrong. At that point the fear and tension she'd felt ever since she'd received her sister's terrifying letter overwhelmed her and, unable to control herself, she began to scream, 'BILLY! BILLY!'

Her sister came tearing into the cottage. 'He's not here, Kit!' she exclaimed.

Kit whirled round on her. 'WHAT?'

'I'm so sorry – he's not here,' Rosie repeated, looking wretched.

Before she could offer any kind of explanation, Mr Murphy came rampaging into the cottage, where with a blow he knocked Rosie to the floor before turning to hit out at Kit. 'Jesus Christ!' he bellowed. 'What the 'ell do you want?'

Suddenly Kit wasn't frightened of her father. The experience of leaving home and working as a Bomb Girl in the Phoenix Munitions Factory, filling fuses for bombs and explosives that were vital for the war effort, had matured her. And for the first time in her life she saw her father for what he really was: a mean, dirty, blustering bully. Looking him straight in the eye she said, 'Where is my son?'

Murphy hit her twice across the face, but Kit held her place, her voice icily calm. 'Where is he?'

Kit would have taken as many beatings as it needed to get the information she wanted out of him, but her poor mother, gasping for breath and coughing up blood, put an end to her husband's repeated slaps.

'He's taken Billy to the Sisters of Mercy in Dublin,' she gasped.

'Shut up, woman!' Murphy roared.

Kit's mother, like herself, was beyond fear; she knew her days were numbered. If she died as a result she was determined that her daughter would know the truth.

'He's after having the child adopted,' she wheezed.

Kit's legs literally gave way beneath her. Grasping hold of the back of a chair for support, she looked from her mother to her sister. 'It can't be true?' she cried.

She'd heard of babies being taken at birth to the Sisters of Mercy, new-borns who never saw their mothers again. Surely her father, however drunk he was, would never do such a thing to her and Billy? When she saw the tears brimming in her sister's eyes, her stomach knotted and her heartbeat quickened in terror. With a tense nod Rosie said quickly, 'You'd better get yourself to the convent right away. You might just be in time to stop it.'

Kit needed no further encouragement. Hoping to God she wasn't already too late, she grabbed her belongings, nodded her thanks to her sister and raced back through the door, praying she wouldn't have to wait too long for the bus back to Dublin.

It was difficult not to notice a new lightness in Violet's step; she walked as if a burden had been lifted from her.

'God forgive me for how I feel about anybody's death,' she thought to herself.

Though still grieving for her former Wood End neighbours, nothing could stop Violet from feeling an intoxicating giddy relief at the loss of Ronnie, combined with a sense of growing hope that crept through her body, making her feel like she was a woman reborn.

It didn't surprise her that Ronnie had come to a bad end, and she couldn't bring herself to feel any sadness about him. She'd seen first-hand the kind of characters he was dealing with: profiteering scum of the earth getting rich on the backs of hard-working men and women living through a harsh war on the bread line. Ronnie had regularly invited the ring leaders into her own home, where they played cards, smoked and drank till dawn; more than once she'd found one of them in her own bed, having sex with a prostitute. She knew Ronnie had a gun and a couple of flick knives; he'd showed them off to her, threatening to cut her if she told anybody about his business. Well, now a gun had been turned on him; there was no way he could have survived that bombing raid. Never again could he hit her or force himself on her, or mock and jeer at her. She wished it hadn't had to take his death to bring that about, but the honest truth was Ronnie's death was the start of a whole new life for her.

After a long afternoon shift, Violet lay in a rather tepid bath, wondering if she should share her news with Gladys and Kit, and Arthur too. She didn't want to deceive them but neither did she want to relive the past. What was the point of digging up disgusting and degrading memories, which she'd much rather forget? 'And what will they think of my feeling such relief that he's been killed,' she thought, the guilt returning. As she soaped her long slender arms and legs, she knew that she would keep her secret of those nightmare years in Coventry and move on. God had given her another chance, a clean sheet, finally to live the life she really wanted.

13. Billy

Kit somehow managed to keep her wits sufficiently about her to trace the Sisters of Mercy to Duke Street. On the slow journey back into Dublin, she'd forced herself to stay calm and think straight. Surely the nuns couldn't put her child up for adoption without her consent? Weak and dizzy as she was after not eating or sleeping for over twenty-four hours, Kit steeled herself to concentrate.

'Everything depends on me coming over as a strong woman capable of bringing up my own child, so don't go in all guns blazing,' she scolded herself.

After impatiently ringing the convent bell, she was admitted by a young nun into a gloomy parlour that was dominated by scenes of the Passion of Christ. Pacing the room, Kit waited for the Mother Superior, who appeared wearing a long black habit and a starched winged wimple. A heavy gold crucifix dangled from a gold chain around her neck.

'Welcome, child. I am Mother Gabriel; how may I help you?' she asked softly.

At the sound of her gentle voice, Kit burst into tears. 'Is my son, Billy Murphy, here with you?' she sobbed.

'Yes, Billy's here,' she answered calmly.

'My father brought him to you without my permission,' Kit said as she took deep breaths and wiped away her tears. 'Billy belongs to me.'

Seeing Kit so distraught, Mother Gabriel called for tea,

then settled the weeping girl in a high-backed wooden chair. As she poured tea into fine china cups, she added, 'Your father produced no birth certificate; he just said he was the child's father.'

Kit sipped gratefully at the hot sweet tea, the first thing that had passed her lips in twenty-four hours.

'He's my son; he was born out of wedlock after I was raped.' She then listed the bald facts for the Mother Superior. 'Mi da forced me to work in England. He said he would look after Billy if I sent money home every week, and I have,' she added angrily. 'I've never once failed to send him money and look what he's done in return.'

'He told me he could no longer bring the child up on his own,' Mother Gabriel informed Kit.

'The lying pig!' Kit cried, then quickly covered her mouth. 'I beg your pardon, Mother Superior.'

Mother Gabriel smiled as she poured more tea. 'I've heard a lot worse than that in this room, believe me.'

'Mi poor ma's dying, so she can't do much, but mi sister, Rosie, would always look after Billy,' Kit explained. 'But I want to take him back to England with me,' she quickly added. 'There are nurseries on the factory site where I work; babies are taken care of there whilst their mothers build bombs. I want to take Billy back to England with me,' she said again desperately.

'There's no doubting your commitment, my child,' the softly spoken nun said. 'But your father said he thought the child would have a better quality of life in America –'

Aflame with shock and indignation, Kit sprang to her feet. 'AMERICA!' she cried incredulously.

'Calm yourself,' Mother Gabriel said as she indicated

that Kit should sit back down again. 'We have a great many adoptive parents in America,' she informed a stunned Kit. 'They are generous with their donations to the convent, money which in part is passed on to the mother or the father seeking adoption for their child. A fine healthy boy like Billy would bring a good price.'

Kit felt all the blood drain from her body before an anger she had never experienced before flooded through her, to the point where she could barely breath. 'A GOOD PRICE?' she spluttered.

With a look of regret in her eyes, the nun nodded. 'I'm sorry. I can see this is a shock. But the truth is, your father signed the adoption papers in this very room. I counter-signed them and we already have a wealthy young couple in New York keen to see Billy. I don't honestly know what I can do for you.'

Feeling like she was in the middle of a bad dream, Kit frantically shook her head. This couldn't be happening. 'But . . . but,' she stumbled on, 'I'm his mother! There must be something I can do.'

Mother Gabriel answered firmly, 'My dear child, the matter is well out of our hands. I'm sorry, but the papers are all signed.'

The room swayed and the china cup she was grasping fell from Kit's hands and shattered on the parquet floor. 'This isn't happening,' she half sobbed. 'It makes no sense that you can push me to one side just because mi da's a filthy rotten liar and a fine young couple in New York are rich enough to buy my son!' she finished scathingly.

Mother Gabriel looked genuinely sad. 'Your absence was your downfall; if you'd been here things might not have gone so far.' Rising to her feet, she extended her hand to Kit. 'I'm sorry, there's nothing further I can do.'

Knowing she was being politely asked to leave, Kit grasped the nun's cool hand. 'I beg you, for the love of God, let me see him at least.'

'He's asleep in the nursery,' Mother Gabriel replied, frowning.

'I won't disturb him,' Kit begged. Seeing a look of alarm pass across the Mother Superior's face, Kit quickly added, 'I won't touch him . . . please just let me see my little boy for the last time,'

Mother Gabriel held Kit's pleading gaze for a few seconds. The least she could do was to let this desperate, bedraggled young woman see her child for the last time.

'Follow me,' she said. 'I'll take you to Sister Clare.'

Stumbling down the dark corridors, too shocked to think of anything beyond her urgent need to see her baby boy, Kit eventually reached a window that gave on to the nursery. Her eyes scanned the few cots arranged around the room, and then she saw her own little Billy peacefully sleeping in a pretty blue-quilted cot. Her stomach lurched with a primeval urge to snatch him up and never let him out of her sight again. Her eyes raked along the length of him as she greedily took in every single detail of his beloved face and body.

'My son,' she breathed. 'My darling boy,' she sighed as she leant against the window, which steamed up with her breath.

Seeing her face pressed to the glass, the nun in charge of the nursery came out to greet her.

'I'm Billy's mother,' Kit quickly told her. Pointing to Billy in his cot, she added with a catch in her voice, 'He's my little boy.

Sister Clare smiled kindly. 'I can see that, for sure, he's the spit of you with his black hair and dark eyes.' Seeing tears well up in the heartbroken young mother's eyes, she added brightly, 'He's grown. He's doing well. Would you be after giving the little lad a cuddle?' Sister Clare asked with a gentle smile.

Kit's eyes opened wide. 'Could I?' she gasped. 'Really hold him?'

'For sure,' the young nun said as she pushed open the nursery door and led Kit to Billy's cot.

Desperate not to disturb his innocent sleep, Kit gently lifted Billy into her arms, and in that split second of holding him, of inhaling the sweet, clean smell of him, she felt for just a few seconds the sheer ecstasy of owning him.

'Remember this,' she said to herself.

Closing her eyes at the intense longing that threatened to overwhelm her, she felt the soft weight of him in her arms and listened to his steady breathing as he snuffled closer to her. Opening her eyes, she marvelled at how much bigger he was. Sister Clare was right: he had grown and his silky hair was longer too.

'All the days I've missed with him,' she mourned. 'Happy days watching him grow, teaching him his first baby words, always being there for him with a kiss and a smile.'

Remembering Sister Clare beside her, Kit murmured, 'He seems content.'

'He is now, thanks be to God,' Sister Clare replied.

'You should have seen the state of the poor child when he arrived in rags and covered in excrement; his hair was matted and he had lice.'

Gazing at Billy's beautiful black eyelashes curling on his rosy pink cheeks and his tiny white hands with clean pearly pink nails, Kit could hardly believe she was hearing right.

'LICE!' she cried in horror.

'Crawling with the things,' Sister Clare retorted. 'I'm sorry to say he'd been dreadfully neglected, Miss Murphy; any longer with that father of yours and the child would be dead for sure.'

Hot scalding tears coursed down Kit's face. Not only had she abandoned her son when he was tiny, she'd allowed him to be maltreated and neglected. What must the poor little boy have gone through in her absence? Slumped against the wall, she realized she owed the convent a great debt.

'Thank you, sister, for taking care of my Billy.'

Seeing the abject agony the young mother was in, Sister Clare's heart melted in pity for her.

'You know,' she started hesitantly, 'you should think about seeking legal advice, Miss Murphy.'

Kit's dark brown eyes locked with her blue ones, hope sparking in her heart.

'I don't know much about the law, miss, but I would make inquiries when you get back to England.'

'But Billy's adoption papers are *here*,' Kit said frantically. 'And I can't wait that long; I've got to stop this right now. By the time I've made inquiries in England, Billy could be on his way to America!' Her heart almost stopped at the horrific thought. 'I don't know what to do!' she wailed, causing the sleeping child to throw up his arms.

Sister Clare wagged a finger at Kit. 'Now, don't go upsetting yourself,' she advised. 'One thing's for sure, adoptions don't happen fast. They go back and forth and back and forth between the Mother Superior and the convent's legal adviser, Mr O'Rourke. I know that for sure, because I've hand-delivered enough to the man myself.'

Seeing the young mother gripping Billy and wondering if it had been a mistake to let her into the nursery in the first place, Sister Clare continued calmly, 'The best thing you can do is go home and see if you can find a loophole in the contract.'

'A loophole?' Kit repeated the word hesitantly.

The young nun nodded. 'It's a word I've heard bandied about between the Mother Superior and Mr O'Rourke in the parlour,' she said as she looked rather pleased with herself. 'Get yourself a top-notch adoption lawyer – no matter what it costs. And fight for your little boy. He should be with you, I can see that,' she added kindly.

Kit held her head high. The little nun was right: Billy should be with her.

'I can pay for a good lawyer,' she announced. 'I saved every penny I didn't send home for Billy. I'll hire the best,' she replied firmly.

Returning her gaze to her beautiful boy, who was by now stirring in his mother's arms, she squeezed him hard, trying to give him in a single hug all the love she had for him, to keep him safe and protected until she could return and claim him as her own.

'I have to say goodbye, darling Little Man', she whispered, tears pouring down her cheeks.

'Lay him down in the cot,' Sister Clare said softly as she drew Kit away. 'I promise I'll take the best care of him,' she added reassuringly.

As she was led away, Kit allowed herself one more glance back at her beloved boy. 'I'll come back for you, my love,' she whispered. 'I promise I'll take you home and keep you by me forever.'

14. Plans

Back at the Phoenix factory, Arthur Leadbetter was in turmoil. He'd virtually fallen in love at first sight with Violet, but he'd been initially rash in his judgement, assuming he could approach her as he would any other woman. Not that Arthur had had many girlfriends: he'd always had high standards and was particular about what he liked in a girl. Violet certainly lived up to all his expectations, but she was a tricky one, like a shadow the way she came and went. At least these days, after several patient months of holding back, Violet now spoke to him, and the other night she'd even allowed him to walk her home, which Arthur considered real progress. He often wondered who had damaged her so much and what had happened in her past to make her so skittish and timid. As these thoughts raced around inside his head, Arthur started self-consciously when Violet walked into the filling shed with Gladys by her side. He stared at her beautiful face, which was looking less tense and preoccupied these days. What had brought about the change in her?

'Morning, Arthur!' she called cheerily. 'When are you going to show me this secret garden of yours that Ivy keeps going on about?'

Her enthusiastic words were music to his ears.

'Any time you want,' he said, slightly taken aback.

'At the end of my shift?' she suggested.

Arthur desperately tried to hide a smile when he caught the stunned expression on Gladys's face.

'What's happened to Violet?' she whispered as she passed him by.

'Dunno,' he whispered back. 'But I'm not complaining!'

It was late the following day when Kit arrived back in Pendleton. Frozen to the bone and utterly exhausted, she staggered up the steep hill to the Phoenix, where the first thing she saw was Edna's blue van parked up in the dispatch yard. Hurrying towards it, she called, 'Edna! Edna!'

'For God's sake,' cried Edna when she saw Kit's ashen face, 'get inside.' She pulled Kit into the van and closed the back doors so they could talk in private. 'What happened?' she asked as she shoved a mug of hot tea into Kit's hands and lit up a cigarette for her.

Tired beyond words, Kit could barely speak, but after a few sips of tea and several drags on her cigarette she said flatly, 'Mi da's handed Billy over to the convent; he's up for adoption.'

Edna could scarcely believe she was hearing right. 'That can't even be legal!'

'Billy's with the Sisters of Mercy in Dublin, who're arranging the adoption,' Kit told her.

Abandoning the tea and cigarette, Kit put her head in her hands and howled like an animal in pain. Edna soothed and petted her until eventually Kit's breathing steadied. Wiping away tears, which smeared her already dirty face, Kit told Edna what Sister Clare had advised.

'She told me to find a top-notch lawyer who might be

able to find a . . .' Kit paused to remember the exact word. 'LOOPHOLE.'

Edna's face visibly brightened. 'A legal loophole – sounds like good advice to me. Look, sweetheart, leave that to me: that's one thing I can help you with, for sure.'

Kit nodded weakly as exhaustion claimed her.

'Right now you need to get some sleep,' Edna urged. 'Come on, I'll drive you home.'

After giving Edna a quick goodnight kiss, Kit crept into the dark digs, where Gladys and Violet were already fast asleep in their rooms. Slipping into bed, she covered herself with a blanket, then fell into a deep sleep in which she dreamt of Billy's gentle breathing as she held him close for those precious few last minutes in the convent nursery.

Kit woke to the sound of Violet's gentle voice. 'Fancy a cuppa, sweetheart?'

Kit nodded as she staggered wearily out of bed and followed Violet into the warm sitting room, where Gladys was busily brewing up.

'How's your mother?' she immediately asked.

Kit shook her head. 'Dying, but I had to leave; Mr Featherstone allowed me only three days off.'

Kit hated telling her dearest friends only half the truth. She was afraid that once she started she'd never stop, and after such an outpouring she would be incapable of any sensible action. Right now her priority was to concentrate on the practical course of action that lay before her. Her secret could be revealed on a later day when she was certain that Billy would be returned to her.

'You must be worried sick,' Gladys commiserated as she handed Kit a steaming hot mug of tea.

Tears flooded Kit's eyes. With all the trauma surrounding Billy, she'd hardly had time to say goodbye to her mother, whom she'd last seen lying in bed, coughing up blood as she gasped for every breath.

'So you won't be with her when she –' Violet's voice faltered.

'No, I won't be with her at the end,' Kit said, finishing the sentence for her miserably.

Violet's sky-blue eyes filled up too. 'I wasn't with my mum at the end either,' she murmured.

Violet bitterly recalled how she'd decided not to visit her mother on her deathbed; the sight of her beloved daughter with two black eyes would be the last thing her mother would have wanted to see before she departed this world. So heartbroken Violet had no choice but to leave her mother to die alone.

The end of June brought more bad news from the war front: Rommel had captured Tobruk and was heading straight for Cairo.

'The lads in the Lancashire Fusiliers are almost certain to be sent overseas to North Africa' Maggie informed her friends. 'Little Elsie on the cordite line told us her fiancé, Tommy, who's in the Fusiliers, would be posted overseas with his battalion to head off the bloody Germans.'

'God help 'em in that heat,' sighed Gladys. 'North Africa must be as hot as hell!'

'Especially when you've grown up in Lancashire, where there are sixteen kinds of rain,' joked Nora.

'You should try living in Ireland,' Kit remarked. 'The grass is not emerald-green for lack of rain, believe you me.'

Normal life resumed. As shifts came and went, thousands of bombs were assembled, dispatched and flown out to war zones urgently in need of fresh ordnance. Back at home, rationing grew harder by the day.

'If I have to face another spam fritter I think I'll scream,' Violet moaned one lunchtime when the menu was spam, spam and even more spam.

'Better get used to it,' stoical Myrtle commented. 'It'll get a lot worse before it gets any better.'

'Now that clothes are rationed we'll never have enough coupons for those glamorous satin ball gowns that Maggie was so looking forward to,' Nora glumly pointed out. 'We'll be playing in the band in our Bomb Girls' overalls until the end of the war.'

'I hate Hitler!' Maggie seethed.

'Don't we all?' sighed Violet.

Unknown to any of their friends, Kit and Edna had whispered discussions most evenings in the dispatch yard. In between frying chips and serving eager customers, Edna told Kit what she'd discovered in Bury's lending library.

'You'll be pleased to hear there are a few lawyers in Manchester who specialize in adoption law,' she said as she flicked through her little note pad. 'An Ian McIvor seems to be the top man, so I suggest you get in touch with him.'

'Oh, Edna,' Kit whispered as she clutched her friend's hand. 'Thanks so much for helping me, I wouldn't have known where to start.'

'When in doubt, go to the library,' Edna chuckled.

With Ian McIvor's phone number written on a scrap of paper in her pocket, Kit suddenly felt elated. 'I'll ask Mr

Featherstone if I can phone from his office,' she said with a new confidence in her voice.

Edna looked alarmed. 'Don't do that! His secretary's the biggest gossip in Pendleton. Use a public phone box: there're a few in town. Or phone from my shop.'

'It's too late to phone now but I'll come to the shop first thing in the morning,' Kit said, impatient to get things started. 'The sooner this clever Mr McIvor is on the case, the better.' She realized that she was placing all her hopes in a man she'd never even met.

Feeling like at least she'd got a plan, Kit hurried home but stopped in her tracks as music came floating out of the cowshed's open windows. She immediately recognized the sound of Violet's lilting clarinet and Glad's bold swooping alto sax. Despite her gnawing pain and constant worry, she was happy to be back with her friends, who quickly laid down their instruments and warmly welcomed Kit. As Gladys popped the little kettle on the wood-burning stove, Violet offered Kit a Woodbine and a mug of hot tea.

'Well, we've got news that might cheer you up,' she announced. 'We've just heard about a competition across the North for the best new dance band.'

Flushed with excitement, Violet took up the story. 'It kicks off in Bolton and ends with the winning band appearing with no less than Joe Loss at the Savoy in London!' she cried.

With her head full of information about adoption law and Mr McIvor in Manchester, Kit was caught off her guard.

'What?' she said blankly.

Gladys flapped a piece of paper in front of her face. 'Each band has to play three pieces to demonstrate their singing and musical skills,' she babbled. 'A foxtrot followed by a jive and closing with a waltz.'

Violet smiled at Kit. 'We thought we could pick the best of three from our very extensive repertoire,' she joked. 'We could improve on them, add a few more harmonies and solo pieces. What do you reckon, Kit?'

Feeling like it was the last thing she wanted, Kit simply said, 'I don't know.'

Remembering that Kit had a lot on her mind, Gladys quickly said, 'You're under a lot of pressure – it's okay, don't worry about it.'

Seeing the hope fade from her face and Violet's too, Kit felt, if possible, even more wretched. Her misery was now affecting her relationship with her friends, who, through no fault of their own, did not know of her secret. Overwhelmed with frustration about how little she could really do for Billy right this moment, she was struck by the thought 'What the hell!' The one thing she felt like doing right now was beating the bejesus out of a set of drums!

15. Mr Ian McIvor

The next day, in between finishing her shift and the scheduled band practice, Kit ran down the hill into Pendleton, and in the privacy of Edna's back room she phoned Ian McIvor's office.

'What shall I say?' she nervously asked Edna.

'Just ask for an appointment with Mr McIvor. Don't get pushed around by his secretary; they always think they're in charge. Why talk to the monkey when you can talk to the organ-grinder?' Edna joked. 'Go on, get on with it,' Edna said as she gave Kit a gentle nudge in the direction of the black Bakelite phone.

Kit took a deep breath, then, thinking only of Billy, she dialled the number. As Edna had predicted, she got through to a very officious secretary who insisted she would personally pass on any messages to Mr McIvor, but Kit steadfastly refused to accept this.

'I must speak to him myself,' she insisted in a firm voice that was so out of character it took Edna by surprise.

Eventually the secretary put her through to the lawyer, who, after Kit briefly outlined her case, arranged to see her the next day after she finished her early-morning shift. Thanking Edna, Kit, with her heart racing and her pulse quickening, hurried back up the hill to the Phoenix. AT LAST she was doing something for Billy, something real and practical; she was sick to death of weeping and grieving – now was the time for action. She had the money; all she needed was the right lawyer to make it happen. And, as far as she could tell from Edna's research, Mr Ian McIvor had all the right credentials!

After a plate of potato hash and boiled beetroot in the works canteen, the girls returned to their digs, where Kit (who yet again hated herself for lying) awkwardly asked a favour of her friends.

'I've got a meeting in Manchester tomorrow – it's a family matter, with my Irish cousins and I've got nothing decent to wear.'

Knowing too well that Kit had only the rags she'd arrived in, Violet and Gladys immediately started to search through their wardrobes for clothes that might fit tiny Kit. Violet found a pale blue tweed suit, which was long on Kit but fitted around her hips and waist. Gladys had a smart cream blouse, which was big across Kit's shoulders but would do; unfortunately neither of them had any shoes that would fit her small feet.

Cheered by the silky blouse and fashionable skirt, Kit shrugged as she joked, 'Never mind – hopefully nobody will look at my feet!'

Ian McIvor, in his early thirties, had been rejected by the armed forces because of his poor eyesight, the result of having contracted measles when he was aged three. As a consequence his thoughtful hazel eyes were partly obscured by thick black-rimmed glasses and partly by an unruly mop of brown hair. He'd studied law at Cambridge, but after he'd finished his doctorate, which had been on adoption law, he'd returned North because of his love of mountaineering in the Lake District. Gazing at the scrap of a girl who sat opposite him barely able to speak, McIvor gently started the conversation, which, he could see, caused his trembling client deep distress. However, as things progressed she became more articulate.

'So are you saying, Miss Murphy, that your father at no point at all consulted with you about his decision to have Billy adopted?'

'I wouldn't have known anything about it if my sister, Rosie, hadn't written and warned me,' Kit replied.

Making notes, McIvor checked Kit's date of birth. 'I see you are twenty-four,' he said, thinking to himself that she looked much younger. 'If you'd been under twenty-one your father would have had total authority over you and the child, but, as you're over twenty-one, you're legally an independent woman and he therefore has no rights.'

'Well, that's a relief,' Kit said. 'But the thing is, sir,' she gulped as she twisted her ragged handkerchief, 'somehow the paperwork has already been signed, and there's a rich couple from New York who are keen to adopt my son – for all I know they could be on their way to Dublin as we speak.'

McIvor gave her an understanding smile. 'I promise you I will move quickly on this, Miss Murphy, but I have to have all the facts before me before I do so.'

'So what can you actually do?' Kit asked anxiously.

'I'll write to Mother Gabriel to find out exactly what has gone on, and how this paperwork has come to be signed, given that you didn't sign anything. It may be that I'll need to travel to meet with your father at some point.'

Kit crossed herself. 'Jesus, Mary and Joseph, he'll knock your block off!'

McIvor couldn't help but smile. 'I can assure you I'm perfectly able to take care of myself. Now,' he said carefully, 'there is the question of payment.'

For the first time Kit felt confident. 'I'm a Bomb Girl at the Phoenix Munitions Factory in Pendleton. I earn good money and I do overtime. I've not spent a penny on anything since I arrived in England other than what I've sent home for my son, I have money to pay you for your troubles.'

The gentle-hearted lawyer's heart contracted at the ring of pride in her voice.

'Excellent. Final question, Miss Murphy: where can I get in touch with you?'

'You can write to me at the Phoenix factory or my digs,' she said as she scribbled down the two addresses on a notepad that he handed her. 'Or you can phone this number: it's Edna's chip shop,' she said, grinning. 'She'll get any messages to me.'

As Kit rose, she fumbled for her purse. 'How much do I owe you for your services today, sir?' she asked, flustered.

Seeing her blushing, McIvor shook his head. 'The first meeting is always free,' he lied.

'Thank you, thank you very much, sir,' Kit said, obviously relieved. 'You promise you'll act soon?' she asked again.

Staring into her sweet trusting heart-shaped face dominated by her sad dark brown eyes, McIvor smiled reassuringly. 'I'll get on to it right away, Miss Murphy.'

Standing at the window, McIvor watched Kit hurry down the dark cobbled street in her wet flapping shoes. He'd do his very best for her, but he was painfully aware that he couldn't guarantee that he could save her son from adoption.

After her meeting, Kit dared to feel positive again, despite her intense frustration at how long it all seemed to be taking. But, short of snatching Billy from the convent nursery, which she knew she would never have got away with, Mr McIvor was her only real hope now and she had to trust him.

'He'll beat the bejesus out of the lot of them!' Kit said to herself as she ran down the track that led to the cowshed. She didn't allow herself to wonder what would happen if clever Mr McIvor couldn't help her or Billy. She did her best to push aside the nagging thought that Mother Gabriel had the upper hand on the destiny of her child. Would she *really* send her son to the rich American couple on the back of what her lying, cheating father had said? It seemed impossible to Kit that anybody in their right mind would believe anything a man such as him had said. Feeling like she would go mad with worry if she allowed these thoughts to fester, Kit took deep breaths. Right now, McIvor was her best and in fact her only hope, so she reminded herself to keep her thoughts on him as she set off walking up the lane.

When she opened the door to the cowshed, Kit knew from the tense expressions on Gladys's and Violet's faces that something was wrong – by their awkward manner she could tell that they were clearly worried about telling her something. Her first thought was for Billy – had he already been taken? Almost hysterical she cried out, 'What is it? What's happened?'

Gladys handed her a telegram. 'It came whilst you were out,' she said softly.

Hardly daring to breathe, Kit ripped open the envelope and read the note, her eyes brimming with tears.

'Ma passed away this morning,' she whispered. Crossing herself, she prayed, 'May God have mercy on her soul.'

Violet and Gladys guided their grief-stricken friend to the sofa, where they sat on either side of her, holding her hands and wiping away her tears. As Kit's tears began to subside, they offered her tea and cigarettes.

'You know what?' Kit murmured as she inhaled deeply on a Woodbine, 'I'm glad it's finally all over for Ma. She's not in pain any more, not coughing up blood and fighting for her every breath, but, most of all,' Kit added sadly, 'at least in heaven she's safely away from my pig of a father's slaps and punches.'

Violet quickly averted her eyes from Kit. She'd run away from endless slaps and punches; poor Mrs Murphy had had no such luck.

'Will you make it to her funeral?' Gladys asked gently.

Kit shook her head. 'Featherstone will never agree to giving me leave so soon after my last trip home. I'll go to mass at St Columba's in Pendleton,' Kit told her friends. 'I can pray for the repose of Ma's soul just as well there as I could in Ireland.'

'Possibly better,' thought Kit, who knew that if she found herself in a church beside her evil father prayers would be the last thing on her mind. She'd be itching to strangle the life out of him for what he'd done to her Billy, herself and her poor long-suffering mother, who in her haste to return to Dublin to see the Sisters of Mercy she hadn't even said goodbye to. Filled with sadness, Kit remembered how much her mother had tried to shield all four of her children – Rosie, herself and her two younger brothers – from their tyrannical father. It had been a wasted effort; as with all bullies, Murphy always did exactly what he wanted and her mother would have got the brunt of his fury before her children did. Poor, poor soul – what a life she'd suffered. Kit prayed in her heart that Ma would understand why she'd rushed off on her last visit without a backward glance at her or the rest of her family.

Gladys cleared her throat as she said awkwardly, 'Kit . . . we'd really understand if you didn't want to play in the band so soon after your mother's death.'

Kit paused, unsure for a moment what she should do out of respect for her mother's departed soul. Lighting up another Woodbine, she asked, 'And who would play the drums if not me?'

Her friends exchanged a blank look, then shrugged.

'There's nobody else,' Gladys admitted.

'I'll play the drums, Glad, for Ma, finally at peace in heaven,' Kit said bravely. 'I know it's what she would have wanted,' she added fiercely.

16. Dance Band Competition

The girls decided that they'd practise every night prior to the competition in Bolton. They all had reasons for wanting to keep busy. For Kit, it took her mind to some extent off her impossible situation, which for now, she told herself, she could do nothing more about. For Violet, it soothed the pain of knowing her entire neighbourhood in Wood End had been blown to pieces as they slept in their beds. And for Gladys, her music was everything – she simply couldn't get enough of it!

'Since we can't wheel the piano up the track into the cowshed,' Gladys joked, 'we'll have to practise in the chapel.'

Fortunately none of them were on night shift, so they were able to practise every night till they dropped from sheer exhaustion. All their hard work and dedication paid off: they were improving their technique and were more confident about improvising too.

Though relieved that she'd done all she could by employing Mr McIvor to fight Billy's adoption case, Kit's thoughts often strayed to imagining things over which she had no control. What if Mr McIvor, clever as he was, found no evidence to support her? What if the American couple offered Mother Gabriel extra money for Billy on condition that she allowed them to claim him sooner? What if her father took Billy to another convent and pulled the same trick on them as he had with the Sisters of Mercy? Worse still, what if her father side-stepped Mother Gabriel by personally taking Billy to America and selling him to the first high bidder he met? When her mind went into any of these nightmare scenarios, Kit missed her cues, lost the beat or failed to join in on the backing. One afternoon, when she missed a sequence of vital drum beats, the band ground to a halt. As the brass section tweeted and hooted discordantly and Myrtle irritably slammed the piano keys, all eyes turned to Kit.

Taking the same sympathetic line she'd taken in the past, Gladys said gently, 'We understand you're still in mourning, Kit, and we really sympathize, so please don't push yourself and play for our sakes.'

On hearing this, Maggie Yates, who – like her sister Emily Yates – always spoke her mind, spluttered, 'And what do we all do if Kit doesn't play? Bang a couple of tin lids together and hope for the best?'

The thought of Gladys improvising the drums with two pan lids made Kit smile despite herself.

'You promised you could do this,' she scolded herself. 'So come on, do it – and do it well!'

'Sorry,' she said. 'Let's crash on!' she joked as she gave the cymbal an almighty whack.

As their music improved and their confidence grew, a buzz of excitement zipped through the band as they became more ambitious about their choreography.

'We should move more!' Maggie urged. 'Really go with the music, like Ivy Benson's girls.'

'And what exactly do they do?' Myrtle asked.

'THIS!' said cheeky Mags, as she tossed her hair, clicked her fingers and wriggled her very shapely bottom.

'God spare me!' Myrtle groaned.

'Mags is right,' said Gladys. 'We could make more of our dance sequences. It's difficult when you're playing an instrument, but the four of us' – she pointed to Violet, Nora and Maggie – 'we could combine to do a bit of chorus-girl style dancing.'

Violet blushed scarlet, 'OH!' she exclaimed.

'I'm not saying we should dance half naked,' Gladys quickly added. 'We'll be covered from top to toe in our overalls!'

'But we could add a bit of glam,' Maggie added eagerly. 'Wear earrings and have our hair loose under our turbans.'

Myrtle rolled her eyes. 'My word!' she chuckled. 'I'm so glad I have my trusty piano to shield me from you Jezebels!'

'BRILLIANT!' Gladys raved at the end of Friday night's practice. Flopping down on to one of the hard wooden pews, she gasped, 'For God's sake! Will somebody make a brew?'

At which point Arthur Leadbetter walked in bearing a loaded tin tray. 'Tea, ladies?' he said with a wide smile.

'You ANGEL!' cried Maggie.

Passing around mugs of hot tea, Arthur said, 'Your music's been booming out across the factory floor; it's cheered up the lasses on night shift. They're the ones who told me to fetch you some refreshments.'

'Much appreciated,' Gladys said as she gratefully sipped the welcome tea.

Arthur crossed the chapel to hand Violet her mug of

tea. 'Mustn't forget you, Violet. He said her name so softly it made Violet's tummy flip.

'You're spoiling me,' she murmured as she accepted one of his Craven 'A' cigarettes.

'The weather forecast's looking good this week,' Arthur continued. 'Do you fancy a walk out on the moors? In between your shifts and your band practice of course,' he added with a laugh.

Violet inhaled the cigarette smoke as she gazed at him with undisguised pleasure. 'I think I'd like that very much, Arthur,' she replied.

'Ooops, nearly forgot, I've got something for you – close your eyes and hold out your hand,' he said as if she were a child.

Violet closed her eyes and extended her right hand. She gasped as she felt something small and cool land in her palm.

'Oooh! What is it?' she squeaked.

'Open!' he cried.

Violet gazed in delight at a little pile of pale green gooseberries.

'First of the season,' Arthur announced proudly. 'Specially picked for you!'

After her recent request, Arthur had proudly taken her to his secret garden, a little bit of spare land behind the dispatch yard looking out over the moors. He'd obviously worked hard on the scrap of land, digging it over, weeding it, then planting out seedlings; he grew vegetables on one half of the plot and flowers on the other. Running down the middle was a neat row of fruit bushes, raspberry, blackcurrant and gooseberry.

'Mr Greenfingers,' she teased as she delicately nibbled a tart gooseberry before she gave him a brief peck on the cheek. 'Thank you.'

The following morning, bleary-eyed from their late-night rehearsal, the girls were busily preparing for work when Gladys called out, 'Anybody know who the car outside belongs to?'

Despite the recent Wood End bombing news, Violet's heart missed a beat. Could it somehow be Ronnie? Could he have escaped the bomb and tracked her down? Then she remembered the reports she'd read: there were literally no survivors from the street, she told herself.

When there was a knock at the door, Kit opened it to Mr McIvor.

'Sorry to call so early, Miss Murphy,' he said as he doffed his expensive black felt hat. 'I just wondered if we could have a word in private, maybe outside?' he suggested.

Still in her old winceyette nightie, Kit grabbed a coat to cover herself; then, looking like a sleepy child with her long dark hair blowing around her anxious face, she followed him to his smart black Ford, which was being buffeted by the wind blowing off the moors. As she sat in the passenger seat beside him, McIvor outlined his plan of action.

'I just wanted to let you know in person how far my plans have developed since last week,' he explained. 'I've already received a letter from Mother Gabriel. We've been lucky – the post often gets sent via very odd places these days – but the gods must have been smiling on you as this one made it through quickly.'

'What did she have to say?' Kit asked eagerly.

'She hasn't said much but has agreed to see me at the

convent. She wouldn't do that if there was nothing to challenge, so I think I should go as soon as I can, with your permission?'

'Of course, of course! I'll pay for your travel,' she gasped. 'Is Billy still there?' she asked anxiously.

'I assume so, Miss Murphy,' he said as he noticed the paleness of her skin underneath the worn nightdress. 'I asked to see him in my original letter and when I get there I shall insist upon it.'

Kit smiled, much cheered by her lawyer's determination to crack the whip on her behalf.

'I intend to examine closely his adoption papers. If there's anything I can do to stop this illegal transaction going ahead, you have my word that I will do it,' he assured her.

Remembering Mother Gabriel's cool business-like certainty, Kit asked, 'Are you sure Mother Gabriel will definitely let you see the papers?'

'She has no choice. That's the point of my journey and, as your lawyer, I'm within my legal rights to peruse the documents,' he explained.

'And what about mi da – will he come to see you at the convent?'

'I'm not taking any chances,' McIvor answered firmly. 'I shall certainly visit him.'

As she looked into his soft hazel eyes flecked with specks of gold, Kit felt a warmth flood through her. This man, a stranger until only a few days ago, was planning on crossing the Irish Sea to fight for her child. Impulsively she took hold of his hand and kissed it. Gripping her tiny hand, the lawyer gazed into Kit's mesmerizing dark eyes that could so quickly move from sadness to happiness, like a cloud passing over the sun.

'I'm grateful to you, sir, and pray that God will go with you,' she said earnestly.

'I'll do my very best for you, Catherine.'

When he said her full name, Kit's eyebrows shot up. Nobody had ever in her whole life called her 'Catherine', and she was surprised at how much she liked it. Having completed his mission, Mr McIvor stepped out of the car to open the passenger door and help Kit out.

'Good day, Catherine.'

'Good day, Mr McIvor,' she replied formally.

Watching her walk away with her battered shoes flapping at the soles, Mr McIvor muttered under his breath, 'I swear I'll buy that young woman a new pair of shoes sometime soon!'

Buoyed with renewed hope, Kit threw herself body and soul into the final rehearsals. Belting out the rhythm on the snare drum and tom-toms, she felt surprisingly elated.

'"In the Mood" one more time,' she urged after yet another late-night rehearsal.

'OHHH, NO!' groaned the weary musicians.

'What's got into you?' Gladys asked.

'I want us to be perfect on the competition night. Come on, it's only the birds on the moors that can complain about the noise!' Kit joked.

With Kit firmly keeping her mind on the extra rehearsals, Gladys took the opportunity to work out the practicalities of their trip over the moors to the competition venue.

'I've been so busy concentrating on the music I haven't given any thought as to HOW we're actually going to get to Bolton,' she confessed to Edna one damp, misty evening.

Edna chuckled as she lit up a Player's. 'Yer daft bugger!'

Gladys frowned as she explained her problem. 'They'll have a piano and a set of drums at the dance-hall, but we'll have to take all the other instruments – trombone, clarinet, trumpet and saxophone. And then there're all six of us lasses too!' she exclaimed. 'WHY didn't I think of transport sooner?' she groaned.

Edna blew out a cloud of smoke before she said, 'I'll take you.'

Gladys gazed at her in astonishment. 'YOU? HOW?'

Edna nodded to her van, 'What do you call this?' she teased.

'But it's a chip shop!' Gladys exclaimed.

'And when it's not a chip shop, it's a big blue van – stinks a bit but it's serviceable. If I take out the range it'll get us all there, for sure.'

Overwhelmed with relief, Gladys flung her arms around the older woman's shoulders. 'What would the Bomb Girls do without our Edna?' she cried.

Then, just as Gladys was beginning to relax, Malc the overseer tracked her down first thing on Monday morning.

'Have you got permission for them girls on't night shift to have time off for't competition?' he asked.

Gladys's jaw dropped. Speechless, she could only shake her head.

'Thou's got a mind like a bloody sieve,' Malc teased.

Seeing Gladys blushing to the roots of her brunette

hair, he said with a reassuring wink, 'I'll have a word with Mr Featherstone, see if I can pull a few strings.'

Later that day he found Gladys with her pals in the canteen. Gladys tensed when she saw him approaching. If he hadn't got permission from the boss, at least three band girls wouldn't be going to Bolton the next night. Looking up at him expectantly, she held her breath.

'Yes . . . ?'

Malc gave her a thumbs-up sign. 'He's agreed that you can all go, on condition that you make up the lost time. He said, I quote, "There's a war on, no concessions."'

Gladys grinned as she stood on her tip-toes to give Malc a kiss on the cheek.

'Bugger!' Malc chuckled. 'It were worth me sticking mi neck out for a kiss like that!'

17. Palais de Danse

On the Tuesday of the dance band competition, Kit forced herself to think about the forthcoming event rather than let her thoughts stray to what Mr McIvor might be doing on her behalf. She was so preoccupied she didn't realize she'd been delegated the task of securing clean, new overalls from the store, which was Malc's domain.

'Why ME?' she cried. 'What if he catches me at it?'

'Malc thinks the world of you,' Gladys assured her. 'Always calls you that poor little Irish lass who needs feeding up! He'd never suspect you of doing anything underhand.'

'Anyway, we'll put them back after the competition,' Violet promised.

Once Kit's mission was successfully accomplished, the girls industriously concentrated on their workload before clocking off the second the hooter sounded.

'Good luck!' their colleagues called as the band girls hurried through the canteen. 'We'll keep our fingers crossed for you,' they promised.

Clutching the leather cases in which their instruments were safely stored, the girls dashed out of the factory gates and ran down the hill into Pendleton, where Edna was locking up her chip shop.

'All set?' she asked as they hurried towards her blue van

parked up in the back street. Suddenly Edna stopped dead in her tracks.

'BUGGERATION! I've got a flat tyre.'

Rolling up her sleeves, Edna took the jack from the back of the van and began cranking it up. 'You'll have to help me lift the van on to the jack,' she told her friends, who had gathered anxiously around her.

'I never had to do this when I was a Sunday school teacher,' fastidious Myrtle grimaced as dirt from the wheel splattered on to her delicate fingers.

Edna expertly replaced the damaged tyre with the spare, then, wiping her greasy black hands on a piece of newspaper, she hustled the girls into the back of the van, where they sat on the floor, apart from Gladys and Myrtle, who'd been delegated to direct Edna over the moors to Bolton. As the giggling girls in the back rolled around and bumped into each other, Gladys and Myrtle in the wide passenger seat gave direction to Edna, who drove along precipitous tracks often blocked by herds of bleating sheep.

An hour and a half later they arrived at the venue with plenty of time to spare.

'Good!' said Edna as she pulled up by the back entrance. 'Mebbe I can find a cuppa for us all.'

As Edna went in search of tea, Gladys and the other musicians dashed inside the dance-hall, eager to check out the musical equipment available to them. Kit stopped short when she saw the elaborate drum kit on the stage.

'Jesus, Mary and Joseph!' she gasped. 'I've never seen one of those things before,' she said as she pointed to a gleaming set of unusual looking cymbals.

The manager appeared from his office and smiled as he

explained, 'It's called a hi-hat – look,' he said as he pressed hard on the foot pedal and the two cymbals, one beneath the other, crashed loudly together.

Wide-eyed, Kit stared at the hi-hat cymbals in sheer delight. 'Well, now,' she said in her soft lilting voice, 'that'll be after making all the difference.'

Myrtle was thrilled to discover she'd be playing a grand piano. 'Oh, if only I'd got a ball gown to set it off,' she sighed wistfully.

'All in good time, Myrtle,' Gladys chuckled.

Edna appeared with mugs of tea and some corned-beef sandwiches she'd brought along with her. 'Got to keep your strength up,' she said as she handed around food to the hungry girls.

They had about an hour to practise before the doors opened at half past seven.

'Time to change,' said Gladys as she ushered her band into the ladies', where they wriggled into their clean over-alls and shoved their hair loosely under their turbans.

'I feel like I'm just about to clock on,' Maggie giggled.

'We're going to look a lot more glamorous than when we clock on,' Gladys said as she produced her make-up bag and started to apply face powder from her gold-coloured compact, then rouge and a sweep of bright red lipstick. 'Kit, come over here, I'll make you up,' she said as she beckoned her forwards.

With her long black hair trailing out from the confines of her turban, Kit's small heart-shaped face looked strained and tired after all the pressure she'd been under, but Gladys's lavish use of cosmetics soon transformed her. The powder made her skin look soft and creamy;

the rosy rouge emphasized her dramatic high cheek-bones; and the glossy red lipstick accentuated her full soft lips.

'I feel like a film star,' she murmured in disbelief after Gladys had turned her around to face the mirror.

'You're a lot better looking than any film star,' Violet enthused as she gazed in admiration at Kit's lovely face.

The girls' finishing touch to their appearance was the addition of long glittery earrings, most of which were begged and borrowed from other munitions girls at the Phoenix. Myrtle resisted all such fripperies and wore only her own three-string pearl necklace with a diamanté clasp.

'This is as good as it gets!' she announced as she patted down her permed curls.

The manager startled them all by banging loudly on the door, 'Five minutes, ladies!' he called.

The Bomb Girls were the third band scheduled to play out of the five who had entered the competition. As the excited audience started to dance to the first entry's open-ing number, the girls along with Edna sat at a table close to the stage, where they critically assessed their competitors.

'They're good,' said wide-eyed Nora, who was a bit red in the face from an over-application of rouge. 'But they're not as good as us,' she added bluntly.

'They've got nicer clothes,' Violet noticed enviously.

'Well, that wouldn't take much!' teased Edna.

'We're far better dancers with a well-rehearsed routine,' Maggie said over-loudly. 'They're dead wooden – just tapping their feet now and then when they remember,' she criticized.

Embarrassed, Gladys hissed across the table, 'For

God's sake, Mags, keep your voice down or you'll get us all thrown out.'

The second swing band on stage were more accomplished than the first, but the musicians were mostly middle aged and played a dull repertoire. A rather lukewarm spatter of applause sounded out as they concluded; then the manager beckoned to Gladys.

'You're on, kiddo!' he yelled.

Clutching their instruments, Gladys, Maggie, Nora and Violet ran on to the stage, where a trembling Kit was doing her best to hide behind the drum kit she was supposed to be playing.

'Holy Mother of God!' she squeaked to Edna, who was enjoying a Player's in the wings. 'I never thought there'd be such a massive crowd.'

'Just pray the air-raid siren doesn't go off or we'll be doing a live performance in the nearest Anderson shelter!' unflappable Edna joked.

Meanwhile Myrtle, in all her statuesque splendour, had swanned over to the grand piano, where she coolly flexed her long bony fingers before taking her seat, rather like Queen Elizabeth taking to the throne!

As the restless crowd mooched about, buying drinks, lighting up cigarettes, chatting up the opposite sex, the manager's voice boomed out: 'Ladies and gentlemen! A new band all the way from the Phoenix Munitions Factory in Pendleton. Put your hands together please for the BOMB GIRLS' SWING BAND!'

As the crowd clapped and wolf-whistled a cheeky young lad shouted out, 'Oi! Didn't you have chance to change before you left work?'

With a loud blast on her alto sax, Gladys drowned him out as she started their opening number, 'PEnnsylvania 6-5000'. As the brass section soared, Myrtle improvised over the top of the chord: vamping with her left hand she played out a riotous but harmonizing melody on the grand piano and the crowd took to the floor and *danced*! When Gladys set down her sax to sing the catchy chorus, the ballroom resounded as the audience clapped and chanted in tune with her: 'PEnnsylvania 6-5000'!

As their opening song reached a climatic crescendo, the Bomb Girls counted the beats into their next song. 'A-1, a-2, a-1, 2, 3, 4,' Gladys sang under her breath.

Swaying and stomping to 'In the Mood', Gladys gave her all to the alto sax; with her fingers running expertly up and down the valves, she ascended and descended the scales, creating rich, rounded notes which sent crowds of couples swirling and dipping around the dance floor. When the number came to an end, the lights dimmed and the same couples, softly illuminated by the fractured light of huge slow-turning silver balls, waltzed to Vera Lynn's caressingly romantic song, 'Yours Till the Stars Lose Their Glory'.

When the lights came back up, the enraptured audience went mad!

'MORE! MORE! MORE!' they bellowed as they clapped and cheered and wolf-whistled.

'They're never going to let you off the bloody stage!' cried the manager. 'Give 'em another song or we'll all be mobbed.'

The laughing girls turned to Gladys. 'Chattanooga Choo-Choo?' she suggested.

'Why not?' cried Kit as she hit the hi-hat cymbals with panache.

Further downstage, Nora, Mags, Violet and Gladys swayed hip to hip, to the left and the right, just as they'd practised over and over again in the Phoenix chapel and in the canteen.

'Stay together, girls,' Mags muttered under her breath. 'Kick, click, shake and tap,' she said as they synchronized their moves.

Their encore brought the house down, and the two groups that followed didn't stand a chance. The judges voted the Bomb Girls the winners, and they took their bow in the spotlight to tumultuous applause.

'We're through to the semi-finals!' gasped Nora.

'You canny lasses have got it stitched up,' the manager remarked as they packed up their instruments and Kit said a very sad goodbye to the hi-hat cymbals, which she'd taken quite a shine to. 'Middle-aged musicians playing middle-aged music is no competition for an all-girls' swing band – they're guaranteed winners.'

Edna proudly threw back her shoulders. 'Believe you me,' she declared, 'they're not called the Bomb Girls for nothing!'

18. Flowers and Birdsong

The Bomb Girls' Swing Band were applauded by their fellow workers when they walked into the canteen after clocking on the day after the play-offs in Bolton.

'You did us proud!' they cried.

'I can't wait for the semi-finals,' Ivy the supervisor in the filling shed laughed as she delivered a tin tray loaded with mugs of tea to the girls' table. 'Here, get this lot down you,' she said cheerily.

'I can bloody wait,' Nora groaned as she lit up her first Woodbine of the day. 'I'm so tired I don't know whether I'm on mi 'ead or mi arse!'

'Oh, but it was worth it,' enthused Kit, who, though exhausted from the long drive home followed by a very late night, was sparkle-eyed with excitement. 'Holy Mother of God – we won!'

For the first time in her life Kit had actually won something, and the feeling was good. Was this an omen of better things to come, she wondered superstitiously. Was her luck finally changing at last?

Later that morning, as Arthur passed through the filling shed, he stopped to congratulate the girls too. As he passed Violet, he stooped to whisper in her ear, 'Meet me in the garden during your next break.'

Before he left, he gently patted her hand with his maimed one. Violet couldn't help but compare him to

Ronnie, who'd dodged conscription, whilst a brave, self-less man like Arthur and millions more beside had not a second's doubt about joining up and fighting for their king and country.

She'd learnt about Arthur's war work on one of their moorland walks up to Witch's Crag.

'Coming from Chester, I immediately joined up – the 2nd Battalion of the Cheshires,' he told her proudly as they wound their way up the steep mossy tracks. 'My unit served in France with the rest of the British Expeditionary Force before fighting in the Battle of Dunkirk – that's where this happened,' he said, holding up his deformed hands. 'I was working in explosives, blowing up enemy bridges and railway lines.'

'God!' Violet gasped. 'I can't think of anything more terrifying.'

He nodded grimly.

'It was truly terrifying, but my unit looked out for each other; we checked and double-checked everything, always looking for booby traps. We learnt to outwit the Germans at their own dirty game . . . until one night . . .' –He took a deep ragged breath.

'Shall we sit down?' Violet asked anxiously.

He nodded and spread his jacket on the heather for her to sit on.

'I was with my mate Ted; we were de-fusing a bomb the Jerries had positioned under a bridge, so our troops could pass over. We'd managed to remove the casing from the bomb, but the damn detonator hadn't gone off. We realized too late we'd been tricked – the bomb had been booby-trapped. I saw a tiny spark and reached over to grab the bomb and throw it into the river, but it went off in Ted's hands. He was blown up right there in front of me,' Arthur added with a catch in his voice. 'I lost two fingers on my right hand and the thumb on my left – and the best friend I ever had.'

Violet took hold of his hands, which even now showed the scar lines of multiple stiches.

'At least you're alive,' she whispered.

'To be honest I wished it was me that had died. Ted had three children and a wife he adored in Southampton. I visited them once I was out of the convalescent home. I don't know how they'll ever come to terms with their loss.' He flung himself back on the heather and gazed up into the sky. 'Once I'd made my recovery, I was declared unfit for the front and sent up here to do my war work.'

'Working with noisy Bomb Girls,' she teased.

'People make jokes about me working with 200 women, and it's embarrassing at times – it doesn't feel like real men's work,' he admitted.

'Don't be ridiculous,' she said crossly. 'What's not real about maintaining factory safety and protecting the workers? It's a specialist job and I'm glad it's somebody as experienced and conscientious as you that's doing it,' she said hotly.

Sitting up, he stroked her face dominated by her large eyes, which were as blue as bluebells in the springtime.

'Really, Vi? Are you glad it's me?' he asked softly.

In answer, she kissed his scarred hand. 'There's nobody better than you, Arthur Leadbetter.'

*

During her break, Violet did as Arthur had asked and made her way to his garden, where she found him watering vegetables.

'What's this?' she teased. 'Depriving me of my break?'

'I've got tea,' Arthur chuckled as he held up a thermos flask. 'And fags too,' he added as he produced a packet of his favourite Craven 'A' cigarettes from his overalls pocket. 'But first, I've got something to show you,' he said with a secretive grin.

Violet smiled to herself. 'It's bound to be his first crop of new potatoes!' she thought.

Instead, Arthur presented her with a huge bouquet of early-summer flowers – carnations, roses, peonies, sweet peas and fragrant white stocks.

'All picked from my garden,' Arthur said proudly.

Violet buried her face in the blooms. 'They're gorgeous,' she cried.

'I wanted to give you a present after last night's success,' Arthur explained.

'Oh, it was marvellous!' she exclaimed as she laid the flowers aside to accept a cigarette and a mug of hot tea. 'We played like we'd never played before,' she said with stars in her eyes. 'The audience went wild; they wouldn't let us off the stage,' she giggled.

'I wish I'd been there to see it,' Arthur said longingly.

'Then you must come to the next round,' she said excitedly. 'And bring us luck.'

Arthur bent to give her a long kiss. 'When you've got talent like the Bomb Girls',' he teased, 'you don't need luck!'

*

That night, Edna came swerving down the moorland track that led to the cowshed. After breaking sharply she jumped out of her blue van and hurried towards the open front door.

'Evening!' she called cheerily to the girls relaxing in the sitting room after their shift.

'Here comes our manager!' Gladys joked.

'Have you signed us up for a million-dollar booking?' Violet teased.

'Not yet, but I will soon,' Edna chuckled. 'Actually I'm here to beg a favour of Kit.' She nodded at Kit, who was lying flat out on the battered old sofa. 'Can you give us a hand to set up, lovie?'

Kit jumped to her feet. 'Course I can,' she said happily.

Once they were in the blue van, Edna's joking tone immediately changed. 'I had a telephone call from Mr McIvor this afternoon,' she said urgently.

Kit's pulse started to race; had he already had a meeting with Mother Gabriel? Had he seen Billy?

'He asked me to let you know that he's safely arrived in Ireland,' Edna added.

Kit's heart dropped in disappointment. She was relieved, of course, that he was there, but she was impatiently hoping for a lot more news than his arrival.

'Oh, is that all?' she muttered.

Keeping her eyes on the narrow winding road, Edna said, 'He's there, Kit – that's something. This time last week, you had nothing. At least he's got the ball rolling for your little Billy.'

Kit agreed. She had to have patience and let the man

she'd begged to represent her do his professional best for her and Billy.

'Just think,' she said, 'he might be with Billy right now.' Her eyes filled up with tears of longing. 'Oh, if only I was with him too, if only I could hold my boy and kiss him,' she sighed, her tears as ever never far away.

Edna gave her a reassuring pat on the arm. 'Come on now, sweetheart, you're in good hands. Mr McIvor knows what he's doing. All you can do now is wait – and pray.'

19. Nora and Nellie

After Les's battalion had been posted to northern Europe, Gladys received quite a few chatty letters from her brother, which cheered her up no end. But after the last couple of letters, which had been opened and heavily censored, there had been no more, which left Gladys feeling very uneasy. Worried as she was, Gladys kept her anxieties to herself in order not to alarm her mother, who was permanently edgy about her son's whereabouts. 'Maybe he's on active duty?' she thought with a shudder.

If that was the case, he wouldn't have time to write letters home whilst he was dodging bullets. She prayed he was safe and resigned herself to the fact that letter-writing might not be his priority at this moment in time.

What with Kit preoccupied with Mr McIvor's visit to Dublin, Violet falling for Arthur Leadbetter and Gladys anxious about her brother, nobody immediately noticed the change in Nora, who turned up for work one day with huge dark bags under her eyes.

It was Maggie who drew their attention to her friend's condition. 'There's trouble at home,' she whispered early one morning in the canteen. 'I can't get any more than that out of her.'

Kit sneaked a look at Nora, who was queuing up at the canteen counter for tea and toast.

'She certainly looks peaky,' she commented, guilty that she hadn't noticed herself.

'Somebody should have a word with her,' Maggie fretted.

Violet volunteered to take Nora to one side, which she managed to do the next evening when she, Nora and several other women were gathered around Edna's blue van in the dispatch yard.

'Can I buy you a cuppa and a bag of chips, Nora?' Violet asked cheerily.

'Er . . . I should go home – mi mam's waiting for me,' Nora said, dithering..

'Go on!' Violet joked. 'It'll only take ten minutes.'

When they'd got their chips, Violet linked arms with Nora and led her out on to the edge of the moors, which were steeped in a warm golden light from the late setting sun. Comforted by the hot chips and the soothing landscape, Nora visibly relaxed. After they'd smoked a companionable cigarette each, Violet broached the subject. 'What's troubling you, lovie?' she asked softly. 'You've not been yourself recently.'

Nora sighed heavily as she slumped back on to the heather and watched tiny silver stars pinprick the darkening sky.

'It's our Nellie.'

'Your younger sister?'

Nora nodded. 'She's only just turned eighteen, but she was mad to go down South and work as a Land Girl – she loves horses and had a romantic notion that working as a Land Girl she'd get the chance to harvest wheat fields with big old cart horses. Bloody mad!' she mocked but in an affectionate voice. 'She's always been a dreamer.'

Violet waited in silence as Nora took a deep breath.

'Any road up, she's finished up on a farm just outside Exeter, milking cows and cleaning cowsheds from dawn till dusk. She's been sending us letters saying she hates it and wants to come home, but the wretched farmer insists he needs her,' Nora dropped her voice. 'He's been behaving indecently,' she whispered.

'What's he been doing?' Violet asked sharply.

Nora looked from side to side to make sure nobody could overhear her. 'Touching her up in the milking shed, well away from where his wife can see him.'

"That's outrageous!' Violet cried. 'She should apply for an immediate transfer North.'

'She has!' Nora retorted. 'But the farmer got in the way of that too – he was 'avin' none of it.'

'Poor girl,' Violet commiserated.

'She was so desperate she tried to run away,' Nora continued. 'She got hauled back by the military police and now the farmer's even harder on her – and it's not stopped him from touching her up.'

Poor Nora gave a long loud sigh.

'It's got so bad mi mam's going down there herself. She's going over the farmer's head, straight to the local authorities,' she added conspiratorially. 'She's going to ask them to let our Nellie transfer North; then, once she's back here in Pendleton, she'll get her a job in't Phoenix, working alongside me and Mags.'

'That's an excellent plan!' Violet exclaimed.

'Better than a slap in't face with a wet fish, as mi dad would say,' agreed Nora, who returned home that night feeling a lot better for her heartwarming chat with Violet.

Early the next morning Violet searched out Arthur in his warm sunny garden that was fragrant with the smell of summer phlox, carnations and sweet peas. Sighing contentedly, she leant against his strong frame.

'Good morning, mister,' she said fondly.

In a preoccupied manner, Arthur smiled and stroked her long hair that had slipped loose under her turban. Sensing his unease, Violet immediately asked, 'What's the matter, sweetheart?'

'The Desert Rat's finally on the run,' he replied.

'Rommel?' she said knowingly.

Arthur nodded as he gave a brief hard smile. 'Turns out the Jerries are an exhausted army after months of fighting in the scorching desert – we're holding the line and repelling Rommel.'

'Victory at last!' Violet exclaimed, but she could see no joy in Arthur's troubled face.

'I should be there, Vi,' he murmured.

Tracing the livid scars on his damaged hand, she patiently listened to him.

'Mates of mine are fighting in the Eighth Army. I should be alongside them, not sitting here digging up carrots and spring onions,' he said self-mockingly. 'What kind of a man does that?'

'Darling, you've made your sacrifice,' she pointed out.

'I can still fire a gun and use a bayonet!'

'Can you?' she asked. 'Really, would you be as quick as your pals when it came to shooting accurately?'

It was a harsh question, but she knew if there was any comfort to be had in this conversation it would be cold comfort. She saw Arthur wince, but she pushed on with her questioning. 'Instead of beating yourself up, be honest,' she urged. 'Don't you think the army would have kept an experienced explosive expert on if they thought it was safe for you to fight?'

She saw his eyes fill with angry tears.

'I just feel so bloody useless, Vi,' he sighed as he laid his head against her soft warm bosom. 'A real Nancy boy, doing nothing but checking safety regulations in a bloody arms factory!'

Violet was wise enough to let him be. He'd had his outburst and she understood his shame, but she was determined that she would make him come to terms with his injuries, which he dismissed as nothing when in fact he'd been maimed for life whilst on dangerous active service. Eventually he pulled away from her and gave her a soft kiss on her full pink lips.

'I don't know what I'd do without you, my sweetheart,' he confessed.

'And do you know what, Mr Grumpy Leadbetter? I don't know what the Phoenix girls would do without YOU!'

A slow smile warmed his dark blue eyes that held her loving gaze.

'I only really care about one Phoenix girl – and that's my beautiful Violet!' he declared as he pulled her back into his arms.

Shortly after Nora's mother had set off on her long journey South to see Nellie in Exeter, Gladys received a troubling letter from her dad in Leeds; he admitted to also being 'concerned' about Les; like Gladys, he'd had no word from his son.

Obviously I've not shared my concern with your mother; she's worried enough as it is. We know Les isn't a natural letter-writer, but it's been nearly a month now since he last communicated, so, Glad, if you should hear from him please notify me right away and then I can set your mother's mind at rest.

Ever your loving, Father X

Gladys felt heavy-hearted as she folded the letter. There was no doubting the triumphant progress of British troops in North Africa, but there seemed to be more losses than victories in the war that raged on in the battlefields of northern Europe, where they believed Les had been posted. Gladys was even more heavy-hearted when she heard another news item. It seemed German bombers had been dropping bombs all over the British countryside. A young boy had witnessed a low-flying plane's bomb bay opening wide and two bombs dropping out. The local boy from a village near Exeter reported seeing one bounce across open fields, then explode in the middle of a row of sheds, whilst the other hit a Royal Ordnance Factory, killing seventeen young women who worked there. As the girls listened to the news on the radio in the cowshed, Violet's eyes grew wide with alarm.

'Oh, my God!' she cried as she leapt from the sofa, where she'd been peacefully smoking a cigarette. 'Did he just say the Exeter area?'

Kit nodded.

'I'm pretty sure he said the boy lived near Exeter.' She looked towards Gladys, who nodded too.

'What's the matter, Vi? Where are you off to?' Kit asked, as Violet headed for the front door.

'Nora's sister's working in that area!' Violet answered quickly. 'And her mother's down there too, visiting Nellie.'

Violet ran over to the dispatch yard, where she found Edna packing up for the night.

'Can you call in on Nora on your way home?' Violet asked the older woman.

'Course I can,' said Edna. 'Is something wrong?'

'I've just heard some bad news on the radio, and I wanted to check that it's nothing to do with Nora's family,' Gladys replied.

Smothering a yawn, Edna said, 'If it's bad news, I'll drive back up here and tell you; if there's nothing to report, I'll snuggle down in my bed for the night.'

An hour later, after Edna hadn't returned, Violet fell asleep, happy in the belief that no news was good news, but when there was no sign of Nora the following morning everybody suspected the worst. Myrtle, who'd become rather protective of Nora over their many trombone lessons, said quite decisively, 'I'll finish my shift, then I'll walk into Pendleton and visit young Nora.'

'Shall I come with you?' Maggie asked. 'I know where she lives.'

'No, thank you, Margaret,' Myrtle replied firmly. 'I shall be fine on my own.'

'Will you let us know how you get on?' Violet said anxiously.

'If it's not too late I shall drop by with an update,' Myrtle promised.

When Myrtle knocked on their door later that evening, the girls ran to open it and immediately knew from the expression on her face that the news was bad. Kit put the kettle on the wood-burning stove, whilst Violet led Myrtle to the battered old sofa, where she wasted no time in beating about the bush. 'Nora's father received a telegram this morning: both his wife and youngest daughter are dead.'

'Oh, Jesus, Mary and Joseph,' Kit cried as she crossed herself.

'The sheds that the first bomb landed on were in fact cowsheds, in one of which was poor Nellie, milking cows; her mother was in there with her too,' Myrtle said as she wiped tears from the corner of her eyes. 'At least they were together,' she continued briskly. 'And it certainly would have been a quick death.'

'Poor Nora,' sighed Kit.

'Poor Mr Barnes,' gasped Violet. 'If his wife hadn't gone down South to help Nellie get away, she'd be alive today.'

'But Nellie would have died on her own, all alone and terrified,' Myrtle pointed out.

'OH, GOD!' seethed Gladys as she angrily paced the room. 'When will this bloody war end?'

'Hitler will only be happy when he's bombed Britain off the face of the earth,' Violet said bitterly.

Myrtle rose to her feet, and like a warrior leader she surveyed the troubled tearful girls before she said with complete conviction, 'There'll *always* be an England!'

20. The Irish Visit

Kit received a letter from Mr McIvor saying he'd returned home from Ireland and asking her to come to see him at the office as soon as possible.

Kit wondered why he hadn't come to see her himself like he had before, or left a phone message for Edna to pass on to her. Letters took so long and they had so much urgent business to discuss. After a long night, Kit got the first bus into Manchester, where she hurried eagerly across Piccadilly to McIvor's office. Shocked by the sight of grey-faced Kit with dark bags under her eyes, McIvor settled her in a chair, then called for his secretary to bring tea and biscuits.

Impatient for news Kit came straight to the point. 'Did you see Billy?'

McIvor nodded. 'Billy looked very well,' he assured her.

Kit smiled proudly. 'Did you give him a kiss from me?' she asked.

'I thought he might not like that but I did sing him a few nursery rhymes,' McIvor admitted with a shy smile.

Kit smiled too at the thought of this kind man spending time with her little boy, but McIvor interrupted her fond line of thought. 'Your father was less than pleased to see me.'

'Well, that's no surprise!' she burst out. 'What did he have to say for his miserable self?'

'He insisted Billy was his and he had every right to choose what was the best course for him.' He paused before he added rather shortly, 'I would have been grateful if you'd told me before I left for Dublin that you'd signed the adoption papers, Catherine.'

Seeing her rendered speechless by his comment, McIvor continued, 'I saw your signature right there on the document, next to your father's and Mother Gabriel's. You can't imagine what a fool I felt,' he snapped. 'With your signature on those documents we simply don't have a case!'

Alarmed and indignant Kit finally got her breath back. 'I did NOT sign any papers!' she insisted, her voice icily calm.

McIvor stared at her incredulously. 'I saw your name, in black and white, "Catherine Murphy",' he declared.

'Then it was forged!' she cried. 'Do you really think I'm that stupid that I would forget that I'd signed my son's adoption papers?'

In the tense silence that followed McIvor beat his fingers on the desktop. 'So, if you didn't sign them, who did?'

'I'll give you three guesses,' she replied angrily.

'Your father?'

'My evil father! Not only did he steal my boy but he also forged my signature,' she cried as tears rolled down her cheeks.

'When I met the Mother Superior I reminded her that you are legally Billy's guardian, not Mr Murphy, and as such you should by law have been legally consulted. I thought we had a strong case until she produced the document with your signature on it.'

'I never signed anything!' Kit retorted emphatically. 'We have to prove that the name on that document was not signed by me.'

Seeing McIvor's brow crinkle, Kit began to panic. 'Do we have a case if we can prove as God's my judge that it wasn't me?' she pleaded.

McIvor's taps on the desktop grew louder and more agitated. 'We'd have to hire a handwriting specialist to prove that it was false.' He suddenly thrust a sheet of thick white paper and a fountain pen at her. 'Sign your name,' he instructed. 'Sign it several times.'

Unused to fountain pens, Kit wielded it awkwardly.

'Take your time,' he warned.

Slowly and methodically, she wrote her name, 'Catherine Murphy', in the formal script she'd been taught at school. McIvor peered closely at the rows of signatures she'd carefully written.

'I believe you that it might have been a forgery,' he sighed. 'We'll know better when we can compare it with the original. But I'll be blunt, Catherine: the time we'll need to prove this isn't your signature is time we don't really have.'

'Why?' she cried impatiently. 'Sister Clare said adoptions take ages – surely we can stop them doing anything illegal?' she cried.

'I'll write straight away to let them know we are contesting the documents. But you need to understand that I have to find a handwriting expert who will have to produce detailed evidence as to why the signature on the adoption papers isn't yours. Then we'll have to present it to Mother Gabriel, who might well challenge it. It's not just a question of revoking the documents on the grounds that they're fraudulent any more; this is all going to take much longer than planned, Catherine. I need you to understand that,' he said with a heavy sigh.

'Holy Mother of God,' she wailed in despair. 'Will this nightmare ever end?'

Feeling desperately sorry for the poor girl, McIvor got up from his chair so that he could put an arm around her shuddering shoulders.

'Catherine,' he said slowly, 'the adoptive couple are making plans to take Billy to America.'

'His home is *not* in America,' she sobbed. 'His home is RIGHT HERE with me!' Almost out of her mind with rage and sadness, she added angrily, 'If that filthy rich couple get to my Billy before you've proved my innocence, I could lose my son forever.'

Keeping his voice calm and steady McIvor replied, 'I don't think Mother Gabriel would dare to go against the law,' he reasoned. 'It would bring disgrace to her order and their adoption agency too. I will contact her right away.'

Furious and frustrated, Kit lost her temper. 'It's not fair!' she cried. 'Here am I, the rightful mother, fighting to keep my son from deportation, whilst Mother Gabriel is busy selling babbies for a big fat profit – and as for my father,' she said as she ground her teeth in fury, 'the thieving pig signed a pact with the devil the day he was born.'

McIvor tried his best to reassure her: 'As I just said, I don't think the order of the Sisters of Mercy would –'

Kit, in a murderously bad mood, muttered as she rose

to her feet. 'Who gives a fiddler's fart about the bloody rotten nuns!'

Before she left the office, McIvor stopped Kit in her tracks. 'Catherine, one other thing. Your sister asked me to pass on a message.'

Wide-eyed, Kit turned to him. 'She said to tell you that your mother had a grand funeral and the chapel was packed with mourners.'

Kit's eyes swam with tears. 'Everybody but me to say a final goodbye to Mammy,' she said sadly.

'And when I saw Billy in the convent nursery, he really did look well. He's a big bonny boy, well taken care of by the nuns. That's something to hold on to, isn't it?'

Despite her misery, Kit smiled. 'He is a beautiful child, isn't he? Has he still got dark hair?'

McIvor nodded as he recalled the baby boy. 'Yes, a mop of it – and dark eyes just like yours.'

'Maybe that's all he'll ever have of me if he goes to America,' Kit said as she left the office in floods of tears.

Before Kit clocked on for her night shift, she managed to have ten minutes in private with Edna, who listened to the poor girl pour her heart out.

'It was complicated enough to start with, but proving my signature's been forged really adds to the pressure,' Kit said as she stubbed out her cigarette under the heel of her threadbare shoes. 'Maybe Billy would be better off with a rich American couple,' she added bitterly. 'What kind of a mother am I? Look at me, with not a decent pair of shoes to mi feet, what have I got to offer?' she cried as her tears flowed once more.

Edna grabbed her by the hands and shook her. 'You've got to stop this, Kit, right now!' she declared fiercely.

'I know, I know!' Kit sobbed hysterically. 'I love him so much – I just want what's best for him.'

'What's best for him, sweetheart,' said Edna modifying her tone, 'is YOU. Nobody can replace a mother; nobody will understand him better than you who carried him inside you and gave birth to him and loved him so much you even left home to provide for him. There is no greater sacrifice than that; leaving him behind was the act of a mother who put her child's safety before herself.'

Kit was surprised to see tears filling Edna's green eyes.

'I'm sorry, Edna, I never meant to upset you too,' she said apologetically.

'It's nowt to do with you, sweetheart; it's something I did years ago which I've regretted every day of my life since.' She quickly wiped away a tear. 'You see, Kit, I had a baby too, a daughter . . .' Edna's voice trailed away as the memories rolled back. 'A beautiful little girl . . . I called her Flora – I don't know what she's called now, or even if she's alive.'

Too shocked to speak, Kit could only gaze in sorrow at the friend who'd always seemed indomitable in her strength; yet here she was, lost in a profound grief that she'd bottled up for years.

'At six weeks she was taken from me, adopted by a rich childless couple in Penrith, or so the agency told me.'

Finding her voice, Kit whispered, 'Did you ever see her again?'

Edna shook her head. 'I tried but there was no Flora Chadderton on any adoption records.' She shrugged as she added. 'The couple who took her probably gave her their own name anyway.'

'And the father?' Kit inquired timidly.

'Edward Pilkington. A local lad. We'd been courting since our school days; We only did it once,' Edna answered with a wistful smile. 'Just before he went off to war, the First World War that is. He never knew he had a daughter; he died at Passchendaele before she was born, blown up in a German rocket attack.'

'God in heaven,' Kit gasped.

'Nobody but my parents knew about my pregnancy; as soon as Flora was born they couldn't get shot of her quick enough. I begged and pleaded, wept and raged, but nothing changed their minds. They didn't want the shame of a bastard in the family.'

'I don't feel like that about my lovely boy!' Kit cried passionately. 'I can see no shame in him, even if I do hate his evil-hearted father,' she said as she clung to Edna, who gently stroked her tired, tear-stained face.

'Keep on fighting for your son, lovie, never let go!' Edna whispered. 'Don't do what I did and live with heartbreak for the rest of your life.'

21. Brave Girl

Preoccupied with Billy's case and all the awful uncertainties, Kit lost interest in almost everything, and that included the Bomb Girls' Swing Band. It was the last thing she could turn her mind to, even though she felt guilty letting her friends down. Gladys, Violet, Myrtle and Maggie talked in private about their friend's change of mood.

'What's got into her?' Maggie snapped crossly. 'She was so gung-ho not long ago, pushing us on, urging us to do better; now she doesn't even turn up for the bloody practice sessions!' she finished angrily.

'It must be something to do with that lawyer fella in Manchester,' Violet commented. 'Every time she has anything to do with him she comes home in a state.'

'I wish she'd talk about this family business with her cousins,' Gladys said. 'If we knew what was worrying her we might be able to help.'

'No chance of that,' Violet retorted. 'Whenever you mention them, she clams up like a shell.'

Maggie, furious that they'd been let down, continued to fume. 'How the 'ell are we ever going to play in the semi-finals without a reliable drummer? Honest to God, I could scream!'

Surprisingly, it was poor heartbroken Nora who brought Kit round. When she returned to work after her sister's and mother's deaths, she was a shadow of her former robust self. Gaunt with grief, she worked slavishly on the cordite line and seemed to find solace only when with her friends.

'We had a church service,' she told them as tears rolled unchecked down her hollow cheeks. 'But there were no coffins . . .' She caught her breath as she added, 'There weren't enough left of them to bury.'

'God in heaven!' gasped Kit as she folded wretched Nora in her arms.

Worried about the girl's health, Gladys gently asked, 'Are you sure it's a good idea to be working, sweetheart? You're not exactly in a safe environment.'

Nora was adamant. 'I'm better off here with you,' she declared. 'It's hell at home with mi dad, who never stops crying.'

'In that case,' said Myrtle firmly, 'let's play some music.'

Inside the chapel during their lunch break, the girls struck up, and, though Nora tried to be brave, she could only weep into her trombone's mouthpiece.

'Sorry, sorry,' she cried. 'It just makes me think of our Nell. Even though I was rubbish, she always used to love me playing; she'd sing along with me when she could.' Waving her hands, she said, 'Ignore me. I'll get through it. Please, let's play.'

Seeing the poor kid heroically struggling through 'South of the Border', Kit did everything she could in her drumming to help Nora through the song. When it was over, Nora looked less miserable.

'Thank you,' she said. 'You're like my family now and I love you all.'

That did it for Kit: if this poor girl could perform with the Bomb Girls, then, by God, she could too!

As they split up at the end of the rehearsal session, Kit gave Nora a big hug.

'Do it for them, sweetheart,' she whispered. 'They'll hear you up in heaven and smile down on you, I know they will.'

Touched, Nora smiled her gap-toothed smile, the first they'd seen all week.

So they slipped back into their old routine of meeting up and practising whenever they could. Unfortunately, this time around the girls' shifts didn't quite coincide with one another; Nora and Mags on the cordite line were working nights, whilst Gladys, Kit, Violet and Myrtle were on afternoon shifts; they stopped work as Nora and Maggie started. Feeling guilty about pushing the girls so hard, Gladys nevertheless made a bold suggestion.

'If you went straight to bed after your shift and slept for four or five hours, we could all meet up before we start our afternoon shift.'

'What? We can't exist on four hours sleep a day!' Maggie cried.

Gladys quickly added, 'You could go back to bed at two, when we're clocking on.'

'We'll be like walking zombies!' Nora giggled.

'You're young, you'll survive,' Myrtle said briskly.

When the two girls finally agreed to Gladys's proposal, the rest of the band were grateful for their sacrifice. As Myrtle put it, 'Your dedication shows true commitment.'

In the precious hours that they did overlap, all six

musicians pushed themselves to the limit, and, in Myrtle's case, she pushed herself far too hard. One afternoon, as they practised in the Phoenix chapel, during a lively jitterbug number Myrtle reached energetically across the piano, then suddenly froze in pain.

'Aghh! My back!' she gasped as she placed a hand on the base of her spine and struggled to keep her composure.

Violet, who'd done a St John's Ambulance course in the Coventry hospital where she'd worked, laid Myrtle carefully on the floor, then tenderly felt along the length of her friend's back.

'Argh!' Myrtle moaned as Violet reached the area around her coccyx.

'Oh, God!' groaned Violet. 'It looks like you might have slipped a disc.'

Myrtle groaned in despair. 'Damn! Damn!' she swore. 'It's happened before. It takes weeks to heal.'

The girls helped poor Myrtle, cringing with pain, to her feet, then half carried her to the Phoenix's infirmary, where the doctor on duty pronounced her unfit for work. 'Bed rest,' he said.

With tears in her eyes, Myrtle, now in a wheelchair, was pushed by the doctor on to the admissions ward.

'Let's face it, ladies, there's no chance of my being fit enough to play the piano at the semi-finals,' she announced flatly.

Her crestfallen friends returned to the factory chapel, where they slumped on to the pews. Though dreadfully sorry for Myrtle, the Bomb Girls stared at each other, wondering how on earth they could possibly proceed. With her head in her hands, Gladys murmured,

'We'll have to let the organizers know we can't attend the semi-finals.'

Surprisingly, it was Nora who showed the most determination. 'We can't give up!' she declared. 'We could ask around the factory, see if anybody could replace Myrtle.'

Smiling at Nora's dogged expression, Kit said, 'It's worth a go; we'll put the word out as soon as we clock on tomorrow.'

Leaving exhausted Nora and Maggie to return to their digs to catch up on their sleep, Violet, Kit and Gladys hurried over to the canteen, where they split up in order to ask every single girl and woman in the building if they could play the piano. Most came back with the same answer.

'I can knock out a few tunes but I'm not up to Myrtle's professional standard.'

With all hope gone, Gladys laid her head on the canteen table they were sitting around and swore. 'BUGGER! BUGGER! BUGGER!!'

At which point Malc walked up. Coming straight to the point, he said, 'I hear you've lost your pianist.'

Gladys nodded. 'Myrtle's slipped a disc,' she told him.

Malc dropped his voice to a whisper. 'Perhaps I can help?'

'HOW?' asked Kit.

Whispering even lower, Malc said, 'Well, I can play the piano.'

As the women stared at him, Malc added somewhat self-consciously, 'I play to a high standard – I was put through all the grades in the orphanage where I grew up.'

Looking nervously around the canteen, Gladys said

quietly, 'Could we have the rest of this conversation in private?'

In the empty chapel, Gladys continued uncomfortably. 'It's good of you to offer, and I don't doubt your skills, but no matter how well you play . . .' Her voice trailed away, in her embarrassment at having to state the obvious.

'I'm a fella,' Malc said, bluntly filling in the blank for her. 'But I'm not averse to wearing a wig and a frock if it helps you out of a tight spot!'

'Are you having us on?' cried Violet.

'Never been more serious,' he retorted. 'Tell you what, whilst you get your breath back I'll play for you . . .' Malc sat down at the piano. 'If I'm not up to scratch, then that's it, end of story.'

Without any music, Malc launched into 'South of the Border'.

'He's not up to Myrtle's level,' Kit whispered from behind her hand.

'But he's all right,' Violet whispered back.

'He'll do,' said Gladys decisively.

Once it was agreed that Malc could join the band, he practised with them as often as he could. The first time he showed up Nora and Maggie were hysterical with laughter.

'How's he going to get away with being a lass?' Nora giggled.

'I'll shave off my five-o'clock shadow – that's a real give-away,' Malc chuckled. 'Though I draw the line at shaving my legs!' he guffawed.

Kit, who was also vastly amused by the prospect of Malc posing as a Bomb Girl, started to giggle as well.

'Don't worry, our overalls cover almost everything up – though you might have to wear a wig underneath your turban!' she finished with a peal of laughter.

'We can stuff a bra with socks to give you a bit of shape!' Violet giggled too.

Getting down to the nitty-gritty, Gladys said rather tensely, 'In order to see if this arrangement's going to work, we *really* need to practise with you, Malc.'

Unruffled, Malc played a rippling chord on the piano. 'Let's get on with it,' he replied.

Gladys was right: a new pianist accompanying them made a big difference to the band. Only now did they realize how much they'd come to rely on Myrtle's skills: apart from her superb musical accompaniment, she was a genius at improvisation and always provided lively backing, particularly for Gladys's alto sax solos. With only two days to go, Malc and the girls practised every available moment, to the delight of their co-workers. Gladys, Violet, Nora and Maggie even used their dinner breaks to play their instruments, whilst laughing Kit beat out a drum rhythm on a steel-topped canteen table. Malc's involvement, however, was kept strictly under wraps.

'If word gets around that our all-female swing band has a male pianist, we'll be the laughing stock of the Leeds Locarno,' Gladys said as she swore her friends to secrecy. 'The less that's known about him playing with us the better,'

The band visited Myrtle in hospital as often as they could, but they didn't dare tell her the truth about the new arrangement.

'Have you got a replacement?' she fretted.

All five girls stared at each other. It seemed mean and underhand to lie to Myrtle, but they knew the truth would incense her.

'Yes,' said quick-witted Gladys as she hid a smile. 'But she's nothing like as good as you!'

22. Semi-final

Malc again persuaded Mr Featherstone to allow the girls to rearrange their shifts so that they could leave work at the same time and travel to Leeds, though this time they left the Phoenix already dressed in clean overalls and turbans.

'We can't risk Malc changing in the ladies' toilets,' Gladys said.

'God forbid!' chuckled Malc as he adjusted an auburn wig over his short-back-and-sides greying hair. 'Will I do?' he joked as he struck a comical feminine pose.

The girls looked him up and down then burst into peals of laughter.

'Oh, Christ!' roared Nora. 'You're taller than the lot of us.'

'And twice as fat,' Malc said candidly. 'Should have stuck to that diet, eh?' he joked.

There was no keeping Malc's identity a secret from Arthur, who was driving Violet to the event in his car.

'Bloody hell fire!' he roared with laughter as Malc settled himself coyly in the back seat of his car.

'For one night only,' Malc joked as he lit up a cigarette.

'What're we going to call you?' Violet asked.

'Molly!' Malc answered as he stuffed his turban over the wig that curled around his ears. Adjusting his hair in the rear-view mirror, he said in all seriousness, 'I'm going to need some lipstick and rouge if I'm to pass for a lass.'

'You'll need a lot more than make-up,' Arthur teased as they drove along the winding moorland tracks into Yorkshire.

Before he went into the Locarno, Malc was skilfully made up by Gladys, who cheekily planted a big kiss on his painted crimson lips.

'WHUMPH! You're gorgeous,' she teased.

Gladys's dad was waiting for them when they pulled up at the back of the dance-hall. Thrilled to see his daughter, he hugged her tightly, then she introduced him to the 'girls', and they all shook hands. He stopped short when Molly gripped his hand.

'Pleased to meet you, sir,' she said in a squeaky high voice.

'She's a big lass,' Mr Johnson whispered to his daughter as they started to unpack their instruments.

'She's a *he*,' Gladys whispered back.

Mr Johnson's jaw dropped.

'Keep it to yourself,' Gladys added with a cheeky wink.

Kit was delighted by the Locarno's stylish drum kit, which included her favourite hi-hat cymbals. Malc was immediately at ease on the grand piano, rippling his very big hands over the keys and pressing the pedals with his broad size-eleven feet!

'As long as I keep 'em under't piano, hopefully nobody will suspect owt,' he told Violet.

'You'll be lucky,' she giggled as she rearranged his wig, which had slipped sideways under his turban, revealing his large red ears.

'Now I get the expression "Keep your wig on"!' he joked.

'Just don't get carried away when you're playing,' she advised. 'You might send it flying into the crowd.'

They were the first of the groups to arrive, which gave them enough time to tune up before Mr Johnson appeared with fish and chips from the shop across the road.

'Never play on an empty stomach,' he advised the hungry musicians.

'Thanks, cock,' Malc said in his normal husky voice as he eagerly took his portion of fish and chips from Mr Johnson, who muttered conspiratorially under his breath, 'I know your secret!'

Malc gave him a cheeky wink. 'Then for God's sake keep it to yourself!'

As the Locarno filled up with a large eager crowd, the manager of the dance-hall clapped his hands to introduce the first act.

In the wings, the tense, nervous Bomb Girls waited their turn.

'We're the fourth to go on,' Gladys whispered down the line to her tense musicians.

'Oh, no! The last,' Maggie groaned.

'Well, we might as well relax and enjoy it,' chuckled Malc as he passed around a packet of Capstan cigarettes.

'The suspense is killing me!' fretted Violet.

'Shhh!' hissed Gladys. 'The first band have started.'

As they listened, Maggie pulled down the corners of her pretty pouty mouth. 'They're rubbish!'

Gladys rolled her eyes in despair as she pressed a warning finger to her mouth. 'SHUT UP!' she hissed.

The second band, from Scunthorpe, were very good,

with a lively and exciting repertoire, but the third band, from Doncaster, were even better.

'We've got real competition this time,' Kit whispered into Gladys's ear.

'It had to happen sometime,' Gladys whispered back.

Nora's heart sank as she realized they could lose this competition. Over the last tragic weeks the Bomb Girl musicians had supported her with their love and their music; they'd become like what she'd called them, her second family. A life without music now would be unbearable. So, not surprisingly, it was Nora who rallied her rather deflated friends as the third swing band left the stage to loud applause.

'Come on, we can do this,' she said forcefully. 'We're good.'

'They were better,' Maggie groaned as she nodded towards the departing Doncaster band.

'Don't say that!' Nora railed. 'We were the best last time; we'll be even better this time. Come on, we're doing this for Myrtle, and my sister Nellie – and my mam too!' she said with tears in her eyes.

'And for my little Billy,' Kit thought sadly to herself.

Then, like a general leading his troops into battle, Nora strode out of the wings and ascended the stage with her head held high.

'What's got into yon lass?' Malc asked.

'She's got fire in her belly,' Edna said as she herded the rest of the band on to the stage. 'Now, come on – get out there and bloody win!'

Kit, with her long black hair already falling loose around her prettily made-up face, played a lively drum number as Violet, Gladys, Nora, Maggie and Malc, with his shoulders drooped in order to reduce his height, took up their positions on stage.

'Ladies and gentlemen!' bellowed the manager. 'It's the Bomb Girls' Swing Band, all the way from the Phoenix Munitions Factory in sunny Pendleton. Let's hear it for the BOMB GIRLS!'

As the crowd politely applauded, Gladys played her alto sax; trilling up and down the scales, she settled on a low vamping note full of rich seductive promise. Caught in her spell, the audience fell silent as her caressing notes merged with the rest of the instruments and the tempo changed to a slinky foxtrot. The audience started to clap as they recognized the rhythm of a favourite war-time number, Frank Sinatra's 'Blue Moon'. Clutching their partners in their arms, the couples swooped and dipped around the ballroom to the slow-slow-quick-quick beat of the music.

As he accompanied Nora and Maggie, who were usually naughty little sprites on the cordite line, Malc's eyes suddenly filled with tears. Here, in the dimly lit Locarno, they played like angels! 'And there is sweet Kit,' thought Malc. So small she was almost hidden from view behind the elaborate drum kit, but hell could she knock out the rhythm. How could somebody so quiet and nervy play like a demon and have the room rocking? As Malc played along with the girls he supervised daily, he felt immensely proud of them and all that they'd achieved in a few short months.

Malc's delight was nothing when compared with the audience's reaction at the end of the number. They cheered and called out, 'MORE! MORE! MORE!'

Turning to her fellow musicians, Gladys grinned. 'Come on, girls,' she said, winking at Malc, who winked back as he adjusted his wig. 'Let's give them a bit of romance.'

Violet's hauntingly sad clarinet notes got the waltz number under way. As Gladys, Maggie and Nora picked up the slow rhythm of Tommy Dorsey's 'I'll Never Smile Again', the lights dipped and the slowly turning silver-mirrored balls hanging from corners of the dance-hall created a shimmering shadow under which couples clung to each other. For ten minutes they lost themselves in the dream-like mood, which allowed them briefly to forget the horrors of war and the gnawing hunger they endured because of ever harsher rationing. Swaying to the gentle 1-2-3 rhythm of the waltz, they held on to each other, prolonging the moment of escapism for as long as they could.

When the band reached a finishing crescendo and the lights came up, the audience blinked as if they'd been woken from their sleep. Keeping the tempo going, Gladys started to tap her finger to the fabulous jive rhythm of the Andrews Sisters' 'Boogie Woogie Bugle Boy of Company B'. Malc grinned as he banged out a quick-paced piano rhythm, whilst Kit crashed the cymbals and scratched the snare drum, and Gladys's gorgeously rich voice soared out. 'The Boogie Woogie Bugle Boy' sent the crowd into a frenzy of excitement; if they couldn't find a boy to dance with, girls happily grabbed hold of each other's hands and spun around the floor. Twirling and circling each other, they sang along at the top of their voices to the 'Boogie Woogie' chorus. Some wildly adventurous couples even swung their partners through their legs, then threw them up in the air!

The final number finished but nobody wanted it to stop. 'ENCORE!' they begged. 'MORE!'

As high as a kite, Malc laughed out loud. 'One more time, ladies!' he cried as his fingers ran up and down over the piano keys, and the band repeated the storming Andrew Sisters' number, at the end of which the entire room echoed to the sound of the audience's repeated chanting. 'THE BOMB GIRLS! THE BOMB GIRLS! THE BOMB GIRLS!'

There was no doubting who the semi-final winners were.

23. August 1942

The Phoenix munitions workers took the Bomb Girls' Swing Band's success to heart. They embraced it with pride and basked in the local publicity as if every one of them had been up on the Locarno stage singing alongside Gladys, Violet, Kit, Nora, Maggie and Malc.

'You've put us on't map,' Ivy said proudly when they clocked on for their first shift after the competition.

'You should have seen them!' Arthur raved. 'They were like real professional musicians, singing and harmonizing, dancing too!' he said with a cheeky wink in Violet's direction.

'Brazen hussies!' teased Ivy as she cackled with laughter.

The mood in the factory was further enhanced by a radio announcement.

'SHHH!' several women hissed as the BBC newsreader's voice echoed around the canteen, which was loud with clattering cutlery and chattering voices.

'It's about the first all-American air attack in Europe!' somebody yelled loudly.

When the news had concluded and was replaced by *Workers' Playtime*, Maggie grinned excitedly at her friends. 'Well, that'll show the bloody Germans! TWELVE B-17s hitting the French coast and railroads too!' she cried as she thumped the table with her fist.

'They call them Yankie planes Flying Fortresses,' wide-eyed Nora added.

After so much recent bad news about the Germans winning the war in the skies, Gladys could hardly take it in.

'About time too!' she cried as she forced back tears.

Could her brother have been on the ground where the American bombs were dropped? Maybe he saw them fall and cheered them on their way? 'Why, oh, why,' she thought for the endless time, 'haven't we heard from him?'

As the waiting turned into weeks, it was getting harder and harder to put on a brave optimistic face. Her mother was so deranged with worry that her father feared for his wife's mental health.

'She'll finish up in't loony bin if it goes on much longer,' he wrote.

Worried Gladys planned to spend her next free week-end in Leeds with her mum and dad, who in their time of need were reliant on their only daughter's love and support.

At the end of their shift, Violet, Gladys and Kit walked up the cobbled lane and along the moorland track that led to the cowshed, which stood steeped in late-afternoon August sunshine. Kit's heart skipped a beat when she saw Mr McIvor leaning against his smart black Ford saloon, admiring the view of the Pennines sweeping northwards.

Violet and Gladys discreetly left Kit to greet the law-yer, who smiled as he shook her hand.

'I thought I'd drop by on my way home from the office,' he said.

Kit imagined him driving home to a neat pretty Mrs McIvor in a smart semi-detached house on the better side of Manchester.

'Any news?' she asked nervously.

'In fact I do have news,' he replied. He nodded towards a pleasant moorland path that wound its way around heather and bracken towards rocks and higher crags. 'Shall we take a walk?'

Feeling self-conscious in her ragged clothes and flapping broken shoes, Kit hid her embarrassed blushes behind her long hair and followed him shyly on to the path.

'I've found an expert handwriting specialist,' he announced. 'The convent's legal adviser has sent on the copies of the papers, but they haven't reached me yet.' He paused, sighing. 'This time the post from Ireland is being tediously slow, but I'll post them straight off to the handwriting specialist as soon as they arrive.'

Kit's head drooped dispiritedly. 'This really isn't working out the way I'd hoped,' she admitted. 'Everything's taking so much longer than I ever imagined, and all the time the clock's ticking. I'm petrified that Billy will be whisked off to America before I've even had a chance to state my case!'

'I'm disappointed too, Catherine,' he said. 'We can do precious little to speed up communications when the post is in chaos and telephone lines are regularly down.'

Seeing her disappointed face, he added gently, 'I understand your disappointment. Believe me, I'm doing everything I possibly can for Billy.' Handing her a brown paper parcel, he said with a cheeky smile, 'I thought these might cheer you up.'

Unused to being given gifts, Kit was flabbergasted. 'For me?' she asked as she fumbled with the string securing the parcel, then gazed in astonishment at a pair of soft brown leather brogues, which were the height of wartime fashion.

'If anybody deserves a new pair of shoes it's you, young lady!'

'They're a perfect fit!' she gasped as she threw off the old shoes and tried on the brogues. 'How did you know my size?'

'I just asked for the smallest size and hoped for the best,' he replied as he watched in delight as she skipped up and down the track like an over-excited child.

'Thank you, sir, thank you from the bottom of my heart,' she said with utter sincerity. 'I've never had anything quite so beautiful.'

'My pleasure, Catherine.' He found he liked saying her name and watching her reaction when he said it. 'I'll be in touch as soon as there's any more news.' McIvor extended his hand. 'Goodbye, Catherine.'

'Goodbye, Mr McIvor.'

Kit watched him drive away, wondering what pretty Mrs McIvor, probably wearing a cool crêpe floral dress and smelling of lavender water, would have waiting for her husband when he arrived home for his tea. Even though they'd eat rationed food, they were bound to have a nice fresh tablecloth and a vase of flowers in the centre of the table. Would they chat happily about his work, then read the evening news together, whilst the help cleared away tea and washed up the dishes? Kit sighed as she thought of their parallel universes, then crossly scolded herself for day-dreaming. As far as Mr McIvor was concerned, her thoughts should be solely centred on Billy's legal battle, not the colour of Mrs McIvor's tablecloth!

The Bomb Girls were surprised and delighted when they walked into the canteen the next morning and found Myrtle waiting for them. As they rushed excitedly forwards to give her a hug, the older woman held up her arms imperiously.

'Careful! Careful!' she warned as they gathered around her.

'Is it safe for you to be back at work?' Violet asked.

'The doctor said as long as I don't do any lifting I'm allowed to resume my shifts in the dispatch yard,' Myrtle replied.

'And is it safe for you to play the piano again?' Kit asked eagerly.

'As long as I don't get carried away and reach for a high C key, I should be fine,' Myrtle assured her.

'Thank goodness for that!' Malc remarked when he saw Myrtle back at work. 'I don't think I'd have the bottle to play the piano at the final!'

'And it would be wrong to do that again,' Gladys replied. 'Though I'll always be grateful to you, Malc,' she added hurriedly.

When Myrtle appeared at the Phoenix chapel for their first rehearsal together in weeks, she clearly had the bit between her teeth.

'I've had plenty of time to consider our repertoire for the next competition,' she said as they assembled.

'Oh, Jesus!' Kit giggled. 'Please don't let it be one of her high-falutin' classical pieces.'

'It's a joint decision, Myrtle,' Gladys reminded the pianist.

'Bear with me, dear.' Myrtle spoke to Gladys as if she was a naughty child interrupting her Sunday school lesson. 'I want to stretch us to our full capacity.'

'There speaks someone who's had bed rest for the last three weeks,' Maggie muttered.

'Duke Ellington's "Take the 'A' Train" for the opening number,' Myrtle announced. 'Lovely foxtrot rhythm, followed by a dreamy waltz, "Begin the Beguine".'

'I've got a jive song!' Kit cried before Myrtle had the chance to organize the entire show. 'Benny Goodman's "Sing, Sing, Sing"!'

Some heated discussion followed. Both Norah and Maggie wanted repeats of 'Boogie Woogie Bugle Boy' and 'PEnnsylvania 6-5000', but Gladys was adamant they were going to play new pieces for the final. 'If we don't extend our repertoire now, we never will,' she insisted.

'We might be better off with numbers we're familiar with,' Violet cautioned.

'And what if somebody who saw us in the audience in Leeds turns up at Stockport and we're playing the same old numbers?' Gladys asked. 'They'll go away thinking we're very limited.'

Eventually it was agreed that they'd go with Myrtle's suggestions, 'Begin the Beguine' and 'Take the "A" Train', which they all loved, and Benny Goodman's 'Sing, Sing, Sing'.

'It's a lot to learn,' Nora fretted.

'We've got time,' Myrtle replied confidently as she played the opening notes of the first song.

In the August heat, the cold wet stone floors of the factory were a godsend, but the Phoenix chapel where they practised daily was baking hot. One afternoon it was so warm the girls stripped off their overalls and played in their underwear! Kit, in her old baggy knickers and vest, looked like an abandoned orphan, whilst Violet, in her elegant lilac silk petticoat trimmed with cream lace, looked like a film star.

'St Anthony in heaven!' Kit cried as she admired the beautiful silk under-slip. 'Where did you get that from?'

Violet blushed in shame as she recalled the underwear they were admiring was part of Ronnie's black market clothing haul. Shrugging, she said lightly, 'I treated myself before I came here.'

She shuddered at the memory of Ronnie touching her. How different it was with gentle Arthur, who treated her like she was a precious work of art. Violet felt constantly guilty about deceiving Arthur. How long before the harsh truth came out – she'd been married and run away from her husband, who (thank God!) had been blown up in a night raid. Would honest Arthur leave her once he knew she'd been stringing him along? The thought of losing him nearly killed her.

'NO!' she'd decided.

It was best to keep the secret to herself, at least for the time being.

McIvor kept his word. As soon as he had news for Kit, he drove up to the cowshed on a warm afternoon, but, finding nobody at home, he walked down to the Phoenix, removing his coat and tie as he did so. In the entrance-way, he asked some passing girls if they knew where he might find Kit Murphy.

'She'll be having her band practice in the chapel, yon-der,' they said as they pointed down a long corridor.

As McIvor got closer, he could hear swing band music, very good swing band music, he thought to himself and when he opened the chapel door he got the shock of his life! The girls, who luckily weren't in their underwear that afternoon, were so engrossed in their music that they didn't even notice him walk in. With his back against the closed door, McIvor smiled as he watched Kit banging out a rhythm to the 'Sing, Sing, Sing' jive number she loved so much. The lawyer could scarcely believe his eyes. How could the mouse of a girl he'd first met in his office play music like this? With her long dark hair tumbling free, she moved from the snare drum to the tom-toms, then back to scratching a rhythm on the snare before crashing the cymbals with wild abandon and very obvi-ous pleasure. This was a Kit he had never seen before. Behind the poor little Irish girl lurked a veritable diva!

After playing and dancing along to the jive number, the girls were sweating with exertion as they came to a cli-matic conclusion.

'Wonderful! Wonderful!' cried Gladys as she flopped like a limp doll into one of the wooden pews. It was only then that she saw McIvor. Not recognizing him at first without his hat and wearing an open shirt, she was taken by surprise. Jumping to her feet, she cried, 'Can I help?'

Smiling, Kit came hurrying forwards. 'It's my lawyer, Mr McIvor,' she said as she shook his hand.

Rather embarrassed by the female musicians all curiously staring at him, he quickly said, 'May we have a word in private, Catherine?'

As they walked along the now familiar moorland track, McIvor noticed how highly polished the shoes he'd bought her were and how they flattered her shapely ankles and strong calves.

As they settled on a wide wedge of a rock that gave a sweeping view of the sun-dappled landscape, across which a cool breeze blew from the high Pennine tops, Kit pushed her mass of long dark hair away from her eyes so she could peer into her lawyer's face.

'So tell me your news, sir,' she said eagerly.

'Ian,' he said firmly.

Blushing, she said his name for the first time. 'Er, all right, Ian it is, then.'

Liking the lilting way she pronounced his name, he smiled as he continued. 'The papers have arrived from Mother Gabriel's legal adviser, O'Rourke. I've sent them straight on to the handwriting specialist, but, whilst we're waiting for the signature analysis, I was thinking we should use this time well. I'd like you to write down exactly what happened to you and Billy, Catherine.'

Kit's eyes flew wide open. 'WRITE!' she cried.

'You can write, can't you?' he asked politely.

Kit felt nettled; his direct question suggested she'd just come off the bog!

'Of course, but I'm no writer!' she exclaimed.

'That's not the point,' he assured her. 'I want to be able

to present to Mother Gabriel and her legal adviser factual evidence. When we have proof and we know for sure that we've got a full-blown forgery case on our hands, the matter might be referred to the courts, which would require documented evidence.'

Kit nodded. 'So what do you want to know? How I got caught with Billy?' she asked with a blush.

'We can leave that out,' Ian quickly replied. 'Include details such as when your father forced you to go to find work in England.'

Looking less panicked, Kit again nodded her head. 'Like a diary?'

'Exactly but keeps to the facts – when you arrived in England, when you left Manchester, when you moved to Pendleton and started at the Phoenix; also quote the letter your sister, Rosie, sent to you.'

'The one when she warned me there was trouble brewing?'

'Yes,' he replied. 'And when you've finished it, post it to me and I'll get my secretary to type it out; then I can refer to the document and quote times and dates, even if you're not with me.'

Feeling stung that she might not accompany Ian on his next trip to Ireland, Kit turned her face away from his so he wouldn't see the flush of disappointment on her cheeks. She didn't turn quickly enough for Ian not to see it. To her astonishment he gently took hold of her chin in order to look at her face, which was once more partially hidden by strands of her long dark hair. Smiling, he stroked the strands off her solemn face, which he had an overwhelming urge to kiss. Thrilling to his touch, Kit felt her cheek burn where he'd touched it.

'I was impressed by your playing back there by the way,' he murmured. 'You sounded very professional.'

Trying to hide her tumultuous feelings, she answered lightly, 'We have to be, sir – Ian,' she quickly corrected herself. 'We're playing in the Northern Swing Band Final next week, at the Stockport Palais. We'll be up against some of the best bands in the area.'

'I wish you luck, little drummer girl,' he said as he held out his hand and helped her to her feet, then briefly held her in his arms before reluctantly letting her go.

As Kit returned home in an emotional daze, Ian drove away from the cowshed, thinking he would certainly check the details of the Swing Band Final in the local paper – it was something he very much wanted to see!

24. Hopes and Fears

With the Bomb Girls' Swing Band on their way to the final competition, the Phoenix munitions workers were keen to support 'their lasses'.

'We can't close down the bloody factory just because they're performing,' Malc blustered to the girls gathered around Edna's blue van one balmy summer's evening, which was so soft and still nobody could face going to bed.

Edna took up her 'managerial' stance: standing arms akimbo, with her bright turban hardly covering her greying auburn curls, she eye-balled Malc. 'Is it our fault that they want tickets for the event?' she asked. 'They're our loyal supporters.'

'That's as may be, Edna,' Malc insisted. 'But they can't *all* go gadding off; in fact very few of them can actually go, as, believe it or not, we have to keep knocking out bombs 'cos nobody's mentioned to bleedin' Hitler that there's a swing band contest in Stockport!'

Irrepressible Edna burst into peals of laughter. 'I bet if the bastard heard about it he'd want tickets too!'

Malc gave up arguing after Mr Featherstone requested two complimentary seats for himself and his wife, as near to the stage as possible.

'Who does he think I am? Your agent?' Malc seethed.

'Stop fretting, cock,' Edna soothed as she handed him

a free bag of chips. 'Get them down you and shut up moaning.'

'Make sure you keep a ticket on one side for me,' Malc said with his mouth full. 'You never know when you might need a stand-in!'

A feeling of pride and excitement hung about the Phoenix in the days leading up to the competition, and the band girls felt the buoyant mood heighten as the big day approached.

'This is *really* tough!' cried Maggie one night during a very hot and sticky band practice as a thunder storm was brewing out on the moors. 'I feel like everybody at the Phoenix is holding their breath waiting for us to win.'

Myrtle, perched regally on her piano stool, flexed her long elegant fingers. 'And what's wrong with giving our co-workers something to take their minds off the vexations of war? We'll perform our very best for the Phoenix munitions workers and all conscripted women in the land!' she finished grandly.

Not having quite as many fine principles as Myrtle, naughty Maggie muttered to giggling Nora behind her hand, 'My motive's a chance to play beside Joe Loss in London!'

After their rehearsal, Kit searched out Edna in the dispatch yard.

Since Mr McIvor's visit she'd been unable to think of anything but him and the gentle way he'd stroked her hair off her face and held her, albeit briefly, in his arms as they said their goodbyes.

'Hiya, cock,' called Edna when she saw the dreamy-eyed

girl approaching. 'You look happy – for a change!' she joked.

Kit smiled as she greeted her friend. 'I'm just so grateful to you for finding me Mr McIvor.'

Edna did a startled double-take. 'Bloody 'ell's fire!' she swore. 'From the look on your face, you seem like you're half in love with the man!'

Turning bright pink, naive Kit whispered, 'What does love feel like, Edna?'

Edna lit a Woodbine, which she drew on thoughtfully. 'It's been over thirty years, and it only ever happened the once, with young Edward Pilkington. It felt wonderful! Butterflies in your tummy, head spinning, pulse racing, heart skipping a beat.'

'Yes! Yes!' Kit laughed. 'That's just how I feel but I know I'm not good enough for him, even if he does like me.'

Edna stared at her friend's beautiful heart-shaped face framed by her long dark hair and slowly shook her head. 'Kit, any man on earth would be lucky to have you.'

A few days before the competition, Ian McIvor drove up to the cowshed. It was a weekend, and Kit hardly recognized him in casual trousers and an open-necked shirt, which showed the top of his strong muscular chest; plus he took his glasses off as he got out of the car, which made him look much younger. With her old faded pinafore flapping around her slender frame, Kit hurried towards him, wondering if he'd brought news of Billy. Seeing her tense expectant face, Ian quickly said, 'Nothing new to report, but I've come to pick up your diary. Oh, and I have a little something for you.'

Knowing her friends might be watching Kit walked on to the moors and he followed.

'I thought you might need something special for the dance band competition,' he said as he handed her another brown paper parcel.

'More presents!' she gasped in amazement.

Unused to the custom of giving and receiving gifts, and despite her disappointment that there was still no more news of Billy, Kit was as excited as a child on Christmas morning. Scrabbling with the paper, she was quite unprepared for what lay within the wrapping.

'A dress!' she whispered incredulously as she shook out a pink-and-lilac flower-printed crêpe silk dress that had little cap sleeves, a nipped-in waist and a short swirly skirt. 'Oh, my . . .' She was lost for words as she gazed in wonder at it. 'Don't move!' she suddenly cried as she darted off and hid behind the large rocky outcrop.

Five minutes later, barefoot and with her waist-length hair flying free, she came running back to him wearing her beautiful new dress.

'Do you like it?' she asked as she posed in all innocence before him.

It was Ian's turn to be lost for words. The dress was lovely indeed; he'd known that when he bought it from a very expensive shop in Piccadilly, but it was Catherine who was stunning. He'd been attracted to her even in rags, but seeing her in stylish clothes made him realize that she had the natural grace and beauty to carry off anything. Having visited her home and met her father and all of her poor family in Ireland, Ian seriously wondered if this gloriously beautiful woman standing before him hadn't been swapped by the leprechauns at birth. She no more belonged to the harsh ugliness of her origins than an angel belonged to the gutter.

'You look beautiful!' he murmured.

'I feel beautiful!' she cried joyously. '*You* make me beautiful,' she said as she grabbed hold of his hands and squeezed them tightly. 'But you must stop spending your hard-earned money on a poor old Bomb Girl.'

Looking her straight in the eye, Ian said softly, 'Catherine, there is no one in this world I would rather spend my money on.'

The radiant smile that transformed Kit's tense face said it all – the man she was falling for liked her too! With Ian's eyes holding her smile, Kit knew for sure that the perfect Mrs McIvor – whose image had been such torture for her – clearly didn't exist.

'Oh!' she blustered. 'I'm . . . I'm so glad!'

Not trusting herself to say another word, Kit gasped as Ian took hold of her right hand and, lifting it to his lips, kissed each of her small fingers in turn.

'I'm very glad too. And I intend to spoil you many more times, young lady. You deserve it!' he said with a soft laugh.

Gladys and Violet couldn't possibly ignore Kit's happy smile or her gorgeous new dress, which she all but slept in.

'It's real silk crêpe,' Violet said appreciatively.

'Nearly as posh as your lovely silk petticoat,' Kit said proudly.

Violet grinned as she held up her finger. 'I'll not be a second,' she said as she headed into her bedroom. When she reappeared, she laid four silk under-slips, in shades of lilac, black, lemon and turquoise, on the dining table. 'For you girls,' she announced. 'Gladys, Kit, Nora and Maggie – I don't think they're quite Myrtle's style,' she added with a giggle.

'Really?' Gladys asked as she gazed at the glamorous lace-trimmed lingerie.

'I'm done with them,' Violet retorted – and she *really* meant it!

25. Stockport Final

As the day of the Stockport final neared, the girls checked their lists in their break times, in between consuming cups of tea and spam butties.

'If anybody mentions the competition just one more time, I think I'll have hysterics,' Violet said as they listened to Joe Loss's 'There'll Always Be an England' on *Workers' Playtime*. 'It's not like I'm not grateful for people's support; it's just I have to keep rushing to the lav as my stomach's in chaos.'

'Nerves are a good thing; they keep you on your toes,' Myrtle replied.

Violet burst out laughing. 'Not in my case, Myrtle, they keep me on the lav!'

'Double-check you've got song and music sheets, make-up, jewellery, clean overalls, musical instruments, brush, comb, lavender water.' Kit stopped to catch her breath. 'Holy Mother, I just wish we were there and getting on with it – all this waiting is having the bejesus with me!' she said as she lapsed into a heavier Irish accent than usual.

'KEEP CALM, LADIES,' Malc said as he passed through the filling shed.

'KEEP CALM – AND DANCE!' the girls called after him.

'Chance'd be a fine thing!' Malc laughed over his shoulder.

When their final shift eventually ended and the hooter sounded, the girls dashed into the ladies' changing room, whilst Arthur, who'd arranged his shift around Violet's, made for the gents'. The girls swiftly changed into their everyday clothes, Kit looking the most stylish in her new crêpe dress and soft leather brogues.

'You're putting the rest of us to shame,' Violet teased as she saw Kit sneak a look at her pretty reflection in the mirror.

'I don't think I'll ever get used to having nice things,' Kit confessed in a whisper to Violet, who always looked gorgeous.

'You'd better: that young man of yours seems intent on showering you with them – and nobody deserves it more than you, dear Kit.'

Outside the factory gates, Arthur and Edna were waiting for their passengers. A small crowd had gathered to wave them off with their high hopes and good wishes.

'You couldn't want for better friends,' Gladys said as she and Myrtle settled in the passenger seats of Edna's blue van and waved back to the munitions girls.

'Right, then, let's concentrate on the route,' said Edna as she threaded her way along the moorland roads flanked by heather and wild ferns almost as tall as small trees.

'I don't like the look of that rain cloud,' Gladys commented.

'Me neither,' muttered Edna anxiously. 'After all the hot weather we've been enjoying, the last thing we need tonight is a thunder storm.'

The sky darkened as they drove, then a thick warm mist descended, obscuring the road ahead.

'Christ!' Edna swore as she braked sharply to avoid hitting a stray sheep nibbling tufts of grass by the roadside.

After Edna beeped her horn, the sheep bolted into the mist and Edna crawled along at less than ten miles an hour. Gladys glanced anxiously at the marcasite watch her brother Les had bought her during their last Christmas together.

'If this damn mist doesn't lift, we'll definitely be late for the competition,' she thought to herself.

Nora, Maggie and Kit inside the van gripped on to each other and groaned as Edna constantly braked, then revved up again. Looking out of the van window, Maggie grimaced. 'Start saying the Rosary, Kit,' she said. 'We need the Almighty to shift this soddin' mist!'

Luckily the mist suddenly lifted on the outskirts of Manchester to be replaced by a light drizzle but at least Edna and Arthur could navigate the roads to Stockport.

When they arrived at the Stockport Palais, they swung into the routine that had become familiar to them over the last months. After Edna and Arthur had parked up by the back door, Kit and Myrtle dashed inside to check out the drum kit and piano, leaving Gladys, Violet, Nora and Maggie to follow with their own instruments. Edna hurried off to find tea for them all, whilst Arthur was dispatched to inquire how many bands were playing and in what order.

Inside the ballroom, a band were already practising; their name, 'The Saddleworth Ensemble', was written in glittering gold on their large impressive base drum.

'They look posh,' said Nora as she gazed enviously at the women wearing beautiful full-length velvet gowns trimmed with tiny sequins.

Knowing all too well Nora's tendency to get distracted, Gladys called sharply, 'Come on, tune up.'

When Edna returned with mugs of hot tea and the usual corned-beef sandwiches, which she always brought along for the girls, Arthur already had the information they needed.

'Six groups are playing,' he announced.

'SIX!' gasped Violet. 'That's more than ever before.'

'And,' Arthur added, 'you're the first on!'

'Oh, no!' squeaked Maggie. 'We'll be a bag of nerves.'

Myrtle gave Maggie a scathing look. 'Don't be defeatist, child,' she said archly. 'What difference does the running order make to the excellence of our music?'

'Get these down you quickly,' said Edna as she handed around sandwiches. 'Then you'd better change right away.'

With hardly enough time for a decent warm-up, the girls rushed into the ladies', where they slipped into their work overalls and turbans. As they lit up cigarettes to steady their nerves, Gladys, who didn't smoke, went along the line applying face powder, rouge, lipstick and eyeliner, and distributing an assortment of long sparkly earrings.

When they heard the sound of the audience surging into the ballroom, the girls fell silent, drawing strength and confidence from each other.

'You know we can do this,' Gladys said softly. 'Don't be overwhelmed by the size of the crowd; just close your eyes and imagine we're all in the Phoenix chapel playing the best music of our lives.'

At the head of the line, with her permed curls tight around her face, Myrtle had the look of a commander-in-chief.

'She looks like she's going to tell us to go "over the top"!' cheeky Maggie whispered to Nora.

Myrtle didn't quite say that but her imperious cry of 'It's now or never, ladies!' galvanized her fellow musicians, who held their heads high as they walked on stage.

As usual, their munitions uniforms were the cause of plenty of raucous teasing.

'Did you leave your frock at work, love?' one cheeky lad called over the wolf-whistles.

Wiggling their bottoms in their tight overalls, the girls played to the audience, who were taken by the fact that there were no male players in sight.

'Eh, don't you know any fellas?' a man at the front of the stage teased.

'Less of that, lads,' chuckled the manager, who'd jumped on the stage to introduce the first act.

'From the Phoenix Munitions Factory in Pendleton . . . the amazing, sensational . . . Bomb Girls' Swing Band!'

Gladys turned to face her musicians and said with a wink, 'Let's give this lot something to remember.'

Myrtle and Kit played a sizzling introduction to 'Take the "A" Train', which Gladys took up on her alto sax, then the rest of the brass section came in, with Violet on her trilling clarinet. The audience stood momentarily stunned by the quality of the music. Gladys, Violet, Nora and Maggie, standing in line and clicking their fingers and swaying their hips, sang in perfect harmony as the audience split into pairs to dance. When the number finished, the mood changed to a dreamy waltz, as Myrtle played out the opening sequence to 'Begin the Beguine' and Kit softly backed the lilting piano chords on the snare drum. Her eyes strayed to the audience, dancing romantically under the dimmed spotlights, and she wondered what it would be like to be held in Ian's strong arms. In the velvety darkness, would she be bold enough to stand on her tip-toes to reach up and kiss his soft full mouth?

As the achingly beautiful song came to a soft close, the musicians felt not unlike the audience: in need of something to really wake them up. Knowing that the jive number came next, Kit hit the drums with a high-stepping tempo, which was immediately picked up by Gladys, who sent her alto sax soaring to the highest notes for 'Sing, Sing, Sing'. That night the Bomb Girls saw jive reach a new level: this was dancing like never before. Holding their partners' hands, the girls on the dance floor spun round and round until they were almost a blur, showing their petticoats as they dropped into the splits, then swooping up and swinging under their partners' outstretched legs before being spun and lifted all over again. Infected by the wild abandon of the audience, the Bomb Girls danced too; at the conclusion of the jive routine, the players were sweating as much as the audience.

'MORE! MORE! MORE!' the crowd demanded.

And at that moment the sound of sirens filled the hall.

'Would you bloody believe it?' the manager cursed. 'OUT! Everybody out!' he bellowed over the din of the crowd running to collect their gas masks. 'AIR-RAID ATTACK!' Turning to the band still on stage, he bellowed, 'Get yerselves into the Anderson shelter down't road. Be sharp!'

Grabbing their gas masks, the Bomb Girls ran out of

the ballroom. Cool, calm and collected, Arthur, firmly clutching Violet's hand, led them to the safety of the nearby Anderson shelter, which was quickly filling up. It was only as they squeezed in beside tired wailing children, rudely woken and dragged scared through the dark night, that an astonished Kit saw Ian McIvor walk in.

'What're you doing here, Ian?' she cried in delight as she ran towards him.

'I was in the ballroom just now, listening to you,' he replied with a grin.

'You never said you were coming!' she gasped in delight. 'I had no idea.'

'That was the point,' he replied with a twinkle in his eye. 'I didn't want to put you off your stroke,' he joked. 'My God, young lady – can you play those drums!'

Delighted by his praise, Kit's glamorously made up face lit up with pleasure and the long dangly earrings she was wearing glimmered brightly against her dark glossy hair.

'You look so beautiful,' he whispered as he gazed into her eyes.

An overweight man pushing past him accidentally sent Ian falling towards Kit, who grasped his arm; then, before he could stop himself, Ian bent down to kiss her softly on the lips. Kit would never need to ask anybody again what love was like. She felt like she was levitating; her feet didn't seem to touch the earth; even with the sound of the siren still blaring she could hear only his voice murmuring caressingly, 'Oh, Catherine, Catherine, you have no idea how long I've waited to do that.'

'Then don't stop now!' Kit giggled as she stood on her tip-toes to reach for his lips and feel his kisses, which she thought if she lived to be a hundred she would never get enough of.

As they sat huddled close in the Anderson shelter, sharing a sip of tea or a nip of brandy from kind strangers, the young couple couldn't take their eyes off each other.

'I could stay here all night close to you,' Kit said as she ran her hand through Ian's thick brown hair.

'And I could stay here all night just looking at you,' he replied as he stroked her silky black hair that fell in waves to her waist.

Ian helped Kit to her feet and, as he did so, he lifted her chin so he could give her another long kiss, then he smiled mysteriously as he handed her a small brown envelope.

'For you,' he said.

Kit's eyes widened as she pulled two tickets out of the envelope.

'Our passage to Dublin at the end of the week!' he announced, beaming. 'I met with the handwriting specialist this morning and he confirms that, after carefully examining the two signatures, the one on the adoption papers is not yours.'

Unable to quite believe what she was hearing, Kit threw her arms around Ian's neck.

'You mean I'm going to see my Billy!'

'More than that, darling, you'll be bringing your baby home!' Ian told her, his eyes shining with love and excitement.

Delirious with joy, she buried her face against his warm chest. She hadn't dared to hope this day would come. But in her hands she held the tickets that would take her back to Ireland, where she would finally claim her son, whom she would NEVER be parted from again. Feeling like she would weep if she moved, Kit stayed pressed against Ian's chest.

'It's just too much to take in,' she whispered.

'Will you look at those two love birds!' Maggie said to Nora as she spotted Ian and Kit clutched in each other's arms.

'Shhh! Leave them be,' Myrtle chided the tittering girls. 'There's little enough joy in an Anderson shelter but those two young things seem to have found it.'

The sound of planes approaching stopped all chatter and laughter. The occupants of the shelter collectively held their breath as the German bombers came closer and closer. Tense, expectant and fearful, they waited in the enclosed space.

'Are they 'eading for Manchester, Liverpool or 'ere?' an old man puffing on his pipe asked, voicing everybody's terrified thoughts.

Gripping Arthur's hand hard, Violet began to panic: if a bomb went off, they might be incarcerated in the shelter, squashed together, unable to breathe, crawling over each other to escape. She'd always suffered from acute claustrophobia, but this was a cloying fear that made her want to hit out and scream. Feeling the sweat pouring out of her, Arthur whispered in her ear, 'Deep breaths, Vi, come on now, my sweetheart, it'll be over soon.'

Hearing his steady voice and doing as she was told, taking deep long breaths, Violet began to calm down. As the planes passed directly overhead and the noise of their mighty engines receded, she let out a deep shuddering sigh. 'Thank Christ for that!' she murmured and then immediately felt guilty.

She was relieved to be alive whilst others hiding in an Anderson shelter less than ten miles away might be the Luftwaffe's target that night.

'God help them,' she prayed.

When the all-clear siren sounded, people rose, and like sleep-walkers, they shuffled out of the shelter bearing babies and yawning children in their arms – one old lady even carried a tweeting canary home!

'Are we *really* going back to the ballroom?' Maggie asked.

'Course we are!' Edna replied. 'The show's not over till the fat lady sings!' she chuckled.

'Move along now,' the warden barked, prodding Ian and Kit, who were the last people to leave the shelter. 'Let's be having you.'

Holding hands, they walked out into the dark starry night, then ran down the deserted street to the ballroom, where fate would decide the Bomb Girls' destiny.

Back in the dance-hall, the manager addressed the re-assembled audience as if nothing had happened at all. 'It's the Stockport Stompers' Jive Band!'

In the wings the Bomb Girls, bleary-eyed with the long wait and the tense hour spent in the Anderson shelter, waited whilst the third, fourth and fifth bands played. Then finally the last band, from Carlisle, took to the stage.

'Well, so far none of the bands got the reaction that you got,' Edna said excitedly.

Gladys held up her hands to show her crossed fingers. 'Let's hope it stays that way!'

The Carlisle band came off-stage to a rousing applause.

'They were the best so far,' Kit said fearfully.

'Due to unforeseen circumstances and the lateness of the hour,' the manager called out, 'we'll skip the break.' He turned to the judges, who were seated at a table close to the stage. 'Have you made your decision?'

One of the judges handed him a slip of paper.

'Gather round boys and girls,' the manager called excitedly. 'As you know, only one band will go forward to the event to be held in the autumn. The winning band will play at the Savoy Hotel in London alongside no less than Joe Loss and his band.'

Impressed, the audience clapped and cheered.

'If he doesn't put me out of my misery soon I swear I'll be sick,' Maggie threatened.

'Shhh!' Edna hissed.

'The winning band are . . .' He smiled as he dragged out the painful seconds. 'The all-girls' band from the Phoenix factory in Pendleton –'

But he got no further – the ecstatic audience took over from him. 'THE BOMB GIRLS! THE BOMB GIRLS! THE BOMB GIRLS!' they cried as they stamped their feet and wolf-whistled.

Ushering the delighted girls on to the stage, the manager muttered, 'Get out there quickly – before they bring the bloody roof down.'

One by one Gladys, Kit, Violet, Myrtle, Nora and Maggie ran on to the stage, where they smiled and waved as they drank in the applause.

'SING! SING!' the audience demanded. 'AGAIN!' they roared.

As they turned to pick up their instruments, Violet stopped dead in her tracks. Out of the corner of her eye she caught sight of a man whose thick black hair was slicked back with Brylcreem, the way Ronnie used to wear it. Blowing into her clarinet, Violet briskly dismissed her ghoulish fears.

'The man's dead! Stop being ridiculous.'

Settling the mouthpiece on her lips, Violet nervously waited for Gladys to give them their cue. As she did so, she caught sight of Arthur, who, feeling her tension, grinned broadly as he gave her a thumbs-up sign.

'I love you,' he mouthed.

Violet smiled back as Gladys called, 'OKAY!' and counted in the beats to the song.

As Myrtle played the introductory chords and Gladys came in on the alto sax, the dark-haired man stepped forward, and even in the half-light he had the stocky familiar look of Ronnie. Feeling distinctly spooked but dismissing the idea, Violet ran her long slim fingers along the valves, then stopped with a sharp squeak as the man walked purposefully towards the stage. He came nearer and nearer, and finally there was absolutely no doubting who he was. As her blood ran cold with terror, Violet gasped. How on earth had he survived that bombing raid? And how had he found her, how had he tracked her down?

With the clarinet dangling limply from her hand, Violet felt like all the air in her body had been sucked away; her bones turned to jelly and she began to tremble uncontrollably as she stared into Ronnie's face, which was suffused with fury. As her band mates, still playing the encore, turned to her in bewilderment, Violet's legs gave way and she grabbed hold of Gladys, crying out, 'It's HIM!'

Following her gaze, Gladys's eyes landed on a man directly in front of the stage. He was glowering with a mixture of malice and hatred at Violet, who was crouching in terror. Scared by the anger in his eyes, Gladys stood protectively in front of her friend.

'Who is he?' she asked.

Almost collapsing, Violet whispered, 'Ronnie . . . my husband!'

26. Stage Fright

Ronnie had had a satisfactory day in Stockport. He'd bought and sold contraband goods from Larry, his black market agent in the North-west, and was planning on returning to Coventry to treat his new girlfriend to a pair of nylons and a bottle of gin. Olive would do anything he asked after such a wealth of gifts, and he had plans in mind for the little brunette he'd picked up months ago in Wolverhampton. He couldn't imagine how he'd put up with snivelling Violet for so long; she certainly had never been fun, in or out of bed. It offended his pride that she'd been the one who'd chosen to leave; he was the man of the house, and he made the decisions for both of them. After she buggered off, he told anybody who asked she'd been conscripted, possibly the first true thing he'd said in years!

Ronnie considered himself a lucky man in more ways than one. By a miracle he'd survived the air attack which had wiped out the whole of Sawley Avenue. The newspapers reported that all the residents had been killed in their beds, something he was thrilled to read. Having run into trouble with a black market operator who was on the rampage for Ronnie, who'd been working his territory, Ronnie was in big trouble. He had no intention of enlightening anybody that in fact he wasn't dead; being dead was a great convenience and prevented him from having his throat slit by his enemy. He'd gone underground for a while and resurfaced in the Manchester area, where he didn't risk being murdered every time he stepped out in public.

He'd been delayed in Stockport by the air-raid warning, and when they'd heard the all-clear Larry had suggested they should pop into the Palais for a pint before Ronnie drove back to Coventry. At first they stuck to the bar, but as the cheering crowd drowned out all conversation they were drawn to the ballroom, where Ronnie had got the biggest shock of his life. Standing on the stage was his wife! But not as he'd ever seen her before: Violet's long silky silver-blonde hair tumbled around her vibrantly happy face as she played the clarinet beside a line of women all dressed in white overalls. Swaying their hips and moving in unison, they vamped to 'Sing, Sing, Sing'. Up until that moment Ronnie hadn't cared whether Violet lived or died, but when he saw her looking so desirable and staring dewy eyed at a man sitting at a table opposite the stage his blood had boiled.

Rendered almost hysterical by the sight of her vengeful husband, Violet tried to scuttle off the stage, but was intercepted by Kit and Gladys.

'What is it, Vi?' Kit said as she crouched low on the ground, where she held on to her friend.

'God help me! Oh, please God help me!' Violet sobbed.

Then everything happened at once. Arthur came forward just as Ronnie leapt on to the stage, where he violently yanked Violet to her feet.

'Never thought I'd find you here, sweetheart,' he snarled. 'Not with all these tarts.'

He turned to sneer at Gladys, Kit, Nora and Maggie, who were wide-eyed with shock. Not so Myrtle.

'I beg your pardon!' she cried indignantly.

'Come along, darlin', I'm taking you home,' Ronnie said in a voice thick with fury.

Almost fainting in terror, Violet begged and pleaded. 'No, no, please, no!'

At which point Arthur came forward. 'Let her go!'

Still grasping Violet in a grip of iron, Ronnie turned to Arthur. 'Who the hell are YOU?'

Arthur simply repeated himself but this time with more menace. 'LET HER GO.'

'The bitch is my wife,' Ronnie leered. 'She ran away last winter, thought she'd got rid of me.' He broke into a mocking laugh.

Arthur gazed down at Violet, who had tears pouring down her face.

'It's true, Arthur, I ran away,' she muttered so quietly only he could hear.

Arthur knelt to wipe away her tears. 'Let's talk about that later,' he murmured. 'Right now I just want to get you out of here.'

'She's going nowhere with you, mate, she's coming home with me,' Ronnie snarled.

Knowing that Ronnie always carried a flick knife, sometimes even a gun, Violet, desperate to warn Arthur off, said, 'He'll hurt you too, pleeeease go,' she implored.

'The lady's right, pal. I'll break every bone in your body if you've been knocking up my wife.'

'You just try!' Arthur said as he confronted Ronnie with his fists clenched.

Seeing a fight brewing, the manager appeared on the stage.

'Break it up, break it up, gentlemen,' he cried as he got between the two men, who looked ready to kill each other. 'I suggest you take your wife home, sir,' he said to Ronnie.

'That's where she belongs!' Ronnie sneered as he jumped off the stage, dragging Violet behind him. With a look of utter helplessness in her eyes, Violet was hauled across the ballroom floor, then pushed out of the nearest exit. The second the door swung shut on them Ian McIvor rushed forward.

'Follow them!' he cried.

Arthur bolted towards the door, but Edna stopped him. 'No, Arthur – he'll recognize you.' She turned to Ian. 'You follow them: he never saw you.'

Without wasting a second Ian ran out of the door, followed by Kit.

'Where are they . . . which way did they go?' Ian gasped once they were out in the sharp night air.

Little Kit darted into the street, where she quickly looked both ways.

'They're getting into a car, down on the right,' she cried.

Ian jumped into the driver's seat of his car.

'Get in, Catherine, and keep down,' he cried urgently as he started the engine. 'We're done for if he recognizes those damn white overalls.'

Crouched in the narrow footwell, Kit held her breath as Ian swung out on to the main road.

'Can you see them?' she gasped.

'I can see them: he's driving a big Bentley,' Ian replied. 'I'm going to slow down.'

'WHY?' she yelled in alarm.

'I need to put another car between me and him so that he doesn't think I'm tailing him.'

When he'd successfully accomplished the manoeuvre, Ian let out a tense sigh as he settled back in his seat.

'He's going at quite a lick,' he told Kit as he upped gears.

'For the love of God, don't lose sight of him,' Kit implored from the footwell.

Back at Stockport Palais, the audience had been swiftly ushered out of the ballroom by the manager and his attendants, leaving the Bomb Girls, Edna and Arthur on the stage. Seeing that they were in a state of deep shock, the manager took a brandy bottle and several glasses from behind the bar. After giving each of them a double shot, he suggested they too packed up and went home.

'You can't stay here all bloody night,' he told them firmly.

Arthur, who was as white as a sheet, couldn't even begin to think straight. WHY? WHY? WHY had she never told him? Nothing in the world would ever stop him from loving her. Why couldn't she have trusted him with the truth? Everything about her neurotic behaviour when she'd started at the Phoenix suddenly became clear. She was a woman on the run from her husband – she was living in terror. Seeing the tears in his eyes, Gladys approached Arthur.

'Why didn't she take us into her confidence?' she asked him.

'I'm asking myself the same question,' he answered weakly. 'If I'd known, I could have protected her; instead' – his voice choked – 'she's out there somewhere with that, that – animal!'

'She must have run away from him,' Gladys mused. 'She was a complete bag of nerves when I first met her.' She gulped back tears that were threatening to overwhelm her. 'What do you think he'll do to her?' she whispered.

Arthur gripped his hands so tight the knuckles of his hands showed white. 'Oh, God, help my poor girl,' he said in an agony of pain. 'How's she going to fight off a brute like him?'

Fearful for Violet's life, Gladys asked, 'Shouldn't we call the police?'

'That would ruin Kit and Ian's chances of tailing Violet,' Myrtle answered sharply. 'For the moment they're our only hope.'

Looking frightened, Edna said thoughtfully, 'I'm not sure the police can interfere in a domestic dispute like this one.'

As the Bomb Girls stared at each other in anguished disbelief, Myrtle added, 'If Mr McIvor manages to successfully follow Violet's wretched husband, we'll soon know where she's been taken.'

As Edna and the girls nodded dumbly, Myrtle, determined to instil in them a shred of hope, continued, 'We can only assume that Mr McIvor will be in touch as soon as he has anything to report.'

Struck by her words, Edna was suddenly seized by a burst of activity. 'Then we'd better get back home right away, just in case they call,' she announced as she started to collect up scattered sheet music and instruments. 'Ian has my number – he's used it in the past. Come along now, let's get everybody back to the Phoenix.'

Arthur bit back tears as he placed Violet's silver

clarinet in its battered old leather case. He ran his fingers tenderly along the name she'd proudly written on it as a young girl: VIOLET MARY MARSDEN. FORM 5. COVENTRY GRAMMAR SCHOOL.

'Darling girl,' he said as he snapped the clips down, then walked out of the ballroom, which he prayed as long as he lived he would never see again.

After Edna had deposited the sad and weary girls at the Phoenix, she turned to hollow-eyed Arthur.

'I'm going to my shop, where I pray I'll get a phone call from Ian sometime soon,' she told him.

'May I join you, Edna?'

'Of course you can, lovie,' she replied.

As Nora and Maggie hurried back to their digs, they exchanged their chaotic thoughts.

'Who would ever have thought it – Violet married!'

'Maybe that's why she ran away, 'cos of the way he treated her.'

'Why didn't Arthur tackle him?' Maggie murmured. 'He's been in the army – he can fight his way out of trouble.'

'He can't go beating up Violet's husband,' Nora protested. 'She's his wife, so legally Violet belongs to him.'

Maggie shuddered. 'Sweet Jesus! That's nothing less than a death sentence.'

Clutching her own and Violet's instrument case, Gladys returned to the cowshed alone. After closing the front door, she slumped on to the old sofa, where she removed Violet's clarinet from its casing, and, putting the mouthpiece to her lips, she played a few notes, which reduced her to tears.

'Oh, Violet! Violet!' she sobbed as she buried her face in the sofa.

Who could ever have imagined that the much longed for final would turn into a nightmare?

In the back room of the chip shop, Arthur and Edna took it in turns to man the phone for what remained of the rest of that long dark night.

As dawn broke over the moors where the curlews called, Edna wearily brewed a pot of tea.

'Oh, God . . .' she sighed, too tired to think straight. 'I can't even remember the town where Violet said she came from.'

'Coventry,' Arthur reminded her.

'Coventry . . .' Edna checked the clock ticking away on her mantelpiece. 'They've been gone eight hours – they must be there by now.'

'If it's Coventry he's taken her to,' Arthur grimly pointed out.

Imagining dark cellars and abandoned sheds in the middle of nowhere, Edna shuddered. 'Maybe we should have gone to the police after all,' she added guiltily.

'And tell them WHAT?' Arthur reasoned. 'Violet was driven away by her husband?' He shook his head. 'They'd laugh in your face – there's nothing the law can do about a man taking his wife home.'

Worried and weary with all kinds of hideous thoughts whirling around inside their heads, the two of them finally dozed off in Edna's comfy armchairs. When the phone shrilled out, Edna grabbed it.

'Yes?' she gasped.

'It's Ian.'

Edna held out the phone so Arthur could listen in too.

'We followed them to an area called Edgwick, to the house where he's holding Violet. I'm phoning from a newsagent's shop just around the corner.' Ian sighed heavily as he added, 'We saw him dragging Violet into the house a few hours ago.'

'Sweet Jesus!' Arthur exclaimed.

'I left Kit keeping an eye on the property whilst I made this phone call,' he added.

'Won't he catch sight of Kit standing guard in her munitions overalls?' Arthur asked sharply.

'She got rid of those almost as soon as we left Stockport,' Ian told him. 'She's wearing an old raincoat of mine. Look,' he added anxiously, 'I need to get back to her.'

'We've been wondering about telling the police,' Edna told him quickly. 'The longer she's with him the more at risk she is.'

'I agree,' Ian retorted. 'But, seeing as we're here now, we'll wait for a few hours in the hope that he'll go out, at which point we'll break in and hopefully rescue Violet.'

'What's the address?' Arthur asked before Ian put down the phone.

'No. 6, Streatfield Avenue, Edgwick.'

Arthur immediately wrote down the address.

'I can't bear this hanging about – I'm going to drive down there right away,' he announced.

'I'd advise you to wait a little longer, Arthur.'

'He could be beating the living daylights out of the poor kid!' Arthur all but yelled down the phone.

'Kit and I have to come back at some point: we're sailing to Ireland and I've a lot to sort out before we leave. If we're not back by eight tonight, then by all means drive down here and take over the watch from us.'

'Okay,' Arthur reluctantly agreed.

Standing shivering in Ian's thin raincoat, Kit double-knotted his scarf around her neck and was instantly comforted by the familiar smell of the lavender soap he used. With her heart clamouring in her ribcage, Kit remained concealed behind a thick hedge while Ian phoned Edna, just as she'd promised him. Peering out, she looked furtively towards the house that they'd seen poor Violet entering in the middle of the night.

'Holy Mother and all the saints,' she prayed, 'look after my sweet dear friend. Please don't let him hurt her, please protect her from harm.'

So deep in prayer was Kit that she jumped when a car went by at top speed. Obscured by the foliage, she managed to peep through a gap in the hedge and saw that the car was Ronnie's big Bentley.

'Jesus, Mary and Joseph!' she gasped.

As soon as the Bentley disappeared around the corner, Kit, with wings on her feet, flew down the length of the street. Terrified of being seen by neighbours, she dashed to the back of the house, where she threw herself at the door and pummelled it with her small fists. When nobody replied, she paused to press her ear to it – holding her breath she was sure she could hear a low grunting noise. Frantic, she looked up to see a narrow kitchen window. Grabbing a shovel that was leaning against the coalhole wall, she stood on an upturned bucket and smashed the window, then opened it by lifting the internal catch. Squeezing in through broken shards of glass, Kit was oblivious to the cuts on her arms and legs. When she jumped off the kitchen worktop, she all but landed on Violet, gagged and trussed up like a chicken on the floor. Bruised and bleeding, Violet lay in her underwear, with her corset and chemise knickers on the floor beside her. When Kit saw the underwear cast aside, her heart skipped a beat – could Ronnie have had his way with Violet after he'd tied her up in the kitchen?

'ARGHHHHH!' Violet cried through her gag when she saw Kit.

Grabbing a knife, Kit quickly cut Violet free, all the time murmuring soothing words. 'All right, darlin', all right, I've got you now, shhh, shhh . . .'

But Violet was hysterical with fear. 'He'll be back!' she cried hoarsely. 'He only left to drop off stuff to his mate in town. He'll be back and he'll kill the pair of us.'

'We'll bloody see about that,' Kit said through gritted teeth as she led her limping, weeping friend to the back door, which she unlocked and then gently guided Violet outside.

Thinking fast, Kit knew it wouldn't be wise to walk back up the street – apart from snoopy neighbours, Ronnie might catch sight of them on his way home. Standing in the back garden, Kit peered around for somewhere to hide. At the back of the row of houses she spotted an Anderson shelter, which seemed to her too obvious a hiding place, but it was surrounded by sprawling allotments. Half dragging trembling Violet, she made her way to the allotments, where under cover of bushes and fruit trees she pushed her friend under a cold frame, which was musky with the smell of tomato plants. Thanking God they were both on the slim side, she pushed Violet inside then squeezed in beside her. Violet's nose wrinkled as she inhaled the heavy smell of compost.

'For God's sake, don't sneeze!' Kit hissed.

Meanwhile Ian had returned to the hedge where he'd left Kit keeping an eye on the house. As he pulled up in his Ford, he did a stunned double-take. Where was she? Where had she gone? In a flash he realized what might have happened. She would only have left their pre-arranged spot for a good reason: Ronnie must have driven away and Kit had seized the moment to get into the house. As the large Bentley with scowling Ronnie at the wheel came roaring back into the avenue, Ian broke into a sweat of fear.

'Oh, God!' he muttered.

27. Edgwick

When Gladys, Maggie and Nora clocked in at the Phoenix the following afternoon, they were met by cheers and applause. Seeing their tear-stained weary faces, the applause faded away as their co-workers crowded round to inquire what was wrong.

'You won the final: we read about it in the morning papers.'

'You're on your way to London!'

'What's up?'

'You look like you've lost a tenner and found a fiver!'

Having agreed on a story with Myrtle, Nora and Maggie, stony-faced Gladys explained as best she could. 'Violet had an accident: she fell off the stage. She's in hospital; Kit went with her.'

After sympathies were offered, the girls managed to slip into the ladies', where they snatched a word in private.

'No word from Edna,' Gladys said before anybody asked.

'Christ!' gasped over-imaginative Nora. 'Violet could be dead and buried by now.'

Gladys glared at her. 'Stop that, Nora!' she cried.

'I still think we should have gone straight to the police,' Maggie maintained.

Myrtle nodded, this time in agreement with Maggie. 'We might have to soon.'

'Let's get this shift over with, then, if Edna doesn't show up, we'll go down to her chip shop,' Gladys suggested.

Malc, who hadn't been able to attend the final due to shifts he couldn't swop, wasn't so easy to fob off.

'What the 'ell's going on, Glad?' he asked as he passed through the filling shed. 'I've got two lasses off and bloody Arthur's not showed up. You've got a face as long as a fiddle, them two kids on't cordite line keep skrikin', and Myrtle looks like she's been up all night.'

Sick with fear, Gladys blurted out the whole horrible story.

'Jesus Christ!' he gasped.

'Arthur's with Edna. We're all praying that Ian or Kit will phone her. They MUST know something by now – it's been well over fourteen hours since it happened,' she added frantically.

Malc dropped his voice to a husky whisper. 'I'll jump in't car when it's mi break and nip down to Edna's.'

Gladys's eyes filled with tears. 'Oh, Malc, it would be such a relief if you could talk to her,' she said with a catch in her voice.

Malc returned as the hooter sounded the end of the break. He hurried up to the girls, who were on the point of leaving the canteen; his grim expression said it all.

Crouching in the cold frame, Kit's heart raced as she saw Ronnie come roaring out of the back door of his house. Incandescent with fury, he shouted as he threw open the shed door.

'I'll bloody kill you when I find you, bitch!'

As he raced towards the Anderson shelter, Kit lay almost on top of trembling Violet to smother her sobs. Popping up to peep through the leafy plants, she saw

Ronnie come running out of the Anderson shelter; then she ducked down as he headed into the allotment. Seeing only sprawling vegetation all around him, Ronnie turned around and raced back to the house.

'Has he gone?' Violet whispered as she came up for air.

'I think so,' Kit answered.

'Shall we make a run for it?' frantic Violet asked.

Kit shook her head. 'We can't risk it; he might drive around the neighbourhood searching for us.'

Sitting in his car, pretending to read a road map, Ian watched Ronnie drive his Bentley slowly up the street, peering from left to right and checking every garden he passed. As he furtively watched, Ian realized with relief that Ronnie couldn't have found the girls inside the house – otherwise why would he be searching the area? Waiting until Ronnie had cruised into the next street and was well out of sight, Ian started up his Ford and drove down the back streets in search of Kit and Violet. When the girls crouching in the cold frame heard the sound of an approaching car, their blood ran cold.

'He's come back,' Violet gasped.

Holding her tightly to stifle her sobs, Kit shivered in terror as she heard a car door slam close by, then the sound of heavy footsteps coming closer and closer.

'I'll stay with you, Vi,' Kit promised. 'No matter what happens I swear I'll never leave you.'

Crouching in order to avoid being seen, Ian crept passed the back gardens of the houses, then stopped short when he saw a shattered kitchen window flung wide open. Desperately hoping that Kit and Violet might be near, he called softly, 'KIT! KIT! Are you there?'

Hearing his voice, Kit leapt like a Jack-in-a-box from the cold frame.

'IAN!' she cried.

'SHHH!' he whispered as she ran into his arms. 'We've got to get Violet away quickly.' Looking around, he asked, 'Where is she?'

'I'll get her,' said Kit.

He nodded towards his car by the Anderson shelter. 'Get her into the car – I'll cover for you.'

Kit had to persuade Violet to come out of her hiding place. 'It's not Ronnie – it's Ian! Come on, quickly, run!'

Grabbing her by the hand, she dragged Violet across the allotments, then shoved her into the back of the Ford.

'Get down on the floor and stay there,' Kit whispered as she crouched low in the passenger footwell.

'Drive!' she cried to Ian. 'For the love of God, get us out of here.'

Ian stuck to the narrow back streets until they were well out of the Edgwick area, then he joined the busy traffic on the main road north. In all that time none of them dared speak. Ian's eyes were constantly on his wing mirror, watching out for a big Bentley hot on his tail. When they finally cleared Stoke, he slumped back in his seat.

'I think it's safe to come and sit beside me, Catherine – and for God's sake please light me a cigarette.'

Kit slipped into the passenger seat, where she lit up cigarettes for both of them.

'How did you know where we were?' she asked.

'I didn't!' he exclaimed. 'When I saw Ronnie driving up and down the streets clearly searching, I assumed Violet had escaped. Once Ronnie was out of sight, I came looking for you,' he added.

'Thank Jesus you did,' she murmured as she inhaled deeply on her cigarette. 'I couldn't have gone much further with Violet; he's beaten her badly.' Then she added in a whisper, 'I think he's interfered with her too.'

'The despicable brute!' Ian seethed.

As tears stung the back of Kit's dark brooding eyes, she murmured, 'I always knew she had a secret – it takes one to know one – but I never imagined anything as terrible as Ronnie.'

Keeping his eyes on the road ahead Ian asked, 'Does Violet know your secret?'

'No . . .' Kit replied. 'But now everybody knows hers.'

Worried that Violet might have overheard her, Kit peered over the back of her seat: her heart contracted with pity when she saw Violet rolled into a tight ball, fast asleep on the back seat. Removing the raincoat she was wearing, Kit gently laid it over Violet.

'Sleep, darlin',' she whispered tenderly. 'We'll be home soon.'

28. Consequences

After her safe return to Pendleton, Violet could not bear to be left on her own. The wounds that Ronnie had inflicted – on her neck, face, thighs and chest – slowly healed, but her mind didn't. She was haunted by the thought that Ronnie would find her and take her back to Coventry, where her life of torture as his abused wife would continue.

'How would he know where to find you?' Edna asked as she, Arthur, Gladys and Kit gathered around the sofa, where Violet lay with her head resting on a pillow.

'Isn't it obvious?' Violet retorted.

Edna snapped her fingers with a loud click. 'In the ballroom in Stockport.'

Gladys threw up her hands as the penny dropped. 'Of course!' she cried. 'The manager's introduction – "The Bomb Girls from the Phoenix Munitions Factory in Pendleton". Violet's right: Ronnie knows exactly where to find her.'

'He could be outside, watching me right now!' Violet cried as she jumped up and rushed to the window that looked out on to the moors, soft and luminous in the sunset's light.

'Darling, darling,' soothed Arthur as he gently took her in his arms. 'If Ronnie were out there, don't you think he would have thrown a brick through the window or kicked the door down by now?' he said as he gently teased her.

Violet's face visibly relaxed. 'Yes, you're right: throwing a brick through the window is Ronnie's kind of calling card,' she said as she clutched Arthur tightly. 'But he could come sneaking up here, and he's always armed.' She paled as she imagined him drawing a flick knife. 'He would kill me if he found me again, I know he would.'

Arthur held her close and kissed her forehead. 'He'd have to kill me first, sweetheart.'

Gladys and Kit exchanged a knowing look: though Arthur could calm Violet down, they all knew she was at risk. Gladys had even talked of police protection, but, as Arthur had pointed out many times, the law can't prevent a man from searching for his wife; and even if Violet pleaded that she was a victim of domestic violence, this would have to be proven to the law. Arthur was virtually living in the cowshed these days, sleeping on Violet's bedroom floor or on the sofa in the sitting room. Though she wasn't fit enough for work, Violet was so terrified of being left on her own that she accompanied Arthur and her friends to the Phoenix, where she lay on a makeshift camp bed in the factory's first-aid room whilst Arthur and her friends worked their shifts.

As Ian finalized all the paperwork he needed to present to Mother Gabriel and Mr O'Rourke, her legal adviser, Kit happily packed her suitcase and counted down the days till she'd see her little boy. Unfortunately, worry for Violet slightly marred her joy – although she pressed her new dress and buffed up her brogues, worry about Violet's delicate frame of mind was never far from her thoughts. And she wasn't the only one who was worried. One evening, after Violet had gone to bed, Arthur announced to her anxious friends, 'We've got to move: she's on a knife edge all the time, waiting for the swine to turn up.' Arthur swiped a hand across his brow. 'She's hardly eating, barely sleeping and when she does she has nightmares. Her screams are terrible; she's always begging him to leave her alone, to stop hurting her.' Arthur put his head in his hands. 'I can't bear to see her this way a minute longer.'

'If she carries on the way she is, she'll have a breakdown,' Edna said grimly.

'I love her too much to let that happen,' Arthur retorted.

'Where will you go?' Kit asked.

'Another munitions factory miles away from here.'

'I still don't know why she never told us,' Gladys said, puzzled. 'I wouldn't have cared less if she was married – why keep it a secret?'

'She was on the run, poor kid,' Arthur said compassionately. 'She probably thought the fewer people who knew about her past, the better.'

Kit's heartbeat quickened; her friends might ask the same thing of her one day very soon. Why had she not revealed her secret? Was it the shame of having had an illegitimate child and abandoning him? They might ask, and she would answer, no, she felt no shame, just joy, especially now when they were so soon to be reunited. She'd tell them the truth: that she'd been forced against all her instincts to leave her baby to provide for her family. She took some comfort from the fact that on her return she would be free to tell her friends the truth and finally there would be no more secrets between them.

*

'Do you remember what Violet was like when she first came here?' Arthur said with a fond smile. 'Like a hen on hot bricks! I couldn't look at her without her taking flight.'

'No wonder,' Gladys replied gloomily.

'I just fell head over heels in love with her,' he confessed. 'Her sweet shy face, her lovely sad eyes – oh, she was worth fighting for,' he added with a tender smile. 'But now it's my job to keep her safe and get her as far away from the Phoenix as possible.'

Knowing she and Ian were due to leave for Dublin at the crack of dawn the next morning, Kit was determined to talk to her friends about what had been troubling her ever since she'd found Violet in Ronnie's kitchen. She waited until Arthur had gone to bed, then she said in a low whisper, 'When I found Violet, she was tied up and gagged. And there was something else too,' Kit took a deep breath before she continued. 'Her corset and chemise knickers were on the floor beside her; the knickers were ripped as if they'd been dragged from her body.'

'Oh, Jesus!' groaned Edna as she lit up a Woodbine.

'She's never mentioned it,' Kit quickly added. 'And I've not either.'

'Don't tell Arthur – he'd take Ronnie apart,' Gladys whispered fearfully.

'I do wish somebody would see off this rotten excuse for a man,' Edna cried wrathfully. 'He deserves to die.'

Kit waited for Edna to calm down before she whispered, 'What if he did interfere with her? What if she's pregnant with Ronnie's child?'

Gladys put her head in her hands. 'That would really push her over the edge.'

'Is it best to talk to her about it or just to wait to see what happens?' Kit asked her friends.

'You mean wait and see if she has her monthlies?' said Edna.

'After the shock she's had and the state of her nerves, it's likely that Violet may not have a period for a while,' Kit replied.

'She's underweight too, which doesn't help,' Gladys added.

'But you do share a bathroom,' Edna pointed out. 'And you use the same changing rooms at work; you'd see tell-tale signs like sanitary towels or blood stains if her monthly started.'

'You're right,' said Gladys.

'Be vigilant,' Edna said firmly.

On the morning she was supposed to sail to Dublin, Kit made sure she said her goodbyes to Violet before Ian arrived to pick her up.

'I pray you'll be here when I get back.'

Violet didn't beat about the bush. 'We'll leave just as soon as we can, Kit,' she said bluntly. 'It's for the best.'

Kit paused before she asked, 'How will you manage, together like?'

Violet gave a bleak smile. 'You mean, not being married?'

Kit nodded.

'We've talked it over and we're going to pretend to be married,' Violet replied. 'I know we'll be living in sin but I HAVE to be with Arthur or I'll just curl up and die!'

'There is no shame or sin about your relationship with Arthur,' Kit said passionately. 'It's a good and beautiful thing!'

Violet smiled proudly. 'He's the dearest most devoted man that ever drew breath. Even now, sleeping by me on my bedroom floor, he's never laid a hand on me.'

Kit gulped; if she didn't ask the question now she never would. 'Vi, forgive me, but it's just that I saw things in the kitchen in that house.' She took a deep breath. 'Did Ronnie, you know . . .'

Violet finished the question for her. 'Rape me?'

Kit blushed and nodded.

'Yes,' Violet answered in a voice that was so remote it didn't sound like her. 'Don't worry, Kit, it wasn't like it was the first time,' she finished bitterly.

'Oh, God in heaven!' Kit exclaimed as she realized the full horror of Violet's nightmare marriage.

'You must NEVER tell Arthur,' Violet insisted.

'But what if you're pregnant?' Kit asked.

'I pray to God I'm not,' Violet cried. 'I could never bring a child of Ronnie's into the world.'

'Have you had your period?' Kit asked.

When Violet shook her head, Kit quickly reassured her. 'Well, that's hardly surprising after everything you've been through; your body must be in shock.'

'What would I feel like if I was pregnant?' Violet asked nervously.

Kit knew that if she talked in too much detail about pregnancy, Violet might guess her secret, so she moderated her language. 'Well, I've heard folks say that in early pregnancy you suffer from morning sickness and have sore breasts,' she said vaguely.

Violet thought for a few seconds, then shook her head. 'Then hopefully you're in the clear,' Kit said confidently.

When they heard the sound of Ian's car rumbling down the cobbled path, the girls clasped each other tightly.

'Good luck, sweetheart,' Kit cried.

'Goodbye, Kit,' Violet sobbed. 'Good luck!'

Kit ran into Ian's arms.

'Before we get carried away,' he said as she reached up to kiss his mouth, 'have you been given official permission to take a few days off?'

Pulling reluctantly away, Kit answered, 'Mr Featherstone was a bit grumpy, but I told him it would be my final visit and I promised I would never trouble him again.' She threw back her head and laughed with sheer joy. 'I didn't say I was going home to pick up my son and had no wish to return to Ireland for a very long time!'

Smiling mysteriously, Ian drew away from Kit and reached into his car.

'I thought you might need something warm to wear on that draughty old crossing over the Irish Sea.' With a twinkle in his eye he draped a pale blue tweed swing coat over her shoulders, then arranged a dark pink velvet trilby at a jaunty angle on her head. 'I want you looking your best when you meet Billy again.'

Thrilled by her new outfit, Kit did a little twirl for Ian's benefit.

'Billy won't be recognizing his owd mother when I walk into that nursery dressed up like a princess!'

Smiling, she wrapped her arms around herself as if she was already hugging her son.

29. A Claddagh Promise

Kit's journey across the Irish Sea was unlike her previous ones home, and that wasn't only because she was travelling with such hope in her heart. This time she was with Ian, who'd had the foresight to purchase medication that kept her sea sickness at bay; plus the September afternoon they sailed out of Heysham Docks was warm and golden, with the sea unusually still. Leaning on the ship's rails, watching the coast of England fade to a blur, Kit and Ian were obviously a couple deeply in love.

'I can't believe this is really happening!' Kit exclaimed as she slipped her arm through Ian's and hugged him. 'Normally I'm in a cabin in the darkest part of the ship being sick,' she said with a grimace.

As the sea breeze lifted Kit's lovely dark hair, fanning it around her sweet heart-shaped face, Ian marvelled at the change in her. Love had given her a new radiance; even their nightmare escape from Ronnie in Coventry had added bloom to her cheeks and confidence to her step. He was proud of Kit's bravery and bold thinking in rescuing Violet – even if at the time she had put the fear of God in him!

'You'll have a first-class cabin all to yourself tonight, sweetheart,' he promised.

Kit tingled with a mixture of pleasure and desire. How she longed to be sharing a cabin with Ian. As passion flared in her for the first time ever, she longed to explore and caress Ian's muscular body. She dismissed the foolish things the nuns at school had said to frighten their students, 'Sins of the Flesh' and 'The Work of Satan'. What could be sinful about loving a man who had irrevocably changed her life? She wanted to love him with her body and her soul, but Ian was not quite so direct: he kissed and cuddled her and delighted in pleasing her, but he never overstepped the mark, even though she often longed for him to do so.

As the deep dark waters churned below them, Kit and Ian snuggled close to keep warm.

'After we land in Dublin, we'll visit Mother Gabriel's legal adviser, who's already had the letter from the handwriting specialist in Manchester, saying that the mother's signature on the adoption papers is not yours and therefore the document is invalid.'

Kit smiled. 'I'm looking forward to hearing you say that out loud!' she said with a gleeful laugh.

'After that,' Ian continued, 'We'll head over to the convent to make the final arrangements for Billy.'

Suddenly alarmed, Kit said, 'Promise me that nothing can go wrong this time.'

'What on earth could go wrong, sweetheart?' Ian asked. 'We've cleared every hurdle; everything is legal and above board. I've been absolutely meticulous; that's why it's taken so long. There's nothing to worry about at all.'

Linking his arm through hers, Ian kissed her warm lips. 'The battle's over, Kit – nothing and nobody can stop you now.'

*

Over supper, which Kit was astonished she could eat and enjoy, Ian broached the subject which he'd been wanting to talk about for some time. Reaching across the table he took her hand in his.

'Darling, I want you to tell me how you became pregnant with Billy.'

Kit snatched her hand away. 'No!' she exclaimed.

Ian's hazel eyes were tender with concern. 'Do you think revealing your secret will make me stop loving you?'

Kit nodded slowly.

'I can only assume you were violated, darling, but look how you fought back! You fought your father, you fought the nuns, you fought the law; a little slip of a girl in rags and tatters, you took them on and you won, my darling.'

'YOU won,' she pointed out.

Seeing a blush rising into her hairline, Ian said softly, 'You don't have to tell me if it's going to upset you.'

'I'm sick to death of keeping secrets,' Kit declared as she decisively laid down her knife and fork and told him her story from the very beginning.

'It was March, wet and windy, as it only can be in Ireland. I was out in the fields, potato picking, along with other estate workers. Himself is a big fat pig of a man, married to an arrogant English woman who looks down her nose at her serfs,' Kit added bitterly. 'I've no time for them or their type, but, according to mi stupid da, we're forever in his lordship's debt 'cos of the cottage he allows us to live in rent free. You've been there – it's nothing but a hovel! Rain dripping through the peat roof and crawling with rats. I swear it was mi da's scraping and bowing that drew the old goat's attention to me. His eyes swept straight over Rosie, mi sister, but they landed on me every time he rode by in his carriage with her ladyship or trotted past on his horse. God only knows why: I was a bag of bones and covered in mud!'

'You don't know how lovely you are, Catherine,' Ian murmured.

'He'd doff his cap and smile as if he was coming a-courtin'. I hated the man and always put a safe distance between him and myself, until that March day. He must have been watching me,' she said as she recalled her actions. 'I'd never allowed myself to be alone with him – I didn't trust him as far as I could throw him – but he must have seen me leave the field and go to the potato shed to collect fresh sacks. That's when it happened. He followed me into the shed, where he locked the door. I begged him to leave me alone but he was having none of it. I stood no chance against him, the big beast that he is. He slammed me against the wall, gagged me with one hand whilst he lifted my skirts then got on with the business.'

Pale-faced Ian raised his full glass of claret and swallowed it in one gulp.

'Christ, I've heard enough,' he said as he topped up both their glasses.

'You know,' Kit added thoughtfully, 'the worst thing was Fitzwilliam didn't doubt for a minute that he had a right to me; because he owns our hovel of a home he thinks he owns me too.'

'*Droit du seigneur*,' Ian growled angrily. 'The ancient right of the aristocracy to take whatever it pleases.'

'What followed was almost as bad as the rape,' she continued. 'When it was obvious I was pregnant, I tried to tell mi da how Fitzwilliam had attacked me, but he said I'd egged him on, enticed him into the potato shed. Can you imagine that?' she said with a hard laugh. 'When I look back now, I marvel that nobody stood up for me. Look at the way we fought for Violet: nobody did that for me or for poor little Billy.' She smiled adoringly at Ian. 'Well, not until I met you.'

Ian lit up a Pall Mall cigarette, which he inhaled deeply. 'One day soon I'd like a word with Fitzwilliam,' he growled.

'Don't go wasting your time,' Kit declared. 'His sort think they rule the world.'

'That may be so, but his sort don't rule me!'

Before they went to their cabins, Ian and Kit took a turn around the deck, where the breeze was getting up. Watching a new moon appear in the dark sky dotted with flimsy transparent clouds, Ian pulled Kit to him.

'I'm sorry I caused you pain, my darling, I just needed to know,' he whispered.

'And I needed to tell,' she whispered back.

'I worry whether you'll ever be able to properly love again, whether you're afraid of . . .' He stumbled self-consciously on his words.

'Giving myself to another man?' Kit replied unselfconsciously. 'I was, for sure, until I met you, but now,' she added with a naughty giggle, 'I can't wait!'

Ian burst out laughing. 'Shameless hussy!' he teased.

'I always believed that falling in love would be as romantic as the poet's words,' Kit said as she recalled her favourite W. B. Yeats poem, which she'd learnt at school.

I would spread the cloths under your feet:
But I, being poor, have only my dreams;

I have spread my dreams under your feet;
Tread softly because you tread on my dreams.

'I will always tread softly upon your dreams,' Ian promised.

'And I, being poor, have only my dreams,' she quoted.

'Not any more, my darling – from tomorrow onwards you have the whole new wonderful world before you,' he assured her.

And as the moon sailed high into the sky, the couple standing by the rails at the prow of the ship sank into each other's arms and kissed.

The following morning, as Kit walked through the streets of Dublin, she recalled the frantic skinny girl in rags running through the very same streets on her way to the Convent of the Sisters of Mercy, where Billy had been taken. Now here she was, a smartly dressed, smiling young woman on the arm of the man she loved on her way to reclaim her son.

'How lucky am I?' she said to herself as she considered her radical change of circumstances.

Suddenly Ian stopped outside a jeweller's shop.

'What kind of a ring is that?' he asked as he peered intently through the shop window. 'It looks like a pair of hands holding a heart.'

Kit followed his gaze. 'It's a Claddagh ring,' she said. 'If it's worn on the right hand with the heart facing inward towards the body, it means that the person wearing the ring is in a relationship – someone has captured their heart!' she giggled.

'That's the ring for you, my sweet!' he laughed and, taking her by the hand, he ushered her inside the shop.

The charming shop girl brought out several velvet trays containing Claddagh rings: some were plain gold or silver; others were more elaborate, and more expensive too, with gems set in the heart clasped between the two hands.

'Amethyst, emerald, sapphire, ruby,' the girl chanted. 'Which will you be after choosing?'

Kit finally opted for an emerald stone.

'Now,' Ian said, trying to recall how she'd explained the wearing of the Claddagh. 'It goes on the right hand.' He smiled as he placed the ring on her finger. 'And if you're spoken for, which you are, young lady, it faces inwards towards the body. See!' he laughed as he stood back to admire the ring on her finger. 'Someone has captured your heart and you're his for life!'

As Kit kissed Ian, she whispered softly in his ear, 'I want no other man but you, my darlin'.'

30. Mr O'Rourke

Though there'd been a lot of talk about the convent's legal adviser, Kit was nevertheless surprised when she met Mr O'Rourke. She'd expected a short, fussy middle-aged man but instead was met by a tall, dark-haired, handsome man with sweeping black hair and a winning smile.

'At your service, ma'am,' he said as he shook her by the hand. 'And nice to meet you in person, sir,' he added as he turned to Ian.

Kit immediately sensed that Ian didn't like the man. He didn't smile and his manner seemed guarded.

'The whole business has taken an extraordinary amount of time,' Ian said rather tersely.

'Come along now, Mr McIvor, you can't be blaming me for the communication problems we've had. It's not my fault the British Government are intercepting letters from Ireland, nor can I be blamed for the German bombs landing on telephone wires.'

Ian tenaciously pushed home his point. 'For something which is essentially quite simple, I seem to have been put to great lengths to prove my client's innocence.'

Feeling like things might get heated, Kit quickly said, 'It was a relief to hear you accept that my name on Billy's adoption papers had been forged.'

'There's no doubting the handwriting specialist's evidence,' smooth-talking O'Rourke replied. 'So now let's be done with them!' he said as he took a set of papers from his desk and tore them in half. Astounded Kit watched as he tore them in half once more before depositing them in the waste-paper basket. The sight of the hateful document lying in shreds in the bottom of the basket should have brought a rush of relief to Kit, but she continued to feel deeply uneasy, as if she was holding her breath waiting for something terrible to happen.

Handing her a heavy gold fountain pen, O'Rourke said, 'If you and Mr McIvor could sign to say you have witnessed my destruction of the fraudulent papers, that will close the matter once and for all.'

Eager to get out of the office and away from O'Rourke, Kit quickly signed her name on to the thick headed paper, as did Ian; then O'Rourke, with an unnecessary dramatic flourish, added his signature.

'I'm sorry for your troubles, Miss Murphy. I hope there will be no more misunderstandings in the future.'

Feeling intensely irritated by his condescending manner, and knowing full well that it had been Ian, with the help of the handwriting specialist, who had in fact done all of the work on her behalf, Kit declared passionately, 'There is absolutely *no* chance of there being any further misunderstanding, Mr O'Rourke!'

Once outside the office, Ian just about exploded. 'Odious pompous fool!' he fumed. 'Blaming the war for his slowness in responding was a cheap trick.'

Kit slipped her arm through his. "Who cares?" she said as she admired her glittering bright Claddagh ring. 'We're done with O'Rourke!'

*

When they stood outside the Convent of the Sisters of Mercy and Ian rang the bell, Kit could hardly believe she was actually there. The moment had finally come: soon she would hold her son in her arms and never be parted from him again. But the minute the pale, nervous young novice opened the door to them, Kit's euphoria started to fade.

'We've an appointment with the Mother Superior,' Ian said politely.

'I'll be after telling her,' the novice muttered before she hurried away.

When she returned, it was with Mother Gabriel herself.

'Please follow me,' the Mother Superior murmured.

At the sound of her heavy voice, Kit's skin began to creep. This was not the reception she had been expecting.

'Something's wrong,' she whispered to Ian. He squeezed her hand but she could tell from the strained expression on his face that he was concerned too.

In the formal sitting room, decorated with lurid images of the Passion of Christ on the Cross, Mother Gabriel didn't call for tea or even ask them to sit down. Instead, she came straight to the point.

'I'm so very sorry, but the truth is . . .' Looking wretched, she finished the sentence. 'Billy's not here.'

As blood pounded through her brain and the room swam before her, Kit cried out, 'What? NO! Oh, Ian, no!'

Ian grabbed hold of her before she fell to the floor, 'Sit, darling! Sit.'

After lowering her into a hard-backed wooden chair, he turned to the nun. 'What happened?'

'The child disappeared in the night.'

Feeling like she would faint or be sick all over the

immaculate grey carpet, Kit concentrated hard on taking deep breaths.

'We have our suspicions,' Mother Gabriel continued. 'Your father was seen on the premises last night, Miss Murphy.'

'Mi da!' Kit gasped. 'What was he doing here?' she demanded.

'One of the novices spotted him in the kitchen quarters; he's often visited in the past and she thought no more about it until early this morning, when Sister Clare discovered Billy was missing from his cot.'

'For sure mi da would steal an innocent child if there was money to be had from it,' Kit said with utter conviction. 'In God's name, where's Billy now?'

'I can tell you for sure he's not with Mr Murphy, whom I sent the police after,' Mother Gabriel retorted with anger in her voice. 'They could get nothing out of the man, but I'm concerned Murphy might have somehow tracked down the American couple who were after adopting Billy.' Turning to white-faced Kit, she added, 'Your father flew into a rage when the adoption proceedings were halted by Mr McIvor.'

Looking white-faced and tense, Ian said, 'So did the American couple actually arrive in Dublin?'

'Yes, they arrived. I myself told them the adoption was held up due to legal reasons. I instructed Mr O'Rourke to communicate with them after that. I assumed they'd returned home, but who knows what they did,' Mother Gabriel answered honestly.

'If mi da ever got the chance to talk to them, I swear to God he would have spun them a line in order to get money out of them,' Kit cried angrily.

'But who would believe a man like him?' Ian asked sharply.

'God forgive me, I did when he brought Billy to me in the first place. He was very convincing, Mr McIvor,' Mother Gabriel confessed.

'And he's kissed the Blarney Stone!' Kit exclaimed. 'Him with his gift of the gab. I can just hear him,' Kit said as she imitated her father's whingeing voice. 'My daughter's under-age, a child herself, the boy is legally mine; he'll have a better life across the water. I'll bring him to you – for a feckin' price!' Kit stopped suddenly, her dark eyes wide with fear. 'Mother Gabriel, do you really think my son could be on his way to America?'

'I've discussed the possibility of Billy's being smuggled out of the country,' Mother Gabriel admitted. 'The police are already searching the docks.'

Kit jumped to her feet. 'I'm going down there right away,' she said.

Ian grabbed her arm. 'Wait darling, we'll go together.' He quickly gave the Mother Superior a card. 'If you have any news, please phone my hotel, the Ship, by the port. The number's on the back.'

Mother Gabriel nodded, then handed Kit a small paper bag. 'These are Billy's things,' she murmured.

With her hands shaking, Kit took the items and breathed in the unmistakable scent of her precious son, her beloved flesh and blood. It was too much to bear after all the hope of the past few days. As her tears now flowed unchecked, Ian steered her gently towards the door.

'We'll be in touch, Mother Gabriel.'

*

Kit had no intention of returning to the hotel, where Ian had booked two single rooms for them.

'I don't care if the police are already checking the docks – we should check too!' she insisted.

Slightly perplexed Ian asked, 'What exactly are we checking for, sweetheart? We haven't a clue what the American couple look like, though we could check the ships' passenger list.'

'You do that, please,' she said quickly as she set purposefully off in the opposite direction to him. 'I'm going to look for Billy.'

Ian shook his head as he watched her go. He didn't dare hurt her even more by pointing out that anybody intent on abducting a baby and taking him out of the country wouldn't be pushing him around the docks in a pram. Sighing, he made his way to the bursar's office, where he ran down the passenger list of the most recent ships that had set sail for New York. There was no sign of a Mr and Mrs Garland, whose names he remembered from the forged adoption papers. Nor was there any sign of a Mr Murphy on the list. He left instructions, as had the police, with the staff to make sure no one going by those names should be allowed to embark on any future sailings, and made his way out into the fresh air, wondering what on earth he could do next.

Ian walked away from the docks and hurried towards the centre of town; he hoped Kit would head that way after her search of the docks proved fruitless. Despite his fears for Kit's baby son, Ian couldn't help but notice how striking it was to walk through a city barely affected by the trials of war. There had been some bombing, but Dublin still remained intact and beautiful. Sitting on a bench in Grafton Street, with no sign of Kit anywhere and at a loss as to what his next course of action should be, Ian put his head in his hands. Heartbroken Kit would insist on scouring every inch of the city, but at some point she would have to go back to Pendleton, possibly without him.

And they would have to talk to Murphy, even though the police had nothing on him; he HAD to be at the root of this, but Ian seriously doubted that the rash, greedy and erratic Murphy had the cunning and intelligence to execute such a complicated plan. Could Murphy book a passage to New York and smuggle a baby on board ship? He'd be more than likely to drink himself stupid at the bar and forget all about the baby!

As Ian pondered, he finally spotted Kit on the other side of Grafton Street: she looked tired and dejected. Poor darling, his heart ached for her; it seemed like whatever she did she was fated not to have her child back. As he got to his feet, Ian scolded himself: he had to remain confident that justice would be done and Billy would be returned to his mother.

When Ian caught up with Kit, he could see the poor girl was almost fainting with nervous exhaustion. Hailing a cab, Ian bundled her inside. 'You need to rest, my darling,' he murmured.

Kit leant her weary head against his shoulder. 'There was I thinking I was the luckiest woman alive not more than a few hours ago,' she sighed as tears slid down her pale cheeks.

Seeing the lost, vacant look in her dark eyes, Ian said

gently, 'Have a rest and some food. You're good for nothing like this.'

Kit was too shattered to do anything but agree.

'We'll resume our search of the city after you've rested,' he promised. 'And tomorrow we'll go to Chapelizod.'

31. Loose Lips

A grim-faced Mr Featherstone had called an emergency meeting at the Phoenix. News that the Battle of Stalingrad was under way had brought the workers' morale to a new low, and it certainly wasn't helped by what Mr Featherstone had to report.

'I've just received stern government warnings concerning the safety of the Phoenix,' he announced to the packed canteen. 'The location of munitions factories throughout Britain is top secret, but recently a surprising number of plants have been attacked by German bombers who clearly knew their exact whereabouts.' He took a heavy breath as he added, 'It appears that government information is being leaked.'

As the assembled workers grumbled angrily, Featherstone continued, 'I hardly need tell you, who are working at the coal face, what damage an enemy attack would cause in a factory like this.'

'We'd all go up like firecrackers,' one woman cried out.

'And so would a good part of Pendleton if we took a German hit,' he said sombrely. 'We already know of the fatal consequences of enemy bombing on the Woolwich Arsenal,' he reminded the workers, who vividly recalled the savage German bombing of the munitions factory in London's docklands.

'How does bloody Jerry know our whereabouts – who

the 'ell's blabbing to the enemy?' an angry young woman demanded.

'It could be spies infiltrating small groups of workers,' Featherstone answered.

'SPIES!' a group of women gasped in terror.

'If I hear of anybody blabbing about their work in't Phoenix, I'll have their bloody guts for garters,' Malc threatened.

Featherstone flapped his hands in an attempt to calm the growing panic. 'Or it could be casual gossip passed on to the wrong person. I can't say it often enough.' He quoted the popular slogan slowly and emphatically: 'LOOSE LIPS COST LIVES.'

After he'd given his gloomy warning, Violet and her friends took the opportunity to grab a cigarette and a mug of hot tea.

'Too many careless young girls are showing off about their war work,' Myrtle remarked crossly. 'They tell their friends down South they're building bombs on the Lancashire moors, word goes around, and before you know it the Luftwaffe have located the site. The more munitions factories they destroy, the less weaponry we supply to our brave boys on the front line. It's a perfect arrangement for the Germans.'

At a nearby table, Malc lit a cigarette as he flicked through a copy of the *Daily Herald*. Suddenly he scraped back his chair and leapt to his feet.

'HELL FIRE! Where's Arthur?' he cried.

Startled Violet nodded in the direction of the filling shed. 'He's working.'

Clutching the paper, Malc bolted across the canteen floor.

'What's up with 'im?' Maggie asked as she stubbed out her cigarette.

'Probably come up on the horses!' Nora joked.

When Malc found Arthur examining trays of packed fuses, he thrust the now crumpled newspaper into his hands. 'Read that, pal!'

Arthur read out loud the bold black headline: MID-LANDS BLACK-MARKET RINGLEADER SHOT DEAD.

'It's HIM!' Malc exclaimed to wide-eyed Arthur. 'It's the swine of a husband that Violet married.'

'It can't be!'

'Read on,' Malc urged.

In a tight tense voice Arthur did as he was told:

In a massive crack-down Midlands Police arrested several black-market operators in Coventry and Birmingham. Thirty-two-year-old Ronnie Walsh from the Edgwick area of Coventry was shot dead whilst trying to wound a police officer, who tragically died of fatal knife wounds some hours later.

Arthur looked up and asked sharply, 'Have you told Vi?'

Malc shook his head. 'No,' he answered quickly.

Unable to take in the information, Arthur looked at the newspaper and shook his head. 'We're supposed to be moving to Scotland on Friday,' he muttered incredulously.

Malc grinned as he clapped Arthur warmly on the shoulder. 'Looks like there's no reason for you to move now!' he laughed. 'Some good news at last.'

In a daze of disbelief, Arthur took Violet to his garden during their dinner break. On a bench he'd cobbled together from old ammunition crates, he showed her the newspaper article, which she read slowly once ... then twice ... then she shook her head.

'He won't be dead, Arthur!' she angrily declared. 'I've fallen for that before.'

He looked at her in disbelief. 'His name's right here in black and white,' Arthur insisted as he pointed to the large headlines. 'Thirty-two-year-old Ronnie Walsh from Edgwick, but originally from the Wood End area of Coventry, was shot dead – it's him!' he cried as he grasped her hand and kissed it. 'He's dead, Vi!'

'That's what I thought before,' she cried bitterly, 'when I read in the newspaper that all the residents of Sawley Avenue in Wood End were dead.' She sighed as she fought back tears. 'Look how wrong I was – all the time he was alive and he found me and nearly killed me.'

Arthur, agitated beyond words, kept pointing to the headlines. 'But here it says his name – Ronnie Walsh, written large for all to see.'

Seeing her stricken face, Arthur dropped the paper and took her in his arms.

'I understand my sweetheart,' he whispered as he stroked her silky long hair.

Staring out across the peaceful garden, fragrant with the last of the summer roses and ripe autumn fruit, Violet said quietly, 'Will you take me to Coventry, Arthur?'

'Of course, my love,' he answered as he lifted her face to his and kissed her lips.

When Arthur explained Violet's sorry predicament, Mr Featherstone looked distinctly fed up.

'I'm not running a holiday camp!' he snapped. 'Young Kit Murphy has disappeared off to Ireland and shows no sign of coming back, and now you want a morning off too!'

'I'll get us both back for our afternoon shift,' Arthur promised. 'It's only Coventry, Mr Featherstone, not t'other side of the moon!'

The short, dumpy factory manager swayed thoughtfully from his toes to his heels; he had a lot of time for Arthur Leadbetter, a war hero who did a good job safeguarding his munitions workers.

'All right,' he agreed. 'But you'd better not miss clocking on for your afternoon shift!' he added grumpily.

Word of Violet's news had been passed around amongst her friends, so when Edna drove her blue van into the dispatch yard Gladys was eagerly waiting to talk to her.

'Is it a sin to celebrate somebody's death?' she asked guiltily.

'Not in this case, lovie,' Edna said as she lit up a Player's. 'Good riddance to bad bloody rubbish!'

'The more I hear about Ronnie, the more shocked I am that our lovely Violet could ever have been married to scum like him,' Gladys said.

'No wonder she was scared stiff of Arthur to start with.'

'When Kit gets back from Ireland, it'll be just like old times,' Edna said with a smile. 'You, Violet and Kit back where you belong,' she chuckled as she added, 'With a bit of luck you might even get down to some regular rehearsals; you'll certainly need to before your show in London.'

For a change Gladys had another more pressing thought than band practices. Dropping her voice to a whisper she muttered, 'Kit's in trouble. Malc told me that

Featherstone's really fed up with her exceeding her official leave.'

'There's got to be a good reason, Glad,' Edna replied, finding it increasingly hard to keep her young friend's secret. Why wasn't the girl back with her boy in hand? 'Kit would never disobey orders – something serious must have happened over there. I only wish I knew what it might be . . .'

32. Chapelizod

After Kit had eaten a little something and briefly rested, she and Ian set about searching the city in a more systematic fashion. Putting the Dublin docklands behind them, they decided to split up at Ha'penny Bridge.

'I'll cross the River Liffey and walk through the other side of the city, whilst you stay this side of the river,' Ian suggested.

Kit looked uncertain.

'We must make the best of the time we've got, sweetheart,' he urged. 'Meet me back at the hotel by suppertime.'

Going their separate ways, they peeped into every pram they passed and scrutinized babies carried in their parents' arms. It was as Ian had imagined: a thankless task. People got annoyed at his interfering questions, whilst others were prepared to gab for hours about their child's amazing achievements. Passing the Jameson Distillery, Ian felt in desperate need of a drink, but he kept on going until he came to a park, where he sat on a bench to get his breath back.

'Where could the little boy be?' he thought for well over the hundredth time. Was he suffering? Was he being taken care of? The long-drawn-out legal exchanges couldn't have helped – they further prolonged Billy's time in the convent nursery, where they'd all believed that at least he would be safe; but now, thought Ian, he could be anywhere. Yet again Ian had a strong feeling that Murphy alone couldn't have executed the plan to steal Billy. It would take complicated arrangements to get a child out of the convent, out of the country and across the Atlantic to a new life with a new name and new parents in America, if indeed that was the plan. Sighing, Ian got to his feet and continued along the Liffey, hoping that Kit might be having better luck.

Outside St Patrick's Cathedral, Kit wondered whether to turn right or left. If she hadn't been so beset by fear and worry, she might have enjoyed the beautiful city, but all she could see everywhere she looked were images of Billy's weeping face. As she stood uncertainly, she spotted Mr O'Rourke crossing the street and walking directly towards her.

'Oh, no!' she groaned as he approached her with his face set in an unctuous smile.

'Miss Murphy! What a surprise,' he gushed. Kit cringed as he grasped her hand. 'My deepest commiserations,' he added in a low voice. 'Mother Gabriel informed me of the child's tragic disappearance.'

Snatching her hand free, Kit moved away from the odious man. 'Are you helping with police inquiries?' she asked curtly.

'Mother Gabriel has instructed me to deal with the police, and with Mr and Mrs Garland, the adoptive party, who have returned to America,' O'Rourke smugly replied.

Kit took a sharp breath. If O'Rourke was in contact with the American couple, he would certainly know where they lived.

'Will you be paying them a visit?' Kit asked sharply.

'I'm sure that won't be necessary,' he responded as he avoided eye contact with her.

Feeling angry enough to hit him, Kit brusquely turned her back on O'Rourke, her skin prickling as she felt his eyes following her as she walked away.

Hurrying by Christ Church Cathedral and the Guinness fermentation plant, Kit's heart began to sink. What she wanted to do was to run into every house and search all the rooms, turn the place upside down just in case somebody had hidden Billy under the bed or in the shed. The thought that he could be anywhere was beginning to drive her mad. She peered into windows, thinking to herself, 'Is he here, or here, or here?' When she saw cars whizz by with a child on board, she ran to see if the passenger was Billy. Drivers looked at her as if she was insane, but Kit didn't care; she had to check everything, and she had to be sure she hadn't missed any vital clues.

Weary and foot-sore, Kit came across a little Catholic church close to St Kevin's Hospital. Dipping her hand into the stoup, she blessed herself with holy water, then went inside. By the light of flickering candles, Kit passed several statues until she reached the statue of the Sacred Heart, before which she knelt and buried her head in her hands.

'Sweet Jesus,' she prayed as tears streamed down her face, 'look after my son. Please keep him safe . . . please lead me to him . . . please let him be alive.'

She could go no further: words failed her, and all she could do was to kneel and sob. Before she left, Kit lit three candles, which flickered into life as she closed the church door and wiped the tears from her eyes.

When Ian and Kit met at suppertime in the hotel, Ian was on his second whisky and soda. He knew immediately from the weary expression on Kit's face that her search had been as fruitless as his. Greeting her with a kiss, he sat her down by the fire in the dining room and rubbed her cold hands.

'Would you like a drink?' he asked.

Kit shook her head.

'Let's order dinner,' he said.

Kit nodded, even though she felt sick to her stomach.

Over a bowl of leek and potato soup, they swopped notes on their separate searches.

'So, nothing, apart from bumping into Mr O'Rourke, which I could have done without,' Kit muttered angrily as she stirred her soup, which had turned cold.

Feeling tired and helpless, Ian leant across the table to take her hand. 'We'll go to Chapelizod tomorrow,' he reminded her. 'We might have more luck there if your father has gone back home.'

The following morning, as Arthur and Violet drove down the A6 to Coventry, Kit and Ian, in the car that he'd hired for their stay in Dublin, drove into the Fitzwilliam estate.

Mr Murphy was indeed at home, and not at all happy to see his daughter or her lawyer friend.

'What the feck are you doin' here?' he said as he stood barring their way into his cottage.

Loathing her father more than she'd ever thought possible, Kit didn't waste time on niceties. 'Billy's gone missing.'

'And what's that to do with me?'

'Quite a lot, according to Mother Gabriel,' Kit retorted.

'The owd bitch sent the police snooping round here; they found nothing to nail on me.'

'Apart from the fact that you were in the convent the night that Billy was taken,' Ian coldly pointed out.

'You're welcome to look for the little bastard,' Murphy mocked. 'The police found nothing, but, if you want to waste your time, feel free.'

Kit clenched her fists so tight her nails cut into her flesh; she had an overwhelming urge to grab her father around the neck and choke the truth out of him. Ian, on another trajectory, continued to challenge Murphy, who remained as cocky as a rooster.

'You do realize that if we were to find Billy in a place where you had concealed him, you would be charged with unlawful abduction.'

'To hell with you and your fancy feckin' talk,' Murphy cursed. 'If it weren't for my whore of a daughter, opening her legs to the lord of the manor, we wouldn't be up to our necks in trouble.'

Before Ian could stop her, Kit flew at her father. Small she might have been, but with a temper on her she was like a wild cat who'd found her cub missing.

'You pig!' she screamed as she repeatedly pummelled his chest with her fists. 'FITZWILLIAM RAPED ME!'

'Bejesus, he did!' Murphy sneered as he landed his fist in her face.

Ian was on Murphy in a second; twisting his arm up behind his back, he cried, 'Touch Catherine again and I'll break your neck!'

'Get off my feckin' land!' Murphy roared. 'Piss off and never come back!'

Ignoring the blood streaming down her cheek and the bruise blooming over her right eye, Kit stood before her father. 'May you rot in hell for what you've done to me and my son.'

Murphy sneered at his elder daughter. 'You might thank me one day.'

Kit paled; she well knew that evil look in her father's eyes. 'What have you done now?' she gasped.

'Me?' he taunted her. 'I don't need to do anything.' He tapped the side of his nose and winked. 'Why would I when I've got connections in high places?'

Knowing how much her father loved to exaggerate his links with the gentry, Kit laughed in his face. 'Connections?' she mocked. 'Who are you kidding?'

Before another fight broke out, Ian led Kit to the car, which he drove away at speed, keen to put a distance between Kit and her now raging father. As he approached the elaborate metal gates that displayed the Fitzwilliam family coat-of-arms, Fitzwilliam himself came riding by on a large dapple-grey horse. His curious eyes landed on Kit, to whom he doffed his cap as he mouthed a lascivious kiss. The sight of him salaciously greeting his girlfriend in this way sent Ian into a frenzy of anger he'd never before experienced.

'You unutterable swine!' he roared as he slammed on the hand brake and leapt from the car.

Standing before scowling Fitzwilliam, Ian reached up and dragged him off his horse. Crying out in fury, Fitzwilliam started beating Ian around the head with his leather riding whip.

'Who the bloody hell do you think you are?' he

bellowed as he lunged at the younger and much stronger man. 'How dare you lay your filthy hands on me?'

Kit, who was out of the car and watching the on-going fight in horror, cried out, 'STOP, IAN! STOP!'

Oblivious to her voice, Ian saw red as his blood boiled in rage. Punching Fitzwilliam hard in the face, he yelled, 'How dare I touch you? Look at the young woman you raped!'

Twisting the overweight man around, he forced him to face Kit, who shrank away in disgust.

'You left her pregnant!' Ian cried.

Swinging round, Fitzwilliam gave Ian a hefty punch in the stomach before raining blows around his head. 'I'll do what I want on my own land, you cocky English bastard!'

'Then remember this next time you rape another innocent girl,' Ian snarled as he crashed his fist into Fitzwilliam, sending him reeling to the ground, where he writhed in pain.

'Holy Mother of GOD!' Kit wailed as she pulled Ian back to the car. 'For pity's sake, let's get out of here,' she implored.

'I'll kill him!' Ian raged as he tried to run back. 'I'll break every bone in his body!'

Knowing that Fitzwilliam had the local gardaí in his pocket, Kit all but wrestled him into the driving seat, then slammed the door hard. As she ran around to the passenger seat, she shouted, 'For the love of God – will you get the hell out of here!'

As Kit and Ian drove away from Chapelizod, Arthur and Violet walked into Coventry Police Station, where Violet sought proof of her husband's death. The policeman behind the desk said, 'Ronnie Walsh's body's in the morgue; as his wife you've every right to see it.'

Violet gasped. She'd somehow imagined that he'd show her a photograph of Ronnie's dead body, or produce his gold watch with his initials on the back.

'The body!'

'There's no better proof that somebody's dead,' the policeman said grimly.

Seeing Violet about to decline the invitation, Arthur caught her by the arm.

'Mrs Walsh would like to see her husband's body,' he said firmly.

As they were led along echoing corridors, Violet whispered nervously, 'I don't think I can go through with this, Arthur.'

'We're not living in fear for the rest of our lives,' he answered. 'Today we lay Ronnie's ghost to rest.'

Once inside the bleak and chilly morgue, the policeman passed along several bodies, all draped in white sheets, lying on stretchered trolleys.

'This is Ronnie Walsh,' he said as he read a ticket attached to Ronnie's big toe. 'I'll leave you to it,' he added as he left the room.

'It's got to be done, Vi,' Arthur said as he gripped Violet firmly by the hand and lifted the sheet to reveal a very white and waxy naked man.

Violet smothered a cry with her gloved hand. 'Oh, dear God' she cried as she saw the gun wound to Ronnie's temple and his wide gaping mouth.

Determined to see the grim business through to the end, Arthur asked, 'Are you sure it's him?'

246

Violet nodded.

'Certain? No doubts?' he persisted.

'No doubts at all.'

Turning trembling Violet to face him, Arthur said with steely purpose, 'Ronnie can never come back, Vi. Your husband is well and truly dead.'

Violet took the end of the sheet from Arthur's grip and threw it back over Ronnie.

'GOOD!' she shouted, and, turning her back on the man she hated, she walked out of the morgue and into a new life.

Kit and Ian arrived back at their Dublin hotel covered in cuts and bruises. Not wanting to be seen, Ian hurried Kit to his room, where he bathed their wounds with warm water.

'Jesus, Mary and Joseph!' Kit cried as he washed her bruised cheek. 'Why did you have to lay into Fitzwilliam? He could have you whipped and imprisoned.'

'He's not God Almighty, Kit, whatever your family and the other estate workers may think. He's an overweight, self-seeking rapist!' He drew in a breath as he continued. 'The way he looked at you, the leering, salacious, dirty old man. He would have taken you again if he'd had his way.' Seething, he dipped the soft cloth in the warm water. 'I would have torn him apart if you hadn't pulled me away.'

'I could see that!' Kit exclaimed.

'I've never actually wanted to kill a man before,' Ian confessed. 'The thought of him touching you, forcing his ugly bloated body on you.' He stroked a finger over her bruised cheekbone as he murmured with tears in his eyes, 'My sweet innocent Catherine.'

Kit took his hand in hers and kissed it. 'Ian, my love, it's over with now: let the past stay in the past. We've got to focus on Billy. We've got to find him,' she added desperately.

Gazing into her earnest, pleading face, Ian nodded in agreement. 'You're right,' he said. 'Fitzwilliam, God damn his soul, is history. Billy is the priority now.'

A knock at the door startled them both.

'Telegram, sir,' said the porter when Ian opened the door.

Ian glanced at the name on the envelope. 'It's for you, darling,' he said as he handed it to her. The wording was brief:

GET BACK TO PENDLETON NOW YOU'RE IN BIG
TROUBLE WITH THE BOSS GLADYS

Kit scrunched the telegram into a ball. 'I am NOT leaving until we find Billy!' she declared angrily.

'Even if it takes weeks?' he asked.

Sticking out her chin, Kit said defiantly, 'YES!'

Ian sighed. He knew from the mutinous look on her face that he was in for a fight. 'If a soldier went AWOL during a battle, he'd be court-martialled,' he started. "You can't walk away, Catherine.'

'There are compassionate reasons for me staying!' she cried angrily. 'It's not like I'm on holiday – my son has been stolen – does compassionate leave cover that?' Slumping back on to the bed, she wailed, 'How can I abandon Billy?'

Ian took out his handkerchief and tenderly wiped away

her tears. 'Darling,' he said softly, 'I'm going to stay here and search for Billy.'

'On your own?' she asked in surprise.

Ian shook his head. 'No, I'm going to employ a private detective.'

'A private detective!' Kit gasped.

'I'll give him all the leads we have so far: your father, Mother Gabriel and the Garlands too. That's a good few to start with.'

'O'Rourke needs watching!' Kit cried. 'He's like a snake,' she gave a little shudder. 'There's something about the man that makes my skin creep.'

'I intend to keep an eye on O'Rourke personally,' Ian assured her.

Kit leant her head against his shoulder. 'Let me stay, Ian, please let me help you,' she implored.

'Sweetest girl,' he said as he kissed her quivering lips, 'the longer you're away from the Phonix, the harder it will be to go back. Believe me, it's the right thing to do.'

Kit sighed. She'd imagined quite another triumphant return home, accompanied by the two 'men' in her life. Now she would have to make that miserable journey back across the sea with all her hopes dashed and without the baby she yearned for and the support of the man she loved.

33. Home

Violet and Arthur raced back from Coventry and clocked on for their shift with only five minutes to spare. When they walked into the canteen arm in arm and wreathed in smiles, everybody knew the news was good. Malc, who was waiting with Myrtle and Gladys said, 'Is he . . .' Unable to say the word, he winked. 'You know . . .'

'DEAD?' Violet asked.

Malc nodded.

'We saw him in the morgue,' Violet told him. 'Like the policeman who accompanied us said, "You can't get deader than that!"'

A loud irreverent cheer rang out. 'That's the best news I've heard in weeks!' laughed Malc.

'She's a free woman,' Arthur said happily.

'At last,' Violet added. 'Is it wrong to feel so relieved?'

Myrtle considered her question. 'I would say it's a gift from God,' she replied. 'He's relieved you of your misery.'

Violet leant over to kiss Myrtle's plump cheek. 'Thank you, Myrtle – you make me feel so much better!'

Kit's crossing back to England couldn't have been more different from the happy one she had so enjoyed on the way out with Ian. Autumn weather had set in, and the rain poured from low grey clouds that churned the waters of the Irish Sea. The medication that had worked so well previously barely touched Kit this time: she was sick throughout the entire journey. Worse than that, she ached for Billy and for all the shattered dreams of the home journey she'd imagined. And for Ian too, whom she'd clung to at the port. Why was it always her destiny to leave Dublin with a heart as heavy as lead? As fellow passengers jostled by, Kit had disentangled herself from Ian, who had kissed her for the last time.

'I'll be back soon with good news, I hope. I'll do everything in my power to get that boy of yours back, I promise.' he'd said solemnly.

'I love you more than I can say,' Kit whispered as she picked up her suitcase and walked up the gangplank like a woman condemned by pirates to drown.

The gangplank was drawn up and the ship slowly pulled away from its moorings. Leaning over the railing, Kit waved to Ian until his beloved face was nothing more than a blur.

Though exhausted by their long hard day, neither Arthur nor Violet was ready for bed.

'Let's take a short walk on the moors,' Arthur suggested.

'Blow the cobwebs away,' Violet joked and slipped an arm through his.

After being cooped up all day, the air was sweet and refreshing. Lengthening their stride, they made their way along sheep tracks that led up to a flat wide crag surrounded by heather. In silence they sat together listening to the cackle of scurrying pheasants and the lonely call of the curlew.

It was Violet who broke the easy companionable silence, 'You know Arthur, I want to live in this area for the rest of my life. I've never known such peace as I have here on these lovely moors.'

'I don't mind where I live as long as I always have you beside me, darling Violet,' Arthur replied.

Violet passionately kissed his beautiful mouth and stroked his strong stubbly jaw line.

'You need a shave!' she joked.

Grabbing her around the waist, he squeezed her to his chest. 'I need YOU!' he teased.

When they finally, rather breathlessly drew apart, Arthur reached for her left hand.

'I bought this for you to wear in Scotland,' he said softly as he slipped a glittering ring on to her wedding finger. 'I wanted you to have a ring on your finger when we moved up there.'

'So people wouldn't think we were living in sin?' she guessed.

He nodded then added, 'And because I love you.'

Violet gazed in wonder at the pearls and diamonds mounted on a golden band.

'Oh, Arthur! It's beautiful,' she murmured.

'Hold on a minute, there's more,' he said, and with a laugh quickly went down on one knee before her. 'Now that you're free, Violet, my sweetest Violet . . . please will you marry me?'

Bursting with happiness, Violet all but threw herself on Arthur, and, clutching each other, they laughed with joy as they rolled on to the heather.

'YES! YES! YES!' she cried in between planting kisses on his nose, his mouth and his eyes. 'Yes, a thousand times over,' she declared.

'Mrs Arthur Leadbetter,' he said playing with the sound of the name.

'Mrs Arthur Leadbetter,' she echoed his words.

'To have and to hold,' he said as he pulled her on top of him and squeezed her tight.

'Till death us do part,' Violet said gently as she sank into the ecstasy of her fiancé's deep, long kisses.

Heartbroken Kit returned to the cowshed the next day to find Gladys washing her hair in the bathroom.

'KIT! KIT!' she cried when she saw her friend. 'Did you get my telegram?'

Kit nodded but could barely speak. When Gladys saw her face running with tears, she quickly grabbed a towel and hurried towards her.

'Kit!' she cried again. 'What's the matter?' she asked anxiously.

Seeing Kit starting to tremble, Gladys led her to the sofa and settled her close to the crackling wood-burning stove, where Kit immediately lit up a Woodbine.

'I need to tell you something, Glad,' Kit started. 'And Violet too.' Her voice dropped and she started to cry all over again. 'But she's probably not here any more,' she wailed.

'She is!' Gladys retorted. 'She didn't go to Scotland after all!' Gladys yelled, 'VIOLET!'

Still in her nightdress, Violet ran into the sitting room. At the sight of Kit, her face broke into a radiant smile, but when she saw her friend's stricken expression she rushed to her, crying, 'What's happened to you, sweetheart?'

With her dearest friends on either side of her, Kit started her story.

'I have a son, a nine-month-old baby boy called Billy.'

'A baby!' Violet cried.

Relieved that she could finally speak the truth, Kit poured out her tragic story – at the end of which, both her friends, who were doing their best to comfort their stricken friend, were in tears too.

'We could have helped each other so much if we'd shared our secrets instead of keeping them to ourselves,' Violet said regretfully. 'I never told anybody about Ronnie. I was so ashamed of running away from him and keeping my identity a secret, and look what happened . . . it nearly killed me.'

'The truth will out eventually,' Gladys said wisely.

'I kept too much to myself too,' Kit confessed. 'I was afraid you'd think I was a loose woman with no morals.'

'As if we would have ever thought that!' Violet exclaimed. 'Everybody's got something hidden in their past, however small. Nobody's perfect.'

As huge sobs ripped through her body, Kit cried out in an agony of pain. 'God help me! I thought I was going back to Ireland to pick up my baby, but now I might never see him again.'

34. Penance

Left with a broken tooth and a black eye, not to mention his wounded pride, Lionel Fitzwilliam was determined to take revenge on somebody, and that somebody was his tenant, Murphy. At the sight of Kit's father doffing his cap obsequiously to him, Fitzwilliam ran into his garden in a rage and hit Murphy repeatedly in the face before he threw him on his back and kicked him hard in the ribcage.

'Take that – and that – and that for your bitch of a daughter!' he yelled.

Curled up in a ball of pain, Murphy begged for mercy, but Fitzwilliam had only just started. Barging into the cottage, he reappeared bearing an armful of bedding and clothes, which he threw on to the ground before re-entering the house. Five minutes later clouds of smoke emerged.

'NO! NO!' screamed Murphy as he ran towards the open door, which Fitzwilliam blocked with his broad bulky body.

'This house's not fit for sewer rats!'

Seeing the flames, Rosie and her younger brothers came running in from the fields.

'Somebody help us!' Rosie screamed as the fire took out the roof and the house caved in.

Fitzwilliam sneered at the distraught weeping family.

'Get off my land and never show your faces round here again!'

Speechless with shock, they watched him walk away – then the youngest boy burst into floods of tears.

'Where will we go now, Rosie?' he said, turning in bewilderment to his big sister, who shook her head in despair. 'What'll we do?'

Seeing her devastated younger brothers and her home in ruins, Rosie, blazing with anger, turned on her father. 'You have cursed this family!' she cried. 'You killed Ma with your beatings,' she screamed. 'You sold Kit's baby, an innocent helpless child, for a pot of gold.' Lowering her voice, she added, 'You're as bad a traitor as Judas himself. You'll go to hell for your sins!'

In Dublin, Ian and his private detective, Ross Dunleavy, had so far drawn blanks on all their leads.

'I'm beginning to think the worst,' Ian confessed as they sat in a local pub drinking pints of Guinness.

'Which is?' asked Dunleavy.

'Billy's long gone with the American couple.'

Dunleavy wiped froth from the stout off his upper lip. 'Do you want me to extend the search to New York?' he suggested.

Ian thoughtfully lit up a Pall Mall cigarette. 'My instincts tell me not to do that until we know for sure we've really closed the door on finding Billy in Ireland.'

'Much as I've enjoyed working with you, sir, I'd say you'd be throwing good money after bad.'

'I'm going to pay Murphy one more visit before I leave,' Ian said as he recalled Kit's father's mean, conniving face.

'Could the old bastard be hiding something there? An address, a name, a number?'

'You're wasting your time on him, man, and on O'Rourke too,' Dunleavy retorted. 'You've got nowhere with either fella.'

Ian took a deep slug of his Guinness. 'Humph!' he snorted, more annoyed with himself than with Dunleavy for his comments.

Nevertheless, before he booked his passage home to England, Ian drove to Chapelizod, where he firmly told himself that if he had the misfortune to bump into Fitzwilliam again, he would exercise more self-control than on his previous visit. When he pulled up outside the Murphys' house, he was stunned to see it reduced to a heap of cold ashes.

'What happened here?' he asked a passing neighbour.

'The big man lost his temper and kicked the Murphys off his land,' the neighbour replied.

'Where did they go?' Ian asked.

'The young ones went west, to find work in Tipperary.'

'And the father?' Ian asked. 'Where did he go?'

The man shrugged. 'Nobody knows. Somebody else came looking for Murphy: a big fancy legal man, he said he was.'

Intrigued Ian asked, 'Did he have a name?'

The neighbour reached into his pocket and pulled out a slip of paper.

'He left this, said I was to call him if I heard anything about Murphy's whereabouts. Gave me a shilling for mi troubles too.'

Completely amazed, Ian read out loud:

'Do you know the man?'

'Yes,' Ian said through gritted teeth. 'Yes, I damn well do!'

Back in Dublin, Ian was aflame with righteous anger. Deep down, he'd known all along that somewhere along the line O'Rourke had been involved. He just had to be the link – but you had to hand it to him, he was devious enough not to get his hands dirty. He'd left thieving Murphy to do the dirty work whilst he handled the seemingly respectable side of things.

If he was to expose O'Rourke, he realized he urgently need Mother Gabriel's help. Hurrying to the convent, he had to wait for her to finish mass with the rest of her order; then she joined him in the chilly visitors' room. When she entered, Ian leapt to his feet.

'I think O'Rourke is connected to the theft of Billy,' he blurted out.

After he'd told the shocked Mother Superior all that he knew, Ian said, 'Do you know where the Garlands can be contacted?'

She shook her head. 'As God is my judge, I have no address for them,' she replied as she laid her hand on the large crucifix that lay against her chest. 'O'Rourke handled that side of the business.'

'I bet he did,' Ian seethed under his breath. Turning to the Mother Superior, he asked, 'Is it at all possible that the Garland couple could still be in Ireland?'

Mother Gabriel thought long and hard. 'O'Rourke told me that they'd left some time ago in great sadness and disappointment.'

'It might not be the truth,' Ian pointed out.

'We put them up in a nice family hotel, close to the convent,' she recalled. 'You could check with the proprietor, a nice young woman and a good Catholic too,' she added. 'She might be able to shed some light on the Garlands' comings and goings.'

'Thank you, Mother Gabriel, I'll do that,' Ian replied.

The 'good Catholic' woman who ran the family business recognized the photograph of O'Rourke that Ian had had the foresight to cut out of a legal magazine he'd found in the local library.

'Did you ever have dealings with this man when the Garlands arrived from America in the hope of adopting one of the convent babies?' he began.

'Oh, yes, for sure,' she retorted.

'Have you seen him or the Garlands again recently?' he continued.

'They were here all the while they were waiting for the adoption to go through, but then something went wrong and they left in a heartbroken state, poor souls.' She sighed heavily. 'Mr O'Rourke spent a lot of time with them at the end of their stay, even drove them to the port himself to take their ship home.'

'Did they leave with a child?' Ian asked.

'No, sir! The missis, she told me that the mother of the child had changed her mind at the last minute and kept the baby to herself. Terrible to drag them all the way over the water to Ireland and then send 'em back empty-handed.'

'They must have been devastated,' Ian commented.

'They were for sure, although Mr O'Rourke had a cheery effect on them, I overheard him say to them more than once, "Leave it with me." I took it into my head that he was going to sort everything out for them. I hope so: they were that desperate for a child, God love 'em.'

Ian left the family hotel and walked along the windy banks of the River Liffey to clear his thoughts, but O'Rourke's smooth assuring words rang loud in his head: 'Leave it with me.'

Ian knew that, since then, O'Rourke had paid a mysterious visit to Kit's father, who was indisputably involved in Billy's disappearance. Could it be that O'Rourke had sent the Garlands back to the States with hope in their disappointed hearts? Could O'Rourke be on one end of the deal and Murphy on the other? Were they working in tandem, running rings around Mother Gabriel, Kit and himself too? If so, where was Billy now?

After she'd clocked on, Gladys dashed to her pigeon-hole, where she found a letter from her father.

We heard from the War Office today. There's no easy way to tell you this, love, but our Les has been reported missing in action in Belgium. Come home as soon as you can, you mother is distraught.

Ever loving,
Dad

Gladys's heart skipped a beat. Intuitively she'd always known this moment was coming. At first she felt relief that the letter didn't say 'Killed in Action'; 'Missing in Action' could mean anything! Shot, wounded, imprisoned, hiding in a hedgerow. Her head whirled with all sorts of terrifying images. It was at least five months since Les had been in touch with his family, and anything could have happened to him in that time. Guilty that she hadn't visited her parents earlier, she vowed she'd take a long-overdue day off and go to Leeds as soon as she could. As she hurried into the filling shed, she wondered what she could do to help her stricken mother. She had a sudden thought: some of Les's pals from the Yorkshire Regiment might still be stationed at the barracks. Though she knew all soldiers were warned 'Loose Lips Costs Lives', Gladys decided she'd visit the barracks anyway; someone just might know something that would give Gladys and her parents hope and pity her enough to tell her.

It was terribly hard to focus on her work in the filling shed. Beside her, Violet sang along to *Workers' Playtime*, chuckling over Arthur Askey's slightly smutty jokes, but Gladys's thoughts were elsewhere. Knowing Les would want her to carry on as normal, Gladys forced herself to concentrate on the job in hand, when all the time her instinct was to run out of the factory and jump on the first bus into Leeds, where she knew she was desperately needed by her parents.

It was a relief for Gladys when Kit joined her and Violet after her meeting with Mr Featherstone. Sitting glumly beside her friends, Kit appeared lost and withdrawn. Gladys and Violet exchanged anxious glances as Kit automatically stuffed one fuse case after another with gunpowder.

'What did Featherstone have to say?' Violet asked gently.

Kit's eyes filled with tears. 'When I told him my baby had been stolen, and I was delayed in Ireland searching for him, he looked shocked but he still read me the riot act because I'd extended my compassionate leave without official permission,' Kit replied with a scowl.

Relieved that it sounded as if there would be no unpleasant repercussions for her friend, Violet said, 'You got off pretty lightly, then, I reckon.'

Kit shrugged. 'I'd risk disobeying orders – even if it meant I had to go to prison – if there was the slightest chance of getting my Billy back,' she said sadly.

After having his home burnt down in front of him and his children abandon him, Murphy had taken to sleeping rough in hedgerows and stealing eggs and spuds from local farms when he could get away with it. As the wet weather set in, he became weak and hungry; then, after collapsing on the road to Dublin, he was taken unconscious to the workhouse. Lying on a truckle bed covered with a greasy old blanket, Murphy recalled Rosie's departing words to him.

'You sold Kit's baby, an innocent helpless child, for a pot of gold. You're as bad a traitor as Judas himself. You'll go to hell for your sins!'

Haunted by both his daughters' curses, Murphy asked to see a priest. After hearing his confession the priest said, 'You have sinned gravely, my son. Your penance is to recompense those whom you have wilfully harmed.'

Murphy nodded; it was time to pay a final visit to Mother Gabriel.

*

Meanwhile, Ian was still in Dublin. With the O'Rourke revelation unravelling, he delayed his return passage, even though he felt guilty about not returning to Kit as he'd promised. Leaving now whilst he was hot on the trail would be disastrous. He decided to visit Mother Gabriel and share his thoughts before visiting O'Rourke himself. He hoped she'd help him fill in any missing pieces of the jigsaw before he took the next step. After he'd told her what he'd found out from the family-hotel landlady and what he ultimately suspected, Mother Gabriel fell quiet.

'Well, I have to say, Mr McIvor,' she finally said, ''tis a bit far flung if you ask me. Mr O'Rourke has been helping us for years; he's never put a foot wrong so far.'

'I agree it sounds far-fetched,' he replied immediately. 'But think about it: we originally feared Billy might have been taken straight to New York – that's the idea we've been working with. But what if O'Rourke realized that course of action was too risky? What if he thought it was safer to hide the child for a few weeks and then smuggle him out of the country when the heat's off? He could have paid Murphy to steal the child because he knows his way around the convent. And then it's just possible, isn't it, that between them they've found somewhere to hide Billy until it's safe to steal him away?' Ian looked animated now, more sure than ever that he might be on to something.

'But the Garlands wouldn't go along with such an underhand scheme. They were a decent law-abiding couple,' Mother Gabriel insisted.

'But what if they have no idea that they're behaving illegally?' Ian persisted. 'O'Rourke's a legal adviser, remember; they've been liaising with him all along, a fine upstanding man of the law who's manipulating them, misadvising them, to his own ends. We know the cock-and-bull story that Murphy spun you: it's convincing if you don't know the facts. He could have spun the same line to the Garlands, who, like you, believed that he has only his grandson's best interests at heart.'

'So you think the child's still here in Ireland?' Mother Gabriel asked.

Ian nodded, feeling physically sick just thinking of where Billy might be holed up.

'That's the feeling I have,' he admitted. 'We've been looking just in case he is still here, but now that we have a better idea of what might be going on, I hope we'll have more luck. If only we knew who might be hiding the child!' he cried. 'We know for sure Murphy would dump him on anyone, but O'Rourke would be more careful of the boy's wellbeing, don't you think? If he was planning to smuggle him out of the country with a false name and a false passport, it would be in his interests that the child was healthy when he handed him over to the Garlands on his arrival in New York.'

Mother Gabriel broke into his thoughts. 'This is all supposition, Mr McIvor,' she reminded him sharply.

'I know, I know,' he agreed with a heavy sigh. 'I've been going on my instincts since I first laid eyes on O'Rourke. All I'm asking of you is to spread the word of Billy's disappearance. Do you have a picture of him?' he asked.

Mother Gabriel nodded. 'We take photographs of all the babies we put up for adoption,' she answered.

'Then please display the photograph of Billy in your

church and ask parishioners if they've seen him. Keep the community aware of a missing baby boy,' he begged. 'And leave O'Rourke to me.'

'And what have you told the poor young mother?' Mother Gabriel demanded.

'Nothing,' Ian confessed guiltily. 'I'll phone her tonight.'

35. Cursed

Ian phoned Edna and asked her to get Kit to phone him at his hotel at her earliest possible convenience.

'Is everything okay?' Edna asked nervously.

'I think I'm on to something, Edna,' he admitted. 'But I must talk to Kit right away. How is the poor girl? She must be worried sick.'

'Oh, she's that, all right,' Edna retorted. 'White as a sheet, hardly eating – we're all worried about her.'

Ian groaned into the phone. 'If only I could give her good news, just for once.'

Kit didn't get Ian's message until much later that night, when she'd finished her shift and had gone into the dispatch yard to have a cigarette with Edna, who was standing by her blue van.

'You need to phone Ian in Dublin,' her friend immediately told her. 'Jump in and I'll drop you off at the shop,' she said quickly.

When Ian's phone shrilled out in his hotel room, he steeled himself as he moved to pick it up. He wondered how on earth he was going to tell Kit what he now suspected. It was bad enough for her to accept that her son had been stolen, but now he was asking her to accept that on top of that Billy had most likely been taken to a place of hiding. 'This really is the stuff of nightmares,' he thought to himself.

'Darling!' he said when he heard her sweet earnest voice.

'What's the news, Ian?' she cried impatiently.

Taking a very deep breath, Ian told her everything. As he finished, he heard a sound like a suppressed sob.

'It's worse than I thought,' she murmured.

'Sweetheart, you must remember a large part of what I've just told you is what I've pieced together myself,' he quickly added.

'But it all makes sense,' she replied. 'O'Rourke, a pillar of the community, helping a disappointed couple and mi da doing whatever's asked of him for a back-hander.'

'Mother Gabriel's on our side,' Ian assured her. 'She's promised to put a photograph of Billy in the Church of the Sacred Heart to keep up an awareness of him in the local community.' Ian paused nervously before he added, 'There's something else, Catherine: I paid another visit to Chapelizod.'

After he'd told her about the fire and the information he'd got from the neighbour, there was a long silence on the end of the phone.

'Kit, darling, are you still there?' he asked anxiously.

Her voice sounded weak and strained as it came down the line. 'Now I have no home, no family and no son. I have NOTHING!' she sobbed.

'My love, you have me,' he whispered.

Kit's response was an angry one. 'Don't you see?' she cried hysterically. 'I'm worth nothing! You would be far better off if I were dead.'

'Catherine, you're upset, and no wonder. I'm upset too! These last few weeks have been too much for you to bear, and the fact that we have nothing to show after all our efforts is devastating, but that doesn't reflect on YOU.'

'Everything I touch turns to ashes,' she said in a strange faraway voice. 'The bad blood in my family courses through my veins, just as it does through my father's. That must be why God took Billy away.' She said the words as if she was talking to herself. 'He knew I'd be a bad mother, so He sent him somewhere far away from me.'

Wondering if she was losing her mind, Ian spoke softly. 'Darling, this is utter nonsense: you're over-wrought. I beg you to stop torturing yourself.'

Kit's voice came back cold and hard. 'I don't want to see you again, Ian. I love you too much to destroy your life like I have my own.'

'This is ridiculous!' he replied. 'You're overreacting, punishing yourself,' he insisted. 'You've done everything in your power to make your life good, but circumstances have prevented this. You can't turn me away on that basis.'

'I can, Ian, and I am. For your own sake, leave me alone!'

As the line went dead, Ian stared into the ear-piece. He'd gone too far, said too much, overloaded Kit's already fragile state of mind. What she'd said about her cursed family and bad blood was melodramatic Irish blarney, but it indicated to him that she was clearly disturbed. Panicking, he tried to phone her back but nobody picked up.

'DAMN! DAMN! DAMN!' he ranted as he paced the room.

No matter how close he was to unveiling O'Rourke's

plot, he couldn't remain in Dublin; he *had* to see Catherine. He had to make sure that his beloved wasn't on the point of losing her senses.

Neither Violet nor Gladys saw Kit after their shift finished. She said she had a headache and rushed off home. Violet held back to say goodbye to Gladys, who was finally going home to Leeds to visit her family.

'Good luck with your parents,' Violet said, squeezing her friend's hand as she and Arthur waved Gladys off on the last bus. 'Seeing you is sure to cheer them up, and I hope you get some news,' she added.

Gladys's face crumpled as she thought of her parents. 'I'm terrified, Vi,' she admitted. 'There's been nothing for so long – could Les really have survived?'

'Hundreds of prisoners on the run do,' Arthur answered confidently. 'Don't give up hope.'

'That's what I say every time I write to my parents, but it's hard to stay strong when you're on your own and thinking the worst,' she admitted.

'Come on now, Glad,' Violet said as she gave her a hug to send her on her way. 'Les wouldn't want you to give up hope.'

'You're right, Vi!' Gladys said as she waved them goodbye, then ran to catch her bus.

When she'd gone, Violet linked her arm through Arthur's and they walked for a few minutes in companionable silence.

'So, sweetheart,' he said as he held her close, 'when are we going to get married?'

'Now, tomorrow, right away!' she laughed. 'Imagine

sleeping with you every night,' she whispered. 'We could even start tonight,' she teased.

'Much as I'd love to, I'm only going to make love to you when you're my very own beautiful wife.'

Violet turned and kissed him passionately on the mouth.

'I can't wait much longer for you, Mr Wonderful Leadbetter – we should fix a date right now!' she declared.

Early the next morning, whilst Violet and Kit slept safely in their beds, Arthur was busy at work in the filling shed.

'Here he comes!' Ivy cackled to the girls working at her table. 'Why've you got a big smile on your face?' she cheekily asked.

'I might be getting married soon, Ivy,' Arthur announced proudly.

'Well, I hope she's good enough for you?' Ivy teased.

'Oh, she's more than good enough!' Arthur retorted.

Ivy nodded towards several trays at the end of the bench, all stacked with fuses awaiting collection.

'Do something useful,' Ivy joked with Arthur. 'Once I've stamped these fuses and got them into the trays, shift 'em out of the way, will you, lad?'

Ivy picked up the stamping machine which she used to imprint the date and batch number on all the filled fuse cases. As Arthur pushed the metal trolley he used to transport the fuses around the factory towards another bench some distance from Ivy, he had no idea that she was using – tragically unbeknownst to her too – a damaged machine. As the stamper hit a fuse stem in the wrong place, Ivy didn't have a split second to move before it exploded and immediately detonated all the other trays on her bench. Arthur watched helplessly as he was thrown backwards by the blast, seeing poor Ivy and the girls she'd tried to shield burn to death, before his eyes. Knowing the slightest wind or vibration could set off further detonations, Arthur scrambled to his feet and hollered at the top of his voice, 'OUT! OUT! EVERYBODY OUT!'

As severed sparking electric cables dangled precariously from the ceiling, the munitions workers ran screaming for their lives. Terrified for their safety, Arthur turned to Malc, who'd run into the filling shed when he heard the explosion.

'Get them right out of the area,' frantic Arthur cried. 'If there's another explosion the whole factory and everybody near it could go up in flames.'

As Malc herded the terrified women to safety, Arthur called after him, 'Come back as quickly as possible – I'm going to need your help.'

As fleets of fire engines dealt with the flames and toxic black smoke, ambulance crews carried out the dead and the wounded whilst the police guided the workers to safety.

'Don't come back till you hear the all-clear,' they told the munitions girls, who, scared they might get caught in another series of explosions, ran screaming in panic down the hill into Pendleton.

As soon as he was able, Malc rushed back into the factory to find Arthur, who'd gathered together a group of male volunteers. Looking white and tense, Arthur explained that they had to get all the fuse trays out of the Phoenix.

'You must be bloody joking, pal!' Malc exclaimed. 'We're talking about more than 12,000 fuses.'

'Exactly,' Arthur retorted. 'If they should ignite, we'll have an uncontrollable blaze that no number of fire engines could extinguish – the flames could even reach Pendleton. It's imperative that we get the fuses out of the building as quickly as possible.'

As fire workers continued to hose the flames that were now licking the factory roof, Arthur continued, 'We have to work swiftly. Carefully load all the fuse trays on to trolleys, then wheel them very slowly – don't bump them, they might explode – out of the factory.'

'Where do we take them?' an edgy volunteer asked.

'One of my duties as fire safety officer was to dig a large explosive pit for an eventuality such as this,' Arthur replied. 'It's in the field well beyond the dispatch yard.'

Hardly daring to breathe for fear of unbalancing the fuses in the trays, Malc, Arthur and the volunteers worked for over three hours trundling loaded trolleys out of the building, whilst the maintenance crew tried to deal with the exposed electric cables and collapsing interior walls.

'God Almighty!' Malc muttered as sweat poured off him.

Working carefully through the batches of fuses that the volunteers wheeled to the pit, Arthur discovered a batch of fuses with damaged stems. Used to handling live explosives, Arthur said to Malc, 'I'll take charge of this faulty batch – I'll remotely detonate them in another pit well away from this lot.'

'I'll come with you,' Malc said.

Arthur shook his head. 'Stay here with the others, and

make sure you stand well back – there'll be a hell of a bang!'

Arthur carefully carried the fuses on a tray to the detonation pit. Lying flat on his stomach, he stretched his arm as far as it would reach in order to gently lay each of the defective fuses deep inside the hole, where he planned to electronically detonate them. As he laid the last fuse, Arthur saw with a sinking heart a trickle of soft earth fall into the pit. He immediately tried to stem the flow with his hand but as he did so a new trickle started on the opposite side. Knowing that the falling earth would shift the position of the fuses, Arthur desperately tried to stretch wide to halt the new flow. But his frantic efforts were in vain. Just as he did so, a fuse disturbed by falling earth went off in his face.

Hearing a loud explosion Malc and the volunteers waited a good ten minutes for Arthur's return. When he didn't show up, pale-faced Malc stood up.

'Stay here, I'll check what's going on,' he commanded grimly.

He found an unconscious Arthur flat on his back with his hair singed and blood oozing from a head wound.

'Jesus God!' he cried. 'HELP! HELP!'

Malc and the volunteers carried Arthur into the dispatch yard, where an ambulance crew were still treating the wounded.

'The fire safety officer's taken a direct hit in the face,' Malc quickly told them, panicked. His voice broke into a sob as he gazed down at his wounded friend. 'For God's sake get him to the hospital!'

*

The first explosion, which killed Ivy and her team, had shaken the ground underneath the girls' beds. Confused and half asleep, they ran into the sitting room, where they saw, through the cowshed windows, flames licking the walls and roof of the Phoenix.

'Arthur's in there!' Violet wailed as she ran out of the door in her nightie.

Grabbing coats and shoes, Violet and Kit ran to the factory, where Violet stopped a woman in her tracks,

'What happened?' she cried.

'Nobody knows owt other than the fire started in't filling shed,' the woman gabbled.

'The filling shed,' Violet gasped in horror.

'We were told to run for it before the whole factory blew!' the woman added melodramatically.

Before Violet could detain her any longer the woman ran off.

'ARTHUR! ARTHUR!' Violet screamed.

As she bolted towards the factory, a burly policeman blocked her path.

'You should be running in the opposite direction, Miss,' he said. 'This is a danger zone.'

'My fiancé's in there,' Violet cried as she pointed at the blaze. 'I've got to find him.'

Seeing Kit and Gladys behind Violet, the policeman called out, 'Best take care of your friend before I have to lock her up for her own safety,' he warned. 'Get yourself down into Pendleton with the other lasses and wait there for the all-clear signal.'

Gladys and Kit half dragged Violet to Edna's chip shop.

Edna firmly sat her down in an armchair in the back room, where she gave her hot tea and a Woodbine.

'We'll get news soon enough,' she said. 'The shop will be packed out within the hour; somebody is bound to know what's going on.'

Edna was right: even before she started cooking, her shop was packed with munitions workers, all swopping notes on the Phoenix explosion.

'Oh, it were terrible,' a woman said to the others gathered around her. 'Somebody said Ivy's gang in the filling shed were blown to pieces.'

Another woman continued in a melodramatic whisper, 'The fire safety officer called for volunteers to help him shift the fuses.'

'Arthur Leadbetter,' a third woman picked up the story. 'I've just seen one of the fellas who helped him.' She paused before adding, *sotto voce*, 'They said Arthur's copped it.'

'Are you sure you've got your facts right?' Edna asked sharply.

'I didn't make it up, if that's what you mean,' the woman retorted crossly. 'Like I said, I overheard it from one of the fellas who carted poor Arthur intert' ambulance.'

Edna turned to Kit, who'd also overheard the gossiping women.

'You'd better tell Violet right away,' she said nervously.

Pacing the back room, chain-smoking, Violet rushed to Edna when she walked in.

'Any news?'

Looking grey, Edna said gently, 'Sit down, lovie.'

Violet refused, sensing the worst. 'Tell me!'

Taking a deep breath, Edna said, 'One of the women in the shop says Arthur's been badly injured.'

Frantic, Violet gripped her hand, 'Is he alive?'

Edna prevaricated: 'Nothings very clear at the moment. But the wounded' – she didn't dare say the dead – 'have been taken to Manchester Royal Infirmary. I think we need to get you there.'

Without saying a word, Violet flew for the door.

'Wait! I'll take you,' Edna cried as she ran after her. 'Look after the shop,' she called over her shoulder to Kit. 'Shut it if you have to.'

36. Manchester Royal Infirmary

The hospital looked like a ghoulish scene from a nightmare film. Exhausted families lay sleeping on the floor or sat tensely waiting on chairs and benches. Frantic doctors, nurses and porters were running everywhere, and there were bodies covered in blood on stretchers all waiting to be seen. Violet, who'd hardly spoken a word on the journey into Manchester, rushed to the front desk, where a frantic receptionist was trying to listen to three people at the same time. When she finally turned to Violet, the panicked young woman could barely speak. Edna quickly stepped in to help her friend.

'We're looking for a Mr Arthur Leadbetter,' she said. 'The fire safety officer at the Phoenix.'

The woman scanned the long list of names on sheets of paper on her desk.

'Nobody down here by that name, though the emergencies haven't all been registered yet; they were rushed straight through to theatre.'

'So he might well be there?' Edna asked.

'Yes,' the receptionist answered. 'If he's not been taken to the morgue.'

Seeing Violet clutching the side of the desk for support, Edna quickly led her to a bench, where Violet slumped in a heap.

'Please God, let him be alive, please, please, God, don't

take Arthur from me, let him be alive,' she prayed over and over again.

Edna held her close, comforting her as she would have comforted a frightened child, but all the time she rocked sobbing Violet she wondered how she could find out what had really happened to Arthur. Nobody seemed to know anything; wild rumours flew around, but the facts were short on the ground. Who could she go to for help? As she gazed wildly around, Edna's eyes landed on Malc, who, hollow-eyed with exhaustion and grey with fire dust, sat on a bench smoking a cigarette.

'MALC! MALC!' she yelled as she jumped to her feet and, pulling Violet behind her, she ran to him.

Without any preamble Violet asked, 'What happened to Arthur?'

Too devastated even to try softening the truth, Malc said bluntly, 'He was detonating a batch of faulty fuses – one went off in his face.'

'But he's alive!' Violet insisted. 'He's not dead?'

Malc wearily shook his head as he mouthed to Edna, 'Not dead – yet.'

On the verge of hysteria, Violet started to shout, 'Where is he? I've got to see him?'

'He's in the operating theatre – having surgery,' Malc told her.

In an effort to avoid the growing panic, Edna said, 'There's no point in hanging around here for now; let's go and find a nice cup of tea.'

In a Lyons Café just around the corner, they sat smoking cigarettes whilst they drank hot, strong tea.

'He wouldn't let anyone go near the faulty fuses,' Malc

said as he recalled the terrible incidents of the morning. 'He said it was his job and he'd deal with it. He took the dodgy batch to a pit, where he planned to carry out a controlled explosion, but something must have happened. He was a hero, a complete bloody hero!'

Violet smiled proudly, 'That's my Arthur: brave, fearless, always putting others first.'

When they returned to the infirmary, there was no further news of Arthur's condition. Edna persuaded Malc to return to the Phoenix, where she thought he might be needed.

'I'll let you know,' she assured him in a low voice. 'One way or another.'

Returning to the bench, the two women sat there for hours and hours, Violet passing the time by frantically praying.

'Arthur's the kindest man on earth. Please God, take me instead of him: he's more use to the world than I could ever be. Please God, let him live.'

It was nearly midnight before the receptionist at the desk directed a bleary-eyed doctor in their direction.

'Violet Walsh?' he asked. 'Arthur Leadbetter's fiancée?'

'Yes, yes, that's me,' Violet said as she leapt to her feet. 'How is he?'

The doctor sighed as he wiped his tired weary face. 'Critical,' he replied.

'Oh, please', she begged. 'Please do all you can to save him.'

The man looked exhausted. 'I assure you we're doing all we can. But he has serious wounds to the right side of his face and the back of his skull; he's lost a lot of blood and has been unconscious since the explosion occurred. The next twelve hours will be critical,' he added, his eyes kind but serious.

Trying to control her rising fears, Violet asked, 'Can I see him?'

The doctor firmly shook his head. 'Mr Leadbetter's heavily sedated; he needs all the rest he can get if he's to pull through. The best thing you can do is to go home and get some sleep; if he's regained some strength you might be able to visit him tomorrow.'

Edna led a weeping Violet back to the van and drove her home where, pressing a finger to her lips to warn Kit not to ask questions, she led Violet into her bedroom, undressed her and tucked her up in bed.

'I know it's hard, sweetheart, but you must try to sleep; you're going to need all your strength for tomorrow.'

After a fitful night, with Edna sleeping on the sofa in front of the wood-burning stove, Violet insisted that she would take the bus back into Manchester early the next morning.

'I can manage,' she insisted. 'You've got your shop to run, Edna.'

'I can come with you,' Kit volunteered. 'The Phoenix is shut and will be for some time from the look of things.'

Violet smiled and nodded her head. 'Thank you, Kit.'

There weren't many people in the vicinity of the Phoenix, where the maintenance men were busy nailing back walls and replacing shattered window frames. The one person they did see was Mr Featherstone, who was deep in conversation with several senior firemen.

'Once we've run safety checks throughout the building

and the maintenance have finished their work, you should be back in business soon, sir,' she overheard one of them say. 'Apart from the filling shed, of course, which will have to be entirely rebuilt.'

Seeing Violet's face pale, Kit gripped her arm. 'Come on,' she said, keen to get her away from the sombre firemen.

But when Featherstone saw the girls hurrying by, he called loudly, 'Violet! Any news of Arthur?'

Violet told him as much as she knew, then added, 'We're on our way to the infirmary to see him now.'

Mr Featherstone looked quite emotional as he said, 'You know your fiancé saved a lot of lives yesterday?'

Violet's eyes brimmed with tears. 'Malc told me what Arthur did.'

'We don't know the full picture as yet, but from what I gather he put his life on the line for others,' Featherstone said with a choke in his voice.

Violet held her head high. 'And he's done it before, sir, serving at the front.'

'The man's a hero; he deserves a medal,' Featherstone declared.

This time instead of waiting in the over-crowded infirmary entrance, Violet was led to the ward. As they sat in a long, echoing corridor loud with the sound of clanking trolleys being wheeled back and forth to the operating theatre, Violet gripped Kit's hand. 'Thanks for coming with me,' she whispered.

'I'm glad to be here with you,' Kit whispered back. Determined to make conversation, she added, 'Anything's better that sitting brooding by myself at home.'

Violet gave her hand a squeeze. 'You mustn't give up, Kit – that's what I've been telling myself all night. Whilst there's life, there's hope.'

Kit, who didn't want to worry Violet with her own troubles, simply smiled. Sensitive Violet took her hand and squeezed it. 'You must be feeling awful, Kit.'

Trying to be brave, Kit replied, 'I do feel awful, Vi. But we must both hold on to hope if we can.'

'How old is your son again?' Violet asked shyly.

Kit drew in a long breath. 'Ten months old. He's probably crawling, maybe saying his first words.'

Though lost in her own worries, Violet's heart ached for Kit; she couldn't even begin to imagine what it would be like to lose a child. How did Kit sleep at night or get out of bed in the morning? How could she even face the day never knowing where her baby was? Violet's thoughts were interrupted by the appearance of a middle-aged sister wearing a crackling starched uniform and a winged cap.

'Violet Walsh?' she asked briskly.

Violet leapt to her feet. 'Yes!' With her heart pounding and her pulse racing, she gasped, 'Is Arthur alive?'

The sister nodded. 'You can see him briefly,' she said as she led Violet on to the ward, where Arthur lay connected to tubes, with bandages wrapped around his head and half of his face.

'Oh, Jesus!' Violet cried.

The sister briefly detained her. 'He's very weak, Miss Walsh, and he's by no means over the worst,' the sister said as she held Violet's gaze. 'It's vital he remains calm.'

Violet nodded. 'I understand.'

Walking quickly to Arthur's bedside, she took hold of

his cold hand. Her eyes swept over his body, which was covered in a hospital blanket. His head was propped up on several pillows, and he was breathing loudly through an oxygen mask. Just the feel of his warm hand and the sound of his breathing gave her hope and happiness; he was alive! Pulling up the bedside chair, she sat as close to him as she could, stroking Arthur's hand in peaceful silence. Suddenly she felt a tiny, barely noticeable squeeze. Leaning in towards him, she whispered, 'I'm right here, my love.'

Looking into his face, she could see tears welling in the eye that hadn't been covered over by a bandage. 'Everything's going to be all right, my darling.'

Soothed by her voice, Arthur drifted back to sleep, and Violet stayed by his side until the doctors arrived and asked her to leave.

37. Connections

The calamity at the Phoenix factory did not get publicized: news such as this was censored by the government, which was anxious not to reveal the whereabouts of vital munitions factories. Even though areas of the Phoenix still smouldered and smoke hung over it like a heavy grey smog, explosive experts were combing the area for fuses, bombs and cartridge cases. The trays of fuses that Arthur and his team had so carefully wheeled out of the factory still lay in the pit a good distance away from the site and would be returned only once the all-clear was given. Word had gone round of Ivy's death and those of the poor girls working alongside her. Families were notified, but, again, government lines were followed: the fact of their deaths and the cause were not made public.

Therefore it was hardly surprising that Gladys in Leeds was totally unaware of the Phoenix explosion. She'd spent every spare hour with her distraught mother, who moved from hysteria to utter despair in a matter of minutes. Seeing her poor dad completely worn out by his wife's wild mood swings, Gladys suggested he left the house and went for a walk.

'Thanks, love, I'd like that,' he admitted in a guilty whisper. 'A breath of fresh air will do me the world of good.'

Gladys made a pot of tea, which she took into the sitting room, where her mum lay slumped in an armchair.

'Tea's up!' she said in a cheerful voice, but Mrs Johnson completely ignored her.

Placing a cup of tea on a nearby side table, Gladys gently shook her mum by the shoulder. 'Come on, Mum, Les wouldn't like your being like this,' she said.

At the mention of her son's name, Mrs Johnson started to weep. 'It's the not knowing,' she sobbed. 'Is he alive or is he dead?' Looking Gladys wildly in the eye, she said, 'Nigel Webster across the way went missing in action at the start of the war; he was shot down when he was flying over Germany. His mother's been waiting for news for three years,' she cried. 'I'll die if I have to wait that long!'

Desperate to cheer her mother up, Gladys said, 'I thought I'd pop over to the regiment's barracks – you never know, one of Les's mates might be home on leave.'

Her mother visibly brightened at this news. 'Good idea, Glad,' she said as she reached for her tea. 'Get over there right away.'

The next day Violet told Kit that she was fine to visit the infirmary on her own. 'There's no point you hanging around waiting with me; I'm sure you've got plenty to do here.'

With the Phoenix still closed and Gladys away, Kit in fact had little to do. She and Violet walked down the hill together, then went their separate ways, Violet to the infirmary and Kit to Edna's shop, where she found her friend soaking peas and peeling potatoes in readiness for her dinner-time opening. Seeing Kit's drained, tired face, Edna immediately put the kettle on and got out the Woodbines.

'How's Arthur?' she quickly asked.

'Violet said it's still touch and go; she's on her way to see him now,' Kit replied.

'And how are you, missis?'

Kit looked at her knowing friend and her eyes swam with tears. 'I told Ian I didn't want to see him again,' she blurted out.

'And why would you go and do a silly thing like that?' Edna inquired as she handed Kit a cigarette.

''Cos I think me and my family are cursed!' she exclaimed. 'And I'm afraid I'll ruin his life with my bad luck,' she added tearfully.

Edna laughed out loud. 'That's the biggest load of superstitious tripe I've ever heard in my life!'

'You can mock!' Kit angrily retorted. 'Just look at the evidence. The curse of the Murphy. No baby, no house, no family.'

'That's not a curse, darlin', that's a series of bad events, all centred around that no-good father of yours. If there is bad luck in any of this, it's the misfortune to have such a bastard for a father.'

Edna irritably dragged on her cigarette. 'God in heaven, child, you're over-wrought, rung out with disappointment and fear,' she cried. 'I lost my child, which was bad enough, but thank God I never had her dangled before me, then snatched away, only to be dangled before me again – that is sheer torture. You need some sleep,' Edna said as she rose to her feet and helped Kit to hers. 'Go home and get some rest.'

'I can't rest!' Kit cried. 'All I do is lie on the bed with my head spinning.'

'Try,' Edna begged. 'And if you can't, well, then,' she said with a grin, 'come back here and help me out in the shop, but at least give it a go – you look done in.'

Kit trailed up the hill to the cowshed, feeling as limp as a rag doll. She stopped dead in her tracks when she saw Ian's black Ford parked up close to her digs. Gasping in shock, she hid behind the nearest hedge. She couldn't face him, not now. She watched him pace up and down the track, checking his watch all the time. He must have heard about the explosion at the Phoenix, she thought, and rushed home after all. Her heart ached for him; it would be so easy to run into his arms and beg him to forgive her mad emotional outburst, but a part of her still believed she was bad news and he'd be better off without her. With tears streaming down her face, she stayed hidden till ashen-faced Ian drove away; then she hurried home, where she found a bunch of roses lying on the doorstep with a note saying simply 'I LOVE YOU, CATH-ERINE. IAN'.

Gladys didn't have much success at the barracks in Leeds. Sighing with disappointment she headed home, but on her way across the city she bumped into several girls whom she recognized as Phoenix munitions workers.

'Hello,' she said in surprise. 'You on leave too?'

The girls gazed at her in astonishment. 'Haven't you 'eard?' they asked.

'Heard what?'

Taking in the disastrous news, Gladys felt so sick she had to hold on to a nearby lamp-post for support.

'We'll be on our way, then,' said the girls. 'Don't hurry back to't Phoenix – it's shut till we get the all-clear.'

Gladys took deep breaths of fresh air to steady herself. 'God!' she thought. 'Thank heavens Violet and Kit weren't on that early-morning shift.'

Gladys decided she might as well use her unexpected time in Leeds well. The next day she returned to the barracks, where she was met by a brass band playing 'Flowers of the Forest' in the courtyard. Gladys smiled sadly as she recalled how happy Les had been when he'd been selected to play his trumpet in the regimental brass band. Loitering by the gates in her smart three-buttoned utility jacket and short skirt, she waited for the band to finish, then scanned the soldiers, who smiled or winked as they passed her by. Feeling deflated that yet again she recognized none of them as Les's mates she stood in the courtyard wondering what to do next. A polite voice gently asking 'Can I help, miss?' made Gladys jump.

'Sorry, didn't mean to give you a fright,' a tall man with a blond moustache and a broad friendly smile said. 'Captain Trevor Horricks, at your service.'

As he clicked his heels in a smart military fashion, Gladys saw a conductor's baton tucked under his arm. She smiled up at the handsome young captain, dazzling him with her beautiful face and big blue eyes.

'I'm Gladys Johnson,' she explained. 'My brother, Les, played the trumpet in the regimental band.'

'Yes,' he replied. 'I remember Les – excellent trumpet player.'

Gladys nodded proudly before she said, 'We recently heard he's missing in action.'

'Oh, bad luck,' the captain responded; then, embarrassed by the seeming hollowness of his words, he quickly added, 'May I buy you a drink in the Officers' Mess?'

Gladys didn't hesitate for a second. 'Yes, please, I'd like that.'

At Manchester Royal Infirmary, Violet spent most of the day in the waiting room. When the sister did appear, it wasn't to call her into the ward but rather to tell her that Arthur had a chest infection that was causing the doctors great concern and no visitors would be allowed that day. With tears in her eyes, Violet left the hospital, then wandered aimlessly into the city centre, where Ian, hurrying across Piccadilly, spotted her familiar face.

'Ian!' she cried. 'You're back.'

'VIOLET!' he called as he ran to catch up with her. 'I heard about the explosion at the Phoenix. I drove up to the cowshed, but nobody was at home.' He paused to take a breath. 'I've been going mad with worry – how's Kit?'

'She's safe, we're all safe . . . apart from Arthur.'

Hearing the catch in her voice, Ian led Violet to a nearby Lyons Corner Café, where over a pot of tea he heard about Arthur's accident at the Phoenix.

'Everybody's calling him a hero,' Violet said as she played with some toast and Marmite the waitress had brought. 'I know it's true – he saved a lot of lives – but I just want my Arthur back!' she exclaimed as she dabbed away the tears with her handkerchief.

Ian leant across the table and took hold of her hand. 'He's tough, your Arthur, a real fighter,' he said with utter conviction.

She gave a little smile. 'He's not the sort who gives up easily,' she agreed.

'And neither are you,' Ian assured Violet. 'Believe me, the pair of you will pull through and live happily ever after.'

'Please God,' she prayed. 'You're right, though, Ian: I must stay strong for my Arthur; weeping and moping are no good for anybody.'

'That's a girl!' Ian said as he poured out more tea. 'Tell me, how's Kit? She won't talk to me,' he admitted. 'She's avoiding me.'

Violet repeated her own words to describe her sad friend. 'Weeping and moping,' she replied.

Ian got out his packet of Pall Mall cigarettes, which he offered to Violet; they smoked for a few seconds in silence, then Ian said gloomily, 'The poor girl's heartbroken – she blames herself for everything. She'd be better off blaming me. I've not come up with a satisfactory answer as to what happened to Billy. Though, please God, I have left good people working on that in Dublin.'

'Not seeing you is doing Kit more harm than good – she's cutting off her nose to spite her face!' Violet exclaimed crossly.

'Will you take a note to her?' Ian asked shyly. 'Maybe she'll read it if you stand over her,' he joked.

'Don't you worry – I'll stand over her, all right,' Violet promised.

Gladys was relieved she'd worn her best jacket and skirt for her visit to the barracks. When she walked into the Officers' Mess, all eyes turned to her, and there was a brief moment of silence as every man in the room stared in admiration at the tall shapely brunette accompanying Captain Horrocks.

'What can I get you, Gladys?' He stopped.

'Sherry, please, Captain,' she answered formally.

'Trevor,' he said as he ordered their drinks. 'Ignore the mob! They're not used to seeing a beautiful woman in the bar,' he added with a grin.

Grateful to be led to a table in a corner well away from the curious staring men, Gladys took a quick sip of the sherry.

'Have you any idea how I can find out what happened to my brother, Les? Or even where he was stationed when he was posted abroad?' she said, coming straight to the point. 'My mother's losing her mind with worry.'

'I'm afraid I can't help,' he answered honestly. 'I have no idea where the men go once they leave here; it's all rather hush-hush. You just have to hope he's managed to escape from the prisoner-of-war camp, if that's in fact where he is,' he added awkwardly.

Seeing Gladys shudder, Trevor quickly reassured her. 'Some of the war camps aren't so bad; when the Germans stick to the Geneva Convention, the prisoners get treated fairly decently.'

Worried he'd say too much and put his foot in it, Trevor took a deep drink of his beer before he added, 'He could be in hiding? I've heard there are undercover cells who shelter escaped prisoners.'

Gladys visibly brightened up. 'That thought will certainly cheer Mum up,' she said gratefully. 'It's the not knowing that's the worst part'.

'I can imagine,' Horrocks sympathized. Doing his best to lighten the mood, he looked up as he lit his pipe. 'Are you as good a musician as your brother?'

'Better!' she laughed. 'Dad taught us both to play, Les the trumpet, me the alto sax.'

Trevor looked impressed.

'I can sing too!' she said. 'In fact I sing in a swing band that we set up in the factory where I work: we call ourselves "The Bomb Girls' Swing Band". We've just won the best new band in a regional competition!' she finished proudly.

'I'd love to hear you play.'

'I'm a bit out of practice,' Gladys admitted. 'Personal events have overtaken the band; we've hardly played in weeks.'

'You can always practise with me whilst you're home,' Trevor suggested. 'I play the guitar and violin.'

'And where would we play?' she laughed.

'Right here,' he replied. 'We have a large rehearsal room.'

'But I left my sax in Pendleton,' she suddenly remembered.

'We've got loads going spare,' he retorted. 'No excuses.'

Gladys gazed at his honest, open smiling face. 'I'd love that,' she said.

When Violet gave Kit the note from Ian, she stood over her as she'd promised Ian.

'Ian asked me to make sure you read this,' she said with a determined smile. 'He's been up here looking for you. He's worried sick, Kit.'

Blushing, Kit opened the letter in front of Violet.

Darling! Please come and see me. I miss you so much.
Ian xxxx

Clutching the note to her heart, Kit smiled for the first time in days.

'Thank God for that,' thought Violet as she put the kettle on for a much-needed brew.

38. Small Gifts of Love

The following morning, Kit and Violet took the same bus into Manchester, where they again went their separate ways, Kit to Piccadilly, Violet to the Royal Infirmary. Wearing all her new pretty clothes, gifts from Ian, Kit considered how awful life had been without him: the terrible explosion at the Phoenix, combined with Arthur's critical condition, made her realize just how precious life was. She needed Ian like flowers need the rain. Edna had been right when she'd said that Kit was talking a load of superstitious blarney! Maybe her brain had become unhinged after the loss of her son, but that didn't mean she should take it out on the man who'd showed his love for her in so many generous ways. Hiding from him, avoiding him, only made things worse; they were a team. Without Ian she'd be lost.

With all of these thoughts swirling around her head, Kit ran across Piccadilly, then through the side streets that led to Ian's office. Seeing him walking out of the doorway, Kit opened her mouth to call to him but stopped short when she saw a glamorous woman behind him. She was tall and slender, stylishly dressed in a navy-blue suit with a natty navy-blue trilby perched on top of her long hair. Turning to Ian, she laughed as she said something which made him laugh too; then she kissed him warmly on the cheek before walking away with her auburn hair glinting in the morning sunshine. Kit darted behind a parked van so Ian wouldn't see her.

'Holy Mother!' she gasped as she slumped against the side of the van. 'What have I done?'

Of course Ian would have found another girlfriend after she had so rudely ditched him. Rich, clever, successful and single Ian McIvor must have women queuing around the clock to court him; he was a catch for anybody. Not daring to look back at his office, Kit hurried across Piccadilly with images of the glamorous woman reaching up to kiss Ian torturing her. Oblivious to the curious expressions on the faces of those who passed her by, Kit muttered out loud, 'She's just his sort: confident, well dressed, rich and clever.'

WHY had he ever been attracted to her in the first place, she wondered. Although she was a scrawny bag of bones in rags, he'd genuinely cared for her, loved her, but she had pushed him away. What an utter fool she'd been. She'd left her decision to meet him too late – Ian had already found another woman!

At the Royal Infirmary, Violet listened intently to Arthur's doctor.

'We were extremely lucky: we managed to obtain some penicillin for him, and he's responded well. His chest infection is much improved and he's breathing easier,' he said.

'Thank God,' she replied.

'You might see a difference in him,' the doctor warned. 'We've had to change the bandages on his face, expose the skin – it might look a little raw.'

Violet entered the ward and glanced around for Arthur, whose bed had been moved and now stood before a high window. She gazed at him peacefully sleeping in a shaft of soft sunlight and her heart ached with love for him.

'My darling,' she whispered as she drew up a chair so she could sit close beside him.

To her amazement, Arthur opened his eyes. 'Violet,' he croaked feebly.

Terrified she'd be asked to leave for over-exciting him, Violet took hold of his hand and whispered, 'Shhh, Arthur, please don't exert yourself. I'm here, and I'll stay.'

As he drifted back to sleep, Violet was able to examine his face, where, as the doctor had warned her, some bandages had been removed. The burnt skin, livid and red, was raised and puffy.

'My poor love,' she thought as she sat in silence watching him sleep. He'd already lost a thumb and two fingers, and now, after the Phoenix blast, it was clear handsome Arthur Leadbetter would be scarred for life. Not that Violet cared – as long as he was alive and by her side, that was all that mattered to her.

Clutching her gas mask, Gladys hurried into the barracks, where she'd arranged to meet Captain Trevor Horrocks. A smart young soldier clicked his heels before escorting Gladys to the rehearsal room, where she paused in the doorway to listen to the beautiful classical guitar music that drifted out. Trevor leapt to his feet when he saw Gladys approaching.

'Just tuning up,' he said with the wide-open smile she'd

come to like very much. 'I've found an alto sax for you – hope it's okay?'

'It's much smarter than my old sax,' she said appreciatively. Taking off her coat, then setting down her bag, she trilled experimentally up and down the instrument's silver valves. 'Perfect!' she announced.

Trevor gazed at her long brunette hair, gathered to one side so as not to get in the way of her playing. 'The girl's a stunner,' he thought. Gladys's question swiftly brought him back to the here and now.

'What shall we play?' she asked eagerly.

'"I Remember You"!' he said without a moment's hesitation.

'From the film *The Fleet's In*,' she cried. 'I love it!'

'The music's right there,' he said as he pointed to a sheet propped up on a nearby music stand.

Gladys ran her eyes swiftly over the score, all the time humming melodically in tune with the notes.

'Just let me tune up,' she said. Then, when she was ready, she counted them in and they started to play one of the most popular songs of the year.

As Trevor's guitar chords carried the song, Gladys, in between bouts of playing, broke into song. 'You're the one who made my dreams come true,' she crooned as she smiled at Trevor gently strumming his guitar.

'Keep singing,' he urged.

Swaying to the romantic rhythm of the music, she sang with unselfconscious ease, as if it was just another form of speaking. Towards the end of the song, Gladys picked up her sax and played out the final chords, ending with a trilling crescendo of high notes.

'WONDERFUL!' he cried as, breathless and laughing, they both stopped.

'Bloody marvellous,' a voice boomed from outside the hall, and then, to Gladys's amazement, an officer with medals dangling from his military jacket walked towards them, applauding loudly.

Trevor quickly laid down the guitar and jumped to his feet.

'SIR!' he said as he gave a smart salute.

'At ease, Captain,' the officer retorted. 'And who's this new recruit?' he asked with a wink.

Gladys smiled easily as she extended her hand and introduced herself.

'Gladys Johnson, sir, sister of Lance-Corporal Les Johnson.'

'The trumpeter,' Trevor reminded his senior officer, who thought for a moment, then nodded as he recalled the soldier.

'Excellent fellow,' he barked. 'Played "The Last Post", as I remember.'

'That's the one,' Trevor replied. 'Miss Johnson came here looking for information about her brother,' he added.

'We were told he's missing in action,' Gladys quickly added.

The officer gazed into the girl's pleading blue eyes.

'We're doing everything we can to track down the soldiers that went missing,' he said carefully. 'We have faith in our contacts out there; they've already safely returned some of our boys by circuitous routes.'

'My mother will be happy to hear that, sir,' Gladys said gratefully. 'We're not ready to believe he's not made it out, not yet, sir', she added.

'Well, much as I'd love to hear more, I must press on,' he said as he gave a quick salute and marched out of the room.

'You're privileged that the general talked to you so openly,' Trevor said after he'd gone. 'A combination of your winning smile and sweet singing must have won him over,' he laughed.

Happy to have slightly more hopeful news that she could relay to her family – at this stage they would take any hope they could cling to – Gladys eagerly asked, 'What shall we play next?'

'You choose,' he retorted.

'"South of the Border"?' she suggested.

He nodded as he played the opening chords. 'I love the lyrics,' he said with a smile. 'They'll be even lovelier sung by you.'

Catching his admiring gaze, Gladys felt a rush of warmth for the handsome young musician who had brought unexpected pleasure to her visit to Leeds.

'A-1, a-2, a-1, 2, 3, 4 . . .' she said as she picked up her sax and played the opening music to Captain Trevor Horrocks's lilting guitar accompaniment.

Before Violet's next visit to the infirmary, she went to Arthur's garden. What remained of it after the explosion was a small bed of flowers and some singed fruit bushes. Her eyes filled with tears when she saw the broken seat they'd sat on together and the shattered fences he'd erected around the vegetable patch. They'd spent so many happy hours here, smoking and talking, kissing and cuddling; he'd be upset to see it like this, she thought. He was so proud of his little garden, his bolt-hole well away from the factory. Suddenly she had an idea: she'd take some of the garden to Arthur in hospital. Picking any flowers she could find – dahlias and late roses – she gathered together a fragrant bouquet, which she wrapped in newspaper. Then she set off for Manchester to deliver it.

Drumming his fingers on the desk, Ian was beside himself. Mother Gabriel's latest letter was lying on the surface before him; picking it up, he read it once more.

Dear Mr McIvor,

You might be interested to hear that Mr Murphy, now a down-and-out homeless person, came knocking on the convent door asking for food. I asked him point blank if he knew of Billy's whereabouts. I swore that God would forgive him his sins if he told the truth. To be honest with you, sir, he looks like a man in fear of meeting his maker. He told me he was not long for this life and I urged him to be at peace with the Lord.

Ian couldn't help but smile; he could just see Mother Gabriel putting the fear of God in Murphy.

He finally admitted he'd taken Billy on the night of the theft to an address in the Maryland district of South Dublin, which O'Rourke had directed him to. Needless to say, I shall follow this information up immediately and let you know the outcome. May God and all his blessed angels protect the child.

Yours in Christ,
Mother Gabriel

He *had* to see Kit. Whether she was talking to him or not, he had to tell her the latest news. Of course nothing was conclusive – Billy might have been moved on since – but with Mother Gabriel on the case it was like working in tandem with a Rottweiler! The phone shrilling out on his desk roused him from his churning thoughts.

'Your next appointment's here, Mr McIvor,' his secretary announced.

Checking his diary, Ian smiled when he saw the name in his appointments diary.

'Please show her in,' he said and stood up to embrace the lovely woman who wore a smart navy-blue suit and had a fashionably long auburn bob.

'Am I too early?' she asked as she bent to kiss the top of his head.

'Better early than late, Sis,' he teased as he settled her into a chair beside him.

Arthur was sleeping fitfully when Violet arrived. Laying the bouquet of flowers on the floor beside her, she sat patiently holding his hand until he woke up. She was immediately struck by how much stronger he looked.

'How are you, sweetheart?' she whispered as his gaze landed on her.

'Vi, oh, Vi,' he said as he gripped her hand.

'You sound a bit better,' she cautiously remarked.

'The penicillin has helped ,' he said with a catch in his voice. 'But look at me . . .'

Violet looked into his damaged face, then swept a hand gently over his singed hair. 'I'm looking, my darling,' she whispered tenderly.

'I don't want your pity, Vi,' he snapped. 'I saw myself in the mirror this morning. It's bad enough having only half a hand but now I'm ugly, scarred and disfigured!' he cried angrily.

Violet was so shocked she couldn't reply for a few minutes. When she found her breath she said quietly, 'My darling, it's you I love.'

He turned his face abruptly away from her.

'Do you think I care about handsome smiles and good looks? I had that with Ronnie, the best-looking man in Wood End – but he had a cruel, twisted soul. You'll always be beautiful, Arthur: it shines through from your soul. Your injuries are a tribute to your selflessness and care for others; there is no man in the world better or more true than you.' With tears streaming down her face, she reached for the bouquet. 'I've brought you a piece of your garden,' she said as she laid the flowers before him. 'Look at the beauty you made and that still remains after the destruction of that terrible explosion.'

Arthur touched the tender blooms, and, as he did so, he smiled. 'My garden,' he said incredulously.

Violet nodded. 'Still there, just!' she joked. 'Waiting for you to come back and restore it to life . . . just like me.'

Arthur reached up to draw her head on to his chest. 'Oh, my Vi,' he sighed as they kissed. 'My love.'

After his sister left his office, Ian cancelled all his other appointments and drove at speed to Kit's digs, where he knocked on the front door, but nobody answered.

'Hello,' he called softly as he stepped inside.

Looking around, he saw Kit fast asleep on the old sofa,

her hair fanned out around her tired face, her eyelashes fluttering against her pale cheeks as if she was having a bad dream, her mouth slightly parted. Unable to stop himself, Ian reached down to kiss her on the lips and, half asleep, she immediately responded to his kiss.

'Catherine,' he whispered.

At the sound of her name, Kit's eyes flew open.

'IAN!' she cried in shock.

'Darling! Why didn't you come and see me after you got my note?'

Sitting upright and pulling her flimsy nightie together at the bodice, Kit answered, 'I did!'

'When?'

'Today: you were in the street, kissing a pretty young woman,' she answered stiffly.

Looking puzzled, Ian repeated her words: 'Kissing a pretty young woman!'

'She had long auburn hair and was wearing a navy-blue suit,' Kit added.

'That was my sister, Ethel!' he cried as he burst out laughing. 'She came to see me about getting a divorce from her wretched flirt of a husband,' Ian explained. Half smiling, he shook his head. 'So you thought I'd taken up with another woman, just like that,' he said as he snapped his finger and thumb together.

Embarrassed, Kit hung her head. 'You did, didn't you?' he persisted.

'It looked like that,' she finally admitted.

'And you ran away?'

Seeing she was embarrassed, Ian draped a coat around Kit's shoulders.

'Let's go outside,' he said. 'I have news.'

They stood on the edge of the moors, listening to the night call of the curlews and the first hoot of an owl as it swooped soundlessly overhead. The light from the setting sun still remained in the sky, and the air smelt of damp autumn leaves and bracken. In the tranquil peace of the evening, Ian related the contents of Mother Gabriel's letter to Kit, who listened wide-eyed and intent.

'Your father has confirmed O'Rourke's been working with him to abduct Billy,' Ian said. 'He's given us an address, and Mother Gabriel may by now have located Billy's whereabouts. We have a real lead, Catherine – at last we have something to go on.'

Kit stared at him, colour rushing into her pale cheeks and her eyes lighting up for the first time in weeks as she cried out, 'Oh, God! Can this be happening? Can it be true?' She took a breath before she asked the next question. 'When will we hear if she's found him?'

Pulling Kit to her feet, Ian half ran back to his car. 'Come on: let's talk to Mother Gabriel together.'

39. Spring Band Wedding

As Ian and Kit telephoned Mother Gabriel in Dublin, Gladys was returning to Pendleton – the Phoenix had been declared safe for work by the maintenance team. She rushed breathlessly into the cowshed, where she found only Violet.

'Oh, I'm so glad to see you safe and sound!' she cried in relief.

When she heard from Violet all that had happened at the factory in her absence, Gladys sighed heavily. 'It could have been us on the early shift instead of Ivy and her girls.'

'We were so lucky,' Violet murmured.

'Featherstone's organizing a memorial service at Pendleton parish church,' Violet told her grimly.

'Poor Ivy!' Gladys exclaimed as she thought of the older woman's patience and good humour.

As Violet poured them both a mug of tea, Gladys anxiously asked, 'How's Arthur now?'

'He's making good progress,' Violet said happily. 'With a bit of luck he might be home this week. So how did you pass your time in Leeds?' Violet asked, helping herself to a Woodbine.

'Trying to calm Mum down,' Gladys answered. 'And I visited Les's barracks, where I met the captain in Les's regimental band,' Gladys said as a tell-tale blush crept up her cheeks. 'He said some nice things about our Les.' Her blushed deepened as she added, 'We practised together; he plays the guitar and violin really well!'

Violet smiled a knowing smile, which Gladys shrugged off. 'I only saw him a couple of times, and I didn't give him my address.'

'I bet you ten bob he'll track you down!' Violet laughed. 'Even if it's only to play the violin with you!'

In Ian's office, Kit was holding her breath.

'We have the police working alongside us now, Mr McIvor; there's no need for you to come rushing back. I promise I'll keep you posted on all developments.'

'But shouldn't I be there, helping you?' he asked anxiously.

'I think your presence in Dublin might send O'Rourke underground,' she replied. 'We need him in "operational mode", as the police would say.' Mother Gabriel, who was clearly enjoying the drama of liaising with the Garda Síochána, replied, 'They've got plain-clothes policemen on the job around the clock outside the address we were given in South Dublin.'

Ian paused. His instinct and Kit's too was to rush back to Dublin for the final uncovering of O'Rourke, but Mother Gabriel, or, more to the point, the gardaí, were quite right. Plain-clothes policemen on a twenty-four-hour watch were far more effective than he could ever be.

'You promise you'll keep us posted, Mother Gabriel?' Ian requested.

'Every step of the way, my child.'

Putting down the phone, Ian turned to Kit, who'd had

306

her ear to the phone receiver throughout his conversation with Mother Gabriel. Seeing the wild look in her eyes, he knew exactly what she was thinking. Taking her in his arms he whispered, 'Catherine, darling girl, don't go down the Irish blarney path. This has nothing to do with curses and retribution; this is good policing instigated by Mother Gabriel. There could be no better team,' he laughed. 'A Rottweiler and an Alsatian – nobody's going to shake the pair of them off!'

Kit pressed her hot face against his chest – could she dare to hope?

'What will we do now?' she asked in confusion.

'Carry on as normal, as much as we can,' Ian said as he bent to kiss her wonderful long dark hair. 'I'm on the end of a phone.'

'But I'm not!' she protested.

'Edna is – you'll know any news just as soon as I do.'

'So it's back to work, even though my world's turned upside down, again?' she cried.

Ian nodded firmly. 'We wait to hear from Mother Gabriel – and we pray, my darling.'

The filling shed was still in the process of being rebuilt, so the girls were sent to work alongside Myrtle in the dispatch yard. Packing bombs of all sizes into wooden crates was a change from filling fuse cases, but they missed Ivy's cheeky cackling laughter and the calm presence of Arthur wandering in to load the filled trays on to his trolley. Violet glowed with happiness when she told her friends during a tea break in the canteen that Arthur was due to be discharged from the infirmary the following day.

'I'll bring him home in an ambulance and nurse him myself, except when I'm working; then I've arranged for Nora or Maggie to keep an eye on him. Myrtle's volunteered to help too.'

Malc burst out laughing when he heard about Myrtle's involvement. 'Bloody 'ell! He'll be terrified of putting a foot wrong with her in charge. She'll be giving him cold baths and cod-liver oil if he doesn't watch himself!'

'She's a good soul, is Myrtle,' Violet protested.

'Heart of gold,' Malc agreed. 'But I wouldn't want her to give me a bed bath!' he chuckled.

Bringing Arthur home was a joy. After the driver pushed Arthur in his wheelchair into the back of the ambulance, Violet and Arthur sat side by side and gazed out of the window. As the vehicle gathered speed and headed north along the winding lanes to Pendleton, Arthur gripped Violet's hand tightly. 'Look, Vi,' he said as he pointed towards the sun drifting out from behind a bank of dark clouds and illuminating the bright green hillsides, where herds of black-and-white cattle grazed.

'The world's a beautiful place,' he murmured contentedly.

Violet smiled at his happy excited face; he was as entranced as a boy with everything around him, pointing out the rich colours of the autumn leaves and the light falling on a vast sweep of the distant Pennines ridge.

When they got to the cowshed, the driver wheeled Arthur into Violet's room, where a bed was freshly made up for him. On the bedside table, Violet had arranged flowers from his garden in a vase and some back copies of the local paper, so he could catch up on the news.

'This is just fine,' he said as he stepped out of the

wheelchair and settled on the comfortable bed, where the pillows were piled high. 'Ahhh,' he sighed contentedly as he lay back and closed his eyes.

'Don't go overdoing it,' the driver warned. 'One day at a time; otherwise you'll be back in the Royal Infirmary with high blood pressure.'

Arthur winked. 'I've got my nurse to look after me,' he joked.

'Lucky you!' the ambulance man chuckled. 'They don't come more stunning than your fiancée.'

When he'd gone, Violet made them both a cup of hot strong tea, then she snuggled up beside Arthur, who looked tired after his exertions.

'Oh, it's so good to be home,' he sighed as he nuzzled her silver-blonde hair.

'If I'm to marry you soon, Mr Leadbetter, I'm going to have to take very good care of you.'

'Have you checked out the dates with the Phoenix chaplain?'

Violet nodded. 'The first date he can marry us is 21 October. I can push you down the aisle in your wheelchair, if you can't walk.'

'It's my face that hurts, not my feet!' he laughed as he pulled her close to kiss her sweet smiling mouth. 'I plan to walk up the aisle with my beautiful bride on my arm,' he assured her.

When the happy couple told their friends of their wedding plans, Gladys immediately said the Bomb Girls' Swing Band would provide the wedding music.

'I can't exchange vows with my husband and play the clarinet too!' giggled Violet, who was as happy as a teenager.

'We'll let you off on this one occasion,' Gladys teased.

There was no time to make wedding clothes, but that didn't bother Violet; she'd worn a perfect Brussels-lace gown for her wedding to Ronnie, which she'd burnt at the first opportunity. For her wedding to Arthur, she'd wear her best dress and they'd have a small reception at the Black Horse pub in town. Though Violet imagined a simple affair with few guests, there were those at the Phoenix who had other plans.

'The man's a bloody hero!' Malc told Mr Featherstone, who nodded in agreement with him.

'If it weren't for his selfless action, many more lives would have been lost,' the factory boss declared. 'We'll have a whip-round and give the newlyweds a fine spread of a wedding breakfast.'

'And a honeymoon in Blackpool?' Malc suggested with a cheeky wink.

Mr Featherstone threw his hands up in the air as he laughed, 'Yes! And that too!'

Just before the wedding, another letter arrived from Mother Gabriel.

The child was not at the address Murphy gave me. The woman told me a pack of lies, saying she'd never heard mention of Billy, but after I'd threatened her with the Garda and the wrath of God she gave me the address of where she'd been instructed by O'Rourke to move the child on to.

'Christ Almighty!' Ian swore as he ran his hands through his thick brown hair. 'Does it ever bloody end?'

'I will not give up, Mr McIvor,' Mother Gabriel's letter went on. 'This is now a matter between me and my God,' she finished.

Ian decided not to tell Kit this latest piece of news. It was yet another dangling carrot to worry and upset her. Poor Billy. Just thinking about how confused and frightened the child must be, dragged from place to place and living with strangers, brought tears to Ian's eyes. No, he would not tell Kit: it could push her over the edge entirely.

One of the best things about the imminent wedding was that the Bomb Girls met to practise for the first time in weeks. They met up to rehearse in the Phoenix chapel, where the band discussed the music for Violet's wedding.

'Obviously, "Here Comes the Bride",' said Gladys. 'And a hymn we can all sing.'

Without a second's hesitation Myrtle said firmly, '"Jerusalem".'

'We'll need another rousing song for when they leave the chapel?' Nora said.

Maggie burst out laughing. '"When the Saints Go Marching In"!' she cried. 'That'll lift the rafters!'

Maggie turned to Kit, who'd been silent throughout the entire discussion. 'Any ideas, Kit?' she asked.

Kit just shook her head. 'That all sounds fine,' she replied.

When Ian drove up to see her later that day, Kit confessed her reluctance to play in the band. 'I'm not in the mood for laughing and singing,' she confessed. 'It just doesn't feel right.'

'I understand, my darling, but I do think that Violet

would be upset if you didn't play at her wedding; after all you are the best drummer in the county!' he joked.

'I just can't put my heart into it,' Kit replied glumly.

'Do it for Arthur and Violet,' Ian urged. 'They've been to hell and back in the last few months.'

Kit kissed his anxious face. 'You're right,' she replied. 'I'll do it for love.'

Before they parted, Ian pulled Kit close and kissed her warm lips. 'I want to take you shopping for some wedding clothes, darling,' he announced.

Kit looked reluctant. 'I can't keep spending your money,' she protested.

'Come on,' he coaxed. 'It's turning cold: if you wear that skimpy crêpe dress I bought you in the summer, you'll freeze to death.'

Kit's eyes lit up. 'Well, if you put it like that,' she conceded. 'How can I say no?'

Neither Violet nor Arthur had any idea of the machinations taking place right under their noses at the Phoenix. Maggie's big sister, Emily Yates, from the cordite line, had joined forces with Edna and between them the two cooks put together a simple wartime wedding breakfast.

'Parsnip soup for starters,' Edna started. 'My neighbour's got a good crop of veg on his allotment this year – cabbages and sprouts too.'

'I could make trays of meat-and-potato pies,' Emily suggested. 'I know we'll never have enough mince for that many guests, but we can bulk out the mixture with onions and carrots and some fresh herbs – at least they're free and growing wild on the moors,' she laughed.

'I'll provide the spuds,' Edna said. 'There won't be enough time to do chips but mebbe we could roast potatoes in lard and dripping.'

Emily quickly said, 'And drain the stock for the gravy.'

'Pudding's going to be a challenge,' Edna said thoughtfully.

'Jelly and custard,' Emily suggested. 'It's the best we can do.'

As Edna and Emily completed their menu, Malc – courtesy of the factory whip-round, which had been much enhanced by Mr Featherstone's personal donation – booked a hotel on Blackpool's breezy promenade for the newlyweds' honeymoon and bought return train tickets for them too.

'They'll probably never get out of bed,' he joked when he told Gladys of his arrangements. 'Don't let on to them,' he whispered. 'We don't want to spoil the surprise. They're in for the shock of their lives!'

It wasn't easy taking Kit shopping; even though she'd expressed interest when he'd first suggested it, her mood swings were unpredictable these days. Frustrated at the little she could do to help in the search for Billy, Kit failed to show enthusiasm when he mentioned a shopping trip to the large Co-operative store in Piccadilly, but, as she walked between aisles of beautiful dresses, her mouth literally fell open in amazement.

'Holy Mother!' she gasped. 'I've never seen such a place in my entire life.'

After assessing Kit's small stature and colouring, the friendly assistant brought several dresses into the changing room, where Kit tried them on. Twirling in front of the full-length mirror, she couldn't make her mind up between a soft dove-pink velvet dress with a nipped-in waist and fitted three-quarter-length sleeves and a stunning emerald-green silk dress with pearl buttons down the bodice and a stylish pleated skirt.

'What do you think?' she asked Ian.

Looking at his breathlessly excited girlfriend, Ian couldn't decide either.

'Have them both!' he laughed.

In the car on the way home, Kit's unhappiness returned and she slumped into silence.

'It feels all wrong, Ian,' she said quietly. 'Me having treats, walking about free as a bird, whilst my son is in hiding somewhere!' she cried in an agony of pain. 'I don't think I can take much more; it would be easier to die than live like this.'

Ian pulled off the main road so that he could park. As he took her into his arms, he murmured, 'I know how much you're suffering, my darling.' As she sobbed wretchedly against his shoulder he added, 'Would it make you feel any better if I was back over there, searching alongside Mother Gabriel? I could leave for Ireland tonight,' he said impetuously.

'It's for me to be over there, not you,' she replied. 'But thanks for the offer,' she added limply. 'God! Doing nothing is a torture.'

Ian stared through the windscreen, which was speckled with rain. Kit was right: this prolonged waiting was a slow form of torture – if there was no good news at the end of it, he seriously wondered if their relationship would survive.

*

On Violet's wedding day, the guests gathered in the Phoenix chapel, where Myrtle played a classical Mozart piece as they waited for the bride's arrival. Smiling, a happy Arthur standing upright at the altar rail looked surprisingly well; and he had walked down the aisle, not been wheeled, as he'd promised. At a signal from the chaplain the Bomb Girls broke into 'Here Comes the Bride' and radiant Violet on Malc's arm walked down the aisle bearing a bouquet of late champagne roses from Arthur's garden. She wore a simple cream woollen dress that skimmed over her slender body, and her hair was loose around her glowing face. When she reached Arthur's side, he turned to her with a look of utter love that immediately had half the guests weeping into their handkerchiefs. After the simple but touching short ceremony, the bride and groom burst out laughing as the band played 'When the Saints Go Marching In', which, as Maggie had predicted, had the chapel rocking.

Expecting to walk down the hill to the pub in Pendleton for their wedding breakfast, the newlyweds were flabbergasted when they stepped out of the chapel to find dozens of munitions girls forming a guard of honour for them. At the sight of Arthur, whom no one had seen since the explosion, the workers quite spontaneously started to clap and cheer the man who had saved so many lives. With tears in his eyes, Arthur drew his wife's arm through his and with pride they processed along the line of smiling women to the canteen, where Edna and Emily awaited them. Amazed, and very moved, Violet and Arthur gazed at the tables set with jam jars of autumn blooms and at the top table decorated with a Union Jack tablecloth and vases containing the last of the autumn dahlias.

'How did this all happen?' Violet gasped.

'After what Arthur's done for the Phoenix, we all thought you deserved something a bit special,' said Mr Featherstone, who was standing by the top table with his beaming wife. 'Congratulations, Mr and Mrs Leadbetter!'

After a loud cheer, the guests, who consisted of a good half of the workforce, settled down at their tables, where they were served Edna and Emily's tasty wedding breakfast, along with bottles of pale ale supplied by Mr Featherstone, courtesy of Malc's local black-market contacts. At the end of the meal, Arthur got to his feet and addressed his smiling guests.

'I think you all know by now that Violet was a hard woman to court,' he started.

'You got there in the end!' Malc called out.

'We've certainly had our struggles,' Arthur said with an understated smile. 'But God brought us through, though there were times in that infirmary in Manchester when I thought I wouldn't make it.' Arthur took a deep breath to steady himself. 'Violet was always there beside me; quiet, strong and determined, she pulled me through.' Reaching for her hand, he said in a voice choked with emotion, 'I will love you always.'

As the rapturous couple kissed and the entire canteen applauded, Ian looked across the table at Kit, who looked so lovely in her new pink dress with her silky dark hair falling around her slender shoulders. Would the day ever come when it would feel right to propose to Catherine, he wondered; or would he always be waiting for the moment when they found Billy?

Showered with homemade confetti, the newlyweds were driven away from the Phoenix in Malc's car.

'What's happening now?' asked giggling Violet.

'You'll find out soon enough,' Malc chuckled as he pulled up at Clitheroe Station, where he handed an envelope to Arthur.

'Get the train on Platform 2 – be sharp now!'

Once settled in an empty carriage, Violet and Arthur opened the envelope, in which they found their hotel reservation and ten pounds in cash.

'It's like a dream,' Violet said as she wiped tears of gratitude from her eyes.

Arthur shook his head in disbelief. 'I've never known such generous people,' he murmured. 'The Bomb Girls' Swing Band and the Phoenix munitions workers have made our wedding a day to remember for the rest of our lives.'

Violet snuggled up close to her new husband. 'And the best bit is yet to come,' she whispered. 'Just you and me, all alone, Mr Leadbetter.'

Pulling her into his chest, Arthur laughed as he joked, 'I'm a sick man, Mrs Leadbetter!'

Nuzzling his neck, Violet giggled, 'Don't you worry, I'll take very good care of you!'

40. Mother Gabriel

Because of the urgent need for fuses, a temporary shed was set up, where the workers could get on with the vital job of filling the fuse cases which – now that the Phoenix was operational once more – were urgently needed on the bomb line.

'It's a relief not to be in the original filling shed,' Gladys admitted to Kit as they worked their shift the week of Violet's honeymoon. 'The thought of standing on the spot where poor old Ivy died makes me cringe.'

'I suppose we'll have to get used to it,' Kit said as she smoothed the fine grey gunpowder with her fingers before stuffing it into the fuse case.

Gladys looked up and smiled at Kit. 'I wonder how the honeymooners are?' she said with a smile.

'Blissful, knowing those two love-birds,' Kit replied fondly.

After a few minutes' silence, Gladys cautiously asked, 'Any more news about Billy?'

Kit shook her head.

Curious about Kit's last visit to the Convent of the Sisters of Mercy, Gladys asked, 'What's Mother Gabriel like?'

Kit thought for a few seconds. 'Holy – and very bossy,' she replied with a dismissive laugh.

Kit might not have been quite so flippant had she

known that at that precise moment Mother Gabriel and Sister Clare were disembarking at Heysham Port.

'Glory be to God!' exclaimed Sister Clare, who'd never travelled further than the outskirts of Dublin and was having trouble negotiating the wobbly gangplank.

With her wimple as white and starched as it had been when she boarded the ship in Dublin, Mother Gabriel walked through the crowd, which parted before her like the Red Sea. A porter hurried forward with their cases, then, bowing at the nun as if she was royalty, he led the two women to their compartment on the train bound for Manchester.

Ian McIvor, in his office, yawned as he went through the notes for his next case in court. As he absently leafed through the papers before him, the telephone on his desk shrilled out.

'Yes?'

'Somebody to see you, Mr McIvor.'

'Who is it?'

'A Mother Gabriel.'

Ian literally reeled when he heard the Mother Superior's name.

'Are you sure?'

'*Very sure,*' his secretary replied.

Smoothing down his hair in an effort to look presentable, Ian hurried to the door.

'Mother Gabriel, come in . . .' Words failed him when the Mother Superior entered, followed by Sister Clare, who held a big bouncing baby boy clasped in her arms.

Without being asked, Mother Gabriel seated herself in a chair, then nodded to the younger nun to do the same. All the while Ian could not take his eyes off the child.

'Billy,' he said as he struggled to find his voice.

Mother Gabriel nodded. 'Himself. I found him,' she announced.

Ian stared at the tired little boy, who had his mother's stunning dark looks and full soft mouth.

'Is he all right?' he asked anxiously.

'The poor wee thing is starving!' Sister Clare cried. 'Would you be having a drop of warm milk I could give him?'

After Ian had instructed his secretary to heat up some milk, he hurriedly returned to his office. Not waiting on courtesies, Mother Gabriel said, 'Where is the mother?'

Rather shaken by the speed of events, Ian replied, 'At the Phoenix factory in Pendleton.' Realizing that the nun would have no idea what he was talking about, he quickly added, 'Nearby.'

As if in a rush to get things over and done with, Mother Gabriel said firmly, 'The child needs to be with his mother.'

'Of course, of course,' Ian agreed. 'But first won't you tell me how you found him?'

'That's for the mother to hear before anyone else,' Mother Gabriel replied.

Ian nodded in agreement with her sentiments. Kit should be the first to hear Billy's story.

'I'll take you to her just as soon as he's finished his milk.'

After Billy hungrily polished off the warm milk, Ian assisted the two nuns into his car; then he took hold of Billy. As he held the infant in his arms, the child gazed up at him and smiled. In that moment Ian's heart melted – Billy had the same brave smile as Catherine and the same enchanting dimple in his cheek.

'Hello, mister,' Ian whispered. 'I'm going to take you to someone who loves you very, very much.'

Ian rather reluctantly handed the gurgling Billy to Sister Clare, then climbed into the driver's seat and set off for Pendleton with his heart pounding in his ribcage.

Frantically trying to remember which shift Kit was on, he drove to the cowshed, which was empty but warm and cosy with heat from the fading wood-burner, which Ian immediately stoked up.

'And where exactly are we, Mr McIvor?' Mother Gabriel asked as she stared around the simple dwelling.

'This is where Catherine lives with the other Bomb Girls,' he explained.

Thinking that the German enemy might be just around the corner, Sister Clare cried out in alarm, 'Oh, Jesus, Mary and Joseph!'

Ian held up his hands to calm her. 'Bomb Girls is just the common name for the munitions girls who build the bombs,' he explained. 'They're conscripted women who work for the government.'

'Might it not be a good idea, Mr McIvor, for you to have a word in private with Miss Murphy?' Mother Gabriel asked. 'We don't want her fainting away in shock when she meets her son.'

'My thoughts entirely, Mother Superior,' Ian said as he all but ran out of the cowshed.

Pacing the entrance hall where the workers clocked off, Ian was in a frenzy of joy and anxiety. Eventually the hooter sounded for the end of the shift, and Kit and Gladys appeared amongst a crowd of noisy laughing girls.

'Ian!' Kit cried in surprise.

'I need to speak to you,' he said as he drew her aside. 'Catherine,' he started. 'There's been a development.'

Hurrying quickly out of the factory and up the track, Kit said, 'I'm parched. Let's go inside and you can tell me, whilst I make the tea.'

'Catherine, if you would just slow down a minute,' Ian panted as he tried to keep up with her. Kit, who was eager to get home, strode ahead.

'Catherine!' he yelled as he ran to catch up with her. 'Just let me –'

But it was too late: Kit was at the cowshed door. Turning, she said with an apologetic smile, 'Sorry, sweetheart, if I don't have something to drink I'll faint clean away!'

And, pushing open the door, she walked in.

As long as she lived Kit would never forget the sight of Billy sitting propped up with pillows on the old battered sofa. Reeling, she grasped the doorpost for support.

'Billy!' she gasped.

Right behind her, Ian caught her before she fell. Struggling free of his grasp, Kit rushed forwards. 'My son! My boy, oh my sweet babby!'

With tears streaming down her face, she scooped up Billy and held him close.

'You've grown,' she said as she both laughed and cried.

'I should hope so too!' Sister Clare declared. 'He's a big boy now, not far off a year old.'

Billy grabbed a strand of his mother's long dark hair, which he chewed. Yearning to kiss and familiarize herself with every part of his small body, Kit knew instinctively that this was not the time to overwhelm him. Instead, swallowing back tears of utter joy, she smiled at him and said, 'Hello, Billy. I'm your mammy.'

Even though Kit wanted to hold on to Billy, he struggled to get down on the ground.

'He's really enjoying crawling,' Sister Clare told Kit, who thought how strange it was that the young nun knew more about her son than she, his mother, did.

Kit set Billy down on the floor, then watched, enchanted, as he got on to all fours and started to crawl very quickly towards the door.

'He wants to go for a walk!' Kit laughed as she hauled the adventurous little boy back.

'He knows no fear,' Mother Gabriel observed. 'A miracle, considering all that he's lived through.'

As Billy set off once more for the door, Mother Gabriel called to Sister Clare, 'Why don't you take the child for a little walk on the moors, whilst I have a word in private with his mother?'

Kit opened her mouth to protest – the last thing she wanted was to lose sight of Billy – but Ian quickly said, 'Good idea. It'll be dark soon and we'll have to think about finding Billy something to eat.'

After putting a warm woolly jumper on the struggling impatient child, Sister Clare carried him outside, leaving Mother Gabriel with Ian and Kit. Gladys, who'd silently come in and tactfully kept in the background throughout the reunion, quickly said, 'I'll just pop down to the canteen to see if they're serving anything for supper that we could feed Billy.'

Kit gave her a grateful smile. 'Thanks, Glad,' she said appreciatively.

When they were finally alone, Mother Gabriel began.

'Your father's dead, child – may God have mercy on his soul,' she said as she crossed herself.

Kit remained impassive; her only thought was that her father was safer dead than alive.

'At least he made his peace with the Lord before he slipped this mortal coil,' the nun added solemnly. 'And he did try to help us find young Billy in the end, for all the good it did.'

'Possibly the only decent thing he's ever done in his whole miserable life,' Kit conceded bitterly.

In a lather of curiosity Ian asked, 'Tell us how you found him?'

Mother Gabriel grinned. 'Sister Clare followed O'Rourke.'

'In her wimple!' he cried. 'Surely he must have suspected something?'

'We dressed the poor girl up in ordinary clothes,' the Mother Superior explained. 'She looked quite smart, actually,' she added with an amused smile. 'It was the only sensible thing to do in the end. Time passing could do the child harm, so we had our so called *legal adviser* followed.' She said O'Rourke's title with contempt. 'There were plain-clothes policemen on the job too; it was quite a palaver,' she said with a hint of a smile. 'But it was Sister Clare who discovered Billy with O'Rourke's sister in the Liberties. He wasn't hidden in the wardrobe,' she assured Kit, who'd grown pale as the story unfolded. 'He'd been fed and decently clothed, but he was a very frightened little boy indeed.'

Kit gripped Ian's hand as she stifled a sob.

'Did O'Rourke's sister just hand him over without an argument?' Kit gasped.

'It wasn't quite as simple as that,' Mother Gabriel retorted. 'We had the help of the Garda in the end; they seized the child and arrested O'Rourke and his sister, who are both at present in police custody.'

'Best place for them!' Kit seethed.

'He'll go to gaol for his crime,' Mother Gabriel announced with relish. 'Have no doubts about that.'

'I'm delighted to hear it,' Ian said as he crossed the room to shake the old nun by the hand. 'I admire your tenacity, Mother Superior!'

Kit also shook the hand of the woman she had fought against for so long.

'Thank you, Mother Gabriel, for bringing my son home to me,' she said as tears brimmed in her eyes; then she added thoughtfully, 'I still can't believe that Da had such a change of mind,' Kit mused. 'What could have turned him about like that?'

'Guilt,' Mother Gabriel replied. 'He told me you'd cursed him the last time you visited him and your sister, Rosie, roundly cursed him too; she said he was no different from the traitor Judas Iscariot himself. Being evicted and seeing his home go up in flames must have been a blow too.'

'And having his entire family turn their backs on him,' Kit added sadly. 'He's ruined so many lives, including his own.'

'Well, he's paid for it, God rest his soul,' Mother Gabriel sighed as she crossed herself. 'I for one would never have known peace if I had not returned the child to his rightful mother. It was an evil, wicked deed, what your father tried to do, which brought a bad name to myself and the Order of the Sisters of Mercy. It had to be rectified in the eyes of the Lord,' she concluded.

Keen to hear all the facts, Ian persisted in his questioning. 'What about the Garlands?'

'I wrote to them myself, once the police prised the address out of Mr O'Rourke, and informed them they'd been misled by his false promises. To be fair to them, they were very much in the dark about the particulars. Anyway, that's all water under the bridge now,' the tired nun said as she rose stiffly to her feet. 'Be sure to get the boy baptized as soon as possible. He is a child of sin born out of wedlock, so it's important he joins the blessed in the sacrament of baptism.'

Kit bit back her tongue – a child of sin indeed! 'I will pray for you, Mother Gabriel,' she promised.

'I'm after thinking I'll be needing all the prayers I can get for that awful crossing home,' Mother Gabriel joked. 'It's not natural in the eyes of God to be floating on cold dark waters for hours on end!'

Sister Clare came back with Billy, whose little cheeks were as red as apples after his outing on the moors. Smiling, she handed the child to his mother, who buried her face in his warm neck.

'Here're his nappies,' Sister Clare said as she set down a bag on the table. 'And a few clothes and his dummy and bottle – and teddy too,' she said with tears in her eyes. 'He's a lovely boy, and a tough one – take good care of him.'

'Oh, don't worry – I will!' Kit retorted with a happy smile as she held her baby close.

After Ian left to drive the nuns to Clitheroe Station, Kit gazed at Billy, who wound a hank of her hair around his fist.

'You're back my precious, you're home with Mammy, and I'm never ever going to let go of you again.'

Gladys picked up food and milk for Billy from the Phoenix canteen; then she ran across the dispatch yard to Edna's blue van.

'You'll never believe it!' she cried. 'Billy's with Kit in the cowshed!'

'Never!' cried astonished Edna.

Gladys laughed with joy as she said, 'Come and see the little lad when you shut up shop!'

When she got back to the cowshed, Gladys was delighted to find Kit bathing Billy in the sink. Pink, warm and blowing bubbles, he looked a picture of health and happiness.

'He is soooo beautiful,' Gladys sighed as she gazed at his glowing smiling face.

'He's a miracle,' Kit murmured in wonder. 'A complete miracle!'

Gladys warmed up the food she'd picked up in the canteen. 'Mashed potatoes, carrots and a bit of mince gravy – will that be all right?'

Kit was no better informed about solid food than Gladys. 'I've only ever breastfed him,' she giggled.

'Well, let's see what Billy has to say about his dinner!' Gladys declared.

Kit dried Billy in a big warm towel, then she got him into a white nightie that looked more suitable for a girl.

'I'll hold him on my knee,' she told Gladys as she balanced Billy on her lap, 'whilst you feed him.'

'Open wide!' laughed Gladys as she offered Billy teaspoons of food, which he polished off with great enthusiasm. When he grabbed the empty plate and tried to lick it, the girls knew for sure that supper had gone down well.

'I brought some milk too,' Gladys told Kit. 'Just in case he needs a bottle in the night.'

'Whoops!' laughed Kit as she felt a warm dampness spreading across her lap. 'I forgot to put a nappy on him!'

Full of food, Billy was also full of energy. He wriggled and giggled as Kit put on his terry-towelling nappy with great difficulty.

'I'll get the hang of it in time,' she told Gladys, who was laughing at her efforts to hold Billy down so she didn't prick him with the nappy pins.

'He was so little when I left him and now he's a big bouncing cheeky boy!' she said as she swept him up and danced around the room with Billy in her arms.

The door opened and Ian walked in to find Kit spinning around in circles with gurgling, giggling Billy. He gazed with love at his happy girlfriend and realized he had never seen her so radiant in all the time he'd known her. Tired from her exertions, Kit flopped on to the sofa, where she cradled the now sleepy and very contented baby. Ian sat down beside her and took the boy's small hand, which he softly kissed.

'Happy?' he whispered.

'Never happier,' she sighed.

As Gladys retired to the privacy of her room, Ian, Kit and Billy stayed side by side on the sofa, where, warmed by the crackling wood-burning stove, they all fell fast asleep.

A gentle knock on the door round about ten o'clock woke Ian and Kit, who smiled sleepily as Edna walked in.

'I've just come to see your little boy,' she whispered as she gazed at Billy, with his arms thrown out on either side of him, deeply asleep beside his mother. 'He's beautiful,' she sighed as tears poured down her cheeks.

Billy yawned, briefly opened his eyes and earnestly fixed his dark penetrating gaze on Edna's smiling face.

'Hello, mister,' she said softly. 'I'm Edna, your godmother!'

41. Happy Family

In a single day, Kit's life had changed forever and for the very best of reasons: she had her son back in her life. After sleeping with him curled up beside her, Kit bathed, dressed and fed Billy early the next morning. Though ecstatically happy, she was nervous and on edge for a variety of reasons, the main one being concern that Billy might have bad memories of where he'd previously been living. Her father would have been thoughtless and brutish with his grandson, but had O'Rourke's sister been any better? Kit had minutely examined Billy's body when she'd bathed him and found no cuts or bruises, but she couldn't forget Mother Gabriel's words, 'Billy was a very frightened little boy.'

Tears stung her eyes. God in heaven, what had her baby been through in the first year of his innocent life? Abandoned by his mother, maltreated by his grandfather, hidden by strangers in Dublin. It seemed to Kit that the only good times Billy could ever have had must have been in the gentle care of Sister Clare at the Sisters of Mercy convent.

But, for all of Kit's constant nagging worries, she couldn't help but laugh along with Gladys, who was trying to help her as she struggled yet again to change Billy's nappy.

'OUCH!' Kit yelped as she stuck the nappy pin in her

thumb for the second time. 'Will I ever get used to these damn nappies?'

Gladys, who was almost as enthralled by Billy as Kit was, laughed in delight as the little boy, happy to be free of his bulky nappy, waved his bare chubby legs in the air.

'Who's a lovely boy?' Gladys crooned as she tickled his tummy, reducing him to helpless giggles.

'You're making it worse!' Kit laughingly protested.

Next was the question of food. The milk Gladys had brought for Billy was almost gone but there was enough left to make a bowl of porridge, which he wolfed back.

'Oh, my goodness!' Gladys exclaimed as she gazed into the empty porridge bowl. 'He's got the appetite of a lion!'

Kit was trying to stem a rising tide of panic. 'I've got to get organized,' she said firmly. 'Billy needs clothes and food, a pram, some shoes.' She stared at Gladys and asked, 'How am I going to get things for him when I'm supposed to be working?'

During the few minutes she'd taken her eyes off Billy, he'd stood up and was wobbling and grinning as he clutched the edge of the sofa.

'He's trying to walk!' Kit cried in delight as she followed the child around to the back of the sofa, where, with her arms extended, she stood, ready to catch him if he fell. 'Clever boy!' she said as she smiled encouragingly at Billy, who looked very pleased with himself.

Kit briefly left Billy with Gladys so she could wash and change for work. Finally, after Gladys sang 'Row, row, row your boat gently down the stream' while sitting on the floor and pretending to row a boat, the girls got out of the house and hurried down the cobbled lane with Billy clasped in Kit's arms.

'I'd go to see Mr Featherstone right away,' Gladys advised. 'And make sure to ask his advice about the Phoenix nursery.'

Mr Featherstone's secretary, Marjorie, was as granite-faced as usual, but this time Kit didn't care. Whilst she waited in the gloomy dark tiled entrance hall, she played games with Billy, who, after his morning exertions, was beginning to show signs of sleepiness.

'I've nowhere to lay you down if you fall asleep, darlin',' Kit fretted as she cursed herself for not being better prepared. 'I didn't even have you this time yesterday,' she said in wonder to Billy, who yawned widely. 'What a difference twenty-four hours makes. Now I'm a mammy with big responsibilities!' she whispered ecstatically to her son.

When she was allowed into Mr Featherstone's office, the factory boss was delighted to discover that Kit had finally been reunited with her baby.

'I know that I have to carry on working – and I want to too,' Kit added hastily. 'If I could leave Billy in the Phoenix nursery, I could do my shift in the filling shed.'

Having been told Billy's tragic story, Mr Featherstone looked from the tired child to the exhausted but very happy mother and shook his head firmly.

'I think you need a couple of days to familiarize yourself with your baby, Miss Murphy,' he advised kindly. 'For a child so young, Billy's seen a lot of changes, and I would think he would benefit from a nice quiet time getting to know his mother.'

Kit couldn't believe her ears.

'Really?' she gasped.

'Just a couple of days,' Featherstone quickly said. 'No more than that. Now if I were you, I'd pop over to the nursery right away to see if there are any free places for Billy.'

Resisting the urge to throw her arms around Mr Featherstone's neck, Kit gave him a grateful smile. Then, carrying Billy, who was quite a weight, in her arms, she made her way to the nursery, where the matron assured Kit that they had several spare places.

'He could start right away, if you like?' she suggested.

'I'll have him with me for a little longer at home,' Kit explained. 'If it's all right with you, I'll bring him along in a day or two?'

'Well, then, in that case,' said the cheery matron. 'I think you might be in need of a pram for the child.'

Kit carried sleeping Billy to the store shed, where the matron wheeled out a big old Silver Cross pram, in which she arranged a small pillow and some warm blankets.

'He'll be as snug as a bug in a rug in that,' the matron joked.

'Thank you so much,' Kit exclaimed in delight as she settled her son in the pram, then rubbed her arms, which had gone dead from carrying him around for so long.

Feeling immensely proud, Kit pushed the pram down the hill into Pendleton, where she wheeled a sleeping Billy to the chip shop so that Edna could see her godson in daylight. Edna insisted on Kit's bringing the pram into the back room, where she was busy simmering peas and butter beans in readiness for the lunchtime opening. Gazing at the peacefully sleeping child, she whispered, 'He's the image of his mam!'

333

'Thank God for that!' Kit said in genuine relief. 'You'd hate the sight of his father!'

'How are you feeling, sweetheart?' Edna asked as she handed Kit a mug of hot tea.

'I've never been happier,' Kit assured her with a radiant smile. 'But I was just telling Gladys I've got to be more organized. Billy needs food and clothes, but I don't know where to start,' she admitted.

Edna quickly checked the clock on the wall, then turned the heat off underneath the peas and beans. 'Come on,' she said as she threw off her pinafore. 'I've got an hour before opening time.' Grabbing the pram handle before Kit could, Edna said almost shyly, 'Can I push Billy to the shops?'

Realizing that Edna had probably never pushed her own little girl around town, Kit instantly nodded.

'With pleasure,' she answered softly.

On the way to the shops, Kit told Edna that Billy hadn't got a ration book.

'Then you'd better send off for one,' Edna advised. 'Otherwise Billy won't get the free cod-liver oil and concentrated orange juice he's entitled to.'

With her meagre ration stamps, Kit got lots of milk, a few eggs, two ounces of butter and a small slice of cheese.

'This will do for now,' she said. 'I can pick up food for Billy in the canteen once I'm back at work.'

'Have you any bread?' Edna asked.

Kit nodded.

'Then toast some for him: let it go hard so he can suck it. He's got teeth coming through and he'll need to gnaw on something,' Edna chuckled.

There wasn't a baby shop as such in Pendleton, but there was a second-hand shop, and Kit bought Billy some little winceyette pyjamas that needed a few patches, a pair of woolly leggings, socks and some vests.

'He could do with some shoes,' she said.

'Leave that till you go into Manchester,' Edna advised. 'He'll have to do with warm socks for the time being.'

After saying a hurried goodbye to Edna, who gave Billy a kiss on the cheek before they left, Kit all but ran back to the cowshed. The day flew by in a whirl of new activities, at the end of which Kit was almost seeing double. She was relieved when Gladys came home from work and started to play with Billy, who held out his arms to her.

'Glad, Glad,' he burbled.

'He's a quick learner,' Gladys said as she rolled on to her back and held Billy high in the air, where she jiggled him whilst he giggled and squeaked with excitement.

'Thank God you're home! I'm gasping for a fag!' Kit exclaimed.

The routine was just as it had been the night before, but this time neither girl was as nervy as she had been; in fact Kit impressed Gladys with her new-found skills – after changing nappies all day she'd become quite proficient.

'I've not seen you prick your finger with a nappy pin recently,' Gladys teased.

'It's all down to practice,' Kit retorted as she undressed Billy in readiness for bed. 'I don't think I'll ever stop revelling in his strong little body,' she confessed to Gladys. 'It's a joy to see how fit and healthy he is.'

'Given the hardships of his early life, I'd say it's nothing short of a miracle that he's so hale and hearty,' Gladys exclaimed.

Kit decided she'd let Billy sleep in his pram. Though she longed to hold him close all night, she instinctively knew he had to get used to sleeping on his own, and she would only be a few feet away if he woke up in the night. After his bottle and being rocked to sleep with an Irish lullaby, the one that Kit's mam had always sung to her as a baby, Kit lowered the heavy-eyed child into his pram.

'PHEWWWW!' she sighed wearily as she joined Gladys by the wood-burning stove, where she contentedly lit up a Woodbine.

'Nora and Maggie are dying to meet Billy,' Gladys told her. 'Wool's so hard to come by that Myrtle's unpicked one of her own cardigans so she can knit Billy a jumper.'

Touched by Myrtle's kindness, Kit said fondly, 'It's kind of her to sacrifice her own cardigan for Billy.'

'Violet and Arthur are due back from their honeymoon tomorrow,' Gladys reminded Kit.

'Of course!' she exclaimed. 'With everything else going on I'd forgotten when they were coming home.'

'They're in for a shock when they see Billy,' said Gladys with a smile.

'We'll be a full house,' Kit giggled. 'Arthur sharing a room with Vi until they find their own place and Billy sleeping with me.'

'Happy days,' said Gladys contentedly.

When the honeymooners returned, they were flabbergasted to find a baby in the house. They stared in wonder at the sturdy little boy, who was clinging to the legs of the living room table as he attempted yet again to make his way around the room. Violet hunkered down so she was on the same level as Billy.

'Hello,' she said. 'I'm very pleased to meet you at long last.'

Billy gurgled as he reached out to grab the pretty diamanté earrings which Arthur had bought for his wife during their stay in Blackpool.

'We had a wonderful time,' Violet sighed dreamily as she drank the tea Kit had brewed for them. 'I didn't want to come home,' she added as she threw Arthur a look of sheer adoration.

Seeing Arthur and Violet so in love made Kit think of Ian, whom she hadn't seen since Billy's arrival; they'd agreed that for the time being at least Billy was the priority and it would be wise to concentrate solely on settling him into his new life. It had been the right decision to put Billy first, but seeing Violet and Arthur glowing with happiness made Kit yearn for Ian.

When Gladys came home from her shift, they ate mashed potatoes, baked beans and the smoked kippers that Violet had brought from Blackpool. Kit mixed some of the food in a small bowl for Billy and again he demolished his supper in no time.

'He's a big growing lad!' Arthur said as he watched Billy try to feed himself some stewed apples that Kit had prepared earlier.

'He goes to the Phoenix nursery tomorrow,' Kit told the Leadbetters. 'I'm dreading leaving him,' she admitted.

'They'll take good care of him,' Violet assured her. 'And he'll enjoy playing with the other children,' she added as she gave Kit's hand a reassuring squeeze.

337

Kit visibly brightened at Violet's words. 'He's probably not played with many other children,' she said thoughtfully.

'With that cheeky smile of his, he'll have them all running around in circles,' Arthur joked as he helped Billy finish off the last bits of his apple pudding.

The next morning, Kit was up at six in order to make sure she could do all her jobs and sort out Billy before she left for work. Bouncing the pram down the track, she parted ways with Violet and Gladys, who went to clock on. Kit made her way to the nursery, which had big French windows that opened on to a sunny courtyard, where the babies were taken in their prams during nap time.

When Kit took Billy from his snug pram, she couldn't stop herself from protectively hugging him close, but Billy seemed to have no anxieties. Squeaking excitedly, he reached out to the other children, who were crawling and rolling around the nursery floor.

'I think he wants to play,' the nursery nurse in charge remarked as Billy excitedly tottered over to his new friends and their toys. 'Off you go,' she said cheerily to Kit, who was hovering in the background. 'We'll see you at the end of your shift.'

Feeling like she'd been dismissed, Kit took one last look at her son, then ran to join her friends in the filling shed.

Kit automatically tapped gunpowder into fuse cases, all the time wondering what Billy would be doing. Maggie, Nora and Myrtle were keen to hear how he was.

'Tell us all about him!' they said when they gathered in the canteen at midday.

'He's so lovely, and always hungry!' Kit laughed. 'I still can't believe it,' she admitted. 'Having him back after all this time – it's like a miracle.'

Her friends exchanged relieved glances: the fearful shadows that had always lurked in Kit's lovely Irish eyes had finally gone.

Towards the end of their dinner break, Gladys said, 'Now that we're all sort of back to normal, I really do think we need to start rehearsing again.'

'Quite,' said Myrtle briskly. 'Especially as we shall soon be expected to entertain guests at the Savoy.'

'It's not a problem,' Maggie said with a flippant wave of her hand. 'We can play all our favourite numbers.'

'But we still need to rehearse them,' Gladys reminded her. 'We've barely played together since Violet's wedding.'

Kit's stomach dropped. What would she do with Billy when she was rehearsing with the band? As if reading her thoughts, Gladys turned to her and said, 'I'm sure Edna or Ian will keep an eye on Billy whilst you're rehearsing.' Then she turned to Violet with a teasing smile. 'I'm sure Arthur can spare you for an hour or two once a week.'

Violet burst out laughing. 'It's more a question of whether I can spare him!' she joked.

And so it was arranged: even though their lives were busier than ever, they would start regular rehearsals once again in readiness for their swing band show in London.

42. Bridesmaids and Bomb Girls

As days slipped into weeks, a pattern, built around Billy's growing needs and Kit's relentless shift work, developed. When Kit was working nights with Gladys and Violet, Ian looked after Billy, who Kit put to bed at seven o'clock so that she and Ian could snatch a few hours together before she headed off to the Phoenix. Alone in the cowshed, Ian usually read the *Manchester Evening News* by the crackling wood-burner with his ear half cocked as he listened out for Billy's snuffles and whimpers. He loved to watch the little boy as he slept, so content and relaxed, his mouth closed in a soft pout which vividly reminded Ian of Kit's lovely mouth; his long eyelashes fluttering as he dreamt, his arms thrown in wild abandon, and his bedclothes kicked off as he wriggled around in the new cot which Ian had insisted on buying for him.

Billy would be always wide awake by six o'clock every morning, standing up in his cot, calling out to Ian, who slept in Kit's bed, which was beside the cot.

'Hello, little lad!' Ian would say as, rather bleary-eyed, he rose to start the busy morning routine.

By the time Kit came home from work, Billy would be changed, washed and fed. After giving Ian and her son a big hug, Kit would reluctantly wave them goodbye before falling into bed, exhausted by her long night shift. Singing nursery rhymes, Ian would drive Billy to the Phoenix nursery, where, later in the day, Kit would him pick and take him home for tea.

Billy was in the nursery during Kit's daytime shifts; it was only when she worked nights that Ian was called on to help out, but those intimate evenings alone with Billy forged Ian's relationship with the child, whom he grew to love as his own.

It was in the middle of one of her night shifts that Kit had an unexpected allergic reaction to a new batch of gunpowder. She'd been fine at first, but gradually the sneezing started and at one point her eyes were streaming so badly that she was sent home from work.

'It's never happened before,' she told Malc, who was supervising her shift.

'Best get yerself out of 'ere – if you carry on sneezing the way you are, you'll blow all the bloody gunpowder in't factory out of't window!' he joked.

As Kit hurried home, she marvelled at the clarity of the stars speckling the sky over the dark moors. The fresh breeze cleared her nose and throat, and she began to breathe more easily. The cowshed was in darkness when she stepped inside, and before she settled down on the old sofa Kit peeped into her bedroom, where first she looked at Billy, fast asleep on his side; then she turned to Ian, dead to the world in her bed. Looking tenderly at Ian's tousled hair and strong muscular chest, which she could clearly see underneath his loose pyjama top, Kit had an overwhelming urge to lie down beside him. Throwing aside her coat and shoes, she slipped into bed, where she curled up in the softness of his embrace. Still deeply asleep, Ian's response to her was completely unrestrained.

Pulling her close to his body, he murmured softly as he ran his hands under her hair, then along the line of her neck and down to her breasts. Kit gasped at his touch: her whole body felt on fire as she responded to his caresses. Pressing herself against him, she almost swooned as his hands slid down her thighs. Suddenly Billy, in the grip of a nightmare, squawked loudly, and Ian stumbled from the bed, barely registering Kit he rushed to soothe the little boy.

'Shhh, darling, I'm here, shhh,' he whispered as he settled Billy back to sleep.

Looking dazed, he joined Kit on the bed. 'Catherine,' he murmured, 'I dreamt I was making love to you.'

Folding herself into his body, Kit giggled. 'If Billy hadn't woken you up, it might have been more than a dream.'

Looking serious, Ian said, 'We need to talk.'

Taking hold of Kit's hand, he led her into the sitting room, where he rekindled the fire whilst Kit made a pot of tea. When they were sitting comfortably on the sofa, smoking cigarettes and drinking hot tea, Ian took a deep breath and began.

'I've loved you almost from the moment I laid eyes on you, and I vowed as I fell more and more in love with you that I would *never* take advantage of your innocence.'

Kit shook her head as she protested, 'Darling, it was ME taking advantage of YOU just then!' she pointed out.

Looking shocked, Ian said, 'Don't say that, sweetheart.'

'But it's true,' she insisted. 'I was sent home from work because I was ill. You looked so sweet sleeping peacefully in my bed; it was as natural as breathing to lie down beside you. I feel no shame, Ian,' she said with dignity. 'I love you and I always will do.'

'Which is why, Catherine, I want to marry you!' he blurted out.

'Marry me?' she gasped as she shook her head. 'What will your respectable family say when they find out that your wife-to-be has an illegitimate child?'

Ian stopped her with a deep kiss. 'Nothing,' he replied. 'Especially after I introduce Billy as my own adopted son.'

Knocked sideways, Kit gasped, 'You want to adopt Billy?'

'I certainly do!' Ian answered with tears in his warm hazel eyes. 'I would cherish him as much as I cherish you, my darling.'

Moved to tears, Kit herself planted kisses on his smiling mouth as she cried, 'YES. YES. YES!' And with each 'yes' she gave him more kisses, then lay against him in a daze of happiness. 'How can this be happening to me?' she murmured incredulously.

Tired out by each other's kisses and declarations of love, they slept on the sofa, locked together, until Billy woke them up in the morning.

Once Ian had proposed to Kit there was no holding him back. As they wheeled Billy to nursery the following morning, he announced excitedly, 'I want a BIG wedding!'

'In church,' she said firmly.

He nodded as he laughingly added, 'You'll be dressed from top to toe in white satin, carrying red roses and wearing a mile-long lace veil!'

Kit smiled in delight at the thought of being dressed like a romantic princess on her wedding day.

'I'll have four bridesmaids – Violet, Gladys, Nora and Maggie – and Myrtle will play our wedding music.'

'We'll have a long honeymoon, and Billy will soon have lots of brothers and sisters!' Ian declared.

Gripping the pram handle tightly, Kit gazed up at him. 'Our children!'

'Yes!' Ian exclaimed as he lifted Billy out of the pram and danced down the lane with him. 'Friends for Billy to play with!'

Kit stared after the man she loved and the baby she adored. Could life get any better than this, she wondered.

Kit's spring wedding plans had a very convenient knock-on effect for the Bomb Girls' trip to London.

'Your bridesmaids' dresses can double up as ballgowns for our appearance at the Savoy,' she told her friends as she showed them the silky blue fabric she'd chosen and an illustration of the dress style which she'd cut out of a magazine. 'Long flowing gowns with a low neck and elegant dropped sleeves.' Ian had, as usual, been very generous, and their wedding budget was large.

'We'll do it only once,' he'd joked.

'Please God!' she laughed.

'So don't stint on things, my darling,' he said as he'd kissed her several times over. 'I want the world to know my bride and her entourage are the fairest in the land!'

'You make it sound like a fairy-tale,' Kit giggled.

'It is a fairy-tale,' he'd retorted with happiness in his eyes.

'Won't Ian mind us wearing our dresses ahead of the wedding?' Violet asked.

'He said as long as you don't spill a pint of beer down the front, he doesn't mind at all,' Kit replied with a smile.

Myrtle eyed the dress pattern and the silky silver-blue fabric suspiciously.

'I hope you aren't expecting me to wear such a young colour?' she said stiffly. 'The expression "Mutton dressed as lamb" springs to mind!'

'No, Myrtle!' Kit laughed. 'But I could have a pretty stole made up for you in the same fabric as our dresses – that would be nice, wouldn't it?'

Myrtle smiled in approval. 'That would be most appropriate,' she replied.

Maggie and Nora, who had been longing for a ball-gown since the band formed months ago, were eager to have their fittings with the dressmaker in Pendleton.

'Oooh, at last!' Maggie cried rapturously. 'Elegant ball-gowns for the Savoy!'

'I'm not sure we should abandon our Bomb Girls overalls,' Gladys remarked. 'They brought us luck in all our performances, and the audiences always loved them.'

Violet, who agreed with Gladys, said, 'We could wear both.'

'How?' Nora asked.

'We could start off as Bomb Girls, then change halfway through the evening,' Violet explained.

Pleased with her idea, the girls nodded; as Myrtle succinctly put it, 'It doesn't feel like we're abandoning our roots that way.'

With December looming, the band's rehearsal sessions increased; whenever they could play together, they did.

After several heated discussions, they decided to play their winning numbers from all of their public performances. Gladys ran down the list she'd put together.

'"Yours Till the Stars Lose Their Glory", "'PEnnsylvania 6-5000", "Boogie Woogie Bugle Boy of Company B" and "In the Mood". Agreed?'

'Agreed!' came the joint response.

'And if they want an encore?' Kit asked.

'An encore at the Savoy – we should be so lucky!' Maggie giggled.

'We've got loads of songs in our repertoire,' Gladys replied confidently.

They all stopped chatting when they heard a resounding bang-bang from Kit's bass drum. Everybody turned in puzzled amazement to Kit, who was sitting comfortably in one of the chapel pews.

'Who's playing?' Violet asked.

'Well, obviously not me!' Kit giggled.

Billy's little face popped out from behind Kit's drum kit.

'Bang! Bang! Mama!' he gurgled.

Kit's face broke into a big smile. 'Little monkey!' she cried as she ran towards her son. 'I can't take my eyes off you for a minute,' she said as she lifted him up and planted a big kiss on his ruddy red cheek.

'He's going to be a drummer, just like his mama!' Maggie remarked as she too kissed the enchanting little boy they all spoilt rotten.

'Let's get started!' Gladys called. 'Otherwise we'll be here all night.'

Picking up her sax, she ran her fingers deftly up and

down the silver valves. '"PEnnsylvania" first, followed by "Boogie Woogie Bugle Boy".'

Halfway through 'Boogie Woogie Bugle Boy', Gladys was singing to Maggie's trumpet accompaniment when she thought she heard a second trumpet playing. Stopping abruptly, she looked around in confusion. Maggie was equally confused.

'Who else is playing the trumpet?' Maggie asked.

Gladys turned very pale. The trumpet music was identical to what Les used to play when he'd accompanied her on the sax; it was their favourite duet, and the very thought of it brought tears to her eyes.

Trying to regain her composure, she shook her head to clear her thoughts, but the music persisted.

'What's going on?' she cried.

In answer, the door opened and, to her utter astonishment, the very brother she'd just been thinking about walked in blasting on his trumpet. Not missing, not dead, but very much alive and well. Gasping with shock, Gladys's legs buckled underneath her and she fell to the ground with a loud cry. 'LES!'

Seeing his sister in a crumpled heap, Les quickly laid down his trumpet and rushed to her side.

'Glad! Don't cry,' he begged. 'Please don't cry.'

Unable to believe her eyes, Gladys ran her hands incredulously over his smiling happy face.

'You're alive!'

Les nodded. 'I made it out, Sis, I came home.'

It was only as Les helped her to her feet that Gladys saw Captain Trevor Horrocks standing by the doorway.

'You brought him here?' she said gratefully.

347

Looking rather self-conscious to find himself amongst so many women who were all staring at him, Horrocks gave a dismissive shrug. 'Just gave the chap a lift,' he replied nonchalantly.

Sensing that brother and sister would want to spend some private time together, Myrtle started to discreetly usher the band out of the chapel.

'These are my friends,' Gladys said proudly. 'The Bomb Girls' Swing Band!'

'Pleased to meet you,' Les replied, grinning cheerfully as the girls passed him by.

'Very pleased to meet *you*,' gushed Maggie, who was clearly taken by the handsome young lad with the same brilliant blue eyes as his sister's.

Throwing her arms around her brother, Gladys hugged him tightly. 'Let's go to the Phoenix bar – I want to hear *everything* that happened to you.'

Sitting between Trevor Horrocks and her brother in the small bar, Gladys listened wide-eyed to Les's escape story.

'Jerry marched us along the road, don't ask me where, I've no idea. We were in a long straggly column, long enough for the guards to be quite a distance away, so me and my mate, Bernie, we took one look at each other, then bunked over the wall that ran along the roadside. We ran like hell, for miles and miles, and when we couldn't run no further we were terrified of being spotted in our uniforms, so we hid in a cabbage field. God, what a stink!'

Gladys burst out laughing at Les's disgusted expression, but she quickly grew serious as he continued.

'We came out of hiding when it was dark and walked

through the night. We were doing all right until we came across some Germans manning a roadside barricade. Bernie pushed me into a ditch and told me to stay put. I crawled through some long grass by the roadside, where I saw the Germans drive off with Bernie in a truck. Poor bugger, I never saw him again.'

Gladys shuddered at the thought of Les's being driven off in the same German truck as his selfless friend, Bernie.

'So what happened next?' she asked tensely.

'I had to get rid of my uniform; it was a dead give-away.' Les grinned as he recalled his actions. 'I stole some washing off a clothes line – baggy old trousers and a shirt – then I started walking, following directions from locals. I finally reached the sea, and after a series of lifts with local fishermen I managed to board a vessel bound for Harwich. I was incredibly lucky; people helped me all along the way. Without their generosity and guidance I could easily have been picked up.'

'God was with you, Les; you really were so lucky!' Gladys cried as she hugged her kid brother for the tenth time. 'Please don't go away again,' she implored.

Les laughed at her rash request. 'Got no choice, Sis, I'm in the army – I go where I'm sent, even though I'd rather stay here with you and the folks a bit longer.

'I truly thought Mother was going to lose her mind when they reported you missing,' Gladys confessed.

'Poor Ma, and Pa too – he looks worn out with worry,' Les remarked.

'Promise you'll tell me when you get your next posting and where you're being sent?' Gladys begged.

Les winked in the direction of Captain Horrocks. 'Do

you want me court-martialled for giving away military information?'

Gladys smiled bewitchingly at the captain. 'You can tell me if he doesn't,' she laughed.

Sad to see her brother go, but so very happy that he was alive and well, Gladys gave the captain a brief kiss on the cheek as they said their goodbyes.

'Thank you so much for bringing Les to see me,' she said as she stared up at him with her dazzling bright blue eyes.

'The pleasure's all mine,' he replied.

'You should visit me more often,' Gladys added playfully. 'Now that you know where to find me!'

Clearly delighted by the suggestion, Trevor gave Gladys a warm smile before he rather reluctantly started to gather up his coat and gestured to Les to come with him.

Before Les climbed into Trevor's car, he whispered to Gladys, 'Who's your pretty friend with the flaming red hair?'

'Maggie,' Gladys laughed. 'She's a terrible flirt.' Knowing her brother was a bit of a flirt himself, she said with a teasing laugh, 'Shall I pass on any messages?'

Les gave her a naughty wink. 'Yeah – ask her if she fancies a date in Leeds before I rejoin my battalion!'

Gladys winked back, delighted to see that Les was clearly unchanged by his ordeal and back to his usual cheeky self. This was the brother she'd grown up with and Les had always had an eye for a pretty girl!

43. Bomb Girls' Christmas

December 1942 saw victories in Europe and North Africa that raised the nation's hopes high. Malc, supervising girls on the cordite line and in the filling shed, openly gloated when they heard on the BBC news of Montgomery's Eighth Army pushing Rommel's German–Italian Panzer Army into retreating further towards Tunis.

'Nice to think we've got the bloody Eyeties on the run and the Huns too – makes a change for our side to be the victors,' he declared.

Despite the freezing cold weather and the winter days growing shorter, there was an unmistakable air of festive joy at the Phoenix

Maggie, who had a permanent glow of excitement about her since she'd accepted Les's invitation to visit him in Leeds, could hardly contain herself. 'It'll soon be Christmas!' she announced cheerfully.

'Not that we've got any money to buy presents,' Nora said, frowning at the thought.

'Or that there're any presents to be had,' Myrtle pointed out.

'But who can resist Christmas?' cried irrepressible Maggie.

Nora, always the realist, grumbled, 'We're all working nights too; I don't see that there's much to get excited about.'

Excited about her first Christmas with her baby son, Kit dismissed Nora's negative comment with a bright smile. 'Well, at least we'll have Christmas Day at home, I can watch Billy open his stocking and play with him all day long!' she said joyously.

Nora's eyes filled with tears. 'I'm dreading the thought of me and mi da being on our own; it'll be our first Christmas without mi mam and our kid,' she said sadly. 'I honestly don't know how we'll get through it.'

'Come and spend Christmas with us!' generous Maggie offered. 'Our Emily's baking a mock goose with parsley legs and sausage-meat stuffing. Bring your father: we'll cheer him up with a pint of our wicked home brew.'

Nora visibly cheered at Maggie's invitation. 'Thanks, Mags,' she said gratefully. 'We'd love to join you, if you're sure.'

'Sure I'm sure!' Maggie laughed.

'We should go carol singing,' Myrtle suggested, 'And collect money for war widows and orphans.'

'That's a very good idea,' said Gladys. 'We could take our instruments and sing in the main square in town on Christmas Eve.'

'I don't think I'll be pushing my piano into town,' Myrtle chuckled.

'And I won't be rolling my big bass drum down the hill either,' Kit joked. 'But I could bring a small drum.'

Maggie blushed as she said to Gladys, 'Do you think your brother might come carol singing with us? We could play a trumpet duet together?'

'Why don't you ask himself yourself when you see him in Leeds?' Gladys answered with a teasing smile.

'I might just do that!' Maggie replied, grinning.

''Tis the season to be jolly!' Violet laughed as she quoted a line from the carol.

'Fah lah lah lah lah lah lah!' her friends sang back.

Christmas or not, nothing stopped work on the Phoenix bomb line.

'Bombs have to be made even though Santa's on his way!' Malc joked when the girls grumbled about not getting time off. 'Our brave lads at the front don't stop for a slap-up dinner,' he reminded his workers. 'And neither should we.'

Maggie was lucky enough to swap a shift in order to go to Leeds to meet Les. Borrowing Emily's make-up, she dabbed rouge on her cheeks, applied glossy red lipstick to her full lips and used a pencil to accentuate her swooping eyebrows; she also borrowed Emily's best blue tweed hat and coat for her date.

'Do you think your brother likes me, Glad?' Maggie nervously asked as she twirled around for Gladys to inspect her.

'Believe me,' she assured the anxious girl, 'Les wouldn't waste his time meeting you if he didn't like you. He was the one that suggested a date in the first place,' she reminded Maggie.

Feeling a lot more confident, Maggie, with her red hair flying around her excited face, ran down the hill to catch the bus to Leeds. As she watched the young girl go, Gladys felt a pang of envy. She wished it was her that was going to see Les, whom she'd barely spent any time with since his return. She hoped he would accept Maggie's invitation to play a trumpet duet at the carol-singing event in Pendleton; if he came, Gladys would get to see him one more time before he was posted back to his battalion.

Later that night, as Violet, Kit and Gladys clocked off from their long afternoon shift, there was no sign of Maggie, who was due to start work with Nora.

'She never came back,' Nora told them anxiously.

Gladys's heart skipped a beat; she hoped impetuous Maggie hadn't done anything inappropriate with her brother, who was a bit of a wild card himself.

'She's bound to turn up,' Violet said reassuringly.

'Knowing Maggie, she's probably missed the last bus home,' Kit added.

Frustrated that she couldn't contact her brother to find out where Maggie was, Gladys went to bed hoping for the best, but the next morning, when she saw the morning paper on the kitchen table, her blood ran cold.

Just after 5 o'clock last night air-raid sirens across Leeds sounded the 'alert'. Firewatchers on the roof of the Turner Tanning Machinery Company in Stanningley Road, Bramley, reported planes flying from the east to the north-west, and shortly after that the city was hit repeatedly and quickly went ablaze. A large number of incendiary bombs, followed by high explosive bombs, fell, causing widespread damage to the bus station, the museum, the town hall and thousands of homes.

Gladys swayed. 'Oh, no, please, God, no!' she cried.

Maggie had told her that Les was meeting her at the bus station; he would have been sure to have dropped her

354

back there after their date, which would have been around 5 p.m., as Maggie was due back at work not long after that. How could she find out what had happened to the young couple? Would Emily Yates, Maggie's big sister, know anything?

Quickly pulling on her coat, Gladys ran down the track to the Phoenix, where she hoped she might find Emily working on the cordite line. Luckily, she was there, albeit with dark shadows under her eyes.

'Did Maggie come home last night?' Gladys quickly asked.

Emily shook her head.

Almost hysterical Gladys cried, 'How can we find out what's happened to them?'

'Mam and Dad went to Leeds after they heard about the bombing raid first thing this morning,' Emily replied, then added with tears in her eyes, 'The kid's only seventeen.'

Gladys gave her a comforting pat on the arm. 'We're bound to hear something soon,' she said with a conviction she didn't feel.

As she walked out of the Phoenix, Gladys had a sudden thought: Captain Trevor Horrocks might know something. Checking the time on her watch, Gladys belted down the hill into Pendleton, where she ran to Edna's shop and used her phone. But all the phone lines in Leeds were down because of the bombing raid.

'I don't know what to do!' she cried in sheer frustration.

Ever pragmatic, Edna said, 'There's nowt you can do, lovie, but wait and see.'

Gladys decided that when she finished her shift she'd go to visit Maggie's parents. Hours later, standing before their front door, she felt nervous about intruding on them, but she couldn't go through another day and night of not knowing what was going on. After apologizing to Mrs Yates for turning up unexpectedly, Gladys was ushered into the back kitchen, where Mrs Yates gave her a welcome cup of tea.

'Do you have any news of Maggie and Les?' Gladys asked as she held her breath in fear of what the answer might be.

'Yes, we do,' Mrs Yates replied quickly. 'Your Les was just leaving when we arrived at the hospital to see our Maggie.'

Gladys let out a huge gasp of relief. 'Oh, thank God!' she cried. 'He's safe. And Maggie? She's in hospital?'

'Suffering from concussion; she'll be a few days more in Leeds Infirmary,' Mrs Yates answered sombrely. 'But if it wasn't for Les shielding her from the blast and stopping her from running off in a blind panic when the bombs started falling, things could have been very different,' she added, as she sat at the kitchen table opposite an ashen-faced Gladys. 'He hurt his arm in the process of protecting our Maggie.' Seeing Gladys's big blue eyes widen in alarm, she quickly added. 'He's all right – his arm's in a sling but they discharged him from the infirmary.' She sighed heavily as she took a sip of hot tea. 'They were both lucky. I honestly think if it weren't for your brother, our Maggie wouldn't be alive today.'

Smiling proudly, and relieved beyond words that the news was nothing like as bad as she'd feared, Gladys gave a little laugh. 'That's my little brother for you: a knight in shining armour! But poor Maggie – she looked so carefree when she ran to catch the bus to meet Les,' Gladys recalled.

'That's the blasted war for you,' groaned Mrs Yates. 'Just when you think there's a little bit of happiness around the corner, the Luftwaffe come flying in.'

Gladys nodded in agreement. 'What a way to spend their first date! And Les is only just home after months of being missing in action. Just when we get him back, safe and sound, he's hit by the Germans in his own town.'

'Poor lad. We'll just have to make sure they have a good Christmas,' Mrs Yates said determinedly. 'With this war showing no sign of stopping, we've got to live every day as if it was our last.'

Gladys raised her cup of tea. 'Amen to that.'

With a little boy in their midst, everybody in the cowshed had plans for Christmas.

'Arthur and I will go to look for a Christmas tree on the moors,' Violet said excitedly. 'We can stand it in the corner and Billy can help us decorate it.'

'We can make paper chains to decorate the sitting room,' Gladys cried.

'And hang stockings for Father Christmas!' Kit suggested.

'We must invite Edna and Myrtle for Christmas dinner, though what we'll eat is a bit of a mystery,' Violet joked.

Undeterred by the pressures of rationing, Gladys announced brightly, 'Everybody can bring a bit of something; it doesn't have to be a grand affair. A tin of corned beef and a piece of cheese will do,' she said as she thought of the recent bombing in Leeds. 'We're alive: that's all that matters.'

Billy couldn't believe his eyes when Arthur walked into the cowshed bearing a little pine tree that was prettily speckled with white ice. He watched in wonder as Arthur planted the tree in a bucket.

'Christmas tree!' Arthur told the enthralled child.

'Tree,' Billy gurgled as he reached up to grab the tree, then burst into tears as the little green spikes pricked his fingers.

After Kit had kissed his fingers better, Billy helped to dress the tree with bits of tinsel and little homemade paper decorations depicting stars and angels and holly leaves, which Violet threaded with string, then hung from the branches. Billy also tried to help Gladys and Kit make some paper chains, but, after he ripped most of them, Kit suggested they finished the job when the little boy was in bed.

Between them, they put together a Christmas dinner. Edna, who knew just about everybody in Pendleton, managed to get two pheasants from a local gamekeeper who'd shot the tasty birds on the moor. Kit spent her ration coupons on some stringy sausage meat, which she mixed with wild thyme and salt and pepper. The sprouts, potatoes and cabbage that would accompany the meat were all from local gardeners who were passionate about 'Digging for Victory', and Violet's big bread-and-butter pudding dotted with sultanas and apples was a fair substitute for Christmas pudding, especially when she promised to serve it up with hot thick custard, even if it was made with dried milk.

'A feast!' Arthur declared as he appreciatively sniffed all

the wonderful smells that filtered through the cowshed in the lead-up to Christmas.

Violet didn't seem to appreciate the festive smells as much as her husband. The smell of the sausage meat that Kit had bought turned her stomach, and the sight of the pheasants dripping blood as they hung in the kitchen waiting to be plucked sent her rushing to the lavatory, where she was violently sick.

'I must have a bug,' she said as she returned weak and white-faced. 'I've been off my food all week – even the smell of chip butties, which I normally love, turned me queasy the other day.'

'Can I get you anything, sweetheart?' Arthur asked. 'Cup of tea perhaps?'

Violet smiled sweetly at her anxious husband. 'No, thanks, lovie,' she replied. 'I'd give my entire ration book right now for some fresh fruit, a juicy orange or a banana,' she said with a yearning sigh.

'Exotic fruits! Listen to you, milady,' Arthur teased. 'Haven't you heard there's a war on?'

Everybody was immensely relieved when Maggie arrived home from Leeds Infirmary. Even concussion didn't dampen her exuberant spirits. 'It's almost worth getting blown up for a week off work,' she joked when her friends went to visit her on her return home.

'Oooh, weren't you scared?' wide-eyed Nora asked.

'I was petrified when I heard them bloody incendiaries.' She added with a cheeky wink, 'But I had Les to keep me safe. He held me tight and sheltered all through the bombing. Left to miself, I'd have made a run for it – and probably joined the dead in the morgue too.' She smiled at

Gladys and said, 'Your brother's a hero – and a good-looking one at that!'

Les, now on extended leave because of his arm injury, did manage to take the bus over the Yorkshire moors to Pendleton to join in the carol service and visit his sister as well as Maggie, who, though covered in cuts and bruises, glowed with happiness when Les gave her a kiss on both cheeks and a Christmas present.

'Not to be opened until Christmas Day,' he teased as Maggie used the gift as an excuse to give him a few more kisses.

'We need to practise our duet before we go into town,' she whispered in his ear.

Les burst out laughing. 'How am I going to play the trumpet with my arm in a sling?'

'We'll manage, somehow,' Maggie answered confidently as she stroked his wounded arm.

In the Yateses' back parlour the young couple stole kisses in between Maggie practising 'Jingle Bells' on her trumpet and Les singing along in his wonderful deep baritone voice. Mrs Yates insisted that Maggie should rest before the carol service, which gave Les the opportunity to walk up the hill to visit his sister.

'How are you?' she cried as she tried to hug him but instead caused Les to wince as she squeezed his arm.

'Sore!' he laughed, returning the hug as best he could.

After admiring the cowshed and playing with Billy, Les joined his sister for a walk on the moors before darkness descended.

'How long will you be home for now?' she asked as she nodded at his sling.

'Not long – my arm's recovering and I should be back in action with my battalion soon,' he replied as they walked over the icy heather, which scrunched under their feet. 'But it's good to have a bit more time with Mam and Dad over Christmas.'

'I wish I could be with you all,' Gladys said wistfully.

'You're needed here in Pendleton, our Glad. I need somebody to keep an eye on that gorgeous Maggie Yates for me,' he chuckled.

'She's a little fire-cracker,' Gladys said fondly.

'You've only got to look at all that wild red hair to know that,' Les joked.

'Thank goodness you were with her at the bus station,' Gladys added on a more serious note. 'God, when I think what could have happened to you.'

'We got off lucky,' he agreed. 'As long as I live I'll never forget the sound of those planes flying low over Leeds.'

Before they set off down the hill to sing carols, Les gave Gladys a parcel. 'From Mam,' he said.

'PORK!' Violet gasped when she opened the parcel and saw a thick piece of fresh pink pork.

'It's Dad's allotment's pig,' Les told his sister. 'They slaughtered it for Christmas, then shared it out between friends and family. Mam kept a bit back for you; it'll be great with a bit of apple sauce!'

With snow falling around the occupants of the cow-shed, they made a happy little procession as they walked together on Christmas Eve. Pendleton looked like a picture postcard, with the high Pennines topped with snow forming a dramatic backdrop to the little town nestled in the valley. Standing in the town hall square, Nora, Kit,

Gladys, Violet and Maggie, with Les at her side, tuned up their instruments, then started to play 'Jingle Bells' to get everybody into the festive mood. Children came running with their families, and in no time a large crowd had gathered. Whilst the band played, Myrtle led the singing, accompanied by Billy, who, wrapped up snug and warm in his pram, clapped and gurgled to 'Jingle Bells' and 'Away in a Manger'. Edna, Arthur, Les and Ian circulated with buckets to collect money for war widows and orphans; then the concert culminated with a rousing chorus of 'Hark the Herald Angels Sing', which reached new heights when Maggie and Nora played a triumphant duet. The audience were so moved they clapped and cheered and cried for more.

Edna dashed back to her chip shop just behind the town square, where she fired up her range in order to cook supper for the hungry and very chilly carollers. After a warming meal of chips, butter beans and fritters, the happy little party made their way home under a starry sky. After Kit had settled Billy down to sleep, Ian put a coat around her shoulders and drew her outside.

'Let's go for a little walk,' he said softly.

They walked over the snowy moors to a high ridge that gave a view of the town, dark with blackout blinds drawn, way down in the valley. The snow had stopped falling, and slanting beams from the rising moon reflected on the glistening white snow. It was certainly bright enough for Kit to see the small velvet bow on the package that Ian held out to her.

'Merry Christmas, Catherine,' he said as he handed her

the parcel. Looking up at the man who had come to mean so much to her, she hesitated before opening it. He nodded at her to go ahead, so she slowly unwrapped the beautifully wrapped box, opening it to reveal the most exquisite diamond ring. Tears in her eyes, she looked up again at a smiling Ian. 'You haven't forgotten that you promised to marry me?' he teased.

Lost for words, Kit gazed in awe at the ring, which seemed to hold the moon and stars in each of its facets. Slipping it on to her tiny wedding finger, she murmured incredulously, 'It fits!' Then she added, 'How do you always know my exact size? My feet, my waist, even my little finger!' she laughed in delight as she admired the dazzling diamond.

'I know every part of you by heart,' Ian replied as he hugged her close.

'Oh, Ian,' she sighed as she leant against him weak with joy. 'To think this time last year I'd just given birth to Billy and had no idea of the nightmare that was ahead of me.'

Kissing her deeply, Ian whispered, 'A nightmare that's turned into a dream.'

44. London

As soon as Christmas was over, the Bomb Girls started to prepare for the trip to the Savoy. Apart from working their shifts and rehearsing their numbers, they had to pack for their performance, which involved two nights in no less a hotel than the Savoy itself. They also had to book a coach to transport the whole lot of them to London and arrange time off.

'It's all getting rather hectic!' Myrtle said with suppressed excitement. 'I was actually wondering whether to splash out on a new pair of glasses,' she added in an uncertain voice that was at odds with her usual robust self-confidence.

Violet, Gladys and Kit looked shocked.

'No, Myrtle! I love your diamanté-tipped specs,' Gladys assured her.

'They remind me of angels' wings,' Kit confessed.

'You wouldn't look the same without them,' Violet added.

'Well, if you put it like that,' Myrtle said as she adjusted her glasses, 'I won't go to the expense.'

In the middle of all the constantly changing arrangements, Arthur and Violet dropped of bombshell of their own.

'Violet's expecting a baby!' Arthur proudly announced as they sat around the table sharing a potato-hash supper one night. 'A playmate for Billy!'

Violet, who was glowing with good health and happiness, blushed.

'There was I thinking I had a tummy bug and all the time I was pregnant,' she laughed at herself. 'You'd think at my age I'd have known better!'

'Wonderful news!' cried Gladys as she hugged Violet across the table.

'When's it due?' gasped delighted Kit.

'Summer,' Violet replied. 'We'll have moved into our own house well before that; the cowshed is already bursting at the seams!'

Watching the happy couple with their arms around each other, thrilled and so excited about their baby, Gladys could hardly believe that Arthur and Violet didn't know each other a year ago. The pain and fear they'd endured was remarkable, and now here they were, blissfully in love, living every day for each other.

'Here's to Arthur and Violet, the parents-to-be,' their friends cried as they raised mugs of tea. 'Congratulations!'

Nora was getting anxious about 'going South'. As the event drew closer, the epic journey became almost the equivalent of circling the dark face of the moon to nervous Nora.

'Will we be safe travelling?' she asked as the excited girls gathered around Edna's van one cold night.

Edna smiled reassuringly at worried Nora. 'What with all of us lasses and their fellas, not to mention Malc, plus Mr and Mrs Featherstone, we'll be like an army on the move! We'll need the biggest charabanc in Pendleton to get us to the capital.'

'I mustn't forget mi make-up and mi jewellery,' Maggie flapped. 'Oh, and the perfume that Les bought me for Christmas,' she added, all dewy-eyed at the mention of her boyfriend's name.

But poor Nora continued to fret. 'Do you think they'll have an iron at the Savoy?' she asked. 'I'll need to give mi ballgown a proper good ironing; it'll be creased as buggery after it's been stuffed in mi suitcase for ten hours!'

'They'll have ten irons!' Edna assured her. 'I hope you've all got a decent pair of shoes to wear under your posh frocks? Don't want you letting the side down and turning up in clogs!' she chuckled.

'Why not? We are lasses from Lancashire after all,' Maggie declared proudly.

'I'll pack a load of spam and beef-paste butties and fill as many flasks as I can lay mi hands on,' Edna promised. 'Can't have the swing band dying of hunger on their way down South!'

'If we leave on 30 December, will we get to London by New Year's Eve?' Maggie asked dimly.

Myrtle raised her eyes to the ceiling. 'Did you never study geography, child?' she asked.

Totally unabashed, Maggie answered, 'Oh, yeah! I just never understood which way was east or west!'

'We'll be in London on 30 December,' Gladys explained. 'The same day that we leave here.'

'It's not like we're crossing the equator,' Edna snorted.

'And the day after we arrive we perform with Joe Loss and his famous orchestra,' Gladys reminded her friends.

'What arrangements have you made for Billy?' Edna

asked Kit when the younger girls had left in a flurry of nervous giggles.

'He's coming with us!' Kit replied. 'Ian will take care of him whilst we're rehearsing, and we're hoping that when Billy's asleep on the big night we can pay one of the staff to babysit, though Ian's keen for Billy to see his mammy bang the drums!'

Edna smiled at newly pregnant Violet. 'Will you be all right travelling, lovie?' she inquired solicitously. 'No morning sickness?'

'I've never felt fitter,' glowing Violet replied. 'Though I could sleep for England when I get home from work!'

'We'll leave the back seat just for the pregnant,' Edna decided. 'Then young Violet can snooze all through the journey.'

Checking her watch, like the mother hen that she was, Edna said, 'You know what, ladies? I think you should get yourselves off to bed in readiness for the morning.'

As barn owls hooted across the moors, Kit, Gladys and Violet linked arms and walked together up the moorland track that led to their digs. Thrilled as a child who was going on holiday, Gladys suddenly let go of her friends and ran hell for leather up the path.

'I'm going to London,' she cried as she lifted her arms to the starry sky. 'I'm going to meet Joe Loss!'

The Phoenix workers gave the Bomb Girls' Swing Band and their companions a rousing send-off. Lining the way out of the factory, they clapped their hands and waved as they sang in unison Gracie Fields's popular song 'Sing as We Go'. The band girls hung out of windows and sang back as the coach drove away; then, as their Phoenix friends receded and their singing faded away, they sank back into their seats and smiled.

'At last!' Kit exclaimed as she cuddled an overexcited Billy on her lap.

'We're on our way!'

The journey to London was long and often depressing. Driving from north to south through towns and cities bombed and burnt by air-raids brought the horror of war even closer. When they drove through Stockport, Violet reached for her husband's hand.

'Remember?' she whispered fearfully.

Though the livid red scars on Arthur's face were healing, his skin still stretched tight when he smiled, which he did now to soothe Violet.

'It's all right, my sweetheart, that's over and done with forever.'

Feeling the baby flutter lightly in her tummy, Violet smiled contentedly as she said, 'Yes, you're right: this is a new life.'

As they drove through Birmingham, the chattering laughter of the passengers fell silent. Shocked beyond words, they gazed in silence as they passed stark black and scorched factories with roofs and rafters caved in and windows blown out. Streets where communities had lived were raised to the ground; church steeples lay toppled; and in between the dirt and ashes children played 'Catch' and 'Hide and Seek'.

'Good grief,' Edna gasped. 'Our cities are in ruins.'

The horrific sights of Birmingham didn't even begin to prepare the travellers for the destruction of London. The city they'd all been longing to reach brought tears to their eyes. Barrage balloons floated everywhere, even over St Paul's Cathedral. Blasted streets and fractured pavements disappeared into deep holes, and broken pipes revealed stinking open sewers. Some of the city's famous buildings and monuments were still standing, but they were strangely juxtaposed against tenement blocks with their façades blown out, revealing shattered homes where curtains still fluttered and peeling wallpaper flapped in the wind.

'They say the bloody Jerries set ablaze nine miles of dockland wharves and warehouses from Tower Bridge to Woolwich,' Malc solemnly told Edna, who couldn't believe the devastation they were driving through. 'They even bombed Buckingham Palace!'

When the coach finally came to a halt outside the Savoy Hotel, which was surrounded by sandbags, the shell-shocked passengers clambered out and looked nervously around.

'I'm terrified a bomb might drop on us,' Nora confessed. 'Nowhere seems safe in London.'

Myrtle, who was also in shock but kept a stiff upper lip, chided young Nora. 'Come along now. We must take on the same spirit that London adopted during the Blitz – never say die!'

Mr Featherstone, who was supporting a visibly upset Mrs Featherstone, nodded in agreement with Myrtle. 'These people are heroes,' he said in a voice thick with emotion.

It was a relief to be inside the elegant hotel with its tall windows and long, velvet drapes. Billy, for the first time in hours, was set down on the floor and was able to crawl around, but soon got in the way of bustling porters and waitresses with loaded tea trays.

'Let's get to our rooms,' Ian urged as he put Billy on his shoulders and set off up the winding staircase.

They were all on the same long corridor, which was fortunate, as the girls were in and out of each other's rooms, swapping clothes and hair rollers, and comparing bath products, which were the height of luxury to Nora and Maggie.

'I've never seen anything as posh in mi life!' goggle-eyed Nora announced. 'Fluffy pink towels, smelly soap, a full-length mirror and a fitted carpet – all in the bathroom!" she spluttered.

Violet, Kit and Gladys exchanged fond smiles; it was a joy to see the young girls so frivolous and excited; too soon these days girls as young as fourteen were forced into growing up fast and taking on responsibilities way beyond their years. Nora and Maggie were having the time of their lives, and nobody doubted they deserved it. Though slightly worried that they might overdo it, Gladys said, 'Get an early night tonight. It's been a long day, and tomorrow will be even longer. What with rehearsals and then the performance, you won't be in bed till well after midnight.'

Not wanting to go out for fear of having to take shelter in a strange air-raid shelter or, worse, a jam-packed tube station, where, they'd been told, rats ran over sleeping bodies, the travellers had sandwiches in their rooms. Gladys, Arthur and Violet joined Kit and Ian, who'd put Billy to sleep in Kit's single bed.

'I wonder when Joe Loss will arrive tomorrow?' Gladys said.

Kit, who was brewing tea with the kettle the hotel had provided for them, said, 'They'll have to rehearse just like we will.'

'We don't want to get in their way,' anxious Gladys protested.

Violet, who was busy ironing her lovely blue ballgown, smiled as she said, 'I'm sure somebody as famous as Joe Loss is used to getting his own way.'

After a treat of a breakfast consisting of coffee, toast and the total luxury of a boiled egg, the girls decided to face the ballroom bright and early. Wearing their normal everyday clothes, they inspected the bandstand, the drum kit and the grand piano, which Myrtle literally purred over.

'A Steinway grand piano – one can't do better than that.'

Kit was thrilled with her drums, complete with her favourite hi-hat cymbals. When Billy started bashing and rattling them, Ian said a quick goodbye to his fiancée and took the little boy off to London Zoo, whilst Arthur went to meet an old army pal in Whitehall. After the men left, the rehearsal started in earnest. Musically they were well rehearsed, but, because the bandstand was so spacious, Violet, Gladys, Maggie and Nora had scope to develop their dance movements. For 'Boogie Woogie Bugle Boy' they went for the same choreography as the Andrews Sisters, who'd created the song. Coming in close, they sang the chorus in harmony, then pulled out to dance their steps. Snapping their fingers and swaying their hips, they moved in sync with each other. By lunchtime, they were hot and sweaty and hungry too.

'Let's go to the nearest Lyons Corner Café,' Gladys suggested.

The tasty mince and onion pie, cabbage and mashed potatoes they were served by the smiling Nippy soon restored their energy, and the vanilla ice cream with two wafers that followed was a real treat.

'This place reminds me so much of my time in Leeds, before the war,' Gladys sighed as she poured them all a second cup of tea. 'I was a Nippy too, just like these girls, happy as a lark, not a care in the world, with no idea what was just around the corner.'

'I was picking spuds in Ireland,' Kit recalled.

'Who could have guessed that as a consequence of the war we'd become a swing band?' Violet mused thoughtfully.

'A very successful swing band!' Maggie boasted. 'The best in the North!'

They didn't return to the ballroom for fear of bumping into Joe Loss, but that didn't stop the girls singing and practising their steps in the long corridor outside their bedrooms. Barefooted, they danced on the fitted carpet, laughing themselves silly as they wriggled and jiggled in line to the beat of their songs.

As the afternoon drew to a close Gladys said, 'I'm going to have a nice long bubble bath, courtesy of Myrtle, who's offered to share her bottle of bubble bath with all of us.'

Violet yawned and said, 'I'm going to have a nice lie-down.'

'I'll have a snooze too,' Myrtle added.

372

There was no luxurious time out for Kit once Billy returned. 'Mama! Mama!' he cried as he came running into her arms, clutching a little woolly giraffe. 'Look, gaffe off Dada.'

Kit's heart melted every time she heard Billy call Ian 'Dada'. Soon it wouldn't just be a name of affection: it would be the rightful name of the man who would legally adopt him when they were married.

Leaving Kit to have a bath with Billy, Ian took himself off to the Savoy bar, where he restored his flagging spirits with a couple of whisky and sodas and the *Evening Standard*, where with a sinking heart he read more about the Germans' mass execution of the Jews, which Anthony Eden had recently disclosed in the House of Commons.

Upstairs, Kit was beginning to panic: she'd fed Billy his supper but after all the excitement of the day he wouldn't settle down to sleep. Glancing at the bedside clock, she realized she hardly had time to get herself dressed and made up. Luckily Violet walked in wearing her Bomb Girls overalls and turban.

'I'll take care of him,' she said as she sat down on the bed and started to sing nursery rhymes to Billy.

As grateful Kit wriggled into her uniform she said, 'We mustn't forget to take our ballgowns down with us; we'll have to leave them in the wings and change there.'

'I've got terrible butterflies,' Violet admitted with a nervous giggle.

'Me too,' Kit admitted.

'We must keep reminding ourselves we've played in public before – this isn't the first time,' Violet said firmly.

'But we've never performed in a grand hotel in front of famous people!' Kit laughed.

Finally they were all ready. Standing in front of the full-length mirror by the lifts, they did a final make-up check and pulled their hair out from under their turbans, so it hung loose and pretty around their excited faces.

When the lift arrived and the automatic doors flew open, Gladys turned to her friends with a smile on her face.

'Time to face the music, ladies!' she announced.

With their hearts fluttering in their ribcages, the girls, all clutching their ballgowns, and Myrtle, draped in the blue stole Kit had promised her, slipped into the wings, whilst Mr and Mrs Featherstone, Malc, Edna, Ian and Arthur sat at a candle-lit table close to the stage, where they ordered cocktails.

'I don't want to get tiddly,' Edna said as she lit a Woodbine.

'Let yer 'air down, lass!' Malc laughed as he downed his Martini cocktail in one.

Eyeing him saucily, Edna said, 'Somebody's got to keep an eye on you!'

As tables filled up and couples sat down to eat supper, a low hum of conversation filled the room, broken by an occasional high tinkling laugh. The entertainment manager appeared backstage with a tray on which were set crystal goblets of sparkling champagne.

'On the house, ladies. You've come a long way – in more ways than one – for this event,' he joked.

'OOOH! This is the life!' cried Maggie as she took her first sip of ice-cold champagne.

Nora sipped her drink too, then giggled as bubbles popped in her mouth and made her hiccup.

'I feel right glamorous!' she laughed. 'Like Betty Grable or Rita Hayworth.'

'TOAST!' Gladys cried as she raised her glass and smiled at her beloved friends. 'Success to the Bomb Girls!'

'SUCCESS!' they replied in unison.

Just before they were about to go on stage, the manager collected their empty glasses, then explained the evening's running order.

'We'll start at eight o'clock sharp, right after Mr Loss has finished his supper with the ENSA scout. You'll open the show, ladies. Mr Loss and his orchestra will follow, then you'll return to the stage, when both bands will play together.'

'What if we're not up to scratch and Joe Loss thinks we're a dead loss?' Maggie joked.

'He'll love us!' replied Gladys with a confident laugh.

'What's ENSA?' Kit asked curiously.

'Every Night Something Awful!' Violet giggled. 'No, not really,' she said as she turned to Gladys. 'What does it stand for?' she asked. 'I can't remember.'

'Entertainments National Service Association,' Gladys replied. 'Singers, dancers, actors, musicians who tour England, entertaining the workers.'

'They tour Europe too, lifting the spirits of the Allied forces on the front line,' Myrtle added. 'It's all part of the war effort.'

'Sounds a lot more fun than filling shell cases,' Kit chuckled.

Their whispered backstage conversation was interrupted by the lights dimming in the ballroom and the manager standing centre stage to introduce the trembling girls.

'All the way from Lancashire, the winners of the Northern competition – the Bomb Girls' Swing Band!'

The bandstand's lights came up as they took up their positions and launched into 'PEnnsylvania 6-5000'. Gladys ran her fingers up and down the saxophone valves, sending out a series of high clear notes that immediately stopped all conversation and made the audience turn to the girls on stage. The unusual sight of real Bomb Girls dressed in their white overalls and turbans brought the house down. Wolf-whistles rang out, followed by loud cheers.

Gladys's beautiful strong voice resounded through the ballroom, enhanced by Maggie's and Nora's harmonizing backing, and Kit hit the drums so hard she almost fell off the tiny stool where she was perched. There was no way the audience could sit through the number: seeing the Bomb Girls tapping, swaying and singing, they leapt to their feet and started to dance. As the dancers swelled into a throng, the musicians looked at each other and their delighted expressions said it all: *They like us!*

Edna, dressed in a pretty sequinned dress, was completely astonished when a smart, slightly balding middle-aged man in an elegant dinner suit asked her to dance.

'Dance? ME?' she gasped.

'If you would do me the honour,' he said politely.

Edna rose and followed him on to the floor as if she was sleep-walking.

Malc's eyes were just about bulging out of his head. 'What the 'ell?' he spluttered. 'The cheek! I thought she was with me.'

On the dance floor Edna's heart fluttered as the stranger laid a hand on her arm and moved into a lively foxtrot, which Edna hadn't done for years, but as she moved around the floor she recalled the steps and really began to enjoy herself.

On stage, the tempo changed when the band began 'Boogie Woogie Bugle Boy', which Maggie opened with a superb piece of trumpet playing; then Gladys, Nora and Violet came in singing the chorus exactly as they'd practised earlier that day. Though the rhythm was faster, Edna managed to keep up with her accomplished dancing partner, who twirled her this way and that, until she was dizzy! When she saw some young couples throwing their partners up in the air, Edna's heart skipped a beat. Surely her partner wouldn't try that with her? She was all of fourteen stone – if he as much as tried, he'd be carried out of the Savoy on a stretcher!

At the end of the number the manager leapt on to the bandstand, where he announced the next act.

'Please put your hands together for Mr Joe Loss and his orchestra!'

As the band played the opening chords to 'Little Brown Jug', the Bomb Girls slipped into the wings, where they hurriedly changed into the silver-blue ballgowns. Myrtle wore a full-length black velvet gown with the pretty blue stole that Kit had had made up for her. Using little powder compact mirrors, they touched up their make-up and brushed their hair.

'Oh, this is wonderful!' Maggie declared. 'I could sing all night!'

'Don't get too overexcited,' Myrtle warned. 'We're only halfway through the show.'

As Joe Loss's orchestra concluded with 'South of the Border', the Bomb Girls reappeared on stage in their fabulous ballgowns, which transformed them from munitions workers into gorgeous, desirable women. Again wolf-whistles and cheers accompanied their change of clothes, which took the Swing Girls' confidence to a new high. As Gladys played the opening chords of 'In the Mood', Glenn Miller's all-time favourite dance tune, the crowd went wild. Jiving all over the floor, they spun and twirled in each other's arms until they were breathless.

Poor Edna, whose feet were killing her by now, was anxiously wondering if she'd survive a lively jive. Just as she was about to suggest to her tenacious partner that she might pop to the ladies', Gladys's soaring sax drowned out her words and once again she was being whizzed around like a rag doll. Mercifully, Malc materialized from nowhere as Violet opened 'Yours Till the Stars Lose Their Glory' with a hauntingly beautiful piece of clarinet playing. Tapping Edna's partner on the shoulder, Malc said in his gruffest Northern accent, 'I think this next one's mine, pal!'

Edna virtually fell against Malc's chest. 'Thank you for rescuing me!' she giggled weakly.

'Just hold on to me and I'll guide you round the room,' he instructed.

At the end of the waltz, the lights came up and the

audience showed their appreciation with deafening, tumultuous applause. It was only when the manager announced the return of Joe Loss and his orchestra that the applause finally died down.

'I think you need a drink,' Malc said to Edna as she tottered back to the table, where Arthur had to cover his mouth to stop himself from laughing at Edna's painful hobbled steps.

'I think I need three!' she announced. 'Yon bugger's knackered me!'

Seizing the opportunity to enjoy themselves, the band girls sneaked out from behind the wings and joined their partners on the floor. Malc, beside Edna, glared at anybody who might make a move for her.

'Bloody Southerners,' he growled as he handed her a double port. 'They don't know when to stop!'

Mr and Mrs Featherstone took to the floor, along with Violet and Arthur, Kit and Ian, and Gladys, who was in the arms of a handsome young RAF pilot, whilst the middle-aged man whom Edna had previously danced with approached Myrtle.

'God help her!' cried Edna as she watched them sweep into a foxtrot. 'She'll be on her knees in ten minutes!'

Blushing Myrtle looked rather thrilled with her partner, who really was very light on his feet. A little distance away Arthur held his beautiful wife close.

'How are you feeling, my sweetheart?' he whispered.

Violet's pale blue eyes blazed with excitement. 'So happy!' she exclaimed.

'You looked wonderful up there playing the clarinet,' he said with great pride.

'You know what,' she said softly. 'I thought of my mother when I was playing that opening piece. Now that I'm having my own baby I suddenly felt so close to her it brought tears to my eyes.'

Kit and Ian drifted round the floor, lost in a lovely romantic waltz number, whilst Nora and Maggie smooched with two laughing uniformed sailors. As the orchestra concluded and the lights came up, Violet noticed Joe Loss approaching the ENSA representative.

'What's he up to?' she murmured to Arthur, as both men turned towards Gladys, then nodded as if in agreement with each other.

The Bomb Girls ran back on the stage, where they tuned up with Joe Loss's orchestra whilst he took the microphone and turned to an astonished Gladys. 'What shall we ask this beautiful young woman and her amazing all-girl swing band to play?' he called out to the audience.

'"I'll Never Smile Again"!' came back the loud reply.

Mr Loss turned away from the microphone and winked at Gladys as he complimented her on her skills.

'I've been listening to you all night: you handle that sax superbly, and you sing like a bird.'

Gladys blushed to the roots of her long tumbling dark hair. 'Thank you, sir!' she said as her vivid blue eyes sparkled with pleasure.

Teasing, he asked with a smile, 'Sure you can handle a Tommy Dorsey number?'

Gladys winked. 'Oh, yes! Quite, quite sure!'

And with that she went rippling up and down the saxophone valves before launching into a sexy vamping number. Mr Loss signalled to both bands, mouthing the word, 'Wait . . .'

He let Gladys enjoy her solo; then, after a few minutes, he waved his baton and the bands struck up. Gladys, totally in her element, dropped her voice to a husky whisper as she sang the lyrics of the popular song and the audience danced in the dimmed lights of the packed ballroom. The music gave them stolen moments to imagine a life where there was no war, no rationing and no death. They could dream of romance and peace, and escape the trials and sorrows of everyday life.

Edna wiped away a tell-tale tear as she thought of what her brave Bomb Girls had gone through to get to this place, to achieve this wonderful success. Violet's and Kit's secrets had nearly destroyed them, but there they were on stage, looking beautiful and playing like real professionals. And if it hadn't been for Gladys's secret, there would be no Bomb Girls' Swing Band. Fulfilling her secret dream had helped her to achieve what many might have dismissed as impossible: that six hard-working munitions girls, working regular long shifts in a factory on the edge of the Lancashire moors, could dedicate so much of their precious free time to music. Her girls, including giggly Maggie, nervous Nora and splendid Myrtle, had taken the words of the war-time slogan to heart: KEEP CALM AND CARRY ON.

Gladys's lovely girls could do that all right: they could make her cry, they could make her laugh; they represented thousands upon thousands of conscripted women who worked till they dropped most days and were, as Churchill himself named them, 'Britain's Secret Army'. And right now she loved them with all her heart. Seeing Edna dabbing tears off her face, Malc flapped his clean hankie before her.

'Stop yer bawling, lass,' he said in an unusually gentle voice.

'I'm just . . . happy!' Edna sobbed.

'Me too, sweetheart,' he said huskily. 'Me too.'

As both bands took a well-deserved break, Joe Loss invited Gladys to join his ENSA guest at a candle-lit table. Goggle-eyed Maggie and Nora watched their every move.

'What's going on?' Nora asked suspiciously.

'I don't know, but it must be good – our Glad can't seem to stop smiling!' Maggie laughingly replied.

In the powder room, which was lined from floor to ceiling in glass and gleaming chrome, the two young girls later pounced on Gladys, who hurried in to reapply her scarlet red lipstick.

'Who are them fellas you're talking to? What do they want?' Nora asked without any preamble.

With her lovely face glowing and her blue eyes wide with excitement, Gladys burst out, 'Time for more champagne, girls!'

After pushing several tables together, the noisy Lancashire contingent waited as Joe Loss helped Gladys pour everybody a glass of champagne. Nora nudged Maggie and whispered, 'Eh, I could get used to this fizzy stuff!'

As the girls started to giggle, Edna called for order. 'I think Gladys might have something to tell us,' she said.

All eyes turned to Gladys, who was radiating excitement.

'Come on now, our Glad,' joked Malc. 'Don't keep us in suspense!'

Turning to Mr Loss, Gladys took a deep breath, then announced in a breathless incredulous voice, 'I've been asked to join ENSA!' she gasped. 'I've been asked to go on tour and entertain the troops!'

Epilogue

The second day of February 1943 was a momentous one in the course of the war. It would be the day when Hitler's armies suffered their first big defeat: the surrender at Stalingrad. It was also the day when Gladys was to leave the Phoenix factory and her friends in the cowshed.

'I don't know whether to laugh or cry,' she blurted out as she packed all her worldly goods into a big old leather suitcase.

'Oh, I'd definitely cry if I was going on tour with Gracie Fields and Arthur Askey!' Maggie mocked. 'I mean, it would be so much more exciting staying on here at the Phoenix, filling fuse cases and working shifts! I'll swap places with you, Glad, if you're desperate to stay?'

Laughing, Gladys threw a pair of woolly socks at cheeky Maggie. 'You might well be joining me on the ENSA trail if you keep up with your trumpet.'

'Really, really?' cried Maggie.

'Though,' teased Gladys, 'for the time being at least I need you to stay put so that our Les has got someone to cuddle next time he's home on leave.'

'Now you're talking,' Maggie said as she recalled Les's stunning blue eyes and wonderful soft kisses. 'On second thoughts, the nearer I am to Leeds the better!'

As Gladys tried to pack the last of her shoes and

clothes, Billy – sitting on the bed beside her case – immediately unpacked them.

'Cheeky little monkey!' laughed Gladys as she kissed the top of the little boy's head.

'Glad! Glad!' he gurgled as he held his chubby little arms out to her. 'Kiss!'

Holding him close, Gladys kissed both of his red cheeks, then handed him over to Kit.

'Go to Mama or I'll never get out of this place!' she cried.

As Billy, now fourteen months and a confident walker, took himself off to play with his toys, Kit marvelled at the sight of him. Almost a year ago she'd been chasing round Dublin trying to find out what had happened to her son; and now here he was, living with her in the cowshed. Though they'd soon be moving out once she became Mrs McIvor and Billy took Ian's name too.

'You promise you'll be back in time to be godmother to my baby?' Violet reminded Gladys.

'And to be a bridesmaid at my wedding?' Kit added.

'Of course,' Gladys replied. 'I've already promised both of you, and I won't let you down.'

'And we know the bridesmaid's dress fits you, 'cos you wore it so well at the Savoy,' Edna said.

Nora, who always went into a dream-like trance the minute the Savoy was mentioned, sighed. 'Oh, the Savoy . . .' For all her nerves about leaving the safe haven of Lancashire, she had never got over the experience of travelling to London and staying at the poshest hotel in town with fluffy pink bath towels in the bathroom.

Violet, who now looked distinctly pregnant, smiled.

'One thing's for sure, my bridesmaid's dress doesn't fit!' she joked.

It had been agreed that Nora and Maggie were to take Violet's place as Kit's bridesmaids at the forthcoming wedding.

'I really don't fancy being a vastly overweight bridesmaid,' Violet had confessed to Kit, who had insisted that even if Vi didn't follow her down the aisle she would still be her chief bridesmaid and sign her marriage lines in the church's vestry.

As Gladys added the last of her jumpers to the pile already in the suitcase, Myrtle and Edna exchanged a conspiratorial wink, then edged Nora and Maggie towards the bedroom door.

'We'd better get a move on,' Edna said as she picked up Billy and settled him on her comfortable hip. 'I'll pop Billy into his pram and take him for a bit of fresh air,' she said to Kit, who quickly nodded.

'What . . . ? Why . . . ?' big-mouthed Nora started to say before she got a dig in the ribs from Myrtle, who bustled both girls out of the room.

'Are you going already?' Gladys asked in surprise.

'Just a few little things to sort out,' Myrtle called over her shoulder.

'We'll meet you at the bus stop to say goodbye,' Edna added as she wheeled Billy's pram out of the cowshed.

Violet and Kit exchanged a knowing look and hid their smiles.

'Right,' said Gladys as she snapped the clips of her suitcase shut. 'I think I'm just about ready.'

Turning, she saw her friends' faces drop. Though she

386

was excited beyond words at the prospect of touring England, then Europe, where she and other ENSA artists would entertain troops in active service, the thought of leaving Kit and Violet brought a lump to her throat. Dropping her suitcase on to the floor, Gladys held out her arms to her friends, who joined her in an emotional group hug.

'How will I cope without you all?' she whispered. 'I love you so much,' she said with a catch in her voice.

'After all that we've been through, we'll always be friends,' Kit said with real confidence.

'No more secrets!' Violet exclaimed joyfully. 'I've got my Arthur!'

'No more lies!' Kit added with a radiant smile. 'I've got my son!'

Grinning, Gladys held her saxophone case aloft. 'And I've got my music!'

Holding hands, they made a promise that they would keep for the rest of their lives. 'We'll always have each other!'

Linking arms like they'd always done on their way to work, the three friends walked down the cobbled lane. Suddenly the air was filled with music, and when they reached the gates of the Phoenix factory Gladys gazed in amazement at the smiling faces of what looked to her like the entire factory workforce. Mr Featherstone stepped forward.

'Couldn't let you leave without a proper goodbye,' he said proudly.

Kit dashed to the drums, which Arthur and Malc had transported, along with the upright piano, the full length of the factory, and Violet picked up her clarinet, which Edna had left on the piano for her. The sight of so many smiling faces completely finished Gladys off, and she burst into tears. Seeing her tears, Billy began to cry too. 'Glad! Glad!' he wailed.

As Ian comforted Billy, Myrtle hit the piano keys. 'We shall miss our little songbird, but we'll carry her in our hearts always,' she announced as she played the opening chords to the workforce's favourite song, 'Sing as We Go'.

As Kit hit the drums and Violet trilled on her clarinet, Maggie and Nora came in on their brass instruments.

'One more time for the Bomb Girls' Swing Band!' cried Malc.

Swallowing back her tears, Gladys's voice soared as she started to sing. She would never forget till the day she died the wonderful sound of 200 women singing alongside her as they sent her on her way into her new life with a song in her heart.

Acknowledgements

My thanks to Clare Marsh in Nottingham for her guidance on adoption information, also to Donna Poppy for her superb copy-editing skills and my editor at Penguin, Clare Bowron, who worked so hard and patiently alongside me on *The Bomb Girls' Secrets*.

The girls of Walsingham Hall
are determined to unlock the secrets
of a country at war, no matter who
tries to stop them.

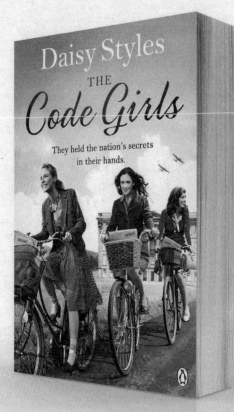

1. Ava

'Friday dinner time,' thought Ava, as she tucked her long, dark hair under her cook's hat and checked her reflection in the small, cracked mirror hanging on the canteen wall. Even smeared with grease, the glass revealed the irrepressible sparkle in Ava's dark blue eyes. She beamed her characteristic wide-open smile, which revealed her small, white teeth and a charming dimple in her left cheek. She was taller than most of her girlfriends, long-legged and shapely with a full bust, softly curving hips and a willowy, twenty-inch waist. Ava was fortunate; her strong frame and athletic build were down to hard work and plenty of walking in all weathers on the wild Lancashire moors.

With her voluminous hair neatly tucked under her cotton hat, Ava wrote the day's menu in white chalk on the canteen noticeboard; two years ago, Friday's menu would always have been fish, cod and haddock freshly delivered from Fleetwood market. Ava had quickly learnt how to skin and fillet fish, but that was before the outbreak of war and the start of food rationing. Nowadays, it was impossible to buy enough fish to feed a family, never mind two hundred mill workers. As rationing got tougher and tougher, Ava had tried variations: parsnip fritters, corn-beef fritters, fake sausage fritters – mince (very little) mixed with oatmeal and herbs made a tasty fritter. But on a Friday, the workers, predominantly Catholics, didn't eat meat; it was a day of abstinence. The best and most popular alternative to fish was Ava's delicious 'scallops', fresh local spuds washed, peeled and thickly sliced then dipped in a thick, creamy, yellow batter made from dried eggs combined with milk and water. Deeply fried in a vat of fat, Ava served the golden-brown scallops with mushy peas or butter beans and pickled red cabbage. It made her laugh when customers asked for chips as well.

'You'll sink like a brick with all them spuds inside you!' she teased.

'You've got to have chips on a Friday, cock,' one of her customers said with a wink. 'It's a bugger we can't 'ave fish like in't th'owd days, but your scallops are bloody beltin'! Give us another, wil't?'

Ava smiled as she dropped a few more of her scallops on his plate; she loved these people and she loved her strong, tight-knit, hard-working community. Half the people queuing up for their dinner lived within a block of Ava, in identical red-brick terraced houses, stacked back to back, row upon row, and reaching up to the foothills of the moors which dominated the landscape of the mill town. Everybody knew everybody else's business; it couldn't be otherwise when outdoor privies were shared and women gathered at the wash house to swap gossip and smoke cigarettes while they did their weekly wash. Then they'd hang it out on washing lines threaded across the network of backstreets, where children played under the wet sheets that flapped like ships' sails in the breeze. The neighbours' over-familiar questions about her future had recently become both an irritant and an embarrassment to Ava.

'So when are you going to get yourself conscripted, our Ava? All't lasses in't town have gone off to do their bit for't war, but you're still here. Can you not stand thowt o' leaving us, like?' neighbours and relatives alike teased.

Ava had self-consciously assured them she was definitely leaving; there was no choice: female conscription was obligatory for women between the ages of eighteen and thirty. Women were being deployed all over the country, and most of Ava's friends had already gone – some to munitions factories in Yorkshire and Wales; others had signed up to work as land girls in Scotland – but Ava had held back. She felt guilty, of course; would people think she was trying to duck out of war work, that she was unpatriotic? She was, in fact, fiercely patriotic and passionately believed in committing one hundred per cent to the war effort, but she was determined to do something big, something bold, something that would push her to the limit in her sacrifice for king and country. Three months after female conscription had been authorized by the government, Ava was well aware that she had to do something soon, otherwise the Labour Exchange would be on her tail and find war work for her.

'*Ava!* Check on them apple pies, lovie!' Audrey, the canteen boss, yelled, as the workers settled down on long wooden benches that ran alongside scrubbed wooden tables to eat their meal.

Ava dashed over to the huge oven, where her pies were browning nicely. She was looking forward to seeing what the customers' reactions would be when they tucked into their puddings. She'd added a surprise ingredient. Last night, she'd ridden Shamrock across the moors to her favourite spot, where wild winberries grew in abundance. Leaving the mare to crop clumps of tough grass, Ava had collected a large amount of the small, fruity berries, and she'd mixed them with baking apples, then covered the mix with a thick pastry crust. As she inspected the pies, she could see rich purple juice seeping through the edges. They would taste delicious served with custard, but she'd have to warn Audrey to cut thin slices if every worker was to have their fair share of her pudding.

Ava loved the Lancashire moors, especially at this time of the year, late spring, when the days were long and the nights were warm. Once work was finished and tea was cleared away at home, she'd change into a pair of baggy tweed trousers and head for the hills. Just a short walk up an old cobbled lane lined with oak and ash trees and Ava was on the moors, where, most evenings, she rode an old cob mare that belonged to a local farmer. He'd asked her if she'd like to take care of his horse Shamrock, who needed exercising now that his daughter had left home. Ava wasn't an experienced rider, but she was certainly not going to turn down the offer. Luckily, Shamrock was willing and patient with Ava, who took many a tumble as she learnt the hard way how to make the mare walk, trot, canter and how to keep her seat over the bumpy moorland terrain. Ava and Shamrock developed a trusting, companionable relationship, both of them enjoying their rides over the rolling moors, with only the skylarks and curlews for company.

It was while she'd been up at the farm the previous evening, tacking up Shamrock in readiness for a ride out, that she'd caught sight of the local newspaper, which had been left lying around by the farmer in the tack room.

WOMEN WORKING IN COMMUNICATION CENTRES

Ava laid down Shamrock's reins and hurried over to read the article.

As the war rolls on, more and more women are required to fill the spaces left by men who have gone to fight on the front line. Conscripted women are needed for training in communications, decoding, Morse, tracking, signalling, administration, interception and mapping intelligence in military-command control centres. Training Centres offering intense six-month training are opening across the country to provide women, potential code girls, with the necessary skills for this vital war work.

Ava's deep blue eyes blazed with excitement. With her heart beating double time and her pulse pounding, she let the paper drop into her lap and gazed out over the open stable door at the arching blue sky.

'*This* is what I've been waiting for,' she said out loud. 'I could be a code girl!'

The first spare moment she had, she dashed into the Labour Exchange in the high street and marched boldly up to the desk.

'I want to be a code girl!' she had announced, with a proud ring in her voice.

The woman behind the desk raised her eyebrows.

'Code girl?' she asked.

'I want to work in communications,' Ava explained. 'Please can I sign up?'

'What's your present employment?' the woman asked.

'Canteen cook.'

There was no doubting the shock on the woman's face.

'Canteen cook!' she exclaimed.

Ava nodded.

'At Dove Mill. I'm second in charge,' she added with a proud smile.

'Cooking isn't exactly the right kind of background for a communications trainee,' the woman retorted. 'They'll be looking for more academic lasses, them with a bit of schooling behind them.'

Ava's eyes flashed with indignation.

'Women are doing jobs nobody ever expected them to be doing all over England right now – why shouldn't I?'

The woman nodded.

'I'm not going to argue with that,' she replied, handing Ava an application form and a pen. 'Fill this in. When it comes to "present employment", you must state your current job.'

'But –' Ava protested.

'You can add that you want to train in communications because you feel you have an aptitude for it,' the woman quickly explained.

Smiling happily, Ava filled in the form, writing 'Canteen Cook' as her profession but adding in big bold capitals that she wanted to switch to communications:

'I want to be a code girl, as I believe it's far more beneficial to my king and country than me cooking in the Dove Mill canteen in Bolton.'

'That should do it,' she said, as she returned the completed form to the woman at the desk.

'Don't build your hopes up, lovie,' the woman advised. 'Be prepared to knuckle down and do anything that's required.'

'I'll knuckle down to anything,' Ava said with a winning smile.

The woman watched Ava walk away. She was a stunning girl, but good looks didn't always pay dividends. With a war on, people got what they were given and did as they were told.

'I've enlisted as a code girl,' Ava proudly told her boss the next day.

Audrey looked up from the mound of pastry she was mixing and burst out laughing.

'And what's a code girl when she's at home?'

Standing by the massive industrial oven, stirring a mince-and-onion stew bulked up with root vegetables such as swede, parsnips and turnips, Ava reiterated what she'd read in the paper.

'It could be anything from operations, tracking, signals, administration, interception, decoding, Morse – even working in military-command control centres,' she said with a bit of a swagger.

'Sounds too much like bloody spying to me!' Audrey joked. 'Here, roll that lot out,' she added, pushing half the pastry across the table to Ava. 'Roll it thin, mind. We've two hundred hungry mouths to feed; a little must go a long way.'

As the two women at either end of the table rolled and cut pastry to fit into huge tin trays, Audrey continued, 'How are you going to cope with all that brainy stuff?'

'I'll learn,' Ava said with conviction. 'I really want to improve myself.'

'Well, good luck to you, lass, but I bet they turn you down,' Audrey said, as she poured the cooled mince-and-onion mix into the trays, now lined with pastry. 'It's not like you went to grammar school and got a good education.' Audrey slapped a pastry crust on top of the filling and neatly nipped in the edges. 'Them stuck-up communications toffs will be looking for brains, certificates and qualifications – none of which you've got, Ava, love!'

Ava smiled confidently.

'Don't worry, Audrey – I'll be a good code girl; it's exactly the war work I've been looking for.'

A fortnight later, Ava was packing her small, cheap suitcase, helped by her mother, who was carefully folding her few dresses before laying them on top of Ava's freshly ironed blouses and new tweed skirt.

'Do you think you've got enough frocks?' Mrs Downham asked.

'They'll do for now,' Ava replied, wrapping her two pairs of battered shoes, which her mother had polished till they shone, in the newspaper.

'I wish I could have bought you a warm twin set,' her mother said wistfully.

'Mam!' Ava cried. 'Stop worrying; it's a communications centre, not a fashion school.'

Seeing the tears welling up in her mother's eyes, Ava took hold of her hands.

'I'll write every week,' she promised.

Her mother nodded sadly.

'I wish you weren't going so far away. Norfolk's the other side of the country, miles away from here.'

'I have to go where the government sends me,' Ava pointed out. 'You should be thrilled it's only Norfolk; I could be in Scotland felling trees like Marjorie Todd from round the corner!'

Her mother gave a bleak smile.

'I always knew this town wasn't big enough for you,' she said, as she stroked her daughter's long, dark hair. 'You were made for better things.'

'Mam, this isn't about daydreams, this is my contribution to beating Hitler,' Ava said with a laugh, and kissed her mother's cheek.

Before leaving, Ava had to say goodbye to Shamrock, something she'd been dreading doing since the moment she'd signed up. The old mare's excited whinny did nothing to lift Ava's spirits.

'Hey, sweetheart,' she said softly.

Shamrock nudged her softly in the chest.

'I haven't forgotten,' Ava murmured, as she produced the mandatory carrot, expected on every visit.

As Shamrock contentedly crunched on it, Ava gulped back the tears that were threatening to overwhelm her.

'I don't know how to say this, sweetheart,' she said. 'You see, I've got to leave you.'

Oblivious to the changes that were about to unfold, Shamrock snickered, then nuzzled Ava's arm. Even though Ava had found a nice, local lass to replace her, she still felt guilty about leaving Shamrock. How could you explain to a dumb animal that your life was about to change for ever. Ava thought about the thousands upon thousands of young men who had joined up in September 1939, when Prime Minister Neville Chamberlain had announced that England was at war with Germany. How many lives had been shattered by their departure? How many homes had been broken, and families wrecked, by the loss of a loved one who never came home?

Sighing, Ava bent to kiss Shamrock's soft, velvety muzzle. Her sacrifice amounted to nothing compared to that of the soldiers, sailors and pilots who were risking their lives fighting the enemy in planes, ships and on land, in armoured tanks. Two years in, and the war was not going well; Britain was ill-prepared and ill-equipped when compared to the organized might of the Third Reich. The evacuation of Dunkirk in May 1940 had shown the true grit of the British. They'd launched thousands of boats into the North Sea on the hazardous mission to rescue soldiers from the Normandy beaches, but the losses on that fateful day had cut deep, as did the continual bombing of Britain's major cities. The nation, no longer gripped with the irrefutable belief that it would win the war, began to fear the worst: an invasion.

'Which is why we all have to do our bit,' Ava said, swiping away sentimental tears with the back of her hand. 'I'll miss you, sweetheart,' she whispered, and kissed Shamrock for the last time. Turning, she briskly walked away, leaving the old mare neighing shrilly behind her.

Ava's last day at home was fraught with emotion. Her little sister kept bursting into tears, and if her mum packed her case once, she packed it twenty times. Their last meal together was eaten in an awkward silence, with none of the usual family banter and easy teasing. It was a relief when tea was over and Ava could busy herself with washing-up while her parents gathered round the big Bakelite radio, where the news reader announced in a grim voice that Operation Barbarossa was underway, the Germans were marching on Russia.

'Bloody 'ell,' said Ava's dad, as he puffed hard on a Woodbine. 'There'll be no stopping the buggers now!'

'The Russians are bound to put up a fight, they're not going to take it lying down,' Mrs Downham insisted.

'Aye, but what guns and weapons have they got against the Huns?' Mr Downham pointed out. 'It could end up a bloodbath for the Bolshies.'

'Thank God it's the summer – at least they won't be fighting in five feet of snow,' Mrs Downham murmured.

Ava boiled up some milk and made cocoa for them all, then sat as usual by the coal fire, with her parents on either side of her.

'We'll miss you, our lass,' her dad said softly.

Ava took hold of their hands.

'I'll miss you, too.'

She would miss them for sure, but – she thought rather guiltily – there was a wonderful new world waiting for her in Norfolk.

The next morning, Ava settled her suitcase in the netted luggage rack of the compartment she was travelling in, then leant out of the open window to smile at her family, who stood on the platform with heavy, sorrowful faces.

'Write!' her mum sobbed, dabbing away her tears with a hankie.

'Don't forget me!' yelled her little sister.

'Take care of yourself, lass,' her dad cried, as the heavy steam train pulled out of the station.

'I love you!' Ava shouted, through a belching cloud of black smoke.

As the platform receded, Ava sat back in her seat and sighed. The goodbyes were over; her adventure was beginning! Having never travelled further south than Rhyl, Ava was wide-eyed as she peered out of the window at the ever-changing countryside. The wild northern moors gave way to the Peak District, with its tidy grey stone farmhouses nestled neatly between green fields, where sheep grazed.

'What wouldn't I give for one of them woolly lambs roasted with potatoes, Yorkshire pud, mint sauce and gravy,' said a young lad in a soldier's uniform on the opposite side of the carriage.

'That's never going to happen,' said an older soldier, who was sitting next to him, puffing hard on a cigarette. 'Them animals will be made into mince and spread thin across half the county. I can't remember when I last had a solid piece of meat put in front of me,' he added, and took a greaseproof parcel out of his overcoat pocket.

'Fancy a beef-paste buttie, sweetheart?' he asked with a wink.

'In exchange for one of my carrot buns,' Ava replied, opening a small tin she'd packed with home-made buns.

'That'll be a rare treat,' said the soldier. He bit into the bun and nearly swallowed it whole.

'You, too,' Ava said, proffering the tin to all the soldiers in the carriage.

By the time it had done the rounds, there was only one bun left, but the soldiers each gave Ava something in return for her kindness: half an orange, a piece of chocolate, a soggy sandwich, a cigarette and cold tea from a bottle.

The cheery soldiers got off at Peterborough, where Ava changed lines. On the slow train to Norwich, her heart began to pound with excitement. She had to keep reminding herself that this was war work, her sacrifice to save the country from fascism. The only problem was, it felt more like a great adventure rather than a painful sacrifice, and she was having trouble keeping the smile off her face. A third and final train took her to Wells-next-the-Sea on the north Norfolk coast. As Ava walked along the platform, she felt the sea air blowing breezily around her and tasted sea salt on her lips. Her stomach flipped with nerves as she joined a few girls standing outside the station.

'Are you going to Walsingham Communication Centre,' a cheery, red-headed, young woman asked.

Ava nodded.

'Join the queue, we're waiting for a lift.'

The lift turned out to be a rickety old jeep.

'Hop in, ladies. I'm Peter, gamekeeper-cum-gardener from Walsingham Hall.'

As he piled their luggage on the roof, the new code girls

squeezed in tightly beside each other. Instead of sitting side by side, they sat on benches facing each other, and when Peter cranked the gears and the jeep bounced forward they all fell towards each other, almost into each other's' laps.

'Hold on tight!' he warned, too late.

Though the sun had set, the light lingered in the eastern sky. Peering through the window, Ava could see the townspeople had dutifully pulled down their black-out blinds. Peter drove to the hall without any headlights to guide the way.

'How do you know where you're going?' laughed one of the girls.

'Instinct,' Peter replied, without taking his eyes off the twisting road for a second.

Ten minutes later, Peter took a sharp left turn and swung into a drive flanked by elaborate metal gates gilded with an elaborate coat of arms.

'That's the hall,' Peter said, dropping down a gear to make his way up the drive, which threaded through a deer park. Even in the half-light, Ava could see fallow deer grazing under ancient oak and horse-chestnut trees. They rattled over a cattle grid, then, with a swoop, Peter came to a halt in front of Walsingham Hall. Ava caught her breath. She'd expected a big place that could accommodate a lot of people, but she hadn't expected *this*.

'It's beautiful,' she breathed, as she stepped out of the jeep and gazed up at the majestic building that towered before her.

'One of the finest stately homes in the country,' Peter said proudly. 'Just wait till you see it in the daylight. It's a sight to behold.'

As the girls tumbled out of the jeep, Peter called out, 'Make your way indoors. I'll follow with your luggage.'

With their feet crunching on the gravel drive, the trainees pushed open the heavy front door and entered the elegant marble hall, which was decorated with ancestral portraits hung in huge, ornate gold frames.

'Nobody mentioned we'd be billeted in Buckingham Palace!' giggled one of the girls.

Her laughter faded as a grim-faced woman dressed from head to toe in black approached.

'Your accommodation is in the south wing,' she said, in a voice that bristled with contempt. 'Follow me.' Then she quickly moved off, as if she wanted no association with any of the newcomers.

'Who's she?' Ava whispered to Peter, who was staggering along with as many cases as he could carry.

'Timms, the housekeeper,' he gasped, under the strain of his heavy load. 'She doesn't like you,' he added with a wink.

'She's made that perfectly obvious,' Ava replied.

The makeshift dormitories in the south wing had been built in what must have been a series of connecting drawing rooms, all with high ceilings decorated with swirling stucco plasterwork and floor-to-ceiling windows draped in blackout blinds.

'In there,' barked Timms, before turning her stiff-as-a-ramrod back on the trainees and walking away, disapproval evident in every step she took.

'She's a regular bundle of laughs!' tittered the cheery red-headed girl.

'Don't worry, you won't be seeing much of her,' Peter assured them with a chuckle.

'Thank God for that,' thought Ava.

The yawning girls selected their bunk beds, then made their way along the dark, bewildering corridors to the bathroom, which had a line of sinks running along one wall and a line of lavatories running along the opposite wall.

'Oooh!' exclaimed an impressed trainee as she switched on a tap. 'Hot and cold water – more than we get at home.'

'Thank goodness!' joked another trainee, as she dashed into the nearest cubicle. 'One minute longer and I would have wet myself!'

Ava cleaned her teeth, washed her face, then dabbed her skin with a few blobs of Ponds Cold Cream, a parting gift from Audrey. As she settled herself in a bottom bunk, Ava pulled a blanket and a scratchy, starched single sheet over her body, then looked nervously up as the woman on the top bunk bounced around, causing the bed springs to sag and twang over Ava's face.

'Will I ever get to sleep?' she wondered, as a few girls started to snore. A few even sniffed, as if they were crying.

Ava eventually slipped into a deep, exhausted sleep, and the smile that had been on her face all day remained there through the night. It was the smile of a girl who just couldn't wait to see what tomorrow would bring.

Emily, Lillian, Alice, Elsie and Agnes.

Five very different young women with very different lives.

But it's 1941 and everyone has to do their bit.

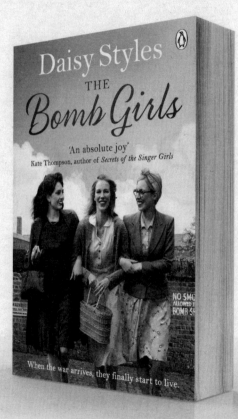

The Bomb Girls by Daisy Styles
is available to buy now

Next from
Daisy Styles